STARSHIP
MAGE

JUDGMENT OF MARS

BOOK FIVE
OF THE STARSHIP'S MAGE SERIES

This edition published in 2018 by:
Faolan's Pen Publishing Inc.
22 King St. S, Suite 300
Waterloo, Ontario
N2J 1N8 Canada

ISBN-13: 978-1-988035-62-8 (print)
A record of this book is available from Library and Archives Canada.
Printed in the United States of America
1 2 3 4 5 6 7 8 9 10

Second edition
First printing: September 2018

Read more books from Glynn Stewart at faolanspen.com

STARSHIP'S
MAGE

JUDGMENT OF MARS

BOOK FIVE
OF THE STARSHIP'S MAGE SERIES

GLYNN STEWART

FAOLAN'S PEN
PUBLISHING
faolanspen.com

CHAPTER 1

THE FRAIL OLD MAN standing by the office window could barely even remember the name he'd been born under. It hadn't been the name he'd used for most of his life, the one he'd entered the Protectorate's service under. Even then, he'd been a double agent, working for Legatus as well as Mars.

That was the name the Keepers had known him by—but that was a man the entire galaxy, including both the Martian and Legatan governments, *knew* was dead.

He'd used many names since. He'd introduced himself to Damien Montgomery at a...*memorable* meeting as Winton, and that name served as well as any. It was even close, he thought, to his birth name.

He smiled thinly as he studied the concourse beyond his window. The transshipment station he stood on saw a lot of traffic into and out of the Alpha Centauri System and the optimistically named New Terra beneath the station.

None of those swarming crowds would have given the old man in the suit with the pure white hair a second glance, never realizing he owned the station.

Others managed it for him, but owning the platform gave him a secure location, only five jumps from Sol, from which to carry out his plans. The closeness was no longer as necessary as it had once been, thanks to the very allies and technology he was now waiting on.

A soft buzz informed him the Link was online, and Winton turned around, walking into the field of hidden cameras needed to send his three-dimensional image across the light years—via a quantum entanglement technology the Protectorate he'd once served didn't even know existed.

"Partisan," a gruff voice greeted him as screens slid down from the roof to encase him, creating the illusion of a conference room with one other person in it.

Another name. Winton smiled. It wouldn't do for any of the people he met to ever connect the various names. That...would cause problems.

"Mr. President," he greeted the President of the Legatan Republic. "You're late."

"I am a busy man, Partisan," President George Solace said calmly. The twice-elected ruler of the most important UnArcana world was a bulky man in his early forties, still hale and vigorous with the muscles of the football captain he'd once been.

"Important as this affair is, I have a star system to run," Solace continued, "and the groundwork for an interstellar nation to build. Your report?"

"The Keepers are done," Winton told him. "Montgomery and Ndosi came close to realizing they were being played, but I had an asset in place. Ndosi is dead and the Archive destroyed. The Royal Order of the Keepers of Secrets and Oaths is broken, its survivors scattered."

"And what would you have done if your provocations had killed Montgomery?"

Winton chuckled.

"The death of a Hand might have delayed the Keepers' fall, but it would also have guaranteed it," he pointed out. "'A Hand falls, another rises,' after all. His Majesty would have sent Lomond or another Hand to seek out Montgomery's killer. There would have been no subtlety, no doubt then. Only fire and the sword.

"No, Mr. President, the Keepers were doomed from the moment you convinced me to turn my hand against them," Winton finished. Earlier, perhaps, but he wouldn't admit that to Solace. He needed the Legatan to believe he was in control.

"Are there any left who can recognize what we've done?" Solace asked.

"It's hard to be certain," the old man said with carefully measured hesitance in his voice. "Some senior members would have been elsewhere, and I suspect the Keepers had backups I might not have been aware of."

"We cannot risk their secrets being turned over to the Mage-King, Partisan," the President told him. "We are not yet ready to declare the wider Republic. No one can be allowed to expose what we have had to do."

"I have assets in place," Partisan told him, "but they are insufficient to guarantee the removal of any surviving Keepers. Additional resources would be helpful."

Solace glared at him for a moment, then sighed and nodded.

"I will have the codes and contacts for an LMID cell operating on Mars forwarded to you," he said. "We have few reliable resources that close to Olympus Mons, Partisan. Do not waste them."

Winton nodded. If he was lucky, those resources were as obviously linked to Legatus as he hoped.

"The Council maneuvering around the deaths of Octavian and Ndosi provides an opportunity," he told Solace.

"Alexander will never permit what they want," Solace replied. "He allows them to run out the rope, but he will hang them with it."

"That is exactly the opportunity I meant. You will never have a better reason than that."

"We are not ready," Solace repeated. "The Fleet continues to be built. It would never do for the Protectorate to realize the new ships exist. There will come a time, but it is not yet."

"You may never have a better excuse," Winton pointed out.

"The Legislature has placed that decision in McClintlock's hands," Solace told him. "They trust him. *I* trust him. He will act when the time is right."

"Of course," Winton murmured. "Do you need anything more?"

"No, Partisan. Make certain the Keepers are destroyed. Their knowledge is our weakness."

"It shall be done."

Once the Link had shut itself down, the screens and cameras folding away to join the technological wonder itself in hiding, Winton finally allowed himself to frown. His conversations with Solace were always fraught.

The President of Legatus's plans worked well for Winton's intentions, but he couldn't afford for Solace's people to realize that "Partisan" was anything but an ex-Keeper turned mercenary, willing to sell out his former allies for money.

He tapped a command on his wrist computer and waited, turning back to the windows over the space station's concourse. As he watched, someone took advantage of the fact that the centripetal pseudo-gravity was only present at the floor to fly a glider over the crowd.

A quick glance down at the computer he wore confirmed that station security already knew. The daredevil would be intercepted. If this was the first time they'd come across security's radar, they'd just get a stern lecture.

If it wasn't, well, Alpha Centauri had laws on the books for reckless endangerment for a reason.

The door behind him slid open without warning, the man entering being the only person other than Winton himself the security system would let through. There were very, very few people left in the galaxy that the old man trusted, but the muscular Mage with the freshly grown beard standing in the door in unmarked gray fatigues was one of them.

Kent Riley wore the gold medallion of a Mage, though this one lacked the man's full qualifications as a Combat Mage. Thin gray gloves covered his hands, concealing the projector rune carved into his palm.

"Was your discussion fruitful, boss?" Riley asked as the door slid shut behind him. The ex-Marine—like Winton, officially dead now—crossed to the concourse and darkened the one-way glass.

"A mixed bag as always with Solace," Winton admitted, settling into a chair with an unconcealed sigh of relief. "He has agreed to provide us with codes for his agents on Mars. An Augment cell, if we're lucky."

"Would the Legatans have actually snuck a cell of cyborg Mage killers onto Mars?" Riley asked. He wasn't disbelieving, just questioning.

That was one of the things Winton liked about his much younger ally. Riley wasn't going to disbelieve something just because it went against what he believed to be true. He'd ask for evidence, but he'd believe it when it was given to him as well.

"More than one, I suspect," Winton replied. "It'll be up to you to find out. I...lack the strength for field work anymore."

"You push yourself too hard as it is," Riley pointed out. "Few knew me on Mars, and I have disguises and false identities. I can handle this for you. You're not a Mage or a cyborg, boss. And we need you."

Winton smiled thinly. Riley, more than any other, knew how carefully Winton kept that true. No one else, not even Riley, knew all of the threads that converged in this office.

Riley knew more than most, and there would come a time when Winton brought the young Mage fully into his confidence. Riley had killed a *Hand* for him, after all, and there were few better proofs of loyalty and commitment.

"The Legatans aren't willing to commit themselves just yet," he told Riley. "They're not ready... We *want* the Republic to be born before it's ready, so I want you to find a spark to push things forward."

"What kind of spark?" Riley asked.

"The Council investigation into Montgomery provides us with tinder," Winton replied. "A threat to the Council itself should light it. You'll have the contact codes for the Legatans, but also..."

He smiled.

"We'll send you with some resources I've long promised some old friends. It's time to fully activate Nemesis Sol."

"It's been a while since we had contact," Riley warned. "They may not be willing to talk to us anymore."

"We promised them ships, Riley," Winton said. "If we fulfill that promise, they'll be willing to talk."

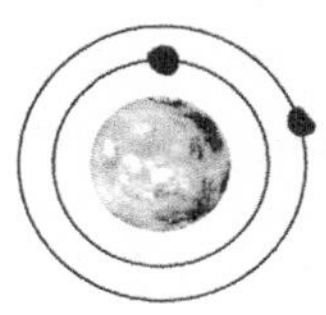

CHAPTER 2

THE ROYAL Martian Navy cruiser *Duke of Magnificence* had been Damien Montgomery's home for over a year. The diminutive Hand of the Mage-King of Mars had dragged the warship from one crisis to another, one space battle to another, and once again, the cruiser was badly damaged and in for repair.

He'd packed all of his things, again, and a pair of ratings from the ship's crew were hauling them to his shuttle. His office, however, still needed to be packed—and the office of one of the Mage-King's roving warrior-judges contained far too many items no one else could see, let alone touch.

Damien had claimed one of the cruiser's observation decks as his office space, allowing him to stand next to the massive window and see the universe outside the ship. Right now, that view was of the Navy yards in high orbit above Mars, mostly of the refit slip *Duke* had been slotted into.

Through the yard, however, he could see Mars itself. The once-red world was mostly green now, terraformed by both technology and magic to support human life. He could even, he was sure, make out the mountains of the Hellas Montes Park.

Thankfully, from this height, he couldn't see the scar where a nuclear explosion had ended his last investigation and killed the traitors he'd chased there. That would only have aggravated his mood.

Damien Montgomery was by nature a calm, if somewhat impulsive, man.

Today he was angry. It was a simmering, unfamiliar thing, a mood that had only built since the moment he'd thought that, perhaps, he could take Hand Charlotte Ndosi alive and finally get some *answers* as to what she and her allies had been up to.

And then one of those "allies" had shot Ndosi and fled, leaving a nuclear bomb to destroy the base. A nuclear bomb Damien had survived only because Ndosi had spent the last of *her* power to get *him* out.

And that left his anger without any target at all. He wanted to be angry at Ndosi for seducing him and betraying him, but she'd saved his life. He wanted to be angry at her killer, but he had no idea who the Mage had even been.

Two Hands had died in a matter of weeks, and while Ndosi had *technically* been killed by someone else, both had died in combat with Damien Montgomery. He had the questionable distinctions of being the *only* Hand to have killed another Hand...and the only person to have ever killed two Hands.

He could have lived without either.

"My lord," a voice interrupted his angry glaring at a world without answers.

"Yes, Romanov?"

Special Agent Denis Romanov, Mage-Captain of the Royal Martian Marine Corps, was the new leader of Damien's bodyguards. He was as slim as Damien himself but with easily forty centimeters on the Hand he was sworn to defend.

"We have news from the MIS's follow-up around the Archive," the Marine told him.

"I'm not expecting them to find much in a nuked ruin," Damien replied. The Martian Investigation Service had received the thankless job of having to clean up after the Keepers' nuke. The Archive may have contained an unknown amount of knowledge hidden from the rest of humanity, but it was all radioactive ash now.

"They also went back over the satellite footage," Romanov said. "Someone, probably Ndosi, ordered an evacuation just after you took off towards the base."

Damien took a moment to process that. If there'd been an evacuation...

"Did any of them clear the blast zone?"

"The nuke was buried pretty deep. The blast zone was contained and directed mostly upwards. So far as we can tell, about forty ground vehicles left the Archive, and all of them made it out."

"So, the Keepers aren't dead yet after all," he murmured.

"Apparently, Director Wong caught wind of this and reran some checks."

Damien finally turned around to face Romanov. Director Wong headed the Martian Investigation Service in Curiosity City, and had been pulled into his investigation of the Keepers when they'd tracked one to her city.

"She didn't..."

"She found Raptis," Romanov told him. "He was being careful, but the encrypted channel he used to access his personal email was designed by *our* cyber-security team."

"Where is he?"

"Safehouse in Curiosity City."

"Is the shuttle we arrived in armed?"

Romanov chuckled.

"My lord, we're *your* bodyguards. Of course the shuttle is armed."

Damien had made the habit a while before of doing most of his traveling in a Royal Martian Marine Corps assault shuttle. It added a layer of security to his personal movements that was useful, and the intimidation factor of the armed spacecraft helped make up for his own unthreatening appearance.

Even though it had been a "safe" trip, just packing up Damien and Romanov's things from the warship, he'd still traveled in the assault shuttle. Now, with suitcases of their personal effects webbed down in the back of the craft, they detached from *Duke of Magnificence* and dropped toward Mars and Curiosity City, on the shores of the Gale Crater Sea.

"The safehouse is in a cheaper neighborhood, an inner suburb that's about due for gentrification to hit any year now," Romanov briefed the mixed squad of Secret Service Agents and Marines sharing the shuttle. "It's a large older home, and our best guess is that the interior has been gutted to allow for security measures.

"We won't have a lot of detail until we're closer and can hit the building with the shuttle scanners, but Professor Raptis accessed his personal email through an encrypted channel from this location seventy-two hours ago.

"I figure the odds are only fifty/fifty he's still there, but remember: the Professor is a Mage. We want him alive, but not at the cost of dead Marines or Agents; am I clear?"

"Yes, sir!"

The men and women started checking their guns and body armor. They hadn't been paranoid enough to pack exosuit heavy combat armor into the shuttle, but they shouldn't need it. Damien was hoping that the Professor, the only senior Keeper he *knew* to be alive, would be willing to cooperate.

As they checked over their gear, he checked his runes. He had eight of them on his body, made of a silver polymer literally inlaid into his flesh. The first two had been the Jump interface runes on his palms that allowed him to interface with a starship's jump matrix and teleport the vessel between the stars.

The five Runes of Power followed. Each was a thaumic feedback loop that dramatically amplified his own magical power. If *those* Runes had problems, he'd probably already know—because he'd be dead. There was a *lot* of power wrapped up in them, and if he was lucky, a failure would only kill him. If he was unlucky, it could take out a city block at least.

The projector rune at the top of his right palm was almost an afterthought, the rune designed to extend a Combat Mage's range, almost overkill on top of the Runes of Power. It was still useful, though, enough that he'd added it after his first two Runes of Power.

A tiny trickle of power ran through them, confirming everything was still working, while Damien doffed his suit jacket and dress shirt for an armored vest and black T-shirt. He'd destroyed a few too many suits over the years to knowingly wear one into combat *again*.

"Touchdown in sixty seconds," the pilot reported. "Linked into the traffic control system; the street should be clear for us."

"Ready?"

"Oohrah!"

The shuttle dropped toward the suburban street at high speed, crashing to a halt in a flare of rockets barely two meters from the ground. It started to descend the last distance, but the rear door was already open and Romanov led his first team out.

Damien was barely a step behind the first four armed men, magic flaring around him as he controlled his descent to land safely. Romanov did the same...but the three Marines following him had no such gifts.

They hit the ground and rolled with the ease of long practice, the impact-absorbing motion *also* allowing them to be well out in front of their commander and their principal. Damien's bodyguards, he noted with a mental smile, knew him *very* well.

"Clear!" one of the Marines announced loudly as the three of them swept the street with the barrels of their guns.

"Move in," Romanov ordered, sensibly gesturing his subordinates ahead of him while he dropped back to stand beside Damien.

The Hand was studying the display on his wrist computer, reviewing the sensor data from the shuttle.

"The entire house is shielded," he told the Special Agent softly. "We're not getting any clean readings."

"That's why we have doorknockers," Romanov replied. "Conner, Chan, secure the door! *Carefully*."

With the shuttle landed, the rest of Damien's bodyguards slash strike team were spreading out around them, watching the street.

The designated Marines moved up to flank the door, rifles at the ready as one of them reached over and gently tried the handle. Conner was already patting his pockets for explosives, but the door swung open at Chan's touch.

"That's...unexpected," Romanov murmured. "Move in by fire teams," he snapped aloud. "Watch your backs. I don't like this."

With the Marine Mage-Captain turned Special Agent standing beside him, Damien was effectively restrained from barging in first or even right behind the lead team. Romanov, however, wasn't significantly more patient than the Hand, and followed the *second* team into the building.

The two Mages arguably each represented more firepower than the rest of the twenty-man detail, but they were no less vulnerable to traps than the Marines and Secret Service Agents.

Eight men and women, half Marines and half Agents, went ahead of them. The entryway and outer portion of the house looked surprisingly normal, though Damien noted that there seemed to be a central core everything was arranged around...and that core didn't have any doors.

"Nothing out here has been touched," one of the Agents noted. "It's a decoy."

There were no stairs, either. The inner section of the house, easily fifteen meters across, was completely cut off from the outside, and any access to the second floor or basement was inside the sealed section.

"Find the access," Romanov ordered. "There has to be one."

The detail spread out, searching the decoy "house" for the entrance to the safehouse itself.

"Here!"

Damien and Romanov followed the shout into the decoy kitchen, where one of the Marines had managed to swing the entire fridge out of place.

"It's on some kind of hinge," she reported. "If it locks... Well, it wasn't locked."

"That's consistent, at least," Damien said. "Romanov?"

"If you'll stand back, my lord," the Marine Special Agent replied, then gestured the fire team in the kitchen forward.

Leading the way with their rifle barrels, they pushed the appliance fully out of the way and moved into the dimly lit space beyond. Lights and scanners reached into the darkness, and Damien waited impatiently for their report.

"Six-meter-long corridor, terminating in a metal security hatch. We've got laser emitters, disabled ones. They're linked up to a row of claymores, but...everything's shut down."

"Disconnect them anyway," Romanov ordered. "No chances."

"On it. Hold on."

Damien tried not to hold his breath as the troopers worked, preparing a shield of hardened air to drop between the Marines and the mines at a moment's notice.

It went unneeded as they did their work slowly and competently.

"We're clear. Advancing on the hatch. No movement on the scopes."

The Hand wanted to charge in right behind them, but he was *starting* to learn better. Instead, he watched down the hall as the four-man fire team reached the heavy steel door and prepared to breach.

And again, the door was unlocked.

"Hatch is open. Scopes have pressure scanners linked to unknown defenses... They were already disabled."

"This is creepy," Romanov told Damien.

"And dangerous," he replied. "We're moving in."

"My lord—"

"We're either already too late or we're running out of time," Damien snapped. "With me, Mage-Captain."

The fire teams fell into place around them as Damien pushed forward through the security hatch, conjuring a mobile shield of hardened air to protect them all from any active traps.

He wasn't particularly surprised, however, when nothing impeded their progress. The disabled alarms, the disarmed traps, it all added up to a very clear picture—and not one he liked.

Once they were past the decoys and the security, the main floor of the safehouse was a drab little apartment with no natural light. A cheap kitchenette, a cheaper set of chairs and a table, and stairs leading up and down.

"Up or down, Captain?" Damien asked.

"If I was living in this place, I'd be up," Romanov replied. "Where there's actual light."

Damien nodded and climbed the stairs, his shield sweeping ahead of him.

Even through the barrier of solidified air, though, the smell of smoke and blood began to reach him, and the Hand suspected what he was going to find. The door at the top of the stairs swung open at the gentlest touch of his magic, and he stepped through into what *had* been a library.

Someone had stripped the shelves, dumping the books and papers into the middle of the room, and then set it all on fire. The still-smoldering pile of debris also included data disks and sticks, all cracked and ruined now.

While the papers and data disks might have contained answers, Damien's main hope for them had been Dr. Periklis Raptis, PhD in Runic Studies. Unfortunately, that worthy lay on the ground just past the impromptu fire pit, his eyes staring blankly into the wall.

"Get me containment on that fire," Damien snapped as he stepped around it to reach Raptis. Kneeling, he closed the swarthy old man's eyes, studying the body and the room.

The Keeper had been shot four times at point-blank range, all from behind.

"He would have died quickly," Romanov said as he joined the Hand. "One of those rounds severed his spine."

"We needed him alive," Damien replied. "Someone else...didn't. Someone he knew."

"You're guessing that because the defenses are down?" Romanov asked.

"That's one factor, yes. Also, the Professor was a Mage," the Hand told him. "He was a Mage, someone killed him, and the room is still mostly intact. He didn't think he was being threatened, didn't fight back."

"That's...not a good sign, boss."

"A Keeper shot Charlotte," Damien reminded his bodyguard. "Everyone may want to blame me for her death, and I'm certainly *responsible,* but she was shot by one of her own."

"Something's rotten in the state of Denmark," Romanov said slowly.

"Agreed. We need MIS Forensics. This mess is outside our expertise now."

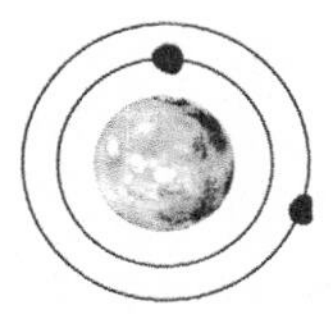

CHAPTER 3

DAMIEN WAS BACK outside by the time the MIS Forensics team arrived on helicopters sweeping in from the local office. The Curiosity City police had been on their way before his shuttle had even touched down, and their blue-and-white cars now blocked both ends of the street, allowing the MIS choppers to land without impediment.

The Lieutenant leading the police detachment saluted Damien as soon as he saw the golden hand hanging on the smaller man's chest.

"My lord," the uniformed officer said swiftly. "I've got twenty officers holding the street clear. What are your orders?"

"Unfortunately, it looks like everyone in the house is dead," Damien told the cop. "You can close your perimeter up to keep this house clear, but this has turned from a raid into a crime scene."

The cop winced.

"That's...only our fifth murder this year, my lord Hand," he admitted. "We're a university town; it's generally pretty quiet here except the drunk and disorderlies."

"I know," the Hand replied. The most excitement Curiosity City had seen in recent months had been when he'd raided the university to try and arrest Raptis the first time. He nodded toward the choppers, where men and women in black fatigues with yellow lettering were off-loading equipment.

"MIS will be handling the investigation," he told the Lieutenant. "We'll need you to keep the house secured, but you can probably start letting the neighbors back in."

"Of course, my lord."

An older woman with graying hair and the mixed ethnic features of a Martian native crossed the street to Damien, looking at him with unreadable dark eyes.

"Director Wong," he greeted the head of the Martian Investigation Service in Curiosity City. "Good to see you again."

"Someday you'll show up in my city for a social occasion, my lord, and then it will be good to see you," she replied sharply. "What have we got?"

"Raptis was exactly where you said he would be, Director," Damien told her. "Unfortunately, someone beat us to him and shot him. They also burned all of the books and wrecked any data storage in the safehouse."

She pursed her lips.

"Not as helpful as we hoped."

"No, but I'm hoping your people can get *something* out of it," he concluded. "Some of the data disks or chips might have retrievable information. Also, I want your people to tear the defenses apart. They were shut down here, and if we know *how*, we can deal with similar defenses elsewhere."

"You think there are more safehouses?"

"If I'd been running the Keepers, my plan for the Archive going up would involve a lot of overlapping partial backups," Damien said thoughtfully. "If we keep looking, hopefully we'll find at least one before whoever is killing the Keepers gets there."

"The life of a Hand is never boring, is it, my lord?"

Before Damien could reply, the pilot stepped out of the shuttle.

"Hand Montgomery, I have Dr. Christoffsen on the secure coms for you," he told him.

Damien shook his head and met Wong's eyes with a small smile.

"Apparently, even less boring than I might think."

The assault shuttle had a small compartment next to the cockpit designed for the platoon officer to communicate with higher command. It had most of the equipment necessary to run a mid-sized combat action, as it wasn't as though the company or battalion commander would have a different type of shuttle.

Closing the door behind him, Damien brought up the secure communications suite and linked into the channel the pilot had set up for him.

"Professor," he greeted Dr. Robert Christoffsen, his political advisor.

Christoffsen was a pudgy older man in the late stages of going completely bald, but he also held multiple PhDs and had spent ten years as the Governor of the Core World of Tara. As far as Damien was concerned, "the Professor" was his local definition of "wiser minds."

"What's going on?" he asked. "I'm guessing it's urgent."

"It couldn't wait for this evening, no," Christoffsen said. "We've been formally notified that you are being summoned before the Council of the Protectorate to be questioned about the deaths of Hands Ndosi and Octavian."

Damien exhaled and nodded.

"Not unexpected," he admitted. "Not that I'm looking forward to it. When do they want me?"

"Oh eight hundred Olympus Mons Time *tomorrow*," his aide told him. "They've only given us sixteen hours' notice."

"To get to Ceres?" Damien considered. "We'll need a fast ship, but we can do it. I'll arrange for one from the Civil Fleet for us."

"I'll take care of it," Christoffsen replied. "*You* need to get to Olympus Mons. His Majesty wants to talk to you, Damien. ASAP."

Damien sighed again.

"Fortunately, I appear to have a high-speed assault shuttle to hand," he told Christoffsen. "I'm not needed here anymore. This is a job for the crime scene people now."

"His Majesty's schedule isn't exactly wide open," the older man told him, "but his secretary said they'd open a spot for you when you made it."

"That is never a good sign," Damien said. "I'm on my way."

Two red-armored Royal Guardsmen were waiting for Damien as he exited his shuttle. He'd changed on the way over, back into the black suit and white shirt that was the closest thing Hands had to a uniform, along with the golden icon of his office, and left most of his own guards behind on the shuttle.

Romanov came with him and would coordinate with the Royal Guard and Secret Service in the Mountain to make sure of Damien's safety. That they were being met by Guardsmen in power armor was disconcerting, though.

"Guardsmen," he greeted them. "Do you know if His Majesty has cleared time for me?"

"He has," a familiar voice replied from one of the suits, and Damien relaxed slightly. He'd worked with Guardsman Han in the aftermath of the Keeper debacle. "If you and the Special Agent will come with us?"

"Of course, Guardsman Han," Damien told her, falling in behind the armored Mage. Every Royal Guard was a fully trained Combat Mage, clad in exosuit combat armor that included runes designed by the first Mage-King to make them more powerful.

Damien was a Rune Wright like the Mage-Kings and could sense the power of the runes woven through the two Guards' armor. There were more effective small-scale amplifiers, like the Runes of Power inlaid in his own skin, but those Runes had to be tailored to the user *by* a Rune Wright.

Outside of the Runes of Power, a Royal Guard's armor was probably the best amplifier in existence smaller than a starship. Their existence, like that of the Rune Wrights who'd designed them, was classified.

As they traveled through the stone corridors of Olympus Mons, Damien noted more runes appearing on the walls around them, runes that were focusing and channeling power toward a specific location. Despite his own skills and experience, they were still over halfway to the Throne Room before he realized where they were going, and he swallowed hard as they reached the massive metal doors that led to the Mage-King's sanctum.

"He wanted to speak to Hand Montgomery alone," Han told Romanov. "We all wait here."

Damien doubted that Romanov was happy about that, but there was nowhere else in the *galaxy* as safe as this room.

"I'll be fine, Denis. Wait here with Han," he ordered.

Taking his bodyguard's silence as assent, Damien pushed open the double doors and stepped through to meet his King.

Damien had entered the throne room at the heart of Olympus Mons more times than he could count, even if the path down from the shuttle pad wasn't as familiar to him as it might have been, but he could count on his fingers the number of times he'd seen the simulacrum in that chamber fully active.

The pyramid-shaped cavern glittered with both electric and magical light as a million pieces of semi-liquid silver sand filled the air, taking the shape of planets, asteroids, ships... Everything in the Sol System was represented somewhere in the room, though there was little smaller than a planet that was more than a few specks of silver.

Olympus Mons was an immense amplifier of incredible power, built by the Eugenicists, who had bred magic back into humanity to allow them to identify even the tiniest scrap of the Gift. They'd misunderstood what they had built, and the first Mage-King had turned it on them.

A simple chair sat in the middle of the room, carved from the stone of the mountain and covered in runes. Once, it had been where the subjects of the Olympus Project had been tested. Now it was the true Throne of the Mage-King.

Desmond Michael Alexander the Third sat in that chair, studying the silver orbiting his head. He was a tall, gaunt man whose hair mirrored the simulacrum above his head.

"You know," he said softly, "people would look at this and think I was omniscient inside Sol."

"A starship is three specks of sand on this scale," Damien told him, ducking under Jupiter as he approached his King. "What's a person?"

"An idea," Alexander replied. "I can *see* individuals, if I know exactly where to look. But I can't find the Keepers. I can't read the Council's minds. I could destroy an entire star fleet from this chair, but I can't protect us from knives in the dark."

"That's why you have us," the Hand said. "And the Royal Guard. And...everyone else."

"I know," Alexander agreed with a sigh. "But I sit here, with near-godlike power at my command, and I find I can do *nothing*."

Damien waited in silence. The King sounded tired and frustrated, but he had to have a point.

"From the moment we decided not to keep the mess with the Keepers secret, this hearing has been coming," he finally said. He didn't even blame Damien for that, which was generous, given that Damien had threatened to resign if they had tried to keep it a secret.

"Factions inside the Council will use this as a lever," Alexander continued. "Some will use it to undermine me, to attempt to accrue more power to the Council itself. The Legatans will use it to undermine the Protectorate itself.

"For a purely advisory body, the Council has become quite the snake pit," he observed.

"There's a reason I'm bringing Robert," Damien replied. "This is not my type of battlefield, my liege."

"This isn't a trial, Damien," his King warned. "You don't get counsel or the protection of law. They will attempt to rip you apart, to mark you as a man who unnecessarily killed two Hands..."

"They have no authority to judge me under the Charter."

"They have the authority to interrogate you and the authority to formally ask me to disavow your actions," Alexander said. "No Mage-King has ever *not* asked a Hand to resign when the Council got that far."

"Meaning that it's arguable if we can even...not," Damien concluded.

"Exactly. The Charter may say one thing, but tradition allows them that power," the King noted. "If I fight them on it, I can be forced to make other concessions. Potentially more dangerous ones. If we open up the tradition and the Charter to negotiation, we don't know where it ends."

"Most of the Council is at least working for the Protectorate," the Hand pointed out.

"We hope," Alexander said, then sighed. "You're right. I don't like the risks inherent in changing the balance of power, but I'll admit some of that is selfish. It's the Legatans I'm worried about."

"We *know* what they've been up to."

"What we know and what we can *prove* are very different things, my Hand."

Damien snarled wordlessly. Legatan spies had been at the heart of every disaster lately *except* the mess with the Keepers, but...

"All of our evidence is circumstantial," Alexander continued. "We can't definitively link surplus weapons and ships back to them. We have enough circumstantial evidence to bury them, but without a solid link, solid proof, there's nothing we can do."

"The answers are on Legatus," Damien pointed out.

"And if we had even one piece of solid damned evidence, I'd send you there with a fleet to find those answers," the Mage-King replied. "If you'd arrested that Augment on Ardennes..."

"She helped us."

"I know. It made sense then." Alexander shook his head. "We suspect. As you say, we *know*. But we can prove nothing, and we cannot move on a *Core World government* without proof—especially not Legatus."

"And this mess with the Council won't help."

"No. Tread softly, Damien," his King ordered. "We are on fragile ground here."

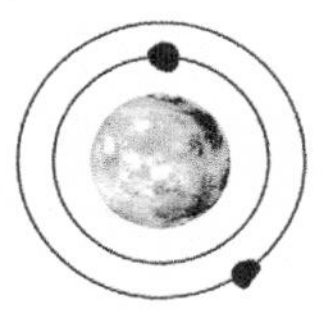

CHAPTER 4

THE MARTIAN GOVERNMENT maintained a small fleet of civilian craft in the Sol System, with crews that rotated between them as needed. While the assault shuttle that Damien used as a personal transport could make it to Ceres, it wouldn't be a particularly comfortable trip for anyone aboard.

Dr. Christoffsen had booked them basically the exact opposite of that instead, and Damien chuckled as the pilot's course lined them on the familiar lines of the jump-yacht *Doctor Akintola*. The ship, named for a Eugenicist scientist who had joined in the first Mage-King's rebellion, was a luxurious ship they'd flown on before.

"Are we going to get shot at again?" Romanov asked as he looked at the ship himself.

"Why would you ask that?" Damien said.

"Last time we were on that ship, we got shot at," the Special Agent pointed out. "And then you did an emergency jump that made everyone throw up."

"We didn't even scratch the yacht's paint, and I'm sure the Civil Fleet has cleaned up the mess inside," Damien replied. "Plus, this time you'll get the quarters Julia did last time. I believe she had one of the en suites, and the bathtubs on *Akintola* could pass for swimming pools."

His chief bodyguard chuckled softly.

"It's lucky for you I'm not so easily bribed," he said virtuously. "Do we have a Civil Fleet crew?"

"*Akintola*'s pretty automated. I'll fly her, though there's no jump involved in the trip to Ceres."

One of the reasons to take *Akintola* was that she had a boat bay more than big enough for two shuttles, and their pilot neatly slotted the assault shuttle into it. Another, less terrifyingly deadly shuttlecraft was already waiting for them, and Robert Christoffsen was standing by the boat bay exit as Damien left the shuttle.

A luxury ship like *Akintola* had gravity runes throughout, providing a steady one gravity everywhere in the ship. The runes were expensive, requiring regular maintenance by a Mage, but the Civil Fleet had a number of Ship's Mages on staff to take care of it.

It was a luxury Damien appreciated, unlike the yacht's gold-plated faucets and wood-paneled bulkheads.

"My lord," Christoffsen greeted him. "Are you feeling ready for this?"

"No," Damien admitted. "But I don't think anyone ever could be. Anything in particular I need to know?"

"How many hours do we have?" his political advisor asked dryly.

"Ten, but I need to be on the bridge for most of them. I can fly while you talk, though."

"Good," Christoffsen said. "Because you're about to walk into a room with over a hundred people where the only requirement to get in was 'my Governor wanted me here,' and the reasons for that vary from Councilor to Councilor."

Damien nodded as he led the way deeper into the ship.

"And I'm guessing that if I want to get *out* of the snake pit intact, I need to know all hundred-odd reasons?"

Christoffsen chuckled.

"About the only good news is that at least half a dozen of them are going to be on your side regardless of their normal allegiances," he noted. "Being a hero is handy."

"I'm not a hero," Damien said quietly.

"We can argue that for months, but the important thing is that people from the places you've helped *think* you are, and that's currency we can spend."

Damien was alone on the bridge when they finally reached Ceres, Christoffsen's lecture percolating in his brain as he maneuvered the jump-yacht toward the Council Station. The dwarf planet beneath the station was uninhabited now, but it had been the gravitational anchor for the shipyards that had built the first colony ships.

Ceres had never been anything beyond a massive industrial and mining complex, and smaller asteroids had proved a more efficient source of materials in the long run. The easy mines had run dry, the shipyards had moved elsewhere as the massive initial diaspora slowed, and the domes of Ceres had become a historical curiosity.

But the Council Station remained and Ceres had become a demilitarized zone. No armed ships were allowed near it, not even those of the Protectorate Navy. Weapon platforms under control of the Council Lictors orbited the station, but Damien's trained eye could tell their scanners and weapons were obsolete.

A single Royal Martian Navy destroyer could have smashed the defenses in minutes, but that wasn't the point. The point was that the Council of the Protectorate was visibly not dependent on the Mage-King for their protection.

The Council Station itself was almost quaint to Damien's eye. His own home system of Sherwood was a moderately prosperous MidWorld, and its orbital infrastructure paled in comparison to the stations orbiting any of the Core Worlds—but its main space station put the Council Station to shame.

The Station was a single ring just over twelve hundred meters across and one hundred and fifty meters thick. It rotated swiftly enough to provide a full gravity at the outside, and a central docking hub had been added some seventy years after it was built.

It wasn't a commercial or economic center, but there were still enough ships around that he'd been assigned a specific course by Station Control. The Council of the Protectorate might not *rule* mankind, but they served an important role in the Mage-King's government. The bureaucracy involved was enough to fill the station, and communications with their home systems kept a small fleet of jump couriers busy.

"*Doctor Akintola*, I confirm you're on the schedule for today. Do you require a docking port?"

"Negative," Damien replied. "I'll be boarding by shuttle with my detail."

There was a pause as the controller realized who she was talking to.

"My Lord Montgomery," she finally said. "Please remember that the Station restricts weapons and armed personnel aboard."

"Check your protocols," he told her. "Those restrictions don't apply to His Majesty or his Hands. I will be boarding with two armed bodyguards. There won't be a problem."

Another pause, and he *heard* the woman swallow.

Even bringing only two guards was arguably a concession on his part, and one that Romanov might complain about. Damien didn't *need* guards, though, and the Mage-King had told him to tread softly.

"Of course, Lord Montgomery," the controller finally replied. "Your shuttle is clear to docking airlock twenty-seven."

"Thank you."

Twenty minutes later, the mostly-empty assault shuttle tucked itself into the docking airlock, and Damien led Romanov, Christoffsen, and one of the senior Secret Service Agents onto the station.

He was unsurprised to discover that the central hub of the Council Station had a full suite of gravity runes. Despite the small scale of the station, it was probably the single most politically important space facility in the Protectorate, and its internal fittings showed it.

The runes were laid into plush blue carpeting that looked out of place in the docking ports of a space station. It was clean enough that either human staff or a fleet of robots had to spend most of their lives just scrubbing and vacuuming the carpet after people came through, and Damien barely managed not to visibly shake his head at the extravagance.

There were luxuries he considered worth it. Then there was everything *else* the rich of the galaxy surrounded themselves with.

"Someone is supposed to meet us," Christoffsen told Damien. "I'm guessing one of the aides."

A couple of moments later, they entered the central lobby of the docking hub and a dark-skinned man with white-streaked brown hair and a navy-blue suit crossed to meet them.

"*Bonjour,* my lord," he greeted Damien with a faint Tau Cetan accent. "Welcome to the Council Station. I am Councilor Granger of Tau Ceti."

Not an aide, Damien reflected. Suresh Granger was a leader of the Loyalist faction in the Council, according to his briefing from Christoffsen, as well as the representative of one of the most economically powerful Core Worlds after Sol and Legatus.

"Councilor Granger, it's a pleasure," Damien told him, offering his hand. "I wasn't expecting so illustrious a welcoming party." He smiled. "Most of the time, I half expect a paper printout with *Your meeting is in this room, Mr. Montgomery.*"

"We offer a slightly higher level of courtesy to those summoned before the Council, Hand Montgomery," Granger allowed. "Your hearing is in just over an hour, in the main Council Chamber."

"That gives us time, thankfully," Damien said. "I'm not sure about Dr. Christoffsen, but I could use some food before I charge into the lions' den."

"Of course." The Councilor coughed delicately. "As it happens, my lord, I have a personal chef aboard station. I would be delighted to feed you and your escort in exchange for, say, ten minutes of your time in private?"

Damien had been quite neatly trapped, he realized. There was no real, polite way to decline, and Granger was almost certainly an ally.

"Of course, Councilor," he agreed cheerfully, exchanging a glance with Christoffsen. "We would be delighted to sample your chef's cooking."

Fortunately, given what Damien suspected he'd been trapped into, Granger's chef was very, very good. Tau Cetan cuisine was...not exactly something he was used to, being normally described as the result of an Indian father and a French mother fighting in the kitchen.

Both the heavily sweetened, spiced, milky tea and the spicy chocolate croissants had been fantastic, however, and Damien had no complaints about the breakfast at all.

As he followed Granger into the Councilor's office, however, he suspected that he wasn't going to be as pleased with the private conversation.

"All right, Councilor," he told Granger as he took in the other man's office and propped himself against the wall, avoiding the many framed photos from the Councilor's long and storied life. "I know when I've been outmaneuvered and trapped. Since I doubt you plan on trying to kill me, I suggest you start talking."

Granger held up his hands defensively.

"I'm not your enemy, Hand Montgomery."

"I know that," Damien agreed. "But you've trapped me neatly regardless, so I'm presuming you have something to say."

The Councilor chuckled. "Fair enough." He dropped into his seat, a powered adjustable chair tucked in behind a massive oak desk. "Have a seat, my lord. Council Station is old, but it doesn't need you to prop up its walls."

"I'm fine," Damien said quickly.

"All right," Granger accepted. "I presume that Christoffsen, being his usual brilliant self, has briefed you on the political nightmare you're walking into?"

"I have some details, yes," the Hand said noncommittally.

The Councilor sighed.

"Look, Lord Montgomery," he said quietly, "the Protectorate is particularly fragile right now. We could argue the reasons for it for months, but the increased piracy, the Navy's apparent failure to contain it despite a series of high-profile successes, the chaos around Antonius... The very fabric of our nation is strained to the breaking point."

Damien waited silently for Granger to get to the point. He was quite certain that all of those issues could be traced back to Legatus, but as Alexander had reminded him, they had no proof. Nothing actionable.

"Now. Two Hands dead. A conspiracy at the heart of the Protectorate." Granger shook his head. "His Majesty said you did the right thing. I have no reason to doubt him or you, but he has already made it clear to us that he will not back down on supporting you."

"I appreciate that show of support," Damien noted, wondering just where Granger was going.

"It is a sign, perhaps, that our King is a better man than he is a wise one," the Councilor told him. "The deaths of two Hands mean it is impossible for the King's allies to prevent this matter coming before the Council...but if the UnArcana Worlds' Councilors throw in with those who would destroy the King's power, this Council *will* demand your censure.

"And if His Majesty refuses to ask for your resignation, a hundred years of tradition will be broken."

"The Council's power is at the discretion of the Mage-King. Defying him is not in their interests," Damien replied.

"But the Mage-King's government is funded by the governments they represent," Granger warned. "Much of that funding is technically voluntary. If even half a dozen Core and MidWorlds cut their funding down to the minimum required by the Charter, the Protectorate would be in an operating deficit for the first time in a century.

"We could stump along for a while, but there are enough governments backing the Councilors who want to take more power for the Council to cause major problems, and that's presuming the Legatans and other UnArcana Worlds don't cease funding the Protectorate entirely, using that as an excuse.

"It is always the purse strings on which monarchies break, Lord Montgomery. If the Council asks for your resignation and his Majesty refuses, the entire structure of the Protectorate is at risk."

Damien remained against the wall, studying Granger. The man was intense but seemed earnest. On the other hand, the wall of photos next to him as a reminder that the Tau Cetan was a politician, one who'd risen to the highest levels of his planetary government. He'd been sent to Sol when he'd lost the contest to become his party's candidate for Governor.

"I'm not certain what you want from me," he finally admitted. "I have every intention of doing everything in my power to convince the Council *not* to ask for my resignation. There is no more I can do."

"You can resign before they ask," Granger told him. "If you step down and return your Hand, this debate and hearing become toothless.

"You have done incredible things for the Protectorate and served His Majesty well, but the best thing you can do now is protect His Majesty from his own desire to protect *you*," the Councilor insisted. "Others can take your place, Lord Montgomery, and there are a thousand ways you could serve the Protectorate that do not require you to be a Hand!"

Granger didn't know that Damien was a Rune Wright. While his rare gift wasn't always directly relevant to his work, it was the reason he had five Runes of Power where every other Hand had one. A Rune Wright could put one Rune of Power on another Mage, but they could only put *multiple* Runes on themselves.

"I have a job," Damien said slowly. "I do the job. I won't say there are no political aspects to it, but largely, the political aftermath is not my problem."

"This one is," the Councilor said flatly. "I'm not saying this is right or just, Lord Montgomery. It is simply what you must do."

"No. It isn't," the Hand replied. "It is my duty to fight the Protectorate's enemies, not surrender to them. My resignation might turn back this particular attack, but it would not stop the forces that move in the shadows around us, Councilor.

"My resignation would not stop wars or arrest rogue governors. I can." Damien smiled thinly. "Don't misunderstand me, Mr. Granger. I appreciate and understand your concern. But I have work to do, and I will not resign."

He would consider it if the Council demanded it. It would still short-circuit the conflict Granger warned of if he took the decision out of his King's hands, but...he couldn't walk away from his responsibilities.

"I swore an oath," he told the other man. "To protect the people of the Protectorate. There was nothing about being more concerned about my own safety or the political consequences in that oath. We will deal with those as they fall.

“Until then, I speak for the Mage-King of Mars, and I will not be intimidated.”

Granger nodded slowly, bowing his head.

“So be it, then, my lord,” he told Damien. “We shall all see what the consequences are, I suppose.”

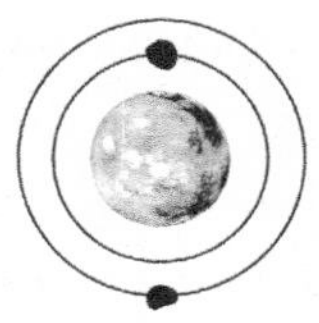

CHAPTER 5

DAMIEN BROUGHT his advisor and bodyguards to the entrance to the Council Chamber, but he wasn't surprised when one of the two Lictors in plain white uniforms stepped forward to bar their way as he approached.

"My Lord Montgomery," she greeted him. "Your name is alone on the summons I have. Your companions will need to wait here. There is a quite comfortable waiting room around the corner, I can show them over."

For a moment, Damien considered arguing. The Lictor was correct in that the Council had only summoned him, but even here he could override that.

Alexander's orders to "tread softly" echoed in his ears, however, and he inclined his head politely to the guard.

"Thank you," he told her. "Gentlemen, I'll let you know when I'm done."

"Of course, my lord," Romanov said with a sharp glance at the Lictors. "One of us will be at this door until you return," he continued. "We'll keep the Council's guards company."

The Lictor looked like she might object, but swallowed anything she was going to say as the Special Agent looked her in the eye. Damien's bodyguards would follow orders, but everyone knew the Council was playing power games, and his people were clearly less patient with it than he was.

"As you wish, of course, Special Agent," the woman replied. "You may enter, Lord Hand."

Checking the time, Damien waited a few seconds to be certain he was arriving exactly on time, then stepped past the white-uniformed guards into the chamber.

He didn't enjoy these kinds of games, but if the Council of the Protectorate wanted to play, he'd learned the rules by now.

The Chamber of the Council might have been built in a space station, but its designers had decided that didn't mean it couldn't have one *hell* of a view. The chamber was built up against the "upper" side of the rotating ring of Council Station, and the entire back side of the chamber had been magically transmuted to be transparent.

The white-uniformed Lictor led Damien across the floor and he looked up at the circular levels leading up towards that transparent wall. Five rows had been set up, though only the first four were fully occupied with thirty seats apiece.

One hundred and twenty seats for one hundred and twenty star systems. Thirteen Core Systems, including Sol and Legatus, whose representatives took up most of the first row. Thirty-three MidWorlds. Fifty-four Fringe Worlds, four of those desks still new enough to look out of place in the chamber.

Behind the risers containing those desks, Damien looked out at the plains of Ceres, currently eclipsing the Sun and haloing the entire room in a gentle gleam of light.

The room was quiet as he followed the Lictor to a plain table in the middle of the chamber, facing the assembled representatives of the Protectorate's worlds.

"Here, my lord," the Lictor instructed.

Damien calmly sat, facing the men and women who had summoned him, and waited.

The quiet stretched out, silence rippling down from the top of the chamber as the conversations died down. Most of the Councilors ceased their conversations as soon as he'd sat down, but others continued on for a good minute.

He continued to wait, his gloved hands crossed on the table in front of him, and studied Ceres behind the Council. Even from here, some of the gouges of the massive open-pit mines that had fueled the initial diaspora were visible. He suspected that had been intentional on the part of the original designers.

"Damien Montgomery," someone finally spoke. Damien turned his attention to the speaker, a white-haired man whose desk declared him the Councilor for Alpha Centauri. "This Council has summoned you to allow us to understand the events that led to the deaths of Hand Lawrence Octavian and Hand Charlotte Ndosi."

"I am at the Council's disposal, Councilor Newton," Damien said politely. If Councilor Paul Newton thought that refusing to grant the Hand his title was going to put him off-balance, the man really needed to up his game.

"So we see," Newton said flatly. "Let's begin at the beginning, shall we? Why were you on Andala IV in the first place?"

"There had been a murder and the Protectorate was asked to investigate," Damien replied.

"But why were *you* there?" the Councilor for Legatus demanded immediately. Raul McClintlock was a red-headed man with tanned skin and dark eyes. He was glaring at Damien as he spoke. "Andala was over fifty percent funded by Legatus. We certainly do not understand why a *Hand* was sent for a regular murder investigation."

"I was available," Damien said simply. "I also have some expertise in runic matters, and we knew that Professor Kurosawa had discovered strange runes before his death."

"You have a minor in Runic Studies," McClintlock pointed out. "What made you more qualified than any of the investigators in Tau Ceti?"

"The fact that I was a Hand and have His Majesty's trust," Damien said. Even in *this* chamber, no one here had need to know about the Rune Wrights. "Hands take on the missions that we feel are appropriate, Councilor McClintlock."

"Hand Montgomery's qualifications are not under question here," Councilor Montague of Tara interjected. "Continue, my lord."

Damien inclined his head towards the Asian-looking woman who spoke for Tara, the Core World Christoffsen had once ruled.

"During my investigation, one of the Marines under my command assisted Kurosawa's murderer in attempting to assassinate me," he told them. "They failed, but the archeological dig came under attack by Octavian's vessel."

"And how do you know the vessel was Octavian's?" Newton demanded.

"That was a long and complex piece of research included in my report, which I know this Council was provided a copy of," Damien noted. "I believe he was attempting to destroy—"

"Stop," Newton ordered. "This Council is not interested in your conjecture or your justifications, Montgomery," he snapped. "The events only, if you please. You do not know that the ship was Octavian's with absolute certainty, do you?"

"I only know of one ship of its type built in the last hundred years," Damien said quietly. "And that ship was owned by Hand Octavian...and Hand Octavian has not been seen since that ship attacked me."

"We are getting ahead of ourselves," McClintlock pointed out. "*A* ship attacked Andala IV. What happened?"

So, *that* was how the Council was planning on doing this. From some of the expressions Damien could see, not everyone was on board with this, but McClintlock and Newton seemed to be running this right now.

"The ship attempted to bombard the dig site, using military-grade munitions," he told them. "I stopped it."

"You'll forgive me, Montgomery, if I find that hard to believe," Newton snapped. "There is no defense against bombardment munitions that I am aware of, and while there is significant damage to the Andala IV site, it is hardly consistent with such a bombardment."

Damien turned his thin smile on the Councilor for Alpha Centauri.

"Councilor Newton, I am repeating myself here, but I am a Hand of the Mage-King of Mars," he said gently. "Not all of the capabilities of the

Hands are available to even the members of this Council. Suffice to say it is within my capacity to stop an orbital bombardment.

"The damage to the site that you noted was inflicted when that ship launched a landing force in an attempt to kill myself and any others at the site."

"Damage to an *irreplaceable* artifact of incalculable value," McClintlock snapped. "Inflicted when your Marines detonated *antimatter* weapons on the surface."

"Yes," Damien agreed. "Because the alternative was to allow an unknown force to exterminate the civilians we were supposed to defend—including several hundred Legatan academics, as I understand."

That shut McClintlock up, at least.

"If this ship was so determined to destroy the facility, what happened to it?" Newton demanded.

"They made two attempts to bombard the facility and landed ground troops to try and kill everyone," Damien said. "After all of those attempts failed, they retreated from the system, presumably surprised at their failure."

And if they hadn't, everyone would have died, because Damien himself had been in a coma triggered by magical overload at that point.

"Again, we are not looking for your conjecture, Montgomery," the Councilor snapped.

"I have no answer for you *but* conjecture," he said softly. "They attempted to destroy the camp. They failed. They left. I and a number of others were medevaced to Tau Ceti, where Mage-Admiral Segal deployed a destroyer squadron to secure Andala.

"To my knowledge, no further attempt was made to attack Andala," he noted.

"You said you were medevaced to Tau Ceti?" Councilor Montague asked. "What happened to you?"

"Thaumic burnout," Damien said simply. Every Mage in the room, roughly forty percent of the Councilors, visibly winced. "Even Hands have their limits, and I exceeded mine by a large margin protecting the dig site."

"That is not relevant to today's discussion," Newton said after a moment, recovering from his own wince. Most Mages had the consequences of thaumic burnout spelled out to them *very* vividly in training.

"What happened on Tau Ceti after you woke up?"

"I was asked to meet with an individual who promised some answers," Damien summarized. There was no need to go into his own questionable actions and the ensuing kidnapping that had *forced* him to meet the man who'd only introduced himself as "Winton."

"The individual attempted to recruit me to an organization he called the Royal Order of Keepers of Secrets and Oaths, even going so far as to offer me the Throne. I declined."

"And this was the first you'd heard of this Order? These 'Keepers'?"

"The assassin who attempted to kill me had used the name before, but otherwise, yes."

"And based on this one discussion, you decided the Keepers were enemies of the Protectorate that needed to be destroyed?" McClintlock demanded. "Rather...abrupt of you, wouldn't you say?"

"My encounters with the Keepers had involved them trying to kill me, trying to blow up the research facility I was standing in, and offering me the Throne of Olympus Mons if I joined them," Damien pointed out mildly. "But no, I did not decide they needed to be destroyed. Identified and contained, yes, but it was quite clear that whatever secrets they were hiding were dangerous and *needed* to be uncovered."

He stopped there before Newton could complain about conjecture again.

"And after this?" the Centauri Councilor asked.

Damien sighed.

"We filed an official flight plan and traveled to Mars, partly to investigate the Keepers and partly to check in with His Majesty. Our flight plan was used to intercept us, and the ship that was at Andala attacked us one jump short of Sol."

"That seems a rather dramatic leap," Newton said dryly.

"I am aware, Councilor, of exactly three living men and women capable of tracking Jumps," Damien replied. "One of them was aboard

Duke of Magnificence. The other two are assigned to special duty Navy task forces.

"In the absence of a Tracker, the only logical explanation for how we were intercepted is that Hand Octavian had access to my flight plan."

"Why are you so certain it was Hand Octavian?" McClintlock asked.

"In truth?" Damien shrugged. "Because no one has seen him *since* the ship was destroyed. Its wreckage gave us more evidence of the existence of the Keepers, and we dug into its history. As my report said, that linked us back to Octavian again."

"So, you returned to Mars in search of vengeance?" Newton asked.

"I returned to Mars in search of answers. I did not expect to find enemies there," Damien admitted. "Our search led us to Curiosity City University and from there to the location we now know was the Archive of the Keepers.

"There, I was intercepted by a squad of Combat Mages and Hand Ndosi."

He sighed. Those were unpleasant memories.

"We talked, we argued, and then we fought," he concluded. "Hand Ndosi had a dead man's switch linking her vitals to the suicide charge in the Archive. On the verge of death, she teleported me clear."

"Most people's discussions don't end in a nuclear explosion, Montgomery," Newton pointed out.

"We were Hands," he said quietly. "I'd sworn an oath to my King. She'd sworn some oath to the Keepers. We did not find a compromise before the situation deteriorated."

By now, Damien was starting to get frustrated with the interrogation.

"All of this was in my report," he reminded them, "with far more detail."

"It is valuable to hear it in your words," Newton told him. "None before you have ever killed two Hands. The situation is without precedent, and we must be certain of our actions."

Damien waited for the Councilor to elaborate.

"A nuclear weapon was detonated on one of our homeworlds," he continued. "Two Hands of the Mage-King are dead. At the center of all of this, one Hand. A very young Hand raised in turmoil and without explanation or qualification.

"We have our concerns and our questions."

"I believe my record speaks for itself," Damien said. "I serve Mars, Councilors, and through her, humanity."

"So do we all," McClintlock told him. "We would be remiss in our own duties, Lord Montgomery, if we did not investigate this situation to make sure there were no more bombs hidden away on us."

That was ironic, coming from the *Legatan* Councilor.

"My job is to find those bombs and defuse them," Damien told them. "Regardless of their source, whether it's pirates in deep space or conspiracies on Mars. In this, I serve our King and you."

"Of course," Councilor Montague agreed, cutting off her colleagues. "We do have more detailed questions as well, Lord Montgomery. Since we have you here."

"I am at the Council's disposal today," Damien replied. "I must warn you that there are matters I cannot discuss, even with this illustrious body."

More of them, he suspected, than any of the Councilors suspected. None of them liked being reminded of that, either—but Newton looked the most offended.

"Fine," he spat. "I'll ask you to refrain from speculation and self-justification as we continue," he warned Damien. "We want the events and the truth, not your *opinion*."

When things finally seemed to be wrapping up, over two hours later, Damien was relatively certain he'd rather be shot again than go through another of these hearings.

"I believe those are our last questions for today," Montague told him. "The Council appreciates your patience and honesty, Lord Montgomery. I imagine this has not been an easy time for you."

Damien smiled mirthlessly. If he was *very* lucky, none of the Councilors realized he and Ndosi had been lovers. "Not an easy time" was a pale descriptor of his last few weeks.

"It is in the interests of his Majesty's servants for us all to work together," he said smoothly.

"The Council will deliberate on this and other evidence," Newton told him. "We will need you to remain on Council Station until our discussions are complete."

Even if Damien had had any patience *left* with the Alpha Centauri Councilor—and his patience was a frayed rope at this point—that wasn't acceptable.

"I'm afraid that won't be possible," he said as gently as he could.

"That was not a request," McClintlock snapped, the Legatan Councilor glaring at him.

Damien returned McClintlock's glare levelly.

"Then perhaps it should have been," he said firmly. "I must remind this Council again, it seems, that I am a Hand of the Mage-King of Mars. I answer to one being in this universe: him.

"He has charged me to continue investigating the Keepers on Mars. That mission continues and requires my full attention. Attention I cannot give it from half a dozen light-minutes away.

"While it is and will always be my intent to cooperate with this Council, my duties as His Majesty's Hand *do* come first. If this Council wishes to interview me again, you may request that through His Majesty's offices and I will attempt to make the time.

"I most certainly cannot and will not restrict myself to this station for your convenience. Like yourselves, I have a job to do."

He let that hang in the air for a long moment and was relatively sure he heard at least one muffled chuckle from the farther desks. Someone had heard the silent "un" in front of his last sentence.

"If that will be all, Councilors, I must be returning to Mars," he told them.

While he was sure at least Newton and McClintlock were tempted, the Council wisely chose to let that be the last word.

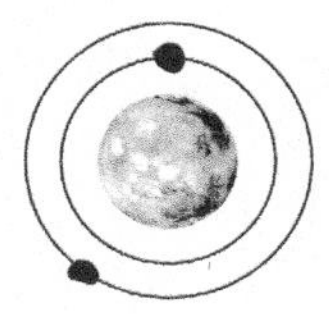

CHAPTER 6

DAMIEN WALKED out of the Council chamber in a silence he *knew* would be read as incandescent rage by anyone who knew him. He could only hope that the Councilors and Lictors didn't know him that well.

Special Agent Romanov did, and the bodyguard fell in behind him in equal silence. Christoffsen and the Secret Service Agent with him emerged from the lounge in response to a signal Damien didn't see, falling into place with Romanov in the Hand's wake as he stalked the corridors of Council Station.

It was apparently lunch break for most of the bureaucrats who populated the station, as the corridors were noticeably more crowded than they had been when he came in. The presence of two openly armed Secret Service Agents opened a path through the crowd, though Damien's localized storm cloud almost certainly helped.

Reaching the airlock where *Doctor Akintola* waited, they found another set of four guards from his detail watching over the jump-yacht.

"Pack it up," he ordered. "We're done here."

"Of course, my lord."

Crossing over into the yacht itself, with its innumerable security systems to make sure no one *else* was watching the cameras, he finally allowed himself to relax slightly.

"I take it your meeting with the Council did not go well," Christoffsen said mildly as the Secret Service Agents began closing the ship up behind them.

"I would place it on par with being shot again," Damien replied. "While we definitely have friends in the Council, I'd say both the Legislaturists and the UnArcana Worlds are out to screw us over."

"That is...roughly the alliance I expected," his aide admitted. "If you have an advantage, it is that Míngliàng is usually with the Legislaturists, but I believe they will take your side in almost any discussion."

Míngliàng had been one of two systems—the other Damien's home of Sherwood—someone had tried to drag into a war over a shared uninhabited system. Like so much else, Damien suspected Legatus was behind it...but had no proof.

He'd stopped the war, so Míngliàng's government thought well of him.

"We'll see if we have enough friends," he admitted quietly. "For now, I intend to return to Mars. If they want to talk to me again, they can damned well do so on *my* availability."

"We should tread softly here," Christoffsen warned.

"Professor, right now, I regard it as treading softly that Councilor Newton didn't get thrown into a wall," Damien pointed out. "We need to work with the Council, but there are limits to the disrespect that His Majesty or his Hands can afford to allow.

"Besides," he concluded grimly, "if I am to be forced to resign, and that is looking far more possible than I'd like, I want this mess with the Keepers cleaned up first."

By the time he slipped *Doctor Akintola* into her orbital slot amongst the rest of the Civil Fleet, Damien was feeling calmer. He could, intellectually at least, see the point where the Council members were coming from—at least in terms of trying to understand just what had happened to result in the deaths of two Hands.

"We show you in final orbital position, Lord Montgomery," the Civil Fleet's controller told him. "Do you need a shuttle directed your way?"

"No, we have several aboard," he told the man. "I'm going to need to keep *Doctor Akintola* on standby for the next few days at least," he warned them. "With *Duke of Magnificence* down for repairs, I'm currently lacking in transport and may need to travel or leave the system."

"We'll reserve her for you," the controller agreed immediately. "If you give us a few hours' warning if you need to leave the system, we can get one of our Jump Mages aboard to back you up as well."

"That would be appreciated," Damien admitted. Despite everything he'd done to upgrade his skills and power, he'd discovered that the one-light-year limit on a jump spell still applied to him—and so did the sheer exhaustion after casting the spell.

Most Mages needed a six- to eight-hour rest in between jumps. Even he couldn't push it much past five, so having a second Jump Mage aboard could easily cut a trip in half.

"I don't expect to need to leave Sol until *Duke* is repaired," he told the controller, "but I will likely need to travel around the system."

"Of course, my lord."

"Thank you."

Letting the channel drop, he made sure that everything was locked down in orbit, then rose and headed for his shuttle.

With *Duke of Magnificence* in for repair, his only "home" was his apartment in Olympus Mons. Unless the world had collapsed while he wasn't looking, he needed to take some time to rest.

Damien managed to make it all the way to his apartment in the Mountain, remove his suit jacket and collapse into his couch before, inevitably, someone caught up to him.

Fortunately, the "someone" was Kiera Alexander, the youngest child of the Mage-King and something resembling a friend, for all that she was fourteen years old to his thirty-plus. She flounced her way past his body-guards, leaving at least one red-uniformed Royal Guard in the vestibule with his own Secret Service crew.

"Dad said to check and make sure you weren't 'spitting nails,'" she told him with the casual bluntness almost unique, in Damien's experience, to younger members of the Protectorate's upper classes. "He... didn't expect your Council meeting to go well."

"And he sent you?" Damien asked.

"Well, no," Kiera admitted blithely. "Gregory's supposed to be by later; I figured I'd check in first. You won't spit nails at me."

Malcolm Gregory was the Chancellor of the Protectorate, the man who ran much of the day-to-day government of Mars and humanity's colonies. Damien could easily see the Mage-King asking *him* to check on a Hand he'd expected to have a bad day.

"I'm not spitting nails at anyone," he told Kiera. "But you're no more immune to an angry Hand than your father is."

Less so, in that the Mage-King had as many Runes of Power as Damien did and had been a stronger Mage before them. Alexander could magically "sit" on Damien if he needed to. Kiera was a powerful Mage but lacked both her father's training and her father's Runes.

"None of you would ever hurt a hair on my head," Kiera replied. "*Especially* not you. You're a big softie."

Damien chuckled. He doubted it was a particularly pleasant sound. He might have been a glorified cop in many ways, but even *he* had lost count of how many people he'd killed over the last ten years.

"You..." He shook his head at her. "You don't really *get* just what your esteemed father uses his Hands for. Even I am not a 'big softie.'"

"I know exactly what my father uses you for," Kiera told him, her voice serious. "I know perfectly well who killed Lawrence and Charlotte, Damien. I'm neither deaf nor blind."

He winced.

"You are very young," he pointed out. "But you're right; I apologize. I'm still not really a softie."

"Remember that I've met *all* of my father's Hands," she replied. "Are you all right?"

"No," he admitted. "But not even your father can fix this one. We'll get through it."

"What do you want me to tell him?"

"That I'm not 'spitting nails,'" he quoted back to her. "I need some rest, that's all."

Fourteen and overly blunt or not, she could at least get that hint. Kiera sprang back to her feet with the easy energy of youth and smiled brightly at him.

"Gregory's going to tell you you're invited for dinner," she noted. "But I'll pass that on."

"Shoo, Kiera," he told her.

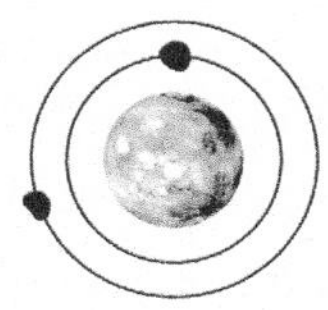

CHAPTER 7

KIERA CLEARLY PASSED on Damien's request for rest to the Chancellor as well as her father, because it was the next morning before the door on his apartment chimed again and he found the immense form of Malcolm Gregory on his step.

"Come in," he told the older man, gesturing Gregory to come inside.

The Chancellor of the Protectorate of Humanity was a grossly obese man noticeably into his second century, his hair long gone and his face marked with a perpetual smile. The unwise read that smile as befuddled and considered him a nonentity.

Malcolm Gregory's rise to power and service to his King was paved with the political and literal graves of the unwise.

Despite his massive bulk, Gregory remained on his feet as he entered Damien's sitting room, glancing around the sparse furnishings. The couch and table were expensive, but they'd been there when he'd moved in. He'd lived in the apartment for three years at one point, but it still didn't truly register as home.

"You know, Damien, if you're not careful, I'm going to sneak someone in here and decorate while you're gone," he observed dryly.

"You presume I would even notice," Damien replied. "So long as I have a bed and a screen to hook my PC up to, I'm pretty happy."

"There may be something fundamentally wrong with you," Gregory noted. "Though it seems to work for you. You threw a few *glorious* wrenches into the Council yesterday."

"My impression was closer to being fed to a herd of piranhas."

"That, my young and innocent friend, is because you were paying attention to who was *talking*," the Mage-King's right hand man told him. "*I*, on the other hand, have spoken with those who were *listening*. You handled that mess as well as anyone could, and the degree to which Newton and McClintlock were pushing you did not go unnoticed.

"I won't say you couldn't have done *better*," Gregory noted, "but you did well. And the fact that you clearly *weren't* being political probably helped as much as handling them more smoothly would have."

"I also got pulled aside by Councilor Granger," Damien said. "Were you aware of that piece?"

"I am well informed," the Chancellor said slowly, "but not omniscient. I was aware you had breakfast with him, but it sounds like there was more than just him reiterating his support for the Mountain."

"He asked me to resign to short-circuit this whole mess."

Gregory started to say something, then cut himself off.

"That is not...unexpected," he finally admitted. "I don't agree with the logic, but I can see it."

"I'm not planning on resigning," Damien told him. "Not until this mess with the Keepers is sorted."

"I'd prefer not even then," Gregory replied. "The man they call the Sword of Mars is not a tool I would lay aside happily."

Damien blinked.

"They call me *what*?"

"The Sword of Mars," Gregory repeated. "It's a nickname that goes around the media, usually attached to the Hand that's seen the most outright military action in the last few years. Lomond was the last one anyone called that, but it's been a few years since they hung it on him, and it seems you've got it now."

"Can I give it back to him?"

"We don't control what the media calls us, but this one is a useful tool," Gregory said. "Even if they push for your resignation, it will be a public relations disaster for many of the Councilors."

"And if their governments back them?"

The Chancellor sighed.

"Then we will have a problem, though I suspect the PR consequences of it would help resolve any such crisis in our favor. His Majesty will back you, Damien."

"And if I decide the price is too high to allow him to?" Damien asked quietly.

"That is a sacrifice neither he nor I would approve of," Gregory replied. "Though it is certainly *your* choice to make."

"We'll keep that in our quiver for a while yet, I think. For now, I think I need to get back to work."

"No one is going to judge you for finding a beach and a martini for a day or two," Gregory pointed out.

"Someone killed the only Keeper I knew was left," Damien pointed out. "I'd like to make sure any of them I've *missed* get found before they share his fate."

"And all of the resources of Mars are yours to command in that quest," the Chancellor agreed. "I worry, Damien, about any secret so powerful it can turn even the *Hands* against us."

"Whatever the cost, I can't help but feel that the first Mage-King would rather the secret was exposed than lost," Damien said. "We'll find the survivors. We'll drag all of this into the light and we will find our answers."

For the "sin" of being the first senior Martian Investigation Service member dragged into Damien's investigation on Mars, Director Wong appeared to have been handed the global responsibility of dealing with the Keeper investigation.

She looked about as tired when Damien called her as he still felt.

"Lord Montgomery, how can I assist you?"

"I need an update on your investigation into the Keepers," he told her. "And if there's any way *I* can assist *you* in that investigation, let me know."

"Right now, we're still in data-compilation-and-analysis mode," Wong replied after a moment's thought. "I don't know if we've got good news or bad news yet, just...data."

"Run me through the highlights."

"Raptis had been dead for roughly ten hours when you found him," she began. "That's both good and bad. Bad because someone beat us to him. Good because they beat us to him by enough that I can be confident *we* didn't betray his location."

That was a more reassuring conclusion than Damien would have expected it to be. With the reach the Keepers themselves had demonstrated throughout his investigations into their operations, it had been a real possibility that the MIS had accidentally betrayed Raptis to his death.

"What about the archives?"

"Destroyed," Wong said flatly. "Some of the data media were recoverable enough for us to establish they had been wiped before being burned. Raptis's murderer was *very* thorough."

"The safehouse was fortified. Cameras?" Damien asked.

"Destroyed. Their data storage wiped, then destroyed as well. No records. No footage. No identifying information."

"I'm guessing the area wasn't under useful surveillance?"

"No. The community association had planned to put in a local security net three times over the last twenty years, but it failed each time," the MIS Director replied. "I can't help but wonder why."

"The Keepers protected the safehouse," Damien concluded. "You're right, Director, that we don't have much good news here. I hate to even ask, but do we have any other comparable murders?"

"I have a team investigating, but their reach is...limited," she admitted. "While the local databases are eventually uploaded into the planetary and system-wide systems, it's not an immediate process. Active, ongoing cases are sufficiently close to home that few police departments like handing their files over to the MIS before they have to."

Damien smiled coldly.

"How big of a stick do you need me to provide, Director?" he asked.

"A Hand's Warrant is probably enough," she told him. "*Most* police officers understand that we're all on the same side here."

"You'll have it," he promised. "I'll be at your office in a couple of hours," he continued. "Mars doesn't see *that* many murders. I want at least high-level details on every one in the last three weeks."

"I'll make it happen."

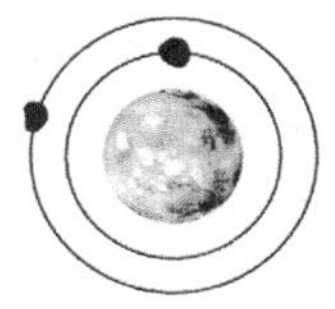

CHAPTER 8

CURIOSITY CITY was starting to be familiar to Damien, though the University's massive heroic bronze of the rover it was named after still seemed excessive to him.

His shuttle swooped over the city, carving a careful course that brought the spacecraft to a halt on the roof of the skyscraper that served as the MIS's headquarters in Curiosity City.

Damien waited, as much tired as patient today, while Romanov and his team swept out to secure the rooftop, then stepped out to meet Director Wong on the rooftop landing pad. The Director looked even older today, her hair frizzing up in the wind on the top of the tower as she directed her companion towards him.

"Hand Montgomery, this is Inspector Munira Samara," she introduced the woman in the dark blue headscarf. "She's been leading my team looking into the details of this mess for you, so I'm seconding her to you for this case.

"She'll be your liaison and continue to head the investigation team as well. Please try not to drag her away from the planet unless necessary, but she is now dedicated to this case."

"Inspector Samara." He bowed slightly to her. "I appreciate your efforts on the Protectorate's behalf. This situation grows more complex every time I look at it."

"My own investigations have not simplified affairs," she agreed, blue eyes flashing as she smiled at him. "Your suggestion to look into other murders has provided unexpected fruit, however. If we can move inside, I've had my team prepare a briefing for you and the Director."

"You haven't been briefed yet?" Damien asked Wong.

"There hasn't been time, my lord," she reminded him. "We only received your Warrant two hours ago, after all. If Samara says this is worth our time, though, I'll trust her."

"I did not intend to imply otherwise," he said apologetically. "Of course, Inspector. Please lead on."

Two more MIS people were waiting when Samara led them into a briefing room. Romanov gestured for two of his Marines to take up guard positions outside the door, then settled himself against the wall next to the door while Damien and Wong took their seats.

"These are Inspector Ryan Cook and Analyst Gunda Daniels," Samara introduced her subordinates. "Ryan has been doing a lot of the grunt work of calling the various local police departments with your Warrant to get them to disgorge their case files. Gunda has been summarizing them for me and you.

"Analyst Daniels spotted the link," the senior Inspector told Damien. "I'll allow her to explain."

Samara took a seat with Wong and Damien, gesturing for her most junior subordinate to speak.

Daniels was a small woman with extremely dark skin and the slanted eyes of a Martian native. She was also even younger than Damien himself, and visibly swallowed as her boss put her on the spot.

"The first thing we noticed," she began, her voice barely above a whisper but rapidly growing louder and more confident as she spoke, "was that the sheer number of murders was unusually high. There's always some variance—people don't decide to kill each other on a neat schedule—but the entire planet normally sees an average of sixty-four murders a week.

"In the three weeks since the destruction of the Keeper's Archive, there have been just over five hundred confirmed murders or deaths otherwise regarded as suspicious," Daniels told them. "This has been the deadliest three-week period on Mars in the last century."

That sent a chill down Damien's spine. Just what *had* he set into motion?

"We don't normally track the movements of our citizens," she continued, "but in the case of suspicious deaths and murders, we try and track backwards as best as we can. One hundred and twenty-two of those murder victims had been in the Hellas Montes Park the day of the Archive's destruction."

"To be clear, Hand Montgomery, so were over eleven thousand other people," Cook interjected. "But I agree with Gunda. That ratio was suspicious."

Daniels nodded to her compatriot, taking a drink of water before she continued.

"That connection I was looking for was based on what I'd been told about the case," she observed. "But since I'd found one connection, I wanted to see if I could find any others."

She tapped a command and a list of names and small photos filled the wall behind her.

About a quarter of the names lit up in orange.

"In orange are the victims we know were in the Hellas Montes Park the day the Archive was destroyed," she noted. "In blue we have individuals who are members of the Grand Eagle's Circle, a small charitable organization present in several northern Martian cities. The group is known for supporting literacy efforts in poorer neighborhoods but has a relatively small membership list."

About a third of the names in orange were now also lit up in blue. Another sixty or seventy of the other names on Daniels' list were highlighted in blue.

"How small?" Damien asked. "If a hundred of them are dead..."

"Something like a fifth of the Circle's membership has been killed in the last three weeks," Daniels said flatly. "None of the rest *appear* to have been involved in anything...but neither do any of the ones who were murdered."

Damien eyed the list of names.

"You have more."

It wasn't a question.

"In green we have the members of the Friends of Hellas Montes Park," Daniels told her audience, lighting up another selection of names. Half of the people who'd been in Hellas Montes Park that fateful day were green. So were about fifty others. At least a dozen names were highlighted in green, orange and blue.

"The Friends are a rather large organization dedicated to raising funds for maintaining and improving the Park," she noted. "These people all appear to have been regular volunteers, putting them inside a core group I can't estimate the size of without far more information than they release to the public."

A fourth group of names highlighted in red. There was a single name that overlapped with the orange, but the red list encompassed at least eighty names.

"*These* are known or suspected members of the Blue Tiger and Dark Sapphire drug rings," Daniels noted. "Both are fragment organizations of the former Blue Star Syndicate that have spent the last month doing their best to exterminate each other. Their war is responsible for a good portion of our spike in murders...and probably unrelated to our investigation."

A final list of names lit up in purple.

"Lastly, and I had to double-check to make sure this group *existed,* as it seemed quite odd to me, these are members of the Steel Library, a social group of ex-military librarians," Daniels said. "Now, not all of our suspected Keepers from Hellas Montes were members of one of those three groups, but ten were members of all three, and there were at least thirty members of each of them among those hundred and twenty possibilities."

There were other names, Damien noted, that were tagged with more than one of her additional colors.

"Based on this, I think that all three of these organizations require further investigation," Daniels concluded. "Without explicit authorization and support, though, there is a limit to what we can do, and, well"—she shrugged—"we ran out of time before your arrival."

"This is good work, Analyst," Damien told her, studying the chart. "Was Professor Raptis a member of any of these groups?"

"He was both a member of the Circle and the Friends of Hellas Montes," she said instantly.

"I take it you need my authority to pull those organizations' membership lists?" he asked.

"That's the starting point, yes," Inspector Samara said, taking over from her subordinate. "Daniels and I will then correlate and see if we can identify persons of interest. What we do from there..."

"Is up to me," Damien concluded. "Would you like your Warrant in writing, Inspector?"

After the briefing, Damien and his people retreated to an empty meeting room where he proceeded to go over the massive pile of data that Wong and Samara's people had pulled together for him. He had no illusions about his skill as a data analyst, but it was still worth it for him to review the data, just in case.

The first thing he checked was the Mages. Raptis was at the top of list, but the fact that it was a list of more than one was statistically significant in itself. The normal ratio of Mages to mundanes was roughly one in five hundred thousand. It was closer to one in eighty thousand on Mars itself, but out of the five hundred murders in the last few weeks, forty-two Mages had died.

Seventeen had been tied up in the drug war. One was an open-and-shut domestic, a suspected abusive husband shot repeatedly in the back by his wife. Of the remaining twenty-six, all made one of Daniels's lists.

Given that the Keepers had managed to produce an entire platoon's worth of Combat Mages to try and take Damien down, he wasn't surprised to discover they'd had a lot of Mage members.

It *was* disturbing, however, to see that many Mages dead without them taking somebody with them. Even the weakest Mage was given some magical self-defense training. That many Mages dead without collateral damage suggested one of two things: they'd either been killed by friends or killed by people who knew *exactly* how to kill Mages.

Like Legatan Augments, the cyborg police and spies Legatus used to maintain their anti-magic laws.

Cyborgs that weren't supposed to be on Mars.

Raptis's murder suggested he'd been killed by someone he knew, someone with the codes to disable his safehouse's defenses. Other deaths were less clean, suggesting professionals but not people the victims had known.

Damien sighed.

"We have at least two players," he said aloud.

"My lord?" Romanov asked.

"Some of the Mages were definitely killed by someone they knew," Damien told him. "Close range, no damage at all, regular police weren't even aware if there were defenses.

"Others were less clean. Sniper shots. Poison. Defenses triggered but without fatalities." Damien shook his head. "We have at least two teams if not two entirely separate *groups* killing Keepers."

"That's...that's not good, boss."

"No."

He still wasn't entirely sure what he'd set into motion, but more and more, Damien was beginning to feel like someone had intentionally pulled the Keepers out into the open and pointed him at them—and was finishing the job themselves now that Damien had scattered them.

The alien runes at Andala IV had been a trigger, but just *what* had they triggered?

Damien's digging into the files they had on the Keepers and the recent murders didn't get him much of anywhere over the ensuing hour before he was interrupted by a buzzing from his wrist-comp.

"This is Montgomery," he answered it briskly.

"It's Inspector Samara," the MIS officer told him. "I think Daniels has made a breakthrough."

"I'm listening," Damien replied. "I'll take anything I can get."

"We've been looking into the three organizations we identified as potential Keeper fronts," Samara explained. "We've got the volunteer list for the Friends of Hellas Montes Park, but the Grand Eagle's Circle and the Steel Library are both smaller organizations and in some degree of disarray right now.

"We're pulling together the resources to raid their offices for files," she continued calmly, "but we found something interesting in the Friends' files.

"The Friends of Hellas Montes Park were a key contributor to a library built in the town of New Andes, just outside the north side of the park. The *other* key contributors were an anonymous donor, the Grand Eagle's Circle, and the Steel Library."

"That sounds suspicious," Damien agreed.

"We also discovered that the head librarian is an ex-Royal Martian Marine Corps Captain: Miles Kessler. We're not sure if he's a member of the Steel Library, but it seems likely."

Damien rose to his feet, folding away his data chips and gesturing for Romanov to pack up his people's gear.

"My shuttle is still on the roof," he told Samara. "Would you care to join me for a quick flight, Inspector Samara?"

"*Inshallah*," she told him. "I'll be there in two minutes."

New Andes was just over ninety minutes' flight away at a regular pace, and Damien was spending the time carefully checking over his runes again.

Around him, his personal detail was checking through their weapons as well. When he realized that Romanov was directing several of his Marines to get into full exosuit armor, he leveled a questioning gaze on his senior bodyguard.

"Overkill much?" he murmured.

"My lord, from what Amiri told me when I took this job, there is no such thing when it comes to your affairs. We'll keep them on the shuttle, out of sight and out of mind, unless we need them."

Damien shook his head but didn't stop the Marines suiting up. The assault shuttle was designed to carry a full thirty-man platoon in exosuit combat armor and actually had suits in lockers aboard for all twenty of his detail.

Not that the Secret Service agents, as opposed to the Marines seconded to his bodyguard, were necessarily experienced in using them. They were *trained* in their use, but his Marines had actually taken them into combat.

"Shouldn't we be getting a strike team of some kind?" Samara asked. The MIS Inspector had thrown an armored vest on over her blouse and tied her headscarf to its straps to secure it, but she was still under-armed and under-armored compared to the crowd.

"I am a Hand," Damien pointed out. "While I do, on occasion, actually need bodyguards, I probably use them more as a strike team than anything else."

He gestured around at the rapidly arming men and women around them.

"They're used to it," he observed.

Before Samara could respond, her wrist computer buzzed. She tapped it and lifted it to her face.

"Samara."

"Boss, it's Daniels," the young MIS Analyst told her. "You're in the air with the Hand, right?"

"Yes. He can hear you," Samara noted carefully.

"Good. We have a problem. A big one."

"What kind of problem, Analyst?" Damien asked. Daniels sounded stressed, so gentle prodding seemed to be the best option.

"I don't know what's going on, but the New Andes Library just lit up a full emergency alert—and then burst into flames."

"Thank you, Analyst," he told her softly. "You're right, that is a problem. We'll deal with it."

"How?" Samara demanded as she cut the channel. "If the building is on fire—"

"Romanov!" Damien snapped, pulling the Mage-Captain back to them. "I take back everything I said about the exosuits. Strap *everybody* into one and tell the pilot to use my overrides to cut us a clear path to New Andes and go to full speed."

"Yes, sir," Romanov said calmly. "That bad?"

"Bad enough."

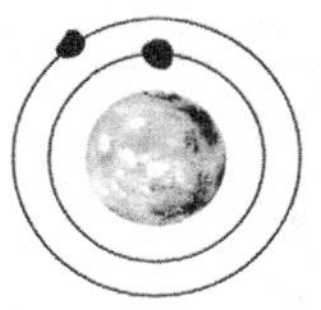

CHAPTER 9

FROM THE VAGUELY sick expression on Inspector Munira Samara's face, the MIS officer had never been aboard a Marine assault shuttle making a combat approach before. Most of the normal torque was missing due to the lack of ground fire, but the variable acceleration appeared to be enough to make her uncomfortable.

It had been a *long* time since Damien's first assault landing. He mostly ignored the maneuvers and acceleration while studying satellite footage of the town they were heading for.

New Andes was a post-terraforming town that had never been domed. It sprawled out in a way few of the older settlements on Mars did, but it was also a tourist town where the economy was driven by the proximity to the Hellas Montes Park.

Ten thousand permanent residents, about the same in transients. The town had probably needed a library long before the Keepers' fronts had built them one. While he was certain their "charity" had been with an ulterior motive, all three of the organizations they'd linked to the Keepers really *had* been doing good works.

"Locals report that the fires are resisting any attempt at suppression," the pilot announced over the intercom. "They're mostly confused, but our scanners are suggesting someone intentionally spread volatile chemicals through the building."

"We need to find the head librarian and any intact Keeper archives we can grab," Damien told him. "This is going to be hot and nasty. Right in the middle of the fire."

"All right." He *heard* the pilot exhale. "Disembarkment will be in forty-five seconds at fifty meters."

Damien heard Samara struggle to raise her head and look at him.

"At fifty meters?" she asked. "Your people have 'suits; how are *we* getting down?"

"Magic," he told her with a smile. "You're with me, Inspector. We'll be fine."

"Twenty seconds."

"The building is still on fire," she pointed out.

"And I plan on fixing that. You don't have to drop with us, but...do you trust me?"

"Five seconds!"

"All right," she agreed.

The time was up. The bottom of the assault shuttle's main cargo bay swung open, dropping out from beneath their feet.

The exosuited Marines and Secret Service Agents went first, plummeting away the moment the floor dropped out.

Damien had released his straps and would normally have dropped right after them, but Samara was still buckled into the shuttle. He held himself in midair and offered her his hand.

She snapped herself free with sudden confidence, dropping away after the exosuits—and Damien followed, gently grabbing her wrist as he wrapped his magic around them both to guide and control their descent.

Beneath them, the exosuits were slamming through the roof of the burning building like drunken meteors, gouts of flame flashing up around the armored men and women. Fire engines continued to soak the area around the building with water, containing the fire as Damien and his people went in.

He inhaled sharply, summoning power and channeling it through his Runes as he began to change the air in the building. Fire needed oxygen to burn, so he starved it, replacing the oxygen in the top floor of the building with nitrogen pulled from the outside atmosphere, working his way down while trying to identify the pockets of survivors and keep the air safe around them.

"The fire is starting to go out," one of the Marines reported.

"And the air is going to stop being breathable," Damien replied. "Find any survivors *ASAP*; I can only keep the fire under so much control while keeping them alive."

"That's why we have armor," Romanov replied. "We're moving in."

Mage-Captain Denis Romanov led his people into the flames, his own magic sweeping a clear path ahead of him. The localized wind gusts he was using to keep the fire off of his armor weren't as broadly effective as the overall starving of the fire that his boss was doing, but they were something Denis could do and sustain.

"Coral, Massey," he snapped crisply as his two senior Marines. "Take a fire team, sweep a floor. Coral take third, Massey take second. Our priority is getting any survivors out, clear?"

"On it."

"The rest of you"—he gestured at the Secret Service Agents, less comfortable in their armor but still effective—"are with me. We keep going down until we hit the ground, then sweep. First call is evac survivors; I doubt any of the attackers are left.

"That said, if someone draws on you, put them down," he ordered. "No unnecessary risks."

He'd have ordered no risks, but they were inside a burning and collapsing building. If any of his people had wanted a risk-free life, they shouldn't have taken the assignment to a *Hand's* personal detachment.

The stairwells were nice broad things, with a meter and a half–wide gap all of the way down. Denis went over the edge before giving himself time to think, dropping three stories to crash into the tiled concrete of the main floor with a ground-shattering crunch.

Most of that floor had been taken up by a large open space filled with bookshelves. Not all of those shelves' contents would have been paper books, but enough were to make the space an inferno...and enough *weren't* to surround that inferno with toxic smoke.

"I've got movement!" someone reported. "Shit, there's *kids* over here."

Denis didn't even react consciously. He pulled his team's sensor reports and located the area, charging *through* the fire toward where his people had identified the class of kids. There were twenty of them backed into a corner of the library where two adults had shoved them before trying, desperately, to keep the fire at bay with handheld fire extinguishers.

A twenty-sixth-century handheld extinguisher was a capable device, but it wasn't *that* capable. Smoke had clearly taken most of the kids down—hopefully nonlethally!—and one of the adults wasn't in much better shape.

The other was still holding one of the handheld extinguishers, trying grimly to get any more foam out of a clearly empty canister while the fire sparked across the barrier they'd already laid. It was a losing battle, and Denis's exosuit's sensors calmly informed him that the roof was only a few minutes from collapse.

He emerged from the fire, probably looking like some kind of troll out of a nightmare, and loomed over the still-standing adult.

"What's on the other side of the wall?" he demanded.

"What?" the man coughed.

"The other side of that wall," Denis pointed past the kids.

"Outside, I think, but it's twenty centimeters of..."

Denis was a fully trained Royal Martian Marine Corps Combat Mage. Short of the Mage-King and his Hands, there were few deadlier or more destructive individuals in the galaxy. His armor might have lacked the amplifying runes of a Royal Guardsman's, but it linked into the projector rune in his palm just fine.

He turned a dozen square meters of twenty-centimeter-thick concrete wall to fine powder with a gesture and slammed more power into the air above him to hold the roof in place.

"Get them out," he snapped, more to his people than the one still-standing teacher. Four exosuited Secret Service Agents were already moving in, while a fifth deployed the fire suppression gear they'd carried down to cover the evacuation.

"All units, report," he snapped. "We have survivors on the main floor, a class of kids."

"Third floor had eight older kids and an adult," Corporal Coral said grimly. "We're evacing now, but I don't know if any of them will make it."

"Second had staff and researchers," Corporal Massey reported. "Eighteen adults. Four *might* make it."

"My lord," Denis linked back to Montgomery. "Do you have contact with the locals?"

"Inspector Samara does," the Hand replied dryly. "I have contained the fire. I'm also maintaining clear zones around the identified survivors." He paused. "Inspector Samara reports the locals say there should have been twenty-two staff and three teachers in the building. We've got the right number of kids, but we're short at least four adults."

There was a loud popping noise above him.

"Second and third floors are clear," Montgomery told him, a flash of fatigue tinging his voice. "I have the main-floor fire contained. Is there a basement?"

"See if the locals can get us floor plans," Denis asked. "Without the plans...time to make another door."

The floor resisted Denis's power about as much as the wall had, a two-meter radius of concrete and tile vanishing into dust and dropping him and five exosuited Secret Service Agents down a full four meters into the inferno below.

His suit was rated to survive deep space, plasma fire, high-velocity bullets...and it started flashing warning signs as they landed in the New Andes Library basement.

"I can see why they can't put the fires out with water," he observed. "The basement has been *flooded* with incendiaries of some kind. Suit scanners can't distinguish, but there's both gasoline and phosphorus down here."

"What the *fuck*?" the Hand snapped. "Can you stabilize it?"

Even Montgomery's trick of stealing the oxygen wouldn't be enough down here. Unless his suit was wrong about the ingredients, this mess didn't even need oxygen to burn; the mix had its own oxidizer included.

"Negative," he admitted. "I don't think even *you* can put this out, my lord. I'm going to sweep for survivors and bodies, but..." He studied the warnings on his suit. "We're going to have to write the building off, sir," he said softly. "This is irretrievable."

"Understood," Montgomery said shortly. "Keep me informed; let me know if you need a rescue."

If anyone would be able to rip open the ground and pull Denis and his people out, it would be Montgomery.

"Yes, sir," Denis replied. "Moving in."

There was no point even trying to give his people instructions by anything except radio. His sensors happily informed him the fire outside was too loud to be heard over.

This was overkill for a library.

"Sweep for cooler spots," he ordered. "Record everything. This mess tells me there was something *else* down here."

It felt like he was wading as he moved, the flames from the noxious mix that *someone* had dumped all over the basement flickering up around his greaves. Even through the armor, he was feeling the warmth as he tried to navigate by thermal scanners and micropulses.

There.

"I've got a cooler zone," he reported. "Looks like there was none of this super-napalm dumped there. Moving over."

The room at the south end of the basement hadn't been covered, but the heat would have been fatal to an unarmored human. There was no oxygen left in the air, only smoke and toxic fumes. Without his scanners, Denis wasn't even sure he'd have been able to see.

There might not have been napalm in the room, but everything that was in the room was burning, with shelves full of books thrown onto the floor...and the fire had reached the bodies in the middle of the room. Three adults; Denis couldn't tell much more in their current state, but they were very dead.

"My lord, I have three bodies," Denis noted. "I suspect we'll want them intact."

"I agree," the Hand told him instantly. "Hold one moment, I'm studying your video feed for angles and... There."

The three bodies vanished in an imploding rush of magic, and Denis was starting to move away... when the wall on the other side of the room *exploded*, the pent-up force of the noxious mix the place had been filled with turning the space on the other side of the concealed hatch into a fuel-air explosive.

Denis threw his magic forward without a thought, focusing and channeling the explosion *down*. In the back of his mind, he felt the Hand's power join him a moment later, their magic capturing the force of the FAE and forcing it downward, containing it in the already wrecked library rather than allowing it to wreck the town.

Finally, it faded. The room was a crater now, the far wall clearly once having been an armored hatch...but that hatch was melted metal, chunks of it stuck to Denis's armor as he moved forward into the wreckage, his suit complaining about every motion.

"Well, there *was* an underground bunker here," he concluded aloud. "But someone beat us to it.

"And they did *not* care about collateral damage."

CHAPTER 10

EVEN DAMIEN was drained by the effort of containing an explosion of the scale that had been buried under the New Andes Library. Nonetheless, he straightened his spine and turned a tired smile on the Martian Planetary Police officer who approached him and Samara.

"Sir... My lord Hand?" she said questioningly. "We hadn't even requested assistance yet."

"We were on the way for other reasons," Damien told her. "Report, Lieutenant."

That was apparently enough to bring her mostly back to the present, and the officer, a tall and graceful woman with long braided blond hair, saluted crisply.

"Lieutenant Marianne Suzuki, my lord," she told him. "I run the New Andes MPP detachment. We...don't see much activity here, but we assist the local fire department when they need the hands."

"What happened here?" Damien asked quietly.

"We got a call reporting smoke and fire in the library forty, maybe fifty minutes ago," Suzuki said, her voice tired. "The fire department got on their way and asked us to help provide a perimeter and extra hands, but..."

She gestured helplessly at the wreckage of the library.

"We couldn't get past the heat or put the fire out, even temporarily," she said quietly. "My son was in a class..."

"My people evacuated everyone who was still in the building," Damien told her. "They're coordinating for medical assistance as we speak."

Suzuki nodded, inhaling a deep, almost sobbing breath.

"We're just a tourist town, my lord," she whispered. "What *happened*?"

"There were military-grade incendiary weapons deployed in the basement," he replied. "We contained the explosion, but *nothing* was going to put that fire out."

"Why?"

"That, Lieutenant Suzuki, is what I intend to find out," Damien promised her. "I'll have questions for you later, but if your son is still alive, he'll be with the medics. Go check on him," he told her gently. "I have a Marine cleanup team on their way."

Suzuki nodded, struggling against tears now, but headed off to check on her son.

"This is insane," Inspector Samara said, her voice shaky as she studied the wreckage.

"This is overkill," Damien replied. "I'm guessing there was some kind of backup archive in the bunker, but unless Miles Kessler is among the survivors, I don't think we're ever going to know for sure."

"This is *Mars*, my lord," Samara said. "What the *hell* is going on?"

"I have a guess," he said grimly. "And we're going to need to go over *every* scrap of sensor data Romanov got in that basement. I need to know what type of incendiary was used—and, if we can, identify the source!"

Barely ten more minutes had passed before the sky filled with thunder as over a dozen RMMC assault shuttles dropped from orbit. A full MASH unit deployed and took over from the exhausted trio of fire department medics as Damien watched, and platoons of Marines, both exosuited and in regular combat armor, took up perimeter positions around the wrecked library.

It took two Marine armorers five minutes after that to detach Romanov from his armor, the combination of literally walking in the incendiary mix and being at ground zero for an FAE rendering his suit basically nonfunctional.

"This looks like a war zone, milord," the battalion commander advised Damien.

"I've seen worse," the Hand replied, "but yes. I want the wreckage swept for any residue—I want to know what the damn weapon was."

"I already have a team on it," Major Calliope replied. "My medics think most of the kids will pull through," he added. "All of the younger ones, at least. The older ones were upstairs, someone said?"

"Yeah."

Calliope shook his head.

"Some might still make it," he said hopefully. "Never expected to see kids tied up in this kind of mess. Not sure how the ones on the ground floor survived."

"Two *very* brave teachers," Damien told him. "Backed the kids into a corner and took on the fire with handheld extinguishers until they were empty."

The Marine whistled.

"Can I recruit them?"

"No, though I'm planning on giving them medals." The Hand shook his head. "We'll have more MIS Forensics people here shortly," he warned the Major. "We're going to go through the ashes of that building with a fine-toothed comb, *and* I want full autopsies on the bodies."

"We can work with MIS," the Major confirmed. "We'll hold the perimeter until they're done. What a gods-accursed mess."

"Agreed. *Somewhere* in there was one of yours, too," Damien told him. "Ex-Marine Captain, Miles Kessler. Pretty sure he's the body we're missing."

"Damn. We'll scan for a dog tag chip," Calliope suggested. "He might have had his ident chip removed when he mustered out, but a lot of our old dogs keep them in to feel part of things still."

"If he died in there, I need to know," Damien replied. "We were coming here to talk to him."

"What a gods-accursed mess," the Marine repeated. "We're going to need hazmat cleanup when the forensics team is done."

"I'll leave that in the Marines' hands. Can you make sure it happens? This town has had a bad-enough day."

"Oohrah, milord," Calliope said firmly. "After a mess like this? The Corps will build them a new damned *library*."

"One way or another, the Mountain is paying to replace the library," Damien agreed.

It took another twenty-four hours before the wreckage of the library cooled enough for the Marine teams to even enter the debris field. The fuel-air explosion in the bunker had opened up the ground beneath the building and collapsed the entire structure into the crater, but it still hadn't been enough to stop from burning the incendiary mix that had covered the library's basement.

Damien joined the Marines in the rapidly assembled campground on the streets and parks around the library. The entire area was locked down, with none of the civilians from the town allowed near as they dug their way in.

"The good news," Calliope finally told Damien, "is that Captain Kessler didn't deactivate his ident chip when he mustered out. The bad news is that chip is definitely not inside the debris—at least, not active."

The Hand looked at the crater. Even now, parts of the wreckage were smoldering, but teams were picking through it in hazard gear.

"What does it take to destroy one of those chips?" he asked.

"They're tough but not invulnerable," the Major replied. "Being, say, in that bunker when the FAE went off would do it."

"What do we know about the bunker?"

"It wasn't supposed to be there," Samara replied, the MIS Inspector sitting cross-legged on a picnic table still incongruously in the middle of the Marines' camp. "It's not on the plans. Not on the work orders. None of the paperwork even suggests when or how they got the materials in."

The cop shook her head.

"They did a damn good job of hiding it, my lord," she told Damien. "At the same time, well"—she chuckled softly—"they built a small town a desperately needed library. Hard to see these folks as the bad guys."

"No one thinks what's *left* are the bad guys, Inspector," he replied. "So, they managed to add a bunker to it in secret? No idea what they had stored there?"

She shrugged.

"Like I said, my lord, I can't even tell when they built it, let alone what they put in it," she admitted. "I would guess, based off my briefings for this mess, a partial backup of the files at their Archive. You don't build a nuclear suicide device into a data storage facility without a backup somewhere."

"Agreed. And where's there one, there's more," Damien replied. "I need your team to find them. Preferably before the people who did *this*." He gestured at the crater behind them.

"Who has the resources to *do* something like this?" Romanov asked.

"Any Mage," Calliope replied. "Wouldn't take much time for you to set this up, Mage-Captain."

Damien smiled to himself. No Marine was *ever* going to call Romanov Special Agent...or at least, if they did, it meant the seconded Marine had *truly* fucked up.

"It wasn't magic," he pointed out. "Trust me on that."

It *could* have been—Calliope was right there—but Damien would have been able to tell. To a Rune Wright, a spell of that magnitude would have left traces. There was nothing here. This had been purely conventional, incendiaries and oxygen mixing in the contained space of the hidden bunker.

"Well, if it was a weapon, we'll find it," the Marine promised. "Casings, chemical residues, all of that adds together. We'll turn it over to Samara's people and we will find out what happened."

The cross-legged woman's computer buzzed, and she checked the holographic screen she had projected in front of her. She was silent for a moment, reading while the three men waited patiently.

"Speaking of 'my people,'" she finally said, looking up at Damien, "they just completed the first of the autopsies of the bodies you pulled out of the basement."

He nodded sharply. Assuming Miles Kessler had died in his bunker, eighteen adults and four teenagers had been killed. Those three, however, were the only ones he was sure had been dead *before* the fire.

"My doctor's best guess is that he was tortured," Samara said softly. "All of the bones in his hands were broken, as were his shins and forearms. He was then shot in the head and the body left to be destroyed in the fire."

"Tortured for information," Damien concluded. He grimaced. "So, it took them three tries to find someone who knew how to access the bunker. Fuckers."

"She says she can't be *certain*," the MIS Inspector continued, "but the style *is* consistent with Legatan intensive interrogation training."

The Hand was silent for a long time.

"Check the other bodies from the basement," he finally ordered. "Let me know if they're the same. And identify the damn incendiary."

If it was Legatan...it was *still* only circumstantial evidence. But it connected two problems he'd thought were entirely separate.

By the evening of the day after the attack, there didn't seem to be any more value in a Hand of the Mage-King hanging around the area. His presence seemed to be reassuring the people of New Andes, but with the Marines present and beginning the hazardous-material cleanup, Damien wasn't really required.

If he ever had been. Really, he'd arrived too late for his presence to make any difference, a situation that was now starting to feel all too familiar.

"Denis, get our shuttle prepped to fly," he ordered Romanov. "We'll return to the Mountain, see if combing through our growing pile of data can produce anything more useful."

"Yes, my lord."

The Special Agent corralled the pilots and headed over to the spacecraft as Damien watched. He wasn't sure he could do more at the Mountain, but all he could do here was stare at the crater created when he was too late.

"I assume there's space on that ship for one more?" Samara asked, the MIS officer looking surprisingly pristine for not having had any more access to fresh clothes the last day than anyone else had.

"We're not going to be swinging through Curiosity City," Damien told her. "One of Major Calliope's birds can get you home if you need."

"I think you misunderstand me, Lord Montgomery," she replied. "I've been assigned to this case until it's done—which also means I'm assigned to *you*. Anywhere you're going, I need to be around to liaise between you and the MIS teams assigned to this mess.

"Until we're done, you're not getting rid of me that easily."

"I don't think I've ever had an MIS liaison before," Damien admitted.

"You haven't worked on Mars before," she told him. "You're right in the middle of our jurisdiction, calling on our resources to deal with a problem *we* should have found. If you don't want me, my lord, we can arrange a different liaison—"

"The problem is not you, Inspector Samara," he said quickly and carefully. "This case is...getting to me. A lot of people have died and I'm not left with many answers.

"There's definitely space on the shuttle for one more," he concluded. "I just don't promise we're going to have any more luck at Olympus Mons than here."

"We keep digging, my lord," she replied. "We've turned up a bunch of loose threads. Keep yanking and something will unravel."

"I hope so," he told her. "Come on. It doesn't take that long for Marines to prep a shuttle for a suborbital flight."

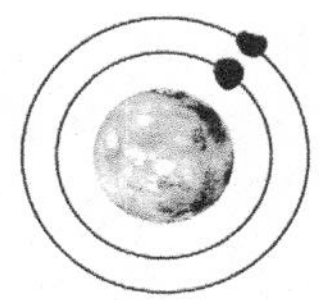

CHAPTER 11

THEY WERE halfway to Olympus Mons when the intercom buzzed.

"Lord Montgomery?" the pilot asked.

"What is it?" Damien replied.

"I have Dr. Christoffsen on the secure channel for you," the man replied. "He says it's urgent."

Damien was sitting at the front of the main troop compartment, only a few steps from the officers' compartment. "Urgent" from Christoffsen could be almost guaranteed to be "confidential". On the other hand...

"I'll be on in a moment," he told the pilot. "Romanov, Samara, with me."

His two subordinates fell in behind him as he moved forward, letting Romanov seal the privacy shield on the tiny room behind them as Damien plugged his security codes into the system.

"Professor," he greeted his political aide as the balding older man appeared on the screen. "We're on our way back to the Mountain. What do you need?"

"You may as well divert up," Christoffsen told him. "The Council is requesting your presence again. How was your trip?"

Damien shook his head.

"My trip saw a lot of people dead because we weren't fast enough," he replied. "I've had better weeks. What does the Council want?"

"Officially, they're asking for you to deliver an in-person update on their investigation into the Keepers," Christoffsen replied. "*Un*officially,

Councilor Montague swung enough votes to give you a chance to run them through *why* everything happened.

"It's the closest thing you're going to get to a chance to present a defense, Damien," he warned. "We have friends on the Council, but just the fact that Montague felt she needed to give you this opportunity is a bad sign."

Damien sighed.

"I don't suppose 'I'm busy actually trying to do my damned job' is a good enough reason to avoid this?"

"Not if you want to keep your 'damned job,'" Christoffsen said bluntly. "I'm not sure how things got this bad, Damien. I don't think it's just the fact that the situation is unprecedented. Too many people see this as opportunity. A weakness."

"And I just love being my King's weakness," Damien snarked. "All right, Professor. We'll divert to *Doctor Akintola*. Will you meet us there?"

"I have Olympus Mons staff loading everyone's travel kit onto a shuttle as we speak," Christoffsen confirmed. "Any special requests?"

Damien glanced over at Samara, who was looking somewhat disconcerted at the frank nature of the discussion.

"MIS Inspector Munira Samara has been assigned to my staff," he told Christoffsen. "Can you make sure there's clothes on the shuttle for her? I don't think she was expecting to get dragged into space."

From her expression, however, she wasn't planning on going anywhere else, and Damien would happily draft one more intelligent, competent agent to his service.

"If she can send me her sizes, I'm sure the Secret Service stockpile has some clothes that will fit," the Professor promised. "If not, I probably have enough time to have something brought up from Olympus City before I launch."

"Make sure there's at least a couple of headscarves in there," Damien told him, eyeing the light blue one Samara currently had wrapped over her hair. While there would be *some* in the Secret Service stockpile—just as there would be turbans and the strange underwear required by certain branches of Christianity—it wasn't something that would be in the basic kit.

"I'll be certain of it, my lord," Christoffsen replied. "I'll be aboard *Akintola* in about eighty minutes."

"I'll check with the pilot, but we'll probably beat you there," the Hand said. "Don't worry; I am *not* going into this mess without you."

Acceleration shifted them around as the assault shuttle turned for orbit, and Damien strapped into one of the seats in the officers' compartment with a sigh that had only partially to do with the sudden increase in force.

"I...am not certain that was a conversation I should have overheard," Inspector Samara finally said after a few minutes of silence. "It appears there are ramifications to this investigation I wasn't aware of."

"There are," Damien agreed. "That doesn't mean it wasn't a conversation you needed to be included in. As I understand it, Inspector, you've been assigned to my staff for at least the duration of this investigation?"

"In theory, I am working solely on this investigation, but both I and my superiors would regard it as a failure if I were not to assist you in anything else that came up," she admitted.

"Exactly," he said cheerfully. "Since I have you, Inspector Samara, I intend to make full and complete use of you. To do so, I need you to be fully and completely informed about what's going on—not least of which, the fact that it is appearing more and more likely that this may be my last investigation as a Hand."

The MIS Inspector looked at him in confusion for several moments.

"That makes no sense, my lord."

"In the context of the politics, it sadly does," Damien told her. "It's possible that if we manage to find out just what secret the Keepers are protecting that makes Mages and Marines and even *Hands* willing to betray, kill, and die for it...it's possible that secret may buy me a stay of execution."

He grimaced.

"It's even possible that in the final accounting, I and the Mage-King will agree that the particular secret needs to be kept, in which case my career becomes the next sacrifice on that altar," he admitted. "I am *far* from having made my peace with that possibility, but I must admit it exists."

"I see, my lord," Samara said slowly.

"If I manage to keep my Hand, you may consider this case an audition," he continued with a smile. "Having a trained detective and analyst attached to my staff could be useful. I prefer, as you can tell"—he gestured towards Romanov—"to keep my personal staff small and as fully in the loop as I can.

"But even if none of this was true," he told her, the smile fading as he considered the screen showing their course to *Doctor Akintola*, "that would still have been a conversation you needed to listen in on.

"This investigation has a political minefield attached, and it would not be just to drag you into it without any kind of warning."

"I appreciate that warning, my lord," she told him. "And the warning that I'm apparently auditioning for a Hand's staff—that wasn't in my brief."

"Working for a Hand is a volunteers-only deal," Damien replied with a smile. "I won't be drafting you."

"I said I appreciated the warning, my lord," she said with a smile of her own. "We'll have to see if I succeed on my audition before I have to decide if I volunteer, won't we?"

He chuckled.

"I see you're going to fit in with my lunatics just fine."

"This is Hand Montgomery aboard *Doctor Akintola*, requesting clearance to exit Mars orbit."

The Civil Fleet controller chuckled.

"Aren't we supposed to be assigning you a pilot, Lord Montgomery?" she asked.

"This is a luxury yacht," he pointed out. "Even if I wasn't qualified to fly her, she can basically fly herself."

A moment of foresight when leaving the yacht after the first Council meeting meant that Damien had been able to shower and dress in a clean suit while the rest of his staff waited for Christoffsen to arrive with their travel kits.

There were few dangers in Mars orbit that worried Damien, and none of them involved anyone attempting to board *Doctor Akintola* under the guns of two of the Martian Squadron's battleships. His entire security detail was currently in the showers, leaving him and the Professor the only people to oversee the yacht's computers and get her on her way.

"You're clear all the way to Ceres, my lord," Control told him. "Olympus Mons filed your flight plan before you boarded. Your course is clear."

"Any leftover War debris nearby?" Damien asked. The Eugenicist War had lasted a hundred years. Even though its battles had been relatively few and its ships tiny by modern standards, the War had littered the space between Earth and Mars—and a lot of orbits that originated between Earth and Mars—with high-speed debris.

Most of the actually hazardous ones had been cleaned up, but the ones that were left were radioactive enough to hide things. The last time he'd flown near one, someone had hidden a missile swarm in it.

"Not even a meteor until you're in the Belt," the woman replied. "Then you're looking at slightly higher than normal density of debris. Charts should be updated, but watch your scanners. Normal precautions."

"Understood. Thanks for the heads-up, Control. I'm bringing antimatter thrusters online in sixty seconds."

"Have a safe flight."

Damien let the channel drop as he plugged numbers into *Akintola*'s computers. Given the power of the yacht's engines, they didn't need to worry about orbital dynamics or anything similar. Their course was slightly more complicated than pointing the ship directly at Ceres and turning the engines on, but not by much.

"Anything I should be worrying about?" the Professor asked from the observer's seat.

"From the flight?" Damien shook his head. "No. Just feeling paranoid today. This meeting, on the other hand, I feel like I should be worrying about. Anything you need to brief me on?"

Cold logic said that the trip out to Ceres was the best time Damien was going to have to catch up on his sleep, but the events of the prior few days and the upcoming Council session kept him awake when he tried.

Aboard *Duke of Magnificence*, he would usually pace the observation deck he'd taken for an office. *Doctor Akintola* was too small to have such a deck, despite its supply of every other luxury he could think of and many he wouldn't have.

The next best thing was the yacht's bridge, which doubled as her simulacrum chamber. All of the walls of the space at the center of the ship were covered in screens, allowing the Mage in the powered chair at the heart of the room to see everything.

Resting just above that powered chair was the semi-liquid silver form of the simulacrum that allowed a Mage to jump *Akintola*. Unlike the simulacrum aboard *Duke*, though, this one would only allow jumps. A Mage could use it to target spells outside the ship, but targeting was all it could do.

An unlimited amplifier, like the one a warship carried, would amplify any spell. They were terrifyingly powerful weapons, which made the ability of a Rune Wright like Damien to *remove* the limits on a civilian jump ship dangerous.

Fortunately, there were only four adult and one minor Rune Wrights in the Protectorate—and all of them except Damien were members of the Royal Family.

"Should I just assume, in future, that if I'm looking for you, I should go to the nearest place one can see stars?" Romanov asked, the Special Agent walking across the bridge and dropping into an observer chair. "Amiri said that was part of your attachment to the observation deck."

"Helps me think," Damien agreed. "And helps remind me of the scale of our affair sometimes." He gestured at the screens. "How many stars can you see from here, Mage-Captain?"

They were over halfway to the asteroid belt, far away from any planets or other obstructions. In every direction, the darkness of space glittered with the pinpricks of distant suns.

"They're not easily counted," Romanov replied. "Hundreds? Thousands?"

"At least. Less than a hundred and twenty have human-occupied worlds," Damien said. "Maybe half again that have outposts of some kind. The entire sphere of human space is perhaps four hundred light years across. We think we are so important, and yet we are so tiny."

"Do I sense a metaphor, my lord?" the Marine asked dryly.

Damien laughed.

"I wasn't intending one, but the point is there," he agreed. "If it came down to it, Romanov, between resigning or letting the Mage-King suffer a constitutional crisis, what would you do?"

"My job is unlikely to trigger a constitutional crisis," Romanov told him. "But...I'd be damned tempted to stick it out. I'd like to think I'd resign in the end, though," he admitted.

"Yeah," Damien said. "That's about where I'm at. You may end up back with the Marines sooner than either of us expected."

"It's bullshit, my lord."

"No one said the joke would be funny, Mage-Captain," Damien replied. "Only that if we couldn't take it, we shouldn't have signed up."

"Fair enough, my lord."

His bodyguard fell back into silence and the Hand returned to his study of the stars. A flashing light on his console caught his attention, and he tapped commands on the arm of the powered chair, bringing the screen in closer and rotating the chair to face the icon the system was identifying.

"And now I wish they'd used a Navy computer for this ship," he murmured as he worked through the unfamiliar iconography. "There we go... A distress signal?"

"In Sol, sir?"

Damien answered Romanov by playing the transmission.

A computerized voice echoed in *Doctor Akintola*'s bridge.

"This is an automated distress signal. Captain Gambon of the asteroid refinery *Callisto* has triggered a Class One distress beacon. This indicates active threat to life and health of *Callisto*'s crew. Message repeats. This is an automated distress signal. Captain Gambon of the asteroid refinery *Callisto* has triggered a class one distress beacon. This indicates..."

"There!" Damien said aloud as he isolated the source. "*Callisto* is about ten million kilometers away around the interior of the Belt. *Akintola*'s sensors can't pick out the problem, but it's not like we have missiles."

A Navy warship could have picked out an attacker and launched missiles at them from there. *Doctor Akintola*, on the other hand, was completely unarmed and so lacked the long-range targeting sensors the warship would have had.

"Detouring."

Damien started plugging the course in immediately, almost absently hitting a command to forward the distress signal back to Mars.

"As the Agent responsible for your safety, I should point out that isn't our job," Romanov said hesitantly.

"There's nobody else closer than Ceres," Damien pointed out. "Our vector's already close enough, we can be there in under an hour, though we won't be anything close to zero velocity. No one else can be there in less than six. If there's a clear and present danger..."

"I'm with you, sir," the Marine agreed instantly. "Just felt the job description meant I had to say something."

"Go get your people in armor," the Hand ordered. "I do not like the look of this."

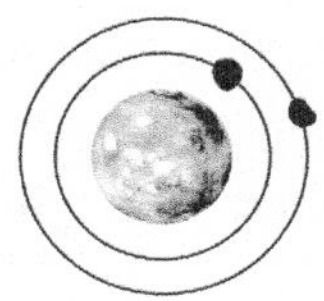

CHAPTER 12

DOCTOR AKINTOLA was an incredibly maneuverable little ship, to a degree that was almost a shame, given that her usual use was flying dignitaries from point A to point B. Her magical gravity was rated to compensate for up to ten gravities of acceleration, and her engines were capable of pulling fifteen.

Damien danced the fleet little ship around one of the asteroid belt's scattered dust clouds, his hands on the controls as he concentrated on the space around him.

He was vaguely aware that Samara had replaced Romanov in the bridge, the MIS Inspector silently taking a seat at the sensor console to help keep an eye on things, but his focus remained on getting *Akintola* to the ship blazing its call for help as quickly and safely as possible.

"I've got a second transmission," Samara told him. "You need to hear this."

A moment later, a new voice echoed in the bridge. Unlike the first message, this was a person instead of a computer. The voice was gravelly, like a man who'd smoked too many cigarettes or caught a couple of whiffs of vacuum.

"I am the Alpha and the Omega," the voice declared. "I speak for the Stone and the Void, the People and the Rock that you have denied for so long.

"*Callisto* now belongs to the people of the Belt. Any of you Martian thugs that come near her or us will meet fire and stone. I, the Alpha and the Omega, have spoken!"

"It doesn't repeat," Samara concluded.

"I'm not familiar with the threat list for Sol," Damien told her. "Do you have any idea who this idiot is?"

"I'm not sure," she admitted. "The Stone and the Void...I've heard that before."

"Anyone who might pull something like this?

"It's come up in the context of the Belt Liberation Front, but they're..." Samara sighed. "They're a bunch of fringe crazies we didn't think even took *themselves* seriously. The last intelligence I saw certainly didn't give them enough resources to pull off a space hijacking."

"It might not be them and it might not be a full-on hijacking yet," Damien replied. "That distress beacon is still going, so I'm guessing they don't have enough control to shut it down. There's a window of vulnerability for them, and I'd say we're arriving right smack in the middle of it.

"We're getting close enough that *Akintola*'s sensors should be able to resolve something," he continued. The yacht might not have warship scanners, but they were better than most luxury yachts of her breed would carry. "See what you can pull up."

It didn't occur to him until after he'd asked that he had no idea if the MIS officer had a clue how the sensor systems of a spaceship worked. From the speed with which the data started feeding to his displays, however, she clearly did.

"*Callisto* is a giant slug of a ship," she said frankly. "Thirty million tons, centrifugal gravity rings for habitation, pure ion thrust. Can't pull more than a tenth of a gravity, but she's the anchor point for Amethyst Star Mining's operations. They've got a dozen mining ships; each of them swings back by *Callisto* at least once a week to deliver their raw ore.

"I'm not reading any of ASM's ships here," she continued, "but I've got at least twenty ships circling her with no IDs—and a debris field that might have been another ship.

"*Twenty* ships?" Damien asked. "How large are we talking?"

"Pocket change and toys," she replied. "A dozen shuttles, six intra-system personnel transports, and two mining ships. I'm *assuming* they've strapped guns of some kind to them, but they won't have the mass or power supply for anything significant."

"But it's not like *Callisto* has any defenses at all," he confirmed grimly. And without weapons or a proper amplifier, his own ability to engage was limited to about fifty thousand kilometers. They weren't going to *enjoy* him getting that close, but they might well be able to shoot at *Doctor Akintola* before that.

"Let everyone know to brace for impact," he told her. "I can take them, but this ride might get rough."

"This ship is unarmed!" Samara objected. "What are you going to *do*?"

"I am a Hand, Inspector Samara," Damien reminded her. "And like you, they might just underestimate what that means in a situation like this."

They were still over a million kilometers away when *Callisto* noticed that the cavalry was on its way.

"Incoming transmission from the refinery ship," Samara told Damien. "The distress beacon is still going; this is a directional transmission straight to us."

"Show me."

One of his screens lit up with a recording of an overweight gray-haired woman. She wore a bulletproof vest and had a gun strapped to her side, both of which looked like she'd worn them before and they were old friends.

"Civil Fleet ship, this is Captain Kayla Gambon of *Callisto*," she said in a gruff drawl. "We have been attacked and boarded by pirates. One Amethyst Star Mining ship has been destroyed with all hands, and I've lost over a dozen of my own crew trying to hold them back.

"They are in control of the engines and the refinery spaces," she continued. "I retain the bridge, communications, and life support, but they are pressing my boys hard at life support.

"Any assistance you can provide would be more than welcome."

The message ended.

"She realizes this ship is unarmed, right?" Samara said, repeating her earlier words with a tone of disbelief.

"She probably only saw the Civil Fleet ID," Damien pointed out. "Most Civil Fleet ships aren't armed, but they do usually have a security detachment."

"What can we do?"

"First, we need to drive off those ships," he concluded, checking his velocity. Burning at fifteen gravities, which even after the gravity runes absorbed ten was an unpleasant experience for everyone aboard, they'd still be moving at just over five hundred kilometers a second when they passed the big refinery ship.

"Second, we need to retake *Callisto*. Romanov." He linked the Marine in. "Are your people ready to go?"

"Shuttle is locked and loaded. What do you need us to do?"

"The shuttle is rated for twenty gravities if you're all in your 'suits, right?"

He could almost *hear* Romanov's wince.

"Yes, my lord."

"Going to kick you out of the door at fifteen minutes and six hundred thousand kilometers away from *Callisto*," Damien ordered. "Burn twenty gees the whole way in; I'll drive the ships off and return for pickup."

"If my math is right, you'll be an hour from zero velocity," Romanov pointed out.

"And you'll be the ones making an assault crash—I mean, boarding," the Hand replied. "I'm not worried about my ability to see off twenty pirates with refitted ships, Mage-Captain. I am worried about losing more of *Callisto*'s people. Understand?"

"Understood. We drop at t-minus fifteen from contact—twelve minutes and counting."

"Good luck, Denis," Damien told him.

"Well, that's nice and obvious," Damien said aloud as the assault shuttle kicked free and lit up its own engines at a third again *Akintola*'s acceleration.

"I'm not entirely unfamiliar with starship sensors," Samara replied, "and I must point out that the bigger ship burning antimatter engines for fifteen gravities is a *bit* warmer and more obvious than the shuttle."

"Oh, I know," he admitted. "I'm waiting to see what they *do*."

"So far, not much of anything," she told him. "Starting to feel ignored."

"Can you get a decent scan of them with those systems?" he asked. "Identify weapons?"

"The mining ships will have lasers, but they're not really designed to hit a maneuvering target," Samara said almost absently as her fingers danced over the console. "If they've gimballed them up to aim better, we're not going to pick it up from here."

"But if they've added bigger systems, you should be able to," he pointed out. "And *those* are what I'm worried about."

If the pirates had any real weapons, he'd have seen them by now. Even cheap missiles had ranges measured in millions of kilometers. A decent military laser could have lit *Akintola* up at over a million.

There were still a lot of things they *might* have that could start messing the yacht up before he could return the favor.

"I'm not sure I'll pick up anything before they fire," Samara admitted after a few more minutes. "There's no major additions to any of the ships that I can see, but we're still pretty far away and they're not exactly standard designs.

"Is this ship armored to even take a hit?"

"We can take a hit," Damien told her. "Maybe two. Depending on what they're shooting at us with."

"That is *not* reassuring."

"I'm not planning on getting hit," he replied, studying his screens and sensor output carefully as they flashed over the half-million-kilometer mark...then throwing the ship into a jinking spiral in time for the sensors to register an energy spike where they *had* been.

"*That* was one of the mining ships' lasers," Samara said instantly. "They've upgraded the power source and presumably the targeting. It's not a military weapon, but nothing civilian is going to like being hit with it."

"And *Akintola* is basically civilian," Damien agreed, studying the sensor screens himself and noticing a very *distinct* pattern he'd only ever seen in training. "Isn't this entertaining." He tapped a command to open up a shipwide intercom channel.

"Everyone, this is your pilot speaking," he said calmly. "I apologize for the acceleration, but I'm afraid things are about to get even rougher. If you're not strapped in, I suggest you fix that."

"Oh, *fuck*."

Samara had finished running the scans and recognized what he'd seen—just as Damien threw *Doctor Akintola* into an even wider spiral, yanking the dextrous little yacht out of the way of the stream of mass-driver rounds launched from the smaller ships.

"Cheap, effective, and dangerous against big freighters and other ships that don't dodge well," Damien said. "That's about what I was expecting."

He twisted the yacht again, distorting her course to make sure the next batch of projectiles missed. The rounds were "only" moving at about one percent of lightspeed, so he could see them coming thousands of kilometers away.

The lasers on the two mining ships were the real threat, but the same twisting course that made it impossible for the mass drivers' metal bullets to hit made it harder for the lasers to connect too.

For now.

The range was dropping rapidly, and every few thousands of kilometers *Akintola* grew closer to *Callisto*'s attackers took a few more fractions of a second off the time elapsed between when they saw the yacht and when their beams would reach her.

Eventually, the lapse wouldn't be enough for him to move the yacht away from their beams, even if they kept failing to guess his dodges.

"What happens if they hit the shuttle?"

"Two things," Damien told Samara, jinking around another burst of high-velocity metal shards. "Firstly, Romanov's pilot is both better at this than I am and behind us, so has more time to dodge. Second, well, the assault shuttle is probably better armored than we are."

"You need to work on your reassurances, my lord."

The ship shuddered as his luck ran out and one of the lasers connected. Damien yanked the controls, twisting the ship out of the way after barely a fraction of a second of contact, but the ship happily informed him that the beam had cut almost entirely through the hull at the impact point.

Leaving the ship's programming to spiral it forward randomly, he stripped off his gloves and lay his hands on the simulacrum. The runes on his palms slotted neatly into place on the semi-liquid silver model, and he exhaled as he linked into the ship.

His options were limited. They were still over a hundred and fifty thousand kilometers away, and even *he* couldn't do much at that distance. Unless he found some way to keep the yacht intact, however, they weren't going to *make* it to the distance where he could reach the pirates.

He'd misjudged, and winced as a second laser beam slammed into *Akintola*. The mining ships had three lasers apiece, and they'd clearly upgraded both their targeting and slew abilities. The beams were still low-power cutting lasers even with their upgrades, or *Akintola* would be debris.

Another salvo of mass-driver rounds bracketed them. The pirates were expanding their field of fire, sacrificing the likelihood of a single salvo kill for a better chance of hitting the yacht at all.

The mass-driver rounds had to come to *him*.

Damien smiled.

A missile would be too fast, too maneuverable for him to do anything.

A laser was begun and over before he could influence it.

Mass-driver rounds, however...

His power flickered out as the next salvo came in. There was *so much* energy in them, a thousand kilometers a second on projectiles that massed everything from fifty grams to fifty kilos.

Another Mage might have been able to deflect them, knocking them aside from the course that would hit *Doctor Akintola*—but Damien Montgomery was a Rune Wright with full command of his powers.

He turned every single projectile back on its course, flinging them back at their originating ships at twice the speed they'd been fired at him.

They had time to see what he'd done and evade, but none of them had expected it. Mass-driver rounds slammed home on the pirate ships. The mining ships and refitted transports had the mass to take the hits; the weapons were only truly deadly in massive quantities.

The fundamentally-civilian shuttles the pirates had stolen had neither armor nor mass. The heavy metal slugs smashed home at over four thousand kilometers a second, ripping gaping holes through the small craft and smashing their wreckage into the asteroids behind *Callisto*.

The transports and mining ships were damaged but functioning... but stopped firing the mass drivers anyway.

"I think you scared them," Samara pointed out. "Wait...you *really* scared them. They're scattering."

"Damn," Damien cursed, studying the screens. The pirates had been watching his velocity, too. All eight remaining ships were scattering on courses where even their lower acceleration could prevent *Akintola* from catching up to them. He could probably catch one...but not the rest.

"That's both better and worse than I hoped," he admitted. "I suppose I'm left hoping that Romanov catches us some prisoners."

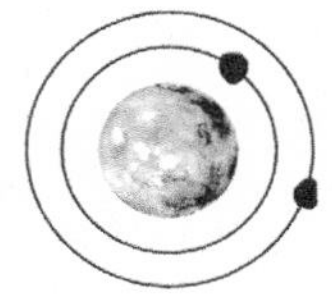

CHAPTER 13

"EVERYBODY HANG ON," Denis Romanov ordered his team as the assault shuttle careened toward *Callisto,* still decelerating toward from the big refinery ship at twenty gravities.

Royal Martian Marine Corps assault shuttles didn't go in for such niceties as magical gravity. They had straps, acceleration couches, and an assumption that their passengers were in armor. The only concession to making sure that Mars's finest survived the assault crash was a one-shot runic artifact at the front of the ship.

It was activated by impact and was *excruciatingly* uncomfortable...but completely neutralized the inertial energy of the shuttle. Once. Then the thing had to be replaced, and it was *expensive.*

But for moments like this, when his shuttle was still traveling at well over four hundred kilometers a second upon reaching their destination, it was an absolute and literal lifesaver.

"Impact in ten seconds," the pilot snapped over the intercom. "If you haven't done this before, open your mouths and clench your guts. This is gonna *suck*!"

Impact.

And then, for a period of time that Denis knew was literally fractions of a second but felt like eternity, the entire shuttle was *wrong*.

There was no other way to describe it. In that infinitesimal instant of time, magic swept through every molecule, every particle of his body, and robbed them of their kinetic energy, converting it into a blast of heat that passed out the rear of the ship like a superheated ghost.

The moment passed, and the Marine turned Secret Service Agent shook himself inside his armor, trying to get the last of the sensation out of his body.

"All right, people, that's never fun, but we have a job to do," he snapped. "Secret Service Agents, back up the Marines; they know this drill better than you do.

"Intel from inside the ship is that engineering is in enemy hands but life support is still holding. Corporal Coral, take your fire team and six of the Service Agents, head to life support. The rest of you are with me."

"Do we have a map?" Coral asked.

"Should be in the download," Denis replied. "So far as I know, she's a standard *MacMurray*-class refinery ship. Interior might be off from the schematics but shouldn't be by much."

"We'll find them either way," the Marine Corporal promised. "Can probably just follow the sound of the guns."

"Don't wait too long," the detail commander replied. "We're headed for Engineering, which means that sound is going to be us pretty damn quickly."

"Oohrah, sir."

Half of his detail split off after the Corporal, suit jets flaring in zero gravity, and Denis turned a smile he knew couldn't be seen behind the faceless mask of his exosuit helmet on the remainder.

"All right, people," he told them. "If these were pirates, I'd be expecting them to surrender. But if these are terrorists...they may try and take us all with them by blowing the fusion plants. Let's go discourage that plan, shall we?"

Overlaying the ship schematic on his helmet view and highlighting the fastest route to Engineering demonstrated to Denis Romanov that he didn't give his pilot enough credit. *Callisto* was an immense vessel, four kilometers around and five kilometers long, that looked more like a mobile factory or city than a spaceship.

Traveling at over four hundred kilometers a second, his pilot had delivered them less than two hundred meters away from the main power plant, a monstrous complex of fusion generators that could handily power multiple cities.

He flipped the route to Corporal Massey, who led his fire team out on point. The Secret Service Agents under Denis's command were decent in a fight and not even particularly bad in zero gravity, but this kind of action was exactly what his Marines trained for.

If Denis had known that Montgomery would have been ordering him to board ships, he could easily have packed another assault shuttle and thirty Marines aboard *Doctor Akintola*. It wasn't a possibility he'd considered in the extremely abbreviated planning for the trip.

"Life signs through here," Massey radioed back to him. "I'm not reading energy signatures of heavy weapons, but could be pirates."

"Could be crew, too," Denis pointed out. "Soft-touch it, Corporal."

"Wilco."

Denis caught up just as one of Massey's Marines locked his boots to a wall and *ripped* a sealed metal hatch out of the way, the other three behind her with their heavy rifles pointed at the hatch.

"We surrender!" a voice exclaimed.

"No need for that, ma'am," Massey barked. "We're Marines. Are you all okay?"

Taking that as a sign they hadn't found pirates, Denis advanced forward to check on the situation. The room was a mess hall of some kind, and easily two dozen men and women in work suits had barricaded themselves in it.

They had no weapons but had wedged a table against the hatch to keep it shut. That hadn't sufficed against exosuit armor.

"I'm Mage-Captain Denis Romanov," he told them quickly. "We've secured local space and are retaking the ship. I'm trying to get to the power complex to make sure the bastards don't blow us all to hell!"

"You're a sight for sore eyes," the woman who'd initially offered their surrender said. "I'm engineer Darlene Matthews, one of the senior wrench jockeys for that complex. In theory, the safety protocols should stop them blowing the plants—"

"Ma'am, I know seven different ways to make a properly-safetied fusion reactor detonate," Denis said gently. "We need to get in there safely and quietly."

"In those suits?"

"Safely is more important," the Marine admitted.

"If you're following the schematics, you're going to walk right into an open area they'll have set up as a kill zone if they're smart," Matthews told him. "But...there are always other ways around a ship of this size."

"Can you show me?"

"No time to walk through it on paper," she snapped. "You lot okay with following a civvie?"

"It's your ship, Miss Matthews."

The engineer might have surrendered immediately on seeing exosuits breaking down the door of her hiding spot, but there clearly wasn't anything wrong with Darlene Matthews's general sense of courage and self-confidence.

She drifted through Denis's team of exosuited men and women without a moment's hesitation, then gestured for them to follow her as she grabbed a handhold.

"Follow the engineer, people," he ordered. "She knows the way and we don't."

The fact that Matthews was also significantly more familiar with the power systems they might need to stop overloading could also come in handy. If she hadn't volunteered, Denis might have had to convince her.

She led them off of the main routes, into a snarl of corridors and tubing that Denis wasn't even surprised didn't match his schematics, then stopped in the middle of one of those corridors.

"I don't suppose one of you fine folks has some kind of cutter?" she asked. "If we cut a hole through here, it'll open up an air exchange pipe used by the main heating system. It's big enough for your suits and will take us right into the center of the complex. They'll be guarding the entrances, not the middle."

"Massey," Denis snapped.

He'd been a Marine officer for too long not to assume that his noncoms had the solution to most relatively mundane problems. He wasn't surprised in the slightest when a compartment on Corporal Massey's armor produced a technically non-regulation vibro-blade easily fifty centimeters long.

The weapon made short work of the relatively frail wall of the corridor and shell of the vent beyond. The piping was slightly larger than Matthews had implied, though still not quite wide enough for the Marines to go two abreast.

"Zhao, you go first," Denis ordered one of his Marines. "Matthews, you can give her directions from behind, but you are *not* going first."

The engineer was smart enough not to argue the point, and the detail moved into the piping.

"Coral, report," Denis requested as he followed his people in. The air in the vent was actually colder than in the corridors. Presumably this was the return pipe, bringing air back to the complex to be warmed by the coolant from the fusion reactors.

"Schematics put us near life support," his subordinate replied. "I'm hearing gunfire, but it's sporadic. We're moving in to relieve the defenders."

"Be careful," he ordered. "I want your people and *Callisto*'s crew intact when this is over. Prisoners would be nice but aren't essential."

"Understood. Point has eyes on bogies," she said crisply. "Coral out."

Smart subordinates were worth their weight in gold.

The schematics he had of the generic *MacMurray* were so far off from the realities of *Callisto*'s interior piping that he had no idea where they'd ended up. This...wasn't really a surprise. Corridors and living spaces weren't consistent from ship to ship of a civilian ship class, and piping wasn't even visible.

There would be true schematics of *Callisto* somewhere. Denis didn't have them—but he was relatively sure Matthews had them *memorized.*

"Here," she announced, shortly after his sensors started to warn him that the vent was getting uncomfortably warm for an unarmored human. "We're right in the middle of the four main plants. If they're going to try and blow us all to hell, they'll at least *start* with those."

Even one of the smaller plants sent into overload would gut *Callisto,* but the big ones would *vaporize* her. Shaking his head, he tagged his people on his wrist-comp, directing each of them in specific directions.

"All right. Matthews, get behind us all," he ordered. "It's warm in here, but I don't want you in the line of fire. Massey, open me a door."

Exosuits weren't designed for stealth or sneakiness. Matthews's route had got them into the middle of the power complex, but Denis had no illusions about his people's ability to try and quietly secure the facility.

His sensors were doing their best to estimate positions of hostiles, and he haloed each one on his screen, marking the potentials for each of his people as Massey went to work with the blade.

Opening up the side of the flimsy vent was easy. Arranging it so a door wide enough for more than a single exosuit opened in one shot without giving too much warning of what was coming...that took a master, and Corporal Massey was just such a master.

When the noncom finally kicked out the panel he'd created, a path wide enough for three exosuited troopers appeared in an instant. His fire team was out of the vent in the same moment, three Marines moving in at high speed with their rifles tracking and their scanners sweeping for threats.

Exosuits weren't designed for stealth. They were designed for assault.

"Drop your weapons!" Massey bellowed over his suit's speakers. "Drop your weapons or die!"

Denis followed the first fire team out, his own suit's computers collating the sensor take from each exosuit around him and layering it over the existing possible contacts it had identified before. A bogie flashed red, raising an assault rifle that probably wasn't a threat to Denis's men.

It didn't matter. Anyone who didn't drop their weapons was a threat to *somebody*. Denis fired, his rifle spitting frangible antipersonnel rounds across the massive open space containing *Callisto*'s power generators.

The rifleman went down. Others went down with him as Denis's people charged in. None of the weapons his scans were detecting were a threat to exosuits on their own, though *enough* fire from even cheap assault rifles would eventually bring down even an exosuited Marine.

The initial break-in over, Denis focused his attention on the sensor data, searching for the threat he was *actually* worried about.

There.

A cluster of three men, none registering as armed, working away at the control console for one of the primary power plants. They might not be trying to rig it to explode, but it was a risk he couldn't take.

He turned off his exosuit's magnetic boots and kicked off, triggering the suit's jets at the same time. His ensuing flight drew fire from all across the power complex, but none of the pirates had penetrator rounds. Their bullets bounced off his armor, and he slammed into the metal floor next to the console, his rifle pointing directly at the center man.

"Step away from the console," he ordered. "It's over."

Then, of course, his sensors went crazy with a threat warning. There was only so much his scans could do to find a concealed weapon, especially one without an active power source. The weapon one of the helpers pulled out didn't even have moving parts. It was a one-shot, close-range weapon that fired a discarding sabot tungsten penetrator triggered by a tiny battery.

Instinct and training took over, the rifle barking as he shot the man on the console and swung an armored fist around to smash aside the man with the penetrator pistol. Both men went down...and his suit warnings informed him that the *third* man had also drawn an identical weapon.

He was out of position. Even with the suit's enhanced speed, he couldn't even get himself around to cast a spell to take the man down.

Then a crowbar, in the hands of a pissed-off engineer, smashed into the thug's arm with a horrible snapping sound as Matthews interjected herself into the fight. She had to have launched into the dive the moment Denis had fired, but she'd arrived in time to save his life.

The pirate went spinning off into the reactor, which he hit with a very final-sounding crunch.

"Thank you, Miss Matthews," Denis said softly. "Can you check the console for me?"

He locked his boots to the metal and surveyed the complex. Despite being abandoned by their peers, it looked like the thirty or so men—and they were all men, he noted absently—had refused to surrender. None of them were still standing and, sadly, it didn't look like they'd taken any prisoners.

"Oh, this is *not* good," the engineer exclaimed. "They mirrored the controls of all four primary plants to this console and shut down the temperature sensors."

Which, if Denis remembered his own training on how to blow a plant like this up, short-circuited about half of the safety lockouts.

"They opened up all of the fuel lines and set the tokamak to maximum pressure," she continued. "They were busy overriding the rest of the safety protocols when you interrupted them."

"That puts us well over halfway to critical overload," Denis concluded. "Can you stop it?"

"Working on it," she snapped.

There was no way he could even evacuate his team. *Callisto* had at least a thousand people on board, and he'd brought twenty more with him. All of them were going to die very quickly if Matthews couldn't stop the process.

"Corporal, start pulling fuel lines," he ordered crisply. "It won't stop the process, but it'll buy Miss Matthews time."

"Wilco."

His people started to jet around the massive open space with its spherical power plants. Denis watched on the schematics projected on his helmet as they detached fuel line after fuel line. There was no way they could remove them all, not in time, but each line removed reduced the amount of fuel being fed into the plants.

His armor's scanners happily informed him that both the temperature and radiation levels in the complex were rising as the containment vessels began to be overwhelmed.

"There!" Matthews exclaimed. "Temperature sensors back online. Oh, *shit*."

"Matthews?"

"Safety venting initiating, but temperatures are *way* over the line. I'm going to have to do a full emergency vent or we're *still* going to have an overload."

That would dump a massive amount of superheated coolant into the very room they were standing in—a process that Denis's exosuited men could survive but Matthews would not.

"Right," he said cheerfully, dropping an armored hand on the engineer's shoulder. "Fortunately, I'm familiar with this system. Shout when you're clear."

"Wait, what?"

Denis's suit computers finished assessing her mass and the necessary vector before she'd finished objecting, and his hand on her shoulder tightened as he picked her up and *threw* her toward an open security hatch.

"Everyone, full seals," he ordered, watching with one eye as the engineer flew across the complex while checking the temperature readings on the console with the other.

They had...about thirty seconds. He spent ten of them making sure Matthews was clear and the security hatch had slammed shut behind her.

It took five more seconds for him to locate the correct commands.

Fortunately, the emergency venting was designed for exactly this situation and only took six seconds to go live, venting superheated coolant into the main engineering space. Alarms blazed across his helmet display again as the temperature skyrocketed toward two hundred degrees Celsius.

Three hundred.

Four.

The exosuit was only rated for five hundred and fifty, and Denis was starting to get *very* worried when the temperature crossed five hundred degrees, but it finally, *finally* peaked.

"Core temperatures are dropping," he said softly, studying the panel. "The venting system for this room is engaging. Congratulations, folks. We get to live today."

Unfortunately, if any of the pirates had survived the clash with his people, they definitely had *not* survived his filling the room with superheated toxic coolant.

Matthews was waiting outside the security hatch when Denis clomped out of the slowly cooling engineering space. Once he was in clean, if still uncomfortably warm, air, he removed his helmet, studying the fair-haired woman with a small smile.

"You were all ready to sacrifice yourself, Miss Matthews," he told her. "There wasn't time to argue or to explain that I was qualified on the system. Needed you out of the danger zone."

"Appreciate that, Captain," she said stiffly. "And thank you. I have a lot of friends on this ship."

"And there was no need for you to die for them today," Denis said. "Tomorrow, well, you remain a power systems engineer."

She chuckled.

"Fair enough."

With a nod to her, he pinged his other team.

"Coral, what's your status?"

"I've had better days, boss," the Corporal replied. "Someone is playing clever buggers. There's almost nobody here, but they've got heavy-enough guns to keep us and the folks in life support pinned down."

"You can take them?"

"Give me time and I can take anything, but I'm guessing they had more and I don't know where they went. But I can guess."

"The bridge."

"Bingo."

"Thanks, Corporal," Denis growled. "Box those bastards in, see if you can force a surrender. We're going to go see if we can find the Captain."

He turned back to Matthews.

"Miss Matthews, you've already helped a great deal, but it seems I may need one more favor," he told her. "What's the fastest way to the bridge?"

"That depends, Captain. Are you feeling up to flying?"

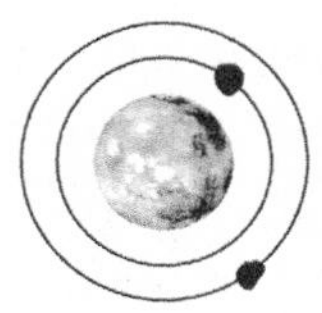

CHAPTER 14

WHILE *CALLISTO'S* overall dimensions were immense, it looked much like a collection of towers and factories linked together by piping and struts and surrounded by two massive spinning rings. The power complex was a squat tower near the edge for easy access, and the bridge was on the "top" of the tallest tower, at the centerline of the ship.

To get from the power-generator complex to the bridge inside would require going "down" to the disk that was the base of the ship and then "up" to the top of the tower. The ship had a decent internal transit system, but it would have been a thirty- or forty-minute trip for Denis and his team.

Their exosuits, however, had begun as combat suits for use in vacuum. They had everything needed to make a three-kilometer EVA jaunt built in, though their fuel tanks were normally kept empty.

The airlock that Matthews led them to was intended for the engineers and repair teams to carry out exterior work on *Callisto*. There were lockers full of civilian EVA suits, one of which Matthews strapped on, and available tanks to fill the exosuit fuel cells.

"Dropping a marker on your maps, but you're still best off following me," the engineer told them. "I've made this exact jump before for maintenance work. It's not just a vector; you need to know the path."

Denis didn't like dragging the civilian into yet *another* firefight, but she was damned useful while they were retaking her ship.

"All right, Miss Matthews. Lead the way."

The airlock cycled, venting the air into space—followed a moment later by the eleven of them. They drifted out for a moment, then Matthews activated her suit jets and took off toward the bridge.

"Follow the engineer, people," Denis ordered, locking his own suit's systems onto her. Her course wasn't a direct path to the marker for the bridge airlock, but he trusted her enough to believe there was a reason for that.

Their course arced them away from the power-generator complex, which was still venting gases as the fusion plants slowly cooled back down to normal operating temperature and pressure, and around several massive storage containers likely holding unprocessed ore. Each of the containers would have easily swallowed a Navy destroyer or two, and the pipes that fed into and out of them were at least thirty meters across.

A *MacMurray* refinery ship represented more spaceborne industry than some entire star systems commanded. There were, at last count, *sixteen* of them in Sol.

"Adjusting course to bear on the airlock; bringing us around Storage Six's feeder pipes," Matthews told them, her suit's computers feeding the vector change back to the Secret Service team following her.

The course twisted them away from the storage containers, dodging them around a set of immense, hundred-and-fifty-meter-wide exhaust flues for the main refinery, toward the central administration tower.

"Even the admin tower lacks gravity," Matthews warned. "The bridge and top few floors have magical grav, but most of the rest is zero-gee."

"Are we going to be in the zone with the runes?"

"Should be."

"Good to know," Denis said dryly. Whether or not they had gravity changed a *lot*.

The ship had a stark kind of beauty from the outside. It was purely functional, with the massive rotating artificial-gravity rings around the outside, and several smaller ones tucked away in various sections of the facility, where some kind of "down" would be needed for either the refining process or the humans themselves.

Lights glowed all over it. It was literally a city in space, though it was home to only a handful of people relative to its size. The massive battleships that stood guard over Mars were heavier, but with their super-dense armor and carefully condensed designs, they were actually significantly smaller than the massive spacegoing structure around him.

"There's the airlock," the engineer told them as they finally came close enough to see it. "I can't raise the Captain," she warned them. "The suit's radio is short range, but I should have got her from there..."

"Understood," Denis replied. At this point, even taking the bridge wouldn't be enough to achieve victory for the pirates, but it would certainly make his task harder if Captain Gambon was dead.

Despite the painful acceleration Damien was putting her through, *Doctor Akintola* was still growing farther and farther away from *Callisto.* Her velocity was shrinking, but they were still almost half an hour away from reaching zero velocity relative to the refinery ship, let alone getting back to her.

"I can't raise Captain Gambon," Samara told him quietly. "She's been checking in every few minutes since we drove the pirates off, but I haven't been able to get in touch for at least five minutes. It's been almost ten since we spoke."

"Damn," he said. "What was the last you heard from her?"

"Life support was being pressed but the bridge was quiet," the Inspector replied.

"That's what I thought. Wanted to be sure."

The Hand studied the diagram of *Callisto* and glanced at the simulacrum floating above him. In many ways, he'd almost be better off if the ship were farther away. He could teleport *Doctor Akintola* using the simulacrum, but the minimum distance he could easily manage was a light-hour.

Jumping a starship was also subject to significant risks from gravity. He could jump the ship from there, but it would be unpleasant and risky. Of course, the matrix just scaled up a smaller spell...

"Romanov," he pinged the Mage-Captain. "We've lost touch with the bridge. Are you in contact?"

"Negative," the Marine replied. "The life-support attack has been cut down to a holding action, too. We're making an exterior approach to the bridge, but we have no coms with Captain Gambon at all."

"Damn."

"We're only a few minutes out, my lord," Romanov told him. "We'll be there soon."

"Understood."

Damien looked over at Samara.

"Ten minutes, huh?"

"At most. At least five, though."

He nodded absently while plugging numbers into *Akintola*'s computer. Two sets of calculations ran side by side, one for the ship's course and one for the exact distance and relative velocity to *Callisto*'s bridge.

Grimly, Damien unstrapped himself from the chair and wove magic around himself to resist the five gravities that had been pressing him down.

"There's a program in the computer that will bring *Akintola* back to *Callisto* on its own," he told Samara. "Should bring to a zero-velocity rendezvous at about fifty klicks' distance."

"Aren't you flying us?" The MIS Inspector was looking at him like he was crazy, and he smiled grimly at her.

"The ship can fly itself for that, and minutes might make all the difference for Captain Gambon," he explained. "I'll see you in a few hours, Inspector Samara."

Before the woman could say anything more, he read the second set of numbers on the command chair's screen and *stepped*.

He teleported directly from one bridge to another, but *Callisto*'s bridge was a *very* different affair from *Doctor Akintola*'s. The yacht's bridge was a gorgeous affair, a simulacrum chamber surrounded by the view of the stars and equipped with the latest in luxuries and electronics.

The refinery ship's bridge resembled a military command center, with four rows of monitors and consoles filling a room more concerned with running the refinery's operations than actually flying the ship.

At the back of the room was a raised area where the Captain could look down over everyone else's shoulders, though it was distinctly too far back for the Captain to be able to see *details* of what anyone was doing.

A dozen men in black fatigues had formed a rough firing line along the front of that dais, their assault rifles pointing at the refinery's command crew to keep them back. Behind them, an unusually tall and pale man, obviously space-born, stood with a gun trained on the heavyset form of Captain Gambon.

The woman was on the ground, already injured, as she glared up at the man threatening her.

Damien threw a shield of force across her as the man, apparently the leader of the attackers, looked up in shock at his arrival.

"I'd recommend you put the gun down and surrender, but the evidence suggests you're not the surrendering type," the Hand told him.

"What the fuck? Who in the Stone and Void are you?" the man demanded.

"I am Hand Damien Montgomery," Damien told him. "And your only chance of living through this is to drop that gun and talk very, very quickly."

"Fuck you. Take him!"

A dozen assault rifles blazed to life, bullets hammering into the shield of force Damien had raised in front of himself as well.

"I'm not sure how many people you've killed today," Damien admitted. "I'm prepared to leave that to a conventional court to assess if you surrender. I'll even promise your lives if you lay down your guns."

The Protectorate used the death penalty only in extreme cases, but piracy and mass murder were on the short list of crimes that could get it dusted off.

"The Belt has listened to the lies of Mars for too long! We will be free."

The speaker yanked his jacket open, revealing that he was wearing an explosive vest. A quick glance at his men suggested at least half had the same accessory.

"Everyone in this room dies when I hit the button. What do you say to *that*, Hand Montgomery?"

"I haven't met many who regard death as freedom," Damien said. "There's been enough death today, I think. We can talk about this, Mister..."

"Go to hell!"

The gun in the terrorist's hand barked, the bullets smashing away from Captain Gambon as Damien tightened his shield around her. Tossing the weapon aside, he suddenly charged at the Hand with the detonator in his hand.

Despite everything, Damien actually *tried* to stop the detonator. He had neither enough time nor enough familiarity with the vest the man was wearing to manage it, but he *tried.*

He didn't account for the fact that the detonator would also trigger the *other* men's vests. Seven sets of explosives went off in one cacophonous blast and he'd shielded only *Callisto*'s crew.

By the time Romanov's people broke through the bridge hatch two minutes later, all of the pirates were dead.

"Keep pressure on that," Romanov instructed, stepping up to where Damien was treating Captain Gambon's wound. The woman had passed out from blood loss, but he was reasonably sure she was going to make it.

"I know that much first aid," the Hand replied. "Tape and gauze, if you want to be helpful."

The Special Agent chuckled but obeyed, handing Damien the supplies he needed to finish binding the ugly wound in the woman's leg.

"She'll live; I did some light cauterization," Damien told Romanov. He glanced up at the shocked-looking bridge crew. "I presume there is a doctor somewhere on this ship?"

"We have an emergency clinic," one of the crew responded. He'd been standing a little too close to where the suicide bombers had blown their vests and was slowly and shakily wiping blood off of his face. Damien's shield had absorbed the blast and the force, but some of the...debris had still ended up all over the room.

"Can you get a doctor up here ASAP?" the Hand instructed. "The Captain will need real attention as soon as possible, though I imagine there'll be a lot of demand for their services today."

Rising, he met Romanov's gaze and jerked his head over to one side.

"Have your people secured the life support section and Engineering?" he asked.

"We have," Romanov confirmed. "No casualties on our side, not least thanks to engineer Matthews's help."

The exosuited trooper gestured to a woman in an EVA suit. She was carrying her helmet while trying to coordinate something out of the confused and traumatized bridge crew.

"Why do you need bodyguards again?" the Secret Service agent asked, surveying the wreckage of the room. "Seems like you handled this without us."

"In my defense, they blew *themselves* up this time," Damien replied. "And I can only be in one place at a time and... Well, one generally prefers not to start with the most powerful weapon in the arsenal. Just in case, say, someone needs to teleport to a specific room to stop the bastards killing the ship's Captain."

Romanov chuckled.

"True enough." The chuckle turned to a sigh. "No prisoners, boss. Only these buggers blew themselves up, but the rest fought to the death."

"I don't know about this supposed Belt Liberation Front Samara linked them to," Damien told him, "but that seems out of character for *any* kind of movement in Sol.

"For that matter, I wasn't aware that we had any kind of resistance movements at *all* in the Solar System, and that *should* have crossed my radar," the Hand continued. "I want to talk to Captain Gambon when she wakes up. This might be something unique to her ship, or..."

"Something bigger."

"Something bigger," Damien agreed quietly, making sure no one on the bridge could hear. "Something, perhaps, *Legatan*."

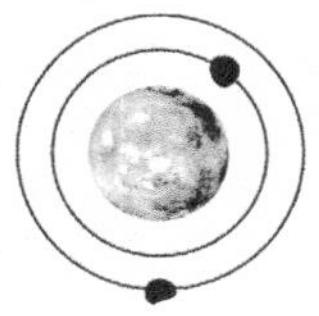

CHAPTER 15

***CALLISTO* WAS** a ship of sufficient size that she actually had docking ports for smaller vessels like *Doctor Akintola*. Once the yacht was close enough, Damien linked in to her by remote control, flying her the last few kilometers to latch the ship on and allow them to connect the two spaceships.

Samara and Christoffsen strode off the ship together, both managing to look concerned and furious at the same time. The MIS Inspector was going to fit *right* in, Damien concluded.

"The ship is secure," he told them. "Romanov's people and AMS's security team is sweeping for any remaining pirates, but the sensors aren't showing any."

"I take it from Dr. Christoffsen's resigned expression that this sort of temporary insanity on your part is normal?" Samara asked.

"I wouldn't call it insanity myself," Damien replied, "but...yes. There are often circumstances where only I have the authority, power, or simply ability to intervene in a timely manner. I would not be doing my job were I not to do so."

"And who does your job if you die, my lord Hand?"

"There remain nine other Hands, despite the events of the last few weeks," Damien told her. "I am...valuable. Not irreplaceable."

She looked at Christoffsen.

"Is he always this dumb?"

"Yes," the Professor agreed instantly. "Smart, powerful, politically connected...but dumb. I talked to his college girlfriend when we were in Sherwood. He hasn't changed much."

"I knew letting Grace anywhere near my staff was a bad idea," Damien said with a sigh. "I try not to be actively stupid, Inspector Samara, but my job requires a significant amount of personal risk. I take these risks so others, less capable, don't have to.

"Had I not intervened, Captain Gambon would be dead. Instead, she is going to live. The doctors say she should wake up sometime in the next few hours and be well enough for at least a conversation, if not heavy questioning."

"She's hardly at fault here," Samara pointed out.

"No," Damien agreed. "But my impression is that the Belt Liberation Front was not regarded as a serious threat—certainly not a serious-enough threat for *me* to be briefed on. And yet they pulled together twenty armed ships and a hundred-person boarding party to assault an *extremely* valuable spaceship.

"I'm hoping there may be some particular reason the Captain is aware of as to why they came after *Callisto*," he concluded. "My hopes are not high. Did you pull what files we have on the BLF?"

He hadn't asked, the thought having occurred to him only then.

"I requested the full file from the MIS on Mars shortly after you decided to teleport off the bridge," she replied. "We received them just before I arrived. I haven't had time to review them in detail, but...there's not much there, my lord."

"I don't suppose any of it links to the Friends of Hellas Montes or the Grand Eagle's Circle?" he asked with a sigh.

"No, my lord. That was the first thing I checked," she admitted.

"If only things were so simple. Shall we go look at your files while we wait for the good Captain to wake up?"

"I'm not sure what you expect me to be able to tell you, my lord," Captain Gambon admitted from the bed.

The bed—the entire room, for that matter—was familiar to Damien. The Charter required a certain minimum medical care for the citizens of humanity's worlds, and one of the ways the Protectorate enabled that was by using the purchasing power of a multi-system government to make certain standardized medical equipment very, *very* cheap for the system governments.

Most clinic rooms in the entire Protectorate looked much the same because of that.

"I don't know either," Damien told her with a chuckle. "These assholes seemed to be from the Belt Liberation Front, but our intel says that the BLF doesn't have the numbers, the gear, or the money for this kind of stunt—let alone the fanatics willing to fight to the death!"

Gambon sighed.

"I can't speak to specifics, but I can say you lot seriously underestimate them," she warned. "I'm Belt-born, Hand Montgomery. I hear the complaints, the problems."

"I didn't think things were that bad in Sol's Belt," Damien said.

"They're not," Gambon replied. "But they aren't perfect, either. Asteroid belts are hard places to make a living. *Hard* places. It's easy to look at that and think you've got it worse off than everyone else. Especially when you're in Sol, and every damned planet seems to be full of the lazy and the rich."

"There can't be many who'd think that being somehow liberated would help," Samara pointed out.

"There aren't," the refinery ship captain agreed. "But there's some. They don't have a goal; they're just striking out at anyone they see as having hurt them."

"Five million people in Sol's Belt," Damien concluded. "It doesn't take much to come up with a couple of hundred nihilistic fanatics out of five million people."

"No," Gambon said. "But your friends with the intel are right, too. They might have had the manpower and the fanatics for this stunt, but they don't have gear and they don't have money. Might be...five hundred folks across the Belt who'd buy into their drivel enough to die for it, but without ships, guns and money, they can't *do* anything."

"They clearly got all three of those things."

"I don't know how," Gambon replied. "We're talking the kinds of folk who drift from ship to ship, working for whatever Captain needs a spare hand this month to put food in their mouths. They don't have money. They don't have ships. They'd need some kind of sponsor—and who's going to sponsor a bunch of idiots?"

"Sadly, I can think of a few people." Damien sighed. "I don't suppose you knew any of them?"

"I wish. I'd be calling their damned mothers."

"Fair enough. Thank you, Captain Gambon. I was hoping for something more actionable, but you provided some clarity I think we needed."

"Those assholes killed over a hundred of my crew, Hand Montgomery. Anything I can do to help you bring them down, I'm in."

"I'll keep that in mind," he told her. "Right now, however, I think your doctor is about to kick us out, so we will gracefully exit before she has to get rude." He rose and offered Gambon his hand. "Thank you again, Captain."

"None of this adds up," Samara told Damien as they left the clinic. "They might have a few fanatics available, but the resources had to come from somewhere, and the Front just plain doesn't *have* them."

The Hand glanced around the hallway, then put a finger to his lips. *Callisto* might have a small crew for her size, with most of her key processes automated, but a large portion of that crew was hovering around the clinic right now, either in for treatment or waiting to hear on friends who were in.

The pair of dark-suited Secret Service Agents accompanying him and the MIS Inspector were giving them some space, but not enough for *that* discussion.

"There are sources," he half-whispered. "But it's not something we can discuss here. We need to return to *Akintola* and get back on our way to Ceres."

"How late are we?" the Inspector asked after a moment's thought and a glance at the strangers around them.

"Late," Damien said. "We were supposed to already be there. Hell, my meeting with the Council was three hours ago now. Without the velocity we sacrificed to get here, we're still six hours away, but..."

Stepping away from the crowd for a modicum of privacy, he brought up his wrist computer and tapped a command.

"Romanov," he hailed his chief bodyguard. "How's your sweep coming?"

"We're about half-done," the Marine replied. "Gambon's people aren't bad; they were just outnumbered and outgunned."

"We're already late," Damien reminded the other man. "How much longer?"

There was a moment's pause.

"I can pull my people out now," Romanov admitted. "We're pretty sure there's no serious threats left; the local security should be able to handle any holdouts."

"But your people are armored against any weapons these idiots have, and Gambon's people aren't," Damien finished the thought for his subordinate. "We're *already* late," he repeated with emphasis. "How much longer?"

"Three hours. Maybe four. It's a damned big ship."

That would make him about twelve hours late and easily bump him to the next day's agenda. Much as Damien wanted to cooperate with the Council, he also couldn't bring himself to regret putting them on a priority below people's lives.

"Three will already bump us to tomorrow. Take four," he instructed. "Then return to *Doctor Akintola*. We'll leave as soon as you and Gambon's people are comfortable the ship is secure."

"Understood, my lord."

Returning to *Akintola,* Damien dismissed the Agents to help secure the ship and gestured for Samara to follow him. Silently, they made their way to the yacht's secure conference room, where he sealed the doors behind them and activated the Faraday cage to prevent eavesdropping.

"A bit of overkill, isn't this?" she asked.

"You asked a question, Inspector," Damien told her. "Do you really want to know the answer?"

"To 'Who might have armed a bunch of right-wing *lunatics* in my star system?' Yeah," she replied, her eyes flashing. "If there's anyone out there arming assholes, that should be in our general briefing."

"It isn't," he said flatly. "And for good reason."

The mess that the Royal Order of Keepers of Secrets and Oaths had made trying to keep *their* secrets was making him twitchy about hiding things from everyone at the moment, but there were some things that *couldn't* be admitted aloud.

"That's a major threat, my lord," she pointed out. "One the system governments need to know about."

"And one we can't tell them about," he replied. "If I fill you in, Inspector, that's the end of the audition," he warned. "You're on my staff and that's not a role that people usually leave upright."

"I am both intrigued and irritated, my lord," she admitted. "But I also have a job to do, and it sounds like the best way to *do* that job is to back you up. If you'll have me, I'm in."

"You may regret that," he told her. But he understood, too. Very few people with enough skill, loyalty, and sense of duty to be *offered* a role on a Hand's staff were inclined to turn it down—any more than those with enough of those things to be offered a *Hand* tended to turn it down.

"*Inshallah,*" she told him. "As Allah wills."

"All right," he sighed and gestured her to a chair. "Have a seat, Munira," he told her, intentionally using her first name for the first time. "This won't take long, but it's not a pleasant set of revelations."

She sat, tightening her headscarf in a nervous gesture he hadn't seen her make before.

"Until about five years ago," he began, "the main source of weapons for revolutions, terrorists, and assholes throughout the Protectorate was Amber."

Amber was a recurring nightmare for the Hands, a world founded by libertarians that acknowledged the rules in the Charter...and had very little more in terms of legal structure.

"The guns and vehicles would run through various hands, but they usually came through Amber at some point. If it came from Amber, somebody paid. There were—still are, for that matter—groups on Amber that will give you discounts or arrange special shipments if they agree with your cause, but to get guns from Amber, you need money."

A set of affairs Damien had been dragged into in a prior life. They'd at least dealt with one of the more ethical gunrunners.

"About five years ago, we started to encounter Legatan gear more and more often," he continued. "It was never all Legatan. There were always cutouts and middlemen. But more and more, the best of the gear we encountered came from Legatus.

"Then, on Ardennes, I ran into a Legatan Agent," Damien noted. "She was an Augment, a cyborg Mage killer, infiltrated into the resistance there. Given the...unusual situation on Ardennes, I ended up working with her to overthrow the Governor.

"But that was our first real clue that more was going on," he admitted, to Samara's disconcerted expression. "We've had other hints since. The whole mess between Míngliàng and Sherwood, for example, was being aggravated by a third party who was using freighters as carriers for ex-Legatan gunships."

He shook his head.

"We dug into those," he said. "*Hard.* But the records were clean. They'd been decommissioned and sold off for scrap. The scrapyard records even showed they'd *been* scrapped, and they were dutifully shocked to discover the ships had ended up somewhere else."

"You're telling me one of our *system governments* is arming rebels and terrorists?" Samara demanded.

"I'm telling you that we *believe* a secret organization known as the Legatan Military Intelligence Directorate, with the full support of their government, is carrying out a covert war to militarily, economically, and morally weaken the Protectorate, likely as a precursor to outright rebellion," he told her.

"We have no solid proof. A pile of circumstantial evidence to reach from Earth to the Moon, but without some sort of solid link, we cannot accuse an entire system government of treason on a grand scale."

"But it sounds like we *know* what they're up to," she objected.

"We *think* we know," he replied. "And the only way we can be sure is to basically occupy Legatus and rip their government files apart. How well do you think that will go over with the rest of the Core Worlds?"

Damien didn't necessarily disagree with his new staff member. The Hands were pretty damned certain that Legatus was behind the Protectorate's recent troubles, and any of them would have happily taken a fleet to Legatus to find out the truth.

The problem was that it would *take* a fleet, and without the rest of the system governments buying into the mission, that level of force and intrusion could easily end up causing more damage to Mars's moral and actual authority than the continued nibbling around the edges did.

"It would go poorly," she admitted. "And most of them have real fleets of their own, don't they?"

"Most of those ships don't have amplifiers, but if they stay at long-enough range, they don't need them," Damien agreed. "If we come down on Legatus the way we want to without some kind of evidence, we could destroy the Protectorate ourselves."

Samara suddenly looked very tired.

"That...sucks, sir. So, you think Legatus armed the BLF?"

"It's definitely a possibility," he agreed. "Acquiring and arming a small fleet of sublight ships is well within the resources we've seen them use before. If anything, it's on the small end—though given that they did it in Sol, right under our noses, that's not entirely surprising."

She shook her head.

"So, what do we do?"

"For now? Nothing," he admitted. "The BLF is the Navy and Sol Security's problem. We pass on everything we've learned here and head to Ceres to talk to the Council.

"But"—he raised a warning finger—"we keep in the loop on their investigation, and if there is even a *hint* of Legatan involvement, we come down like a ton of bricks. Any chance of getting that solid link is worth its weight in gold for us now."

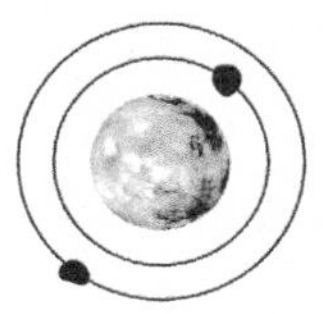

CHAPTER 16

THIS TIME, as *Doctor Akintola* approached Council Station, Damien studied the defenses with a critical eye. The assumption had always been that anywhere in Sol was safe, that any threat to Earth or anything else would end up facing the Martian Squadron's battleships long before it could endanger anyone.

Now, however, he had evidence that perhaps humanity's home system wasn't as safe as they'd thought. The obsolete defense platforms orbiting the Council of the Protectorate's home concerned him. They were *old*, the youngest well over twice his own age, with nothing except station-keeping drives and a primarily laser-based armament.

The ships he'd run off of *Callisto* wouldn't be a threat to much and *shouldn't* be a threat to even those obsolete platforms, but he couldn't help but worry. There were ways, after all, that even those crude ships could knock out most of those defenses from a distance.

"I suppose trying to convince the Council to allow the Navy to position a destroyer or three at the Station is unlikely to go very far," he said to Christoffsen as he piloted the ship in.

"Not a chance," his advisor agreed. "Especially not right now. I'm not sure even any of the Councilors are a hundred percent sure how this whole mess is going to shake out, but having a royal warship hovering over the station threatens their independence in a way they won't permit."

"Wonderful."

Damien shook his head and opened up a channel to the station.

"Council Station Control, this is Hand Montgomery aboard *Doctor Akintola*," he announced. "We are inbound for docking for a requested meeting with the Council."

"*Doctor Akintola*, this is Council Station Control. We had you on the list for yesterday."

"We were delayed due to the duties of my office," Damien explained shortly. The Council members should have seen at least a precis report of the incident by now. They knew where he'd been.

"I'm afraid docking at the station is restricted, sir, I'll need to confirm if your authorization is still valid."

Damien hit a mute button and looked over at Christoffsen.

"They're playing games?" he asked.

"Yes. And it's your move. They'll let us aboard eventually, but..."

"But we're still playing games as to who is in charge."

"Exactly," the Professor agreed.

Damien sighed. "You're the expert, Professor," he admitted. "Are we weaker if we play along or play hardball?"

"You'll convince different Councilors of different things," Christoffsen replied. "I suspect it's a wash either way, but...I don't think giving in to their authority is likely help our long-term case."

"I was *hoping* you'd say that," Damien said with a grim smile, then removed the mute key.

"Council Station Control, I appear to have to repeat myself," he said slowly. "This is Damien Montgomery, *Hand of the Mage-King of Mars*. We *will* be docking with Council Station."

"I...I can't allow that, sir," the controller told him. "You do not have authorization to dock!"

"I just gave myself authorization to dock. I remind you that Council Station is a Protectorate facility and you answer to *me* before you answer to the Council," Damien said firmly. "Again, we will be docking, our ETA is just over two minutes. Please let me know which docking port to use."

There was a long silence on the other end of the channel. There was no time for the controller to go to a superior. No time for him to do anything but either concede to the powerful official on the com or, most likely, end his career.

"Docking port nine, my lord," he finally replied.

"Thank you," Damien said. "And Control?"

"Yes, my lord?" the man said hesitantly.

"If you get in shit for this, contact me. This isn't your damned fight."

Damien and Christoffsen waited on the bridge after docking for someone from the Council to reach out to them. Damien even resisted the urge to try and get his political aide to bet on how long it would take.

The Professor would probably have won. Damien's guess would have been an hour, but it was barely ten minutes before the computers chimed, informing him he had an incoming high-priority communication.

"This is Hand Montgomery," Damien greeted the image of the white-uniformed and shaven-headed woman who appeared on his screen. "To whom am I speaking?

"I am Lictor-Constable Cande Lucas," she told him, her voice flat. "I am in charge of the Lictors of the Council of the Protectorate and of security for this station. Security that you have violated."

"I was summoned by the Council to appear before them," Damien told her. "I am required by the Charter to do so, though I am expected to do so as *my* duties allowed. I saw no reason to delay the meeting while your staff rectified an obvious error."

"We control docking and access to Council Station very carefully," Constable Lucas replied. "You were not authorized to dock. You will undock from the station until such time as the Council has approved your arrival here."

"Lictor-Constable," Damien said, letting his voice drop and chill as he met the woman's gaze, "you have no authority over me. None. Your power is only what the Council gives you, and the Council cannot give you power they do not have.

"They have the authority to summon me before them, and I have arrived in response to such a summons. You may inform the Council that I have twenty-four hours I can spare for them, but then I must return to Mars.

"If they cannot see me in that time, I am not certain when I will next be able to make time for them," he said harshly. "We serve the same masters in the end, Constable Lucas: the people of the Protectorate.

"Don't make me cause more trouble than I have to."

"This station's security is *my* responsibility," Lucas snapped.

"And I have no intention of violating it," Damien told her. "But I am here to speak with the Council. I will not be bullied or ignored. Do I make myself clear, Constable?"

She glared at him a moment longer but then nodded.

"Very well, Lord Montgomery," she allowed. "I presume the Council Secretariat will be in touch with you shortly to arrange your meeting."

The channel cut.

"I'm almost starting to feel bad for the flunkies they're throwing at us," Damien said.

"Lucas is no flunky and she should know better," Christoffsen replied. "We're better off if the Secretariat deals with me."

"Let me know what you arrange," the Hand replied. "I wasn't joking about twenty-four hours either, Professor. Everything going on right now is making my shoulders itch."

"Well?" Damien asked when Christoffsen reentered the bridge an hour or so later.

"Bureaucrats," the ex-Governor said dryly. "Even with a deadline, a crisis, and a Hand to hammer them with, getting anyone from the Secretariat to consider, gods forbid, rearranging the Council's schedule is a nightmare."

"And?"

"We're up for tomorrow morning at ten AM Olympus Mons Time," Damien's aide replied. "About two hours inside your deadline. I'm not necessarily sure Secretary Bernstein *believed* me that you would actually leave if they didn't meet with you inside it."

"Wouldn't that have been a shock," the Hand said. "But we're scheduled in?"

"*You*'re scheduled in," Christoffsen noted. "Again, no companions, no representation. This isn't a trial, though I know it feels like one."

"This one should be friendlier, I'm hoping?" Damien asked.

"Might have been, before we showed up a day late and somebody clearly decided to set up a pissing match." The older man shrugged. "The reasons look good for you, but I guarantee someone's going to spin it against you."

"And I'll deal with it. Until someone takes it away from me, I have a job to do."

Damien shook his head.

"If I've got time, I'm going to see if Inspector Samara's team back on Mars has any updates. This whole mess with whoever is killing the Keepers isn't going away because the Council wants to, as you put it, arrange pissing matches."

The updates weren't pretty.

Analyst Daniels had managed to identify over forty more people she believed to be potential Keepers...and every one of them was dead.

It was entirely possible that Damien was going to run out of Keepers to find, if he hadn't already—and sitting half a star system away as he was, there wasn't anything he could do about it.

Thankfully, however, this was Sol and he wasn't alone.

"Your Majesty," he said into the camera as he began recording. "I'll be attaching the analysis the MIS has carried out at my request to this message, but the key takeaway is this: we have now identified over two hundred individuals that we believe were highly likely to have been members of the Keepers.

"They are all dead. Most murdered. The remainder died in accidents, some more suspicious than others, but all of which I must now question.

"The conclusion was obvious before, but it is inescapable now: someone is hunting down and wiping out the remnants of the Keepers."

Damien shook his head.

"Charlotte turned on us," he admitted, "but she was a loyal and competent servant to the Mountain for years before that. The same with Octavian. Your Hands are not men and women to be easily turned, my liege, and I must wonder what secret the Keepers held that led my fellow Hands to believe they had no choice but to betray their oaths so dramatically."

He sighed.

"And I now fear that someone is attempting to make certain that secret is never exposed. We haven't run out of clues and links to follow yet, but we're finding them too late now. Whoever is hunting the Keepers knows who they all are.

"We don't."

Damien tapped a few commands, making sure that the message he was recording for the Mage-King did include all of the files he needed to send while he marshaled his thoughts for what needed to happen.

"If we continue to chase after the Keepers, we will fail, and they will all die," he concluded flatly. "We need them to come to us. The only option I can see is for you to make a public appeal to them, warn them that they are being hunted, and *beg* them to come in from the cold.

"I don't know what secret they hold, what betrayals they have committed or what oaths they have sworn, but they remain citizens of your Protectorate. We owe them our protection if that is to mean anything."

He paused to think, then sighed.

"I'm running short of other ideas, my liege," he admitted. "Reaching out to them publicly is the only course I see that could bring us into contact with the survivors.

"I meet with your Council tomorrow, and then I will return to Mars to continue my investigations.

"Montgomery out."

CHAPTER 17

THE LICTORS didn't say anything this time as Damien stalked up to the doors of the Council Chamber. One gestured for Romanov and Christoffsen to follow him, and two waited for Damien to be ready.

They clearly suspected that the Hand was furious with their bosses, but their loyalties were clear. He didn't blame them, either. Their *bosses,* on the other hand...

"I'm ready," he told them. "It's time, isn't it?"

"It is, my lord. They're waiting for you."

Damien nodded and walked forward as the doors were swung open for him.

Mutters echoed around the room as he followed the white-uniformed guardian to the same plain table as before, taking a seat without a word and facing the Council. Frustrated as he was with the games, these people remained the representatives of the member governments of the Protectorate. He owed them respect.

"This Council, Mister Montgomery, is not used to being dictated to in our own Station," Councilor Newton snapped. The last few days didn't seem to have done the white-haired old man any favors. He looked exhausted.

"I do not, Councilor, recall issuing any dictates," Damien replied. He felt as exhausted as Newton looked, and he wondered if there was something else going on. The Alpha Centauri Councilor shouldn't be looking like he'd been through a battle.

"We issued an invitation for you to attend this Council two days ago. Yet we were informed yesterday that we would have to meet with you today, on a deadline of yours," Newton reminded him.

"I will remind this Council that while you have the right to summon me before you, such an appearance is dependent on the duties of my office," he said. "I attempted to attend at your requested time. I was forced to detour to intervene in a developing situation and, upon my arrival, advised your staff of my own time limitations.

"I am attempting to be cooperative, but to have adhered to the original schedule would have cost the lives of an unknown number of civilians and permitted a terrorist organization to carry out the hijacking of a spaceship that unquestionably qualifies as a strategic asset," Damien continued.

"While I have no idea what they were planning on doing with a thirty-million-ton mobile refinery, I doubt it involved leaving any of *Callisto*'s thousand-odd crew alive.

"Until and unless His Majesty decides to fire me, I am bound by an oath to honor his Protectorate by *protecting* our citizens, Councilors. That oath required the delay, for which I apologize. My continuing responsibilities on Mars require my expeditious return, hence the time limit.

"I have made myself as available as I can be, Councilors, but my duties remain."

"The dedication to duty of His Majesty's Hands is not in question," Councilor McClintlock said sharply. "Your *judgment*, however, we are less certain of."

"If this Council questions my intervening in an active pirate attack, I am forced to question what this Council would expect me to do," Damien replied.

"Nothing else," a shaven-headed man with pitch-black skin in the front row snapped. Councilor Farai Ayodele represented Earth and, from Christoffsen's briefing, often refrained from speaking, as he understood the weight the homeworld's words carried.

"I think I speak for us all," Ayodele continued, "when I thank you for your intervention, Lord Montgomery. There were no Navy vessels nearby to intervene. No friends waiting in the wings to save Captain Gambon and her crew—no one except you.

"My colleagues are unused to having their neat schedules interrupted; you must forgive them," the black man told Damien, "if they have perhaps missed the grander scheme."

"Of course," Damien allowed with an exhaled sigh. At least someone in this Council appeared to be sane.

"Now, Hand Montgomery"—Councilor Montague took advantage of Ayodele's interruption to take control of the meeting—"we summoned you here before to speak of the events leading to the deaths of Hands Lawrence Octavian and Charlotte Ndosi.

"You understand that these are momentous events. It is unusual for Hands to die. Almost unheard of for Hands to betray their oaths—and never before has a Hand killed another Hand, let alone two.

"We understand, I think, what events came to pass," she concluded. "But you were at the heart of all of this, from the attack at Andala to the Archive at Hellas Montes.

"We need to understand not only the what and the how, but the *why*. Two of the highest officials of our nation died at your hands, Lord Montgomery. His Majesty may have granted you the authority to investigate Hands, but you took it upon yourself to fight them.

"I, unlike others, do not *question* your judgment... but I must ask you to explain it."

Damien inhaled deeply and laid his hands on the table as he looked up to meet Montague's gaze. He was relatively sure she was on his side, at least, and he had an idea of how much political capital she'd burned to give him this opportunity.

To waste that would be...both rude and unwise.

"Very well, Councilors," he began.

"Let me make certain that I understand where we sit at the moment," Councilor Newton said after Damien's course of explanations and analysis had reached Ndosi teleporting him clear of the explosion her death triggered.

"After all of this chaos, the deaths of two Hands, the bombardment of a civilian outpost and threats made to the Mage-King himself...we have no idea what secret these Keepers were charged to keep by the first Mage-King?"

"We do not," Damien confirmed. "The Keepers, including the Hands who had joined their order, died before revealing that secret. Dead man's switches are an effective means of keeping secrets if you're prepared to die for your cause.

"All we know for certain," he continued, "is that it had something to do with the alien runes we discovered at the Andala IV outpost—enough that they were prepared to, as you said, Councilor, bombard a civilian outpost to destroy them.

"I believe that the key may be related to why those runes appear to be Martian Runic despite predating human magic."

"No offense, Mr. Montgomery," Newton replied, "but your qualifications as a Rune Scribe are...unimpressive. That's a rather dramatic conclusion to have reached, isn't it?"

Damien sighed. While he suspected many of the Councilors *knew* about Rune Wrights, none were officially cleared for the information... and the fact that *Damien* was a Rune Wright had been kept from many who knew the Mage-King was one but hadn't worked with Damien himself.

"I was trained by Desmond Alexander himself," he reminded the Council. "Not all of my qualifications are on paper, Councilor Newton. Suffice to say that there are few people in the Protectorate more qualified to draw that conclusion.

"That said, it is a dramatic conclusion," he conceded, "and a new expedition, under Royal Navy escort, is already on its way to the Andala System to confirm that analysis and to study those runes in far more detail than I had time to.

"If the answers to the Keepers' fanaticism lies in the catacombs of Andala IV, we will find them," he assured the Council. "If not..." He sighed again. "We have reason to believe that the remnants of the Keepers are being hunted by a third party. We are doing all within our power to find and protect them, but...if they won't talk to us, we can't help them.

"And if we can't help them, their secrets may very well die with them."

Newton grunted, apparently mollified.

"Thank you, Montgomery," he said. "Is there anything this Council can do to assist in finding the remaining Keepers?"

"His Majesty should be making a public appeal for any survivors on Mars to come into protective custody," Damien replied. "If there are Keepers outside Sol, we will need to make sure that offer—and knowledge of the danger—is spread as widely as possible."

"That we should be able to assist with," Councilor Montague told him. "We will pass that information on to our governments.

"Does anyone else have any questions for Hand Montgomery?"

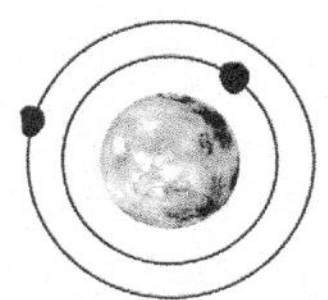

CHAPTER 18

DAMIEN RETURNED to *Doctor Akintola* feeling utterly drained but somewhat less completely raked over the coals than he had after his first encounter with the Council.

"This one went better, I take it?" Christoffsen asked once they'd reached the ship and were out of reach of prying ears.

"Better," Damien agreed. "I'd hesitate to say *well*; there are still only four of them talking to me, and I'm pretty sure both McClintlock and Newton want to hang me out to dry."

"With a hundred and twenty Councilors, they can't all do the talking," his aide reminded him. "Usually, you'll see a few of the Core World Councilors asking most of the questions. Make no mistake, though: they make decisions as a body."

"And I have no idea what they're thinking," Damien admitted. "*Politicians.*"

"Hey!"

"Present company excepted, I suppose," the Hand said with a forced smile. "It's been one hell of a month, Professor, and it isn't over yet."

"No."

"My lord!" Samara intercepted them. "We just got a ping on the news net. His Majesty is going to speak in about ten minutes."

Damien sighed in relief.

"I asked him to make an appeal to the Keepers," he told his staff. "There might be something *else* going on that calls for an unscheduled speech by the Mage-King of Mars...but I hope not!"

He nodded to the Inspector.

"Thank you, Munira," he told her. "How's our own digging going?"

She shook her head.

"The same. Everyone we find is already dead," she answered sadly. "I think...I'm afraid we may be entirely too late, my lord. I think whoever is hunting the Keepers may have completely wiped them out, at least in the Sol System."

"Let's hope someone is left and listening."

Twice a Terran year, the Mage-King of Mars ascended the public throne in the Grand Hall of Olympus Mons—not the true Throne, the one hidden in the chamber that contained the simulacrum for the most powerful amplifier in existence, but the plain chair raised six inches above the room where he would meet dignitaries and reporters—to speak to his people.

Those speeches were carried as live as possible after light-speed delays throughout the Solar System and sent across the Protectorate by ship. News couriers would be standing by to bring the video recording to the Core Worlds and most of the MidWorlds. They were scheduled, preplanned events.

It was unusual for Desmond Michael Alexander the Third to give a public speech outside of those two scheduled events, though not unheard of. Today, the gaunt old man settled into that chair and faced the cameras—and, Damien presumed, a gathered horde of fascinated reporters.

"My people," he greeted them.

"The events of recent weeks on Mars have shaken us all to our core. A nuclear explosion in one of the largest natural parks on Mars. The deaths of two Hands. These are not events We can conceal, nor should We try.

"We do not pretend that We have shared all details and secrets of these events," Alexander continued, his lips quirking in what probably counted as a smile. "But We assure you that Our best men and women continue to investigate them to learn the true nature of what has happened.

"What We can tell you today is that these events were tied to an organization created by Our grandfather, known as the Royal Order of Keepers of Secrets and Oaths. We remain uncertain of the purpose of this organization or, indeed, of whether or not they are Our friends."

He shook his head.

"But. They remain Our subjects and hence under Our Protectorate."

Damien felt his shoulders stiffen as he watched the video. This was a different Protectorate from the nation. When the Mage-King spoke of *his* Protectorate, he meant the oath he had sworn to guard and protect all of humanity.

The nation might fail. The worlds of humanity might go their separate ways. Men and women might betray their worlds and their race. But the Mage-King of Mars and his sworn servants would honor that oath to their deaths.

"Since the Hellas Montes disaster, someone has been hunting these Keepers," Alexander told the cameras. "Dozens, if not hundreds, are dead. We do not know who hunts them—but We also do not know who they are.

"So, We speak now to any survivors of Our grandfather's order: We do not know what oaths you have sworn or what burdens you carry. What We do know is that you are in danger and We cannot protect you if We do not know who you are.

"We beg of you, come in," the Mage-King of Mars said softly. "Find an MIS station, a Marine barracks, someone in Our service you believe you can trust. We will see you safe—but We must know who you are.

"We cannot protect shadows from knives in the dark, but come into the light and We swear, upon Our own royal honor, that you will not be harmed."

The yacht pulled slowly away from Council Station under Damien's careful hand, his mental turmoil easing as he went through the practiced motions. He'd always enjoyed flying, and now it was becoming a refuge.

While he was flying, he didn't need to think about politics or the future. No conspiracies, no knives in the dark, just a ship, engines, and the dark of space.

Ceres glittered in the sunlight beneath *Doctor Akintola* as he watched his distance, waiting until he was far enough away to bring the antimatter engines online. The numbers crossed the thresholds and he flashed a text notification to Council Station.

Then he opened up the throttle, feeding antimatter into the ignition chamber and smoothly increasing the yacht's acceleration up to eight gravities. His Sight showed him the power of the runes under his feet flaring as they adjusted, compensating to keep the entire ship at a single gravity.

They'd maintain that for an hour, then coast for a while before decelerating into Mars orbit. It was a simple-enough course, though someone would have to remain on the bridge to watch the proximity alarms. The asteroid belt might be sparser than even twenty-sixth-century media liked to portray it, but there were still more rocks there than anywhere else.

He was settling back to try and relax when his wrist computer chimed, warning him of a critical message. There shouldn't be anything that needed his attention right now, but he pulled up his PC anyway.

He went from concerned to confused when he saw the message had arrived on a communication channel restricted to Hands. There was a network and an encryption key the Hands kept to themselves. Even the Mage-King didn't have access to that network—he had his own priority ways of reaching his Hands—and there were no other Hands in Sol.

Damien opened the message, and his computer happily produced a tiny hologram of an unfamiliar woman. She was an older woman, with long dark hair and the mixed-tone skin of a Martian native, wearing a sleek black dress.

"My Lord Montgomery," the recording greeted him, "you do not know me. I...am not going to give you my name in this message, either, as a precaution.

"You are wondering, I am certain, how I am able to reach you on this channel. The reason is simple and may have already occurred to you: Charlotte Ndosi gave me the codes."

That meant the woman in the recording was a Keeper. She already had Damien's undivided attention, but that certainly didn't hurt.

"I am a member of the Royal Order of Keepers of Secrets and Oaths, but not in the usual fashion," she continued. "I was recruited by Hand Octavian and later introduced to Hand Ndosi. To my knowledge, those two were the only ones who were aware I was a member."

Because what Damien's headache needed was a conspiracy within a conspiracy and secrets within secrets.

"This...appears to have saved my life," she told him. "I have far more information on the rest of the Order than they have on me, and every Keeper I am aware of is dead.

"So far as I know, I am the last Keeper. I was recruited for this exact circumstance. I am the final failsafe, Lord Montgomery, the last backup. My job is to make certain that no matter what happened, our secret was not lost.

"I will not... I *can* not reveal anything over even this encrypted channel. But I will meet with you, Lord Montgomery, and I call upon you to honor our King's promise of protection. I will be at the Sunrise Mall in Olympus City at nine oh six tomorrow morning. You know my face now, so we will find each other.

"It is safer that way, my lord."

She shook her head, her eyes downcast.

"I am the final backup, Lord Montgomery," she repeated. "To my knowledge, I am the only Keeper left—but I am a Keeper, and my oaths will be kept."

The message ended, freezing the hologram of the beautiful older woman above Damien's computer as he stared at her.

The last time he'd heard that phrase, Charlotte Ndosi had blown herself up. If there was one thing he knew about the Keepers, it was that they *meant* their oaths.

CHAPTER 19

THE ASSAULT SHUTTLE returned to Olympus Mons's government landing pads roughly fourteen hours before Damien needed to be at the mall in the city below. He had time to sleep and catch up on what progress Samara's people had made while they were gone.

The sight of the gawkily tall young man standing by the doors into the Mountain shattered *those* idealistic plans. There weren't many blonds on Mars, but if you changed the hair from gold to silver and added a few wrinkles, Desmond Michael Alexander the Fourth, Des to his friends, was the spitting image of his father.

"Damien," he greeted the returning Hand, offering a friendly handshake. "It's good to see you."

"You, too, Des. Getting yourself in trouble again?" Damien asked. The last time he'd seen the youth, Des had been trying to talk himself into Damien's investigations of the Keepers. Damien had ended up using him as a courier to keep the heir to the Martian throne *out* of trouble.

"Not today," the youth told him with an irrepressible grin. "My esteemed father sent me to meet you. *He* is currently on an RTA call with the Governor of Tau Ceti, but I am to inform you that you are 'invited and *required*' to join the family for dinner tonight."

"I don't suppose I can beg off due to work?" Damien replied with a chuckle. He wasn't actually serious this time. His liege and mentor was not *quite* a friend, but the Royal Family were...relaxing to be around.

"Dad expected you to say that," the younger Alexander said. "He said, and I quote, 'Remind him that he works for me.' I think you're stuck."

"Well, then, I can only obey my liege's commands," Damien told him. "I do need to drop some things off and sort out *some* work, but I'll be there."

"Eight o'clock," the Crown Prince instructed. "Or I'll send *Kiera* after you."

Damien's staff scattered to their own quarters, though, as always, two Secret Service Agents tailed him as he headed to his own apartment. The Marines who guarded the rooms regardless of whether he was home or not greeted him with crisp salutes.

He changed into a fresh suit, tossing the several he'd worn since leaving in a chute that would feed them into the Mountain's housekeeping systems. Between the ever-present automation and ever-competent staff, his clothes would be returned, cleaned and pressed, by morning.

The apartment wasn't much and he'd done nothing to it in the years it had technically been home. He didn't feel settled on any planet anymore. "Home" was the tiny room and massive office aboard *Duke of Magnificence,* not this suite of luxurious rooms buried under a mountain.

Home wasn't where the heart was—home was where the *job* was.

If he got to keep it.

Shaking his head to clear his frustrations, Damien linked his wrist computer into the Mountain's computers, checking to see if any messages that hadn't been forwarded to *Doctor Akintola* were still important enough for him to address immediately.

There was a large report from Analyst Daniels on what she'd learned of the Keepers' activities prior to their effective destruction, but nothing had been flagged as urgent. Useful background, he was sure, but not important enough to be late to dinner over.

With his wrist-comp still linked into the Mountain, he looked up a department in the directory and then linked through to the motor pool.

"Olympus Mons Civil Fleet Ground Vehicles, Melissa Chan speaking," a cheerful Martian woman answered immediately. "My Lord Montgomery!" she greeted him before he could speak. "How may I help you?"

"Good evening, Miss Chan," he replied with a smile. "I'm going to need a pair of vehicles in the morning for myself and my detail. Low-profile armored cars by preference, the kind that don't draw attention."

Most of the Mountain's vehicle fleet was made up of black sedans, the standby of governments for over half a millennium. There were a small number of low-profile armored cars of other colors, and given the level of risk for the next morning's meeting Damien needed to be sure he had them.

"A lot of the low-profile cars are already out or reserved, my lord," she admitted. "Give me a moment." She pecked away at a screen he couldn't see.

"It looks like I've got two Ford Runabouts, one blue and one green," Chan concluded. "They're pure electrics, utility vehicles, not as heavily armored as some of our cars, but they're the only low-profile armored ones I've got."

The Runabout would seat six, so two of them *should* handle a large-enough detail for a quiet meeting in a public place.

"They'll do," he told her. "I'll be down to pick them up in the morning with my Secret Service team."

"Of course. I'll have our maintenance team go over them tonight, make sure there's no problems," she promised.

"Thank you, Miss Chan."

"Anything for the Mountain, my Lord Montgomery."

Damien arrived for dinner before the Mage-King himself, entering the private dining room the Alexanders used for family dinners, to find only the younger two members of the royal family.

"Dad's been delayed," Kiera told him. "Come in; have a seat."

Obedient to the princess, he took a seat at the simple table—plain but made of oak imported from Earth—across from Des. Like the table, the plates and cutlery were plain but of the highest quality.

Some types of simplicity were cheap, born of necessity. Other types of simplicity were *very* expensive, born out of a desire for tools that would last forever.

"Will the Chancellor be joining us this evening?" Damien asked.

"No, he's occupied," Des told him. "It's like most of the people Dad invites to dinner are important senior officials in the Protectorate government or something."

"Just like," the Hand, a warrior-judge who spoke with his King's voice, murmured softly.

Further conversation was interrupted by a steward—an armed member of the Secret Service, according to Damien's briefing—delivering a basket of bread and three bowls of soup.

"His Majesty called to let us know his meeting has finally wrapped up," the suited young man told them. "He should be joining you in a few minutes."

"Thanks, Richard," Kiera told the steward-guard with a smile.

They dug into the food, and the three had managed to clear the soups by the time the Mage-King himself arrived, walking into the room with the careful gait of an exhausted old man and dropping into the empty chair.

"I'll have my soup, Richard," the senior Alexander told the steward with a smile. "Thank you."

Once the bowl had arrived and the Secret Service man had left, however, the Mage-King of Mars leveled a fierce look on his eldest child and only son.

"Des, how old are you?" he asked.

The Crown Prince swallowed. "Nineteen, Dad. You were at my birthday party."

"An adult," the elder Alexander agreed. "So, I understand, Des, that adults have relationships, and that adults of your age especially have *drama* around them. I trust you to be an adult.

"I *also* trust you to be the Crown Prince of Mars and be aware when those relationships—and more importantly, the attached *breakups*—will have political consequences and *warn me*."

Des winced.

"I...didn't think anything recently was going to," he admitted.

"I thought you were dating Councilor Montague's daughter? Why am I getting complaints from the Tau Ceti Governor?!"

"Denise and I are...back together," Des said slowly. "We were on a break. David Granger and I went on a couple of dates and hit it off." He shrugged. "David got a bit clingy, then Denise and I sorted through some of our problems, so I broke things off with David and got back together with Denise."

Damien's university love life, he was grateful to recall, had not been *nearly* so complicated.

"Apparently, David complained to his father, who complained to his Governor, and *I* got a twenty-minute spiel on 'my son's lack of respect and decorum' tacked on to a three-hour meeting on financing Project Mjolnir."

The whole conversation didn't involve Damien directly, but that made him wince. Project Mjolnir was the Protectorate's attempt to secretly assemble a new generation of warships in case the Legatans actually *did* secede and declare war. Since they couldn't ask the broad Council for money, a handful of the Core Worlds were helping fund the project.

But since that funding was as black as black came, it gave that small handful of worlds outsized influence.

Des sighed.

"I didn't think things between David and I were that serious," he admitted. "David apparently thought differently. Sorry, Dad, *I'm* kind of blindsided by this, too!"

"Outside of political complications, I don't need to know about your love life," the Mage-King told his son. "But if you're going to break up with the son of a Councilor, can you at least let me know?" The elder Alexander shook his head. "I wish you didn't have to, but that's the reality of dynastic politics, Des."

"I understand, Dad. I'll remember."

"Good. Now that's settled and my soup has gone cold, I think we should have Richard bring in the main course."

The meal was quiet. After the last few weeks, Damien was content simply to be around people he could trust and stay silent, enjoying the good food.

"How are you holding up, Damien?" Kiera finally asked. "That's twice now you've been hauled in front of Dad's collection of old fogies."

"Kiera," the King warned his daughter in a tired tone. "Whether or not they're my biggest headache is irrelevant; the Council *does* speak for the people they represent and are an important part of my government. Please show them *some* modicum of respect. We all have to work with them."

"You and Des have to work with them," the teenager pointed out. "I intend to follow Aunt Jane into the Navy or, well, *something* not on Mars."

Damien chuckled. Her Highness Mage-Admiral Jane Michelle Alexander, Princess of Mars, commanded a pair of cruiser squadrons roughly as far away from Mars as it was physically possible to get and still have a command worth a full Admiral. The Mage-King's sister had been his heir until Desmond the Fourth was born, and remained the regent-designate until Desmond was twenty.

The Olympus Mons Simulacrum would only answer to a Rune Wright, which meant that only a Rune Wright could stand as Regent for Mars. The Charter required that the Mage-King be twenty-one on full ascension to the throne, though none of three so far had been under forty.

"Where you will *remain* your brother's heir until he has children," the King pointed out. "Given that you can both expect to live over a century and a half, having children upon ascending the throne would give us someone who'd been heir for a hundred years!"

Alexander shook his head. "I was heir for twenty, and that was difficult enough to handle," he pointed out. "The dynasty must be secured, but we are best served by having children older. That is why I have two children. That is why my father had two children.

"I love you both very much," he continued softly, "and I loved your mother more than life itself, but you must always remember that duty, Kiera. It is unlikely you will be called upon to sit the Throne in the Mountain, but...you must always be ready to."

Kiera's expression had turned unusually serious for a fourteen-year-old girl, and she nodded firmly.

"I understand, Dad," she replied. "I really do. I even promise that I don't refer to Our Esteemed Council"—Damien could *hear* the capital letters—"like that in public. But...they are *so* annoying."

"They can be, yes," Alexander agreed. "But we still need to work with them. That said, how *are* you holding up, Damien?"

"It's been a rough few weeks, since before Charlotte died," Damien admitted. This was probably the only room in human space where he'd admit that. "I didn't expect to find her working for the Keepers. I certainly didn't expect her to have a dead man's switch but still choose to save me instead of herself."

"That's about the only thing in this mess that didn't surprise me," the Mage-King replied. "Charlotte Ndosi was always loyal to her friends and her oaths. That was just somehow turned against us," he concluded grimly.

"I have...reason to believe the Keepers are all but wiped out," Damien told his King. "I was contacted via Charlotte's own codes by someone who claimed to be the final backup. I'm meeting with them tomorrow.

"If we can get them to come in where we can protect them, I think we might finally have some answers."

"I want to know what secret can turn even my Hands against me," Alexander said grimly.

"The scariest part to me," Damien admitted, "is the fact that I think the Hands and the Keepers have always been intertwined from the beginning. The man who bought the land for the Archive was a Hand. This 'final backup' appears to have been selected by the Hands.

"And it was a Hand that decided to bombard a world to keep their secret," he concluded grimly. "I want to know what would make one of us decide *that* was the best option."

"It seems we may find out tomorrow," Alexander replied. "If you need anything, all the resources of my government are at your disposal."

"I think I have everything in place," Damien told him. "We shall see."

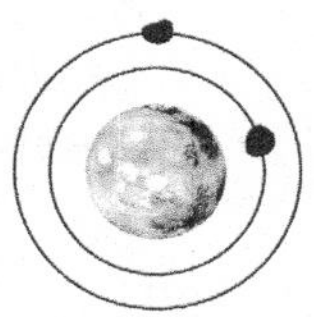

CHAPTER 20

ROMANOV WAS WAITING outside Damien's quarters with four Secret Service Agents in the morning, falling into step with the Hand in companionable silence as they moved through the Mountain.

Inspector Samara was waiting for them at the garage with another team of bodyguards, and a third team was already standing by the vehicles with the official Damien had been speaking to the previous night.

"Good morning, my lord Hand!" she greeted him. "As promised, two low-profile armored Runabouts."

The big electric utility vehicles were ubiquitous across the Protectorate and even more so on Mars, high-based six-wheeled vans designed to carry an entire family or a business's supplies. In their most common setup, which included the two vehicles behind Melissa Chan, they could carry eight.

Romanov had clearly been paying attention when Damien had sent him the specifications of the vehicles, because with all of the Secret Service Agents they'd collected along the way, they had exactly sixteen people for their trip into Olympus City.

"You don't travel in a small group, do you?" Chan continued, looking around the collection of bodyguards in suits almost identical to Damien's own.

"I am a Hand," Damien told her. "I may not contain multitudes, but I appear to bring them with me. Any concerns with the vehicles?" he asked.

"None. They're both fully charged, should be good for thirty hours or so of driving. Not the most heavily armored vehicles we have, but the Runabout is a sturdy vehicle to begin with. Ford still at least tries for 'Built Ford Tough'.

"The panels will stand up to anything short of anti-armor rockets. The windows are more vulnerable, but you'd still need one of the penetrator rounds designed to take down exosuits. They'll keep you safe, my lord."

"Thank you, Miss Chan," Damien replied. "Romanov?"

"Massey, Coral, you're driving," the head of his detail snapped, sending his Marine Corporals to work. "My lord, Inspector Samara, you're with me in the second car. Lead car is detail only."

Chan smiled quickly.

"I suspect I don't need to know these details," she told him cheerfully. "Have a safe drive, people."

The two vehicles emerged from the dark underground of the Mountain's parking garages into the weak sunlight of an Olympus Mons summer. Carefully calibrated greenhouse-gas effects kept Mars *habitable*, but the sun was still small and weak compared to most worlds Damien had visited.

Driving into it still wasn't fun and he was, for once, glad to surrender that task to someone else as he gazed out the window, taking in the city below.

The Mountain itself was an underground complex home to over three hundred thousand souls, but it was a center of government that employed over twice that. There were no fewer than a hundred different garages and entrances, and traffic between them and the city of millions that encompassed the lower reaches of Olympus Mons was always heavy.

There was no problem slotting the pair of electric SUVs into the middle of the flow, the drivers linking the cars into the traffic control net but keeping their hands hovering over emergency overrides.

Despite almost two hundred years of growth post-terraforming, you could still see the denser pockets where the original domes had sat. The rising skylines in each section were still shaped by the memories of those ancient structures.

Of course, the city now sprawled out from those domes, office towers and apartments and houses and suburbs encircling each of the old dome centers and wrapping around the base of the Mountain in an interlinking web of homes, businesses and parks.

Damien had seen bigger cities, on Earth if nowhere else, but Olympus City itself remained stunningly impressive to him.

"We've got quite a ways to go still," Massey reported back. "If anyone needs to catch up on their sleep, now's the time. We'll be at least forty minutes to the mall."

Sunrise Mall wasn't going to break any records in terms of size or crowds—Olympus City alone had a dozen larger malls—but it was definitely a *gorgeous* shopping complex, a T-shaped structure carved of glass and Mars's native red rock.

It was tucked into an area of newer office and apartment towers, surrounded on three sides by structures that towered fifty or more stories above it. The fourth side opened out over the mountain, giving the long edge of the T an incredible view.

"Somehow, I'm not expecting discount stores and cheap trinkets," Samara noted as the Runabouts came to a stop in the parking lot.

"No. But if you ever wanted to price-shop between French and Tau Cetan designer clothing, this is the place," Damien told her. "We're meeting this Keeper in the food court, at the center of the mall. Let's move."

Exiting the vehicles, Romanov studied the area around them.

"This is damned exposed, my lord," he murmured to Damien. "I doubt that glass is rated for bullets, and I don't think there's anywhere in the mall that isn't visible from some of those rooftops."

The Hand *wished* he could pretend his bodyguard was being paranoid.

"Do we have overhead?" he asked.

"Of course," Romanov confirmed. "Being relayed to my contact lenses. Everything looks clear so far; it just makes me twitchy."

Damien might generally use his personal detail as a strike force, but their primary job was to keep him alive.

"There isn't much negotiating with a recording, Denis," he told his bodyguard gently. "She said she'd meet us here and I doubt we'll get a second chance."

"She won't meet us again?"

"To contact us, she came out of hiding," Damien said grimly. "I don't know who's hunting the Keepers, but I have every reason to suspect they have a *lot* of reach and knowledge. By meeting us, she's exposing herself."

"Right now, *I'm* feeling exposed," Romanov replied, gesturing his team out to form a loose cordon around them.

"Keep your eyes open," Damien ordered. "I don't think this is a trap, but it wouldn't be the first one the Keepers have laid for me if it is."

"It's very public, my lord."

"That isn't necessarily to our advantage."

"I agree," Romanov told him. "Sending Massey and his team in first, the rest of us will follow. We'll maintain a perimeter around you and try *not* to look like an invading army."

"Fortunately, the place is full of enough suits, your team should blend in," Inspector Samara pointed out, looking at the crowd rushing into the mall. "I assume everyone is armed?"

"Penetrator carbines hidden in their suit jackets," Damien told her. "Designed to punch through exosuits." He shrugged and clasped his gloved hands together. "I am unarmed, but..."

"He doesn't need a weapon," the head of his bodyguard concluded. "Do you have a sidearm, Inspector, or do you need to borrow one?"

Samara smiled and twitched her jacket back, revealing she was wearing a concealed holster with a good-sized pistol tucked under her arm.

"It won't go through exosuits," she observed, "but it's served me well so far."

"Come on," Damien ordered. "I want to meet this Keeper and get this whole mess out of sight."

The Marines were doing their best, Damien knew, but they couldn't help being more obvious than the Secret Service Agents. The two groups he'd absorbed into his bodyguard were cross-training thoroughly, but just as his Marines were better for an exosuit assault on a space ship, his Secret Service Agents were better for covert protection in a mall.

He could pick out his escorts in the crowd easily, but he knew them all by face and gait by now. Hopefully, someone less familiar with the small army of bodyguards he'd brought along would miss the loose circle they formed around him and his core companions.

"We have interface with mall security," Romanov reported through Damien's earpiece. "No threats pinging their radar, but they've let us into their camera systems. We have eyes on the crowd."

"Good. Can you sweep for our Keeper friend?" he subvocalized back, studying the crowd around him as they moved up to the second floor and headed towards their food court.

"Running a pattern match now." Pause. "There are a *lot* of people in here, boss. I make it at least two thousand in the building. If this goes sideways..."

"We have a real problem," Damien agreed. "Find our guest for me, Romanov."

"Scanning."

They kept moving through the crowd, the circle of bodyguards tightening as the crowds grew denser. Light was flickering down from the skylights and Damien glanced up at the towers around them.

"Ping," Romanov said sharply. "In the food court, she's got a table and a plate of fries. Looks like she's waiting for someone and is an exact match for the images you gave us."

"As expected," Damien said, sighing with relief. He'd half-expected this to be a trap. "With me, folks. Let's go say hi."

The food court was on the third and highest floor, at the center of the T that made up the mall. Damien took a set of old-fashioned escalators up one more floor and stepped into the naturally-lit hall that contained Sunrise Mall's food court. A ping flickered on his wrist PC, directing him toward their contact.

Stepping through the crowds, he finally saw her himself. Romanov was right. She was definitely the woman who'd sent the recording on Ndosi's channel, claiming to be the last Keeper.

He opened his mouth to say something—and then the fist of an angry god slammed into his shoulder and everything went black for a moment.

Marine or Secret Service, it was *never* a good sign to have the principal you were protecting go down to the sound of shattering glass and screaming crowds.

Denis Romanov was moving the moment Montgomery went down, his weapon swinging free from under his jacket as he searched for a shooter.

"Cover the Hand!" he snapped, his own magic flaring to life as he wrapped a shield of force around himself and the man he was sworn to protect—just in time for another high-speed bullet to hammer into it with crushing force.

Everything seemed to be moving in slow motion as he *felt* his spell come apart, the bullet itself insidiously *melting* the solidified air and magic he'd emplaced to defend Montgomery. The spell, which Romanov had used to stop *tank rounds,* only bought him a few moments.

Those moments were enough for him to reach Montgomery and yank him across the tiled floor, leaving the second bullet to smash harmlessly into the tiles—with far more force than it should have had after passing through Denis's spell.

"My lord," he hissed at Montgomery. "Are you all right?"

The Hand didn't respond. He didn't need to. Montgomery was *writhing* on the floor and the Combat Mage could *feel* power rippling off him.

Montgomery's eyes suddenly snapped open and he grabbed Denis's shoulder.

"They've damaged the Runes," he hissed. "Evac the building."

A chill ran down Denis's spine as the full meaning of both the warning and the order sank in. He'd been briefed on the Runes of Power the Hand wore—and the concern of just what would happen if one of them *broke,* unleashing its thaumic feedback loop in an uncontrolled manner.

"Massey," Denis snapped at his subordinates. "Coordinate with mall security, start a full evacuation. Coral, perimeter close, *now*!"

Leaving his subordinates to their work, Denis pulled up another channel.

"Mountain Security Control, this is DM Security Actual," he said grimly. "The principal is down, wounded by a sniper. I am requesting air and ground support to sweep the surrounding buildings."

There was a shocked silence on the radio for a moment, and then he *heard* the controller on the other end swallow.

"Understood, DMS Actual," the woman replied. "I'll have aircraft on their way in thirty seconds, ground contingent to follow.

"What is your status?"

"We are evacuating Sunrise Mall and maintaining a perimeter around the principal," Denis replied. He considered his next words very, very, carefully. "There is a risk of...an extreme thaumaturgic event," he concluded. "*No one* is to enter the mall until we confirm the area is safe; do you understand?"

"Agent, that—"

"That is under *Hand Montgomery's authority*," Denis snapped. "I don't like it, MSC, but I don't have a choice. My team is in the zone. Everybody else gets out and nobody else comes in until either I or the Hand say otherwise, understand?"

Silence for a moment.

"Yes, sir. Your air support is en route. What are we looking for?"

Denis looked up, studying the damage in the skylights.

"One shooter, probably with spotter, in a building on the east side," he reeled off quickly. He paused. "We want them alive, Control. These assholes just shot a Hand.

"We want them alive."

Damien's world was pain.

He wasn't quite sure just *what* he'd been shot with, but it was interfering with his Runes of Power. The feedback loop was...*leaking.*

Sparks of power kept escaping from his Runes, and the normally contained flow of power was now backlashing into his body at random intervals, feeling exactly like he was being repeatedly electrocuted.

He was only vaguely aware of telling Romanov to get everybody out as he twitched in pain, his shoulder slamming into the tile floor, bruising his skin and shattering the ceramic underneath him. The fragments of tile tore into his suit, only the armor weave keeping his skin intact as his own magic tried to kill him.

Releasing some of the power would *help* but only at the cost of destroying part of the building and potentially killing innocents...and that was if he maintained control of it. He could tell that he was running far too close to the edge of completely losing control.

An uncontrolled feedback loop would, at a minimum, destroy the entire damned mall. Quite possibly a good chunk of the city. The Rune Wrights were *careful* designing the Runes of Power; it shouldn't be *possible* for the loop to be damaged like this.

A hand settled on his shoulder and he tried to jerk away from the touch, only for the grip to tighten and hold him in place.

"How can I help?" Munira Samara asked softly, using her body to shield his eyes from the light as he looked up at her.

"Bullet. Shoulder. Interrupting the Rune," he gasped, then spasmed in pain and yanked himself from her grip.

"Right," she replied. "Guessing you've got to stay conscious?"

"Lose control...everybody dies."

"*Inshallah*," Samara whispered, stepping *into* him and using her knee to pin him to the ground. It *hurt*, but compared to the lightning rippling through his body, the sharp pressure of her knee driving him into the tile floor barely registered.

He was losing control, the waves of power rippling through him more frequently and his awareness of the world fading in and out with it. He barely registered Samara producing a knife from somewhere and cutting away the wreckage of his suit while she carefully judged.

"I'd warn you this will hurt," she told him, "but I think we're out of time."

Damien felt the knife slice into his skin. The bullet wasn't just on the surface; it was embedded in his skin and shoulder blade, stuck in place in a way that could not be normal.

Samara cut the bullet out. Probably along with a good chunk of his flesh, but Damien barely registered that compared to the flash of uncontrolled power that ran through him as the bullet yanked free of the Rune of Power it had embedded itself in the middle of.

There was no containing it this time—but there was, now, a chance to control it. Damien flung his arm upward, pointing away from Samara, away from the Secret Service Agents, away from the surrounding towers...and channeled pure magic.

Every molecule in a pillar six centimeters across and a kilometer high suddenly flashed to plasma, hyper-compressing and accelerating with heat as his power tore through the air.

A second wave of power, this one *fully* under his control, followed. His magic encased and contained the inevitable explosion, sending it farther into the air as his burst of uncontrolled energy became a pillar of light and fire easily ten kilometers tall.

But Samara, only twenty centimeters away from it, was unharmed.

Damien inhaled, sucking in surprisingly cool air as another ripple of uncontrolled power tore through him. This one was weaker. Without the bullet embedded in his skin, his Rune was damaged but wasn't actively being distorted.

"Stand back," he told Samara.

"I just cut a hole in you," she snapped. "You need medical attention."

"Not yet. Stand back," he ordered.

Thankfully, she obeyed, and Damien closed his eyes, focusing on the flow of power through his skin, testing the channels, the Runes, the silver polymer.

The Rune of Power on his right shoulder had been severed in two places, but the bullet had clearly carried runes that had been actively distorting it. Without the runes on the bullet, the Rune was still *broken*, but it wasn't attacking him.

A broken Rune of Power was bad enough. Uncontrolled power continued to ripple through him, and he was quite sure it would kill him very, very quickly if not stopped.

With his eyes closed, he found the broken ends, where the bullet had snapped the *almost* indestructible silver polymer inlaid into his skin...and then melted them again, pulling the strings of molten metal out of his skin and linking them again across the bloody gash in his flesh.

The ends joined. Thinner than they had been, but they were connected again, and the ripples of power slowly, ever so slowly, faded.

Damien opened his eyes, looking up at the terrified face of his newest subordinate.

"All right, Munira," he half-whispered. "*Now* you can do first aid."

Then he passed out.

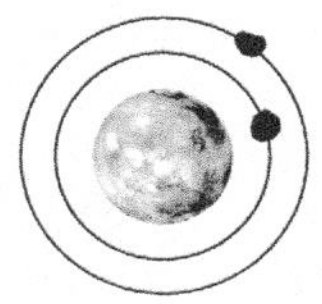

CHAPTER 21

"WHERE'S MY air support?" Denis snapped into his radio, staring up at where a neat hole had been vaporized through the roof of the building by a multi-kilometer line of fire. "Please tell me no one got caught in that."

"Air above you was clear," a new voice replied. "This is Colonel Adam Tsukuyomi, commanding officer of Air Defense Squadron Seven. I have four interceptors dropping into high-altitude cover and eight helicopter gunships moving in low and fast."

Tsukuyomi paused.

"What the hell *was* that, Agent Romanov?"

"As soon as the Hand is conscious enough to ask, I'll ask," Denis told the Colonel, glancing over at where Inspector Samara was beginning to bind up the gaping hole in Montgomery's shoulder. "Montgomery was shot by a long-range sniper. They took two shots that I'm aware of, using some kind of runic round that went clean through my thaumic defenses."

"I can sweep for hostiles, but I can't track down a runner with gunships and jet fighters, Agent," Tsukuyomi warned.

"There should be boots coming from on high," the Hand's bodyguard replied. "Watch out for falling shuttles and keep in the loop; it's looking like this was a one-shot deal, but I'd have arranged a second wave if *I* was going after a Hand."

"Understood, Agent Romanov," the Air Defense officer replied. "We are in position above you and available on this channel if you need fire from above. I'm not reading any moving aircraft, and the only thing of any threat I've seen so far was that lovely pillar of fire."

"Thank you, Colonel."

Romanov shook his head at the circumstances that resulted in his effectively giving orders to a Colonel, a man who outranked him by several dozen kilometers in military terms, then switched over to the Marine Corps channel.

"This is Special Agent Romanov," he barked. "I was promised boots on the ground here. What's the ETA?"

"Six shuttles bearing two companies of Marines just detached from the battleship *Song of Justice*," he was calmly informed. "They'll be on the ground in two minutes. It's going to be a rough ride."

"I have a Hand down and critically wounded," Denis pointed out. "The shooter is still out there. I need those boots."

Silence.

"They'll be on the ground in seventy seconds," the flight controller said grimly. "Just don't expect any of those boys and girls to buy you beer."

"All I want them to do is find the son of a bitch who shot my charge," Denis replied. "We have the Hand secure."

"We've been informed medevac is coming from the Mountain," the other Marine replied. "Should be there just after the Marines."

"Understood. Thank you."

"All part of the service. Just not a service we *want* to be providing."

Thunder echoed in the sky as the assault shuttles rode pillars of fire down from orbit. Landing in an inhabited area, they would normally avoid full-tilt assault landings. With a Hand down and potentially bleeding out, and a sniper on the loose, those niceties were thrown aside.

Sonic booms echoed through the city, rattling the damaged window panes above Denis as the shuttles hammered their rockets to land safely at the last moment. The map being fed to his contact flashed with new icons as five of the shuttles dropped into a perfect pentagram pattern around the mall. The sixth dropped into the mall parking lot, Marines spilling out of all six spacecraft to begin establishing a perimeter.

"We're on the ground, Mage-Captain," a voice said in his ear. "This is Mage-Captain Alistair Lear, senior officer on the deck. Perimeter is in progress; what are we looking for?"

"Lear, this is Romanov," Denis greeted him. "I wish I could give you more clarity, but we have no idea what we're looking at. Minimum of one shooter, took a shot from one of the towers on the east side of Sunrise Mall with a high-caliber rifle."

"Can you send me an image of the impact zone?" Leary asked. "We'll backtrack as best we can. No sonics?"

"Image on the way," Denis told him. "No sonics," he confirmed. "Either too far away or well silenced; I'm guessing on the former—those towers are tall."

"Understood." Leary paused. "Orders are to take the bastard alive, I take it?"

"Unfortunately."

"Understood," the Marine repeated. "We'll try not to kick down any doors we don't have to, but if anyone can find your shooter, we will."

"Good luck, Mage-Captain."

"Likewise, Mage-Captain," Leary replied to Denis's smirk. The Marines *still* figured that rank was more important.

Another sonic boom caused him to look up again—and his smile vanished as he recognized the blood-red aircraft screeching down from the upper tiers of the Mountain.

There was only one force in the area that used that color of *anything*. Only one force equipped with the Hawk-type gunships.

And even if Denis hadn't known that, there was only one force in the area that used the red, rune-encrusted suits of exosuit armor that dropped out of the back of the shuttle as it came to a halt above the Sunrise Mall.

The Royal Guard had arrived.

There were only three of the red-armored Mages striding through the shattered debris of the mall's glass roof, but those three were probably more dangerous than the two entire companies of Marines dropped outside. Denis crisply saluted.

"Guardsmen."

"How is he?" the familiar voice of Guardsman Han asked.

"Shot," Samara replied crisply. "I've staunched the bleeding, but he lost a lot of blood and something *seriously* messed-up was going on with those godawful Runes of his."

"Something managed to damage his Runes?" Han questioned.

"I'm not pretending to understand; that's just what *he* said," the MIS Inspector pointed out. "He had me yank the bullet out, then fixed the Rune himself before he passed out."

"That is not good," the Guardsman said grimly, kneeling next to the unconscious Hand and producing a medical kit from inside her armor. Her gauntlets retracted, freeing up her hands as she quickly and competently got to work on Montgomery.

"We need to get him back up to the Mountain quickly," Han concluded after a few moments. "He's going to live, but he needs a Mage-Surgeon, not a Combat Mage with battlefield first aid training."

She stood back and waved for the gunship to land inside the mall. Her pilot had no hesitation, carefully smashing through the glass in a spot that wouldn't spray the bodyguards with debris and landing the aircraft next to them.

"Romanov, I presume you're with us?" Han asked.

"Of course," he agreed. He looked around, a thought hitting him.

"What happened to the bullet?" Denis asked.

"I have it," Samara replied, holding up an evidence bag with a bloodied round in it.

Of course. She was a cop.

Then Denis finally remembered *why* they'd come and looked around.

"Damn it," he swore. "We completely forgot about the Keeper!"

"Go with Han," Samara told him. "The rest of your team won't even fit in that chopper, so we'll sweep the building for the Keeper and see what else we can find. You make sure Montgomery stays alive—we'll see if we can find out who tried to kill him!"

"Thank you," Denis replied.

"Go!"

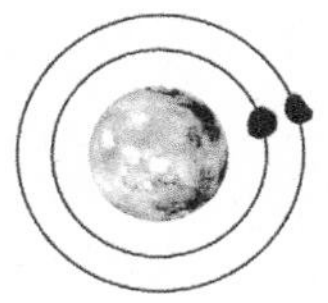

CHAPTER 22

DAMIEN WOKE UP feeling like he'd been on the receiving end of a stampede...that had proceeded to urinate in his mouth.

It wasn't an entirely unfamiliar feeling, though the last time he'd experienced it, he'd stood off an orbital bombardment and pushed himself into a coma.

"Please do not attempt to move," a precise male voice told him before he'd done much more than become aware of his own existence. "Your shoulder is currently immobilized while my work sets.

"I am Dr. Nguyen," the speaker continued. "We have met before, though on that occasion, I was taking blood and gene samples, and I have not treated you previously. I am His Majesty's personal physician, fully briefed on your Runes and your special abilities."

"Given that something specifically screwed with my Runes, that's actually reassuring," Damien admitted.

"His Majesty was here while I was working on you," Nguyen replied. "He has checked over your repairs to the Runes of Power and informed me that you should be fully functional. I cannot speak to that, as I do not share your Gift."

The doctor paused.

"The muscles, bones and skin damaged by the bullet, however, I am qualified to speak to. They have healed well under my ministration, though your shoulder will need to remain immobilized for at least another day, and I would prefer you remain in bed rest for at least eight more hours."

"How long was I out?"

"Twelve hours," Nguyen replied. "I am *very* good at my job, my lord Hand."

"So I see," Damien confirmed, opening his eyes and blinking against the soft light of the clinic. "Any idea what hit me?"

"I understand your staff are continuing to sweep the site of the attack," the Healer told him. "However, *you* were struck by a fourteen-millimeter metal-jacketed hollow-point sniper bullet. A nasty hit, especially as whatever magical tricks they were playing lodged it in your body."

Damien whistled softly. That should have gone right through him without something stopping it. Even his shoulder blade should have fragmented under that impact unless, as Nguyen said, some form of magic had been tied into the bullet.

The truth was that whatever it had been doing to his Runes had actually been more likely to kill him than the bullet punching through him would have been. Whoever had shot him had known *exactly* what they were doing. Given everything the Keepers seemed to know about the Hands, he suspected he'd walked right into someone's neatly set trap.

They'd used his desire to protect them as bait, and he'd walked *right* into it.

"Any update from my staff?" he asked.

"Special Agent Romanov asked that I inform him as soon as you were awake," Nguyen admitted. "So long as you promise that you will not attempt to so much as sit up without my assistance and supervision, I will permit them to brief you."

Damien sighed. Somehow, he suspected he wasn't going to win an argument with the man stubborn enough to be responsible for Desmond Alexander's health.

"Very well, Doctor. I'll be good."

Nguyen helped Damien into an upright position, the Hand wincing against the pain radiating from his immobilized shoulder. If he'd had any inclination to argue with the doctor, the amount of discomfort involved in sitting up, even with help, would have changed his mind.

"I'll send your staff in," the doctor promised. "I'll be just outside the door, monitoring your vitals. If I say your briefing is over, my lord Hand, your briefing is over, you understand?"

"Yes, Doctor," Damien acquiesced.

"Good."

The doctor swept out of the room in a carefully dramatic flare of his white lab coat, returning a moment later with the mismatched set of Damien's current trio of senior staff. Romanov held up the middle, as tall and skinny as ever, though he looked almost as tired and abused as Damien felt.

Samara barely came up to the Marine's shoulder. She was wearing a light green headscarf today, Damien noted, and he didn't know her well enough yet to read the flat look in her eyes. He doubted it was good, though.

Christoffsen just looked...old. Even more so than usual. Weariness exaggerated the lines in Damien's political advisor's face, and the Professor was showing his age badly today.

"None of us look in top form today," Damien told them. "Are you all all right?"

"I'm supposed to keep you from getting shot," Romanov replied. "And you're worried about *us*?"

"I'm alive," Damien pointed out. "Hurts when I move, a lot, but Dr. Nguyen assures me I will heal quickly. That second shot *would* have finished me off, Denis. You're why I'm alive."

"You shouldn't have been shot once," the Secret Service man said. "We've grown so used to being used as a strike team, we've started forgetting that, powerful as you are, you have bodyguards for a reason—and snipers and knives in the dark are the reason!"

"I'm alive," Damien repeated. "What exactly were you going to do, Denis? Sweep every tower around Sunrise Mall for snipers? Make a big show and dance of what was supposed to be a quiet meeting?

"No," he concluded. "We were hit by someone who knew our procedures, knew their target, and wasn't taking any risks. The Keepers know us far too damned well."

"You think they set us up?" Romanov asked.

"I can't think of anyone else with the resources and the motive."

"I can," Christoffsen told them grimly. "The Legatans, for one. Hell, Damien, some of His Majesty's allies would see your 'unfortunate death in the line of duty' as removing a lot of obstacles."

"Great," Damien muttered. "Because I *need* a longer list of suspects."

"Whoever did this," Samara told him, "had a lot of access to our equipment, our protocols, and to magic I haven't seen before. I can't say that rules out the Legatans, but the last makes it unlikely."

The head-scarfed Inspector laid two evidence bags on the table next to Damien. One held a block of circuitry and the other a bloodied bullet.

"This"—she tapped the circuitry—"is a remote-activated homing beacon. All Civil Fleet vehicles have trackers built in. As a matter of course, the Secret Service disables them and scans for active beacons before allowing one of their principals to take a Civil Fleet vehicle.

"This beacon was tagged with a radio transmission after we left the Mountain, turning it on after we had scanned for bugs in the car. There was one on both vehicles," she noted. "Someone was making very sure they would know where you were."

"The shooter was on the fortieth floor of an apartment tower," Romanov explained. "We believe they arrived at the tower after we arrived at the mall, took the elevator up, and then set up in the hallway. The shots were fired from a common-area window. The bullet casings were collected and chemical residue was wiped, but there were still holes in the window."

He sighed.

"The surveillance equipment in the building had been professionally disabled," he noted. "That helps us pinpoint the shooter's arrival time but isn't otherwise useful."

"So, they knew which cars we were taking and they knew Secret Service protocol with those cars," Damien concluded. "Damn. That does suggest Keepers."

"So does this," Samara said, passing him the second bag. "I'm not fully briefed on your abilities, but I understand that you're one of our better experts on Runes. The bullet was covered in silver. A lot of it is damaged, but..."

He took the bullet and studied it, trying to ignore the fact that chunks of it were still marked with his own blood. As Samara had noted, the runes were damaged but intact enough for him to see the flows of power with his Gift.

Damien turned it around, studying it from each angle. "Anyone got a magnifying glass?" he asked distractedly.

"Here," the Inspector produced a multi-tool from inside her jacket and pulled out the magnifier. "What do you see?"

He continued studying the runework under the magnifier.

"I would very much like to meet the Mage who forged this bullet," he finally concluded aloud. "It's *very* fine work; some of the lines are literally as close together as they could be without losing structural integrity."

"A Rune Wright's work?" Romanov asked.

"No," Damien said slowly. "And that's what's truly impressive about it. Most highly complex pieces of new runework are created here on Mars by the handful of Rune Wrights the Protectorate has. Those of us who know that tend to forget that it's entirely possible to craft highly complex and powerful runes and enchantments just using the runic language the first Mage-King created."

Or stole. The fact that it was quite possible the early human Mages had stolen the language humanity knew as Martian Runic from someone else was *definitely* tied into the Keeper's secrets.

"This was done with Martian Runic," he explained. "Very fine, micro-scale runes, but still Martian Runic. It was written by a Rune Scribe, but one with either access to the limited literature on Runes of Power or an actual Rune of Power."

"Whoever forged that bullet handed it to someone who tried to kill you, my lord," Romanov pointed out.

"Oh, yes," Damien agreed with a chuckle. "Make no mistake, people: this bullet was enchanted to do one thing and one thing only: kill a Hand.

It would work better on myself or another Rune Wright, as it would need to impact close to the Rune, though not necessarily actually sever it as this one did mine."

"And what does it do?" Christoffsen asked.

The other two had watched Damien writhe across the floor with the bullet in him. They could probably guess.

"It destabilizes the thaumic feedback loop at the core of a Rune of Power," the Hand explained. "At best, the Hand is forced to manually contain the feedback until someone can yank the bullet out—as happened with me. At worst..."

Damien sighed.

"When I first carved a Rune of Power into myself, I was concerned that I would destroy the ship I was on if I got it wrong," he told his staff quietly. "I overestimated the potential energy release, but not by much. If I had failed to stabilize the Rune, or if Samara hadn't been there and able to yank the damn thing out, the best-case scenario is that I would have been vaporized.

"The worst case is that I would have briefly resembled an atomic bomb."

The room was silent for a long moment.

"They knew exactly who and what they were going for," Samara said grimly. "Except...if it was the Keeper who contacted you, they'd have been more prepared. They'd have known exactly where you were going to be."

"That adds to the theory that the people wiping out the Keepers *are* Keepers," Damien replied. "Which is...an entirely different layer of nightmare."

He sighed, leaning back against the wall.

"I'm told I need at least eight more hours on bedrest," he told them. "But we *need* to find that Keeper. I have a lot of questions and she may be the only person who can answer them."

"She disappeared in the evacuation," Romanov admitted. "I'm sorry, my lord, my priority—"

"Was my safety and the safety of the civilians," Damien interrupted. "Which is exactly what it should have been. Once someone was shooting bullets designed to kill Hands, meeting with the Keepers dropped down the priority list.

"But now we need to find her," he continued grimly. "Has there been any contact on the channel she used previously?"

"None," Romanov told him.

"Okay. Samara, I'll need you to start searching through the footage we have of the evacuation. See if you can trace where she went. Otherwise, all we can do is wait."

"What about the assassin?" Christoffsen asked.

"Do we have *anything* we can trace them with?"

"No," Romanov admitted.

"Then, for now, we leave that in the capable hands of MIS while *we* deal with the Keepers," Damien told his people grimly. "I don't *like* knowing there's someone out there taking potshots at me, but for the moment, we need to prioritize *answers*.

"And hope that the answers to some of our questions help with the rest."

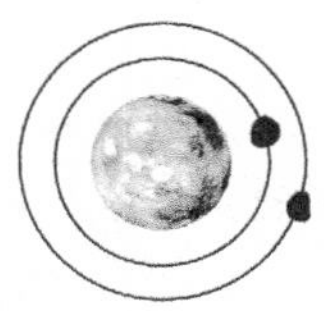

CHAPTER 23

"ANYTHING?" Samara asked, but the team she'd left behind shook their heads.

Denis wasn't entirely surprised.

"It was *very* professional," Inspector Cook reported over the video link. "Cameras in the building were hit with a virus via the planet-net sixteen seconds after Hand Montgomery and his detail arrived at the mall. One minute, forty-eight seconds later, the cameras themselves were physically disabled at the primary router.

"The elevators maintain their own records of floors, so I know that one went from the basement, where the primary router was located, to the fortieth floor seventy-two seconds after the cameras were disabled.

"The shot was taken two minutes, ten seconds after that elevator reached the fortieth floor. It was almost thirty minutes before the Marine sweep teams hit that building, by which point the area had been wiped for chemical residue and any casings collected."

Cook shook his head.

"If it wasn't for the hole in the glass, we couldn't even be certain that this was where the shot was taken from," he admitted. "I'm guessing we're looking at two, a shooter and a spotter, but that's only a guess.

"We have no evidence on which to assume a specific weapon, no evidence on which to assume any details of the shooter. I'm sorry, Senior Inspector, Special Agent, we have *nothing*."

"Someone *shot* a Hand and we have nothing?" Samara demanded.

"I'm not surprised," Denis told her. "Anyone who knew who they were going after knew how far we'd go to hunt down the people who took the shot. That leaves you with two options for this kind of attack: a sacrifice gambit, with the shooter either knowingly or unknowingly certain to die before arrest, or throw every resource you have at it and get *everything* right."

"They got everything right," Cook concluded. "And I mean *everything*. This is the fourth major assassination attempt I've run in my career, but I've never seen anything this clean before."

"They didn't get everything right," Samara objected. "Montgomery's still alive."

"Thankfully," Denis agreed. "Because I doubt we could tear things apart more than we already have, and I'm going to dislike telling Damien we have nothing bad enough. If Damien was dead, I'd be telling the Mage-King we had no idea who killed him."

Everyone on the call winced.

"Do we know anything more about our Keeper?" Samara asked.

"Yes," Analyst Daniels replied instantly. "There was enough distortion on the original transmission to prevent us identifying her, but once Hand Montgomery flagged her in the mall's cameras, we were able to pull enough to get an ID."

The image on the screen of Daniels and Cook slid to one side, replaced with a standard government identification photo.

"Miss Eleanor Meir," Daniels concluded. "Thirty-two. Member of none of our identified groups, but works as a senior librarian and research analyst at Olympus City University. She hasn't flagged *anything* on our records—she's not a Mage, not involved in any political groups, not even a speeding ticket.

"Miss Meir is a model citizen," the Analyst said. "She also went through university with Lawrence Octavian. Several, though by no means a majority, of her research grants were funded by the Octavian Foundation—though I have to point out that the Foundation funds just over a thousand research grants a year on Mars alone."

"So, she had an existing relationship with him, one he leveraged to bring her into the Keepers," Samara guessed. "Do we know where she is?"

"She's currently on vacation, but she might be home. According to her address on file with the University, she rents an apartment in one of the old dome districts," Daniels replied. "Should I have OCPD investigate?"

"Negative," Romanov snapped. He checked the time. "The Hand is still down for at least four more hours, but I think we need to move on this immediately.

"Inspector Samara, would you care to accompany me and one of my teams on a house visit?"

She smiled grimly.

"Of course, Special Agent. We even still have those Runabouts—and I *guarantee* you they aren't bugged this time."

The building the address brought them to was nicer than Denis had been expecting, a ten-story structure of carefully painted and shaped concrete that probably dated from after when the dome had been taken down.

It was still shaped inside the curve of the nonexistent dome. That was just how the dome districts on Mars worked, and no one argued with two-hundred-plus years of tradition now.

"Research professor pays better than I expected," the Marine muttered to Samara as they stopped the electric SUV and his Secret Service agents swarmed out.

"That depends," she replied, looking the building up and down. "I'm betting she's in a one-bedroom on the sixth floor. Plus, she rents and this is a co-ownership building, which means she probably can't afford to own."

Denis checked the address.

"Fifth floor," he pointed out. "But you're probably right. Massey, are we in the BMS yet?"

The Building Management System in every apartment building on Mars had overrides built into it for police, firefighters and Hands to take over control as needed.

"We are," the Corporal confirmed. "But..."

"What?"

"Hallway cameras are down," Massey reported. "I'm getting minimal reports from the building systems, and there doesn't seem to be anyone *accessing* the systems."

"Shit. Massey, take Coral and Earhart, sweep the security station. The rest of you, with me. We're taking the stairs."

The team split up with the ease of both practice and adrenaline, all six of them moving through the building's front door at a brisk pace. They were far enough into the BMS that the doors simply swung open for them as they approached, a map dropping down on Denis's contacts as he headed in.

"Stairs are this way," he barked, leading Samara and his last Secret Service Agent towards the side door and drawing his own weapon.

Marines, MIS and Secret Service alike did enough exercise to make four flights of stairs a trivial challenge, but it still took *time*. Massey made it to the control room first and pinged them.

"There was a janitor and a security guard on duty," the Marine Corporal informed them. "Both are dead—necks snapped."

"Time of death?"

Massey sighed.

"At least two, three hours ago, boss. I'm not sure what you're going to find upstairs, but I doubt it's going to be good."

Denis left that unanswered as he shoved the door open onto the fifth floor, his carbine barrel leading the way.

"Hallway clear," he reported. "Move up."

"I've got a broken door," Samara told him a few moments later. She paused. "It's Meir's."

"Move up, move up," Denis snapped to his Secret Service agent. "Do we have any signs of life?"

"Negative," the agent replied, checking a scanner mounted on her wrist. "I've no movement or human-sized thermals on this floor." She pointed down the hallway. "Two cats in the apartment at the end, a dog over here. That's it."

It was the middle of the day. *Hopefully,* that just meant everyone was at work.

Either way, the threat level was low, so Denis moved forward himself, stepping past the kicked-in wreckage of Eleanor Meir's front door to survey the professor's apartment.

As Samara had guessed, it was a small single-bedroom suite, crammed full of the miscellaneous possessions most adults managed to accumulate if they weren't careful. There was bric-a-brac, paper, a fixed computer screen to link into a wrist PC...

All of it was wrecked and scattered. The front room had been ripped apart, even the couch cushions slashed apart to make sure nothing was hidden inside them. Paper and books were everywhere.

"Check the bedroom if you please, Inspector Samara," Denis asked.

The MIS Inspector nodded, stepping through the door into the other room to look around. She stepped back out and shook her head.

"She's not here. Her room is in the same shape as the rest of this"—she gestured around—"but it looks like she slipped out before whoever did this arrived."

Damien sighed and nodded as Romanov finished his report.

"Thank you, Denis," he told the other man. "Is there any sign of where she may have gone?"

"We'll check," the Marine replied, "but I imagine if there was, whoever ransacked the place will already be on their way."

"That's what I'm afraid of," Damien admitted. "I'll try and reach out to her again, but if she isn't willing to talk to us, we're running out of options."

Romanov snorted.

"I'm getting used to that feeling, boss. Behind the ball and sprinting at the wrong side of the curve," he told Damien. "Not sure I like the feeling."

"I know I don't. Check to see if you can find anything at her apartment and then get back here," Damien instructed. "I have a feeling we'll be moving sooner rather than later."

"Wilco, my lord."

Damien closed the channel with another sigh. He was still restricted to his bed on Dr. Nguyen's orders, and he couldn't even argue particularly hard. Movement was better than it had been when he woke up, but it still hurt.

Nonetheless, he'd pulled enough rank to get his computer returned to him. It sat on his lap instead of his wrist, but he could still use it with his uninjured arm.

He pulled up the channel and protocols the Keeper had reached out to him on and activated them.

"Miss Meir," he said into the camera. "I am giving you the benefit of the doubt and presuming you had nothing to do with the assassination attempt on me. If that's the case, then you are running right now.

"We know who you are. So do your enemies. Someone other than us has ransacked your apartment. If there were any clues there as to where you went, they're coming after you now.

"My reach is long, but it is not infinite and we are not omniscient. I can't help you unless I know where you are." He paused. "Help me help you, Miss Meir. I swear to you, by the honor of the Mage-King of Mars, that you will not be harmed."

He stopped recording and transmitted. He wasn't even sure if Meir could receive on those protocols—it depended on just how much Ndosi had given her.

But if the Keeper didn't reach out to him...there was nothing left for him to do.

Damien had finally managed to drift off into an only somewhat painful slumber when the computer resting in his lap chimed and vibrated, jerking him awake with another spasm through his injured shoulder.

Groggily blinking away sleep, he hit ACCEPT—and a recorded message started playing, popping up a now-familiar dark-haired woman.

"Lord Montgomery," Eleanor Meir greeted him formally. "I received your message. To be honest, I expected you to blame me for the ambush, though I swear I had nothing to do with it.

"Regardless, though, I have nowhere left to turn. I was aware my home had been raided," she admitted. "From the moment I came out to meet you, I knew I could not return there. I have retreated to a safehouse Octavian had set aside for me, but I fear that all of the Keeper safehouses have been compromised.

"There is nowhere left for me to turn but to you. I will answer all of your questions, Lord Montgomery. My oaths would require me to regardless.

"But I must ask you to save me," she concluded, then reeled off an address.

"I do not know how long it will take our enemies to find me," she warned. "They could be breaking down the outer defenses as you listen. I have nowhere else to turn.

"Help me, Hand Montgomery. You are my only hope."

The screen shut down, the hologram disappearing as Damien stared at the computer, then checked the time.

He was supposed to be on bed rest for another hour, but he was out of time. He paged Dr. Nguyen.

"You should be asleep," the doctor told him, but something in the way he regarded Damien said everything.

"I have to go," Damien replied. "Duty calls."

Nguyen shook his head.

"I have treated a King and nine Hands in my time here," he noted. "You are all the same."

"I'm not exaggerating," Damien pointed out.

"I know," Nguyen told him. "Hold still." A hypodermic appeared from somewhere in the lab coat and stabbed into Damien's flesh just beneath the cast immobilizing his shoulder.

"That will block the pain," the doctor continued. "The cast will keep your shoulder in place, stop you from doing *too* much damage. Try not to get in any fistfights. Do not let the drugs fool you—you are weak and your magic is undermined by it. If you are not careful, you could easily injure yourself further by both magical and physical exertion."

"Thank you," Damien said.

"Like I said, you are all the same," Nguyen told him. "I have learned when I can be stubborn and when duty must call. Go!"

Damien carefully rose from the bed, testing the limits of his shoulder as the doctor helped him into his clothes. He couldn't move much, but he could move.

Even weakened, there were few threats he wouldn't back his magic against.

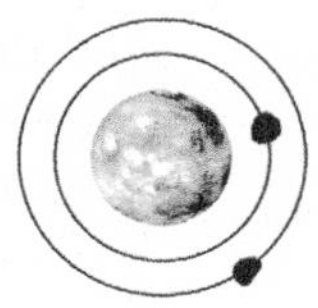

CHAPTER 24

DAMIEN MET his people at the assault shuttle, Romanov and Samara having barely returned from their trip into town to check on Meir's apartment.

"Isn't this a bit of overkill?" Samara asked, looking over the armed spacecraft behind him.

"I have the feeling we're going to want every bit of firepower we can scrape together shortly," Damien told her. "Romanov, I called the regular detail together; they're going to be arriving over the next couple of minutes. As soon as we have the team assembled, we're going to be in the air. I want the Secret Service Agents fully kitted out and the Marines in exosuit armor."

Romanov nodded.

"You think it's going to get that bad?" he asked.

"I hope not," Damien admitted, "but so far, we've been arriving too damned late and too damned short to make a difference. This time, I want to go in fast and loaded for bear."

"It'll take us at least five minutes to get the Marines in armor," Romanov pointed out.

"That's about how long the pilot said it will take us to get there, so I suggest you get started," Damien replied.

As soon as Damien saw the vehicles, he knew they'd lost the race. The safehouse, like the one they'd found Professor Raptis in, was a large older house in a suburb. The four SUVs out front stood out like a sore thumb...but the small surface-to-orbit shuttle was *completely* out of place.

"Take that shuttle out," he snapped. "The cars, too. If I'm wrong, I'll *happily* replace someone's wheels, but I'm pretty sure those are our hostiles."

"Done," the pilot replied crisply.

A moment later, a panel on the bottom of the assault shuttle opened up and five missiles blasted away. The shuttle and SUVs erupted in fireballs as the weapons struck home, shattering the vehicles and the ground underneath them alike.

"Marines first," Romanov barked. "Slow down and drop us out, then sweep back for second wave deployment."

"Roger."

The Special Agent's armored finger swung around to point directly at Damien.

"And *you*, my lord, go in the second wave. Clear?"

"Clear," Damien replied meekly.

"Good."

The shuttle swept across the neighborhood ten meters above the ground, still traveling at well over a hundred kilometers an hour when Romanov led the rest of the exosuited Marines out the back of the shuttle, falling like homesick meteors to the shattered ground below.

Damien tried to keep a watch on the situation, but the shuttle continued on in a wide sweeping turn that would bring them back onto the ground in a few moments.

"We are under fire," Romanov reported calmly. "Nothing that's a threat to exosuits yet, but we're moving in to suppress hostiles."

"You'll be on the ground in sixty seconds," the pilot told Damien. "Hang on."

Acceleration pressed him to the side of his chair as the shuttle turned, continuing to slow as the pilot brought the spacecraft towards the open street.

"Man down," Romanov reported. "Two men down, shit! They've switched to carbines with penetrator rounds. Go suppressive! Suppressive!"

Fire lit up the street as the shuttle swept around, and Damien caught himself holding his breath. They needed to rescue Meir, not level the building, but...

"Pilot, relay from Romanov's suit scanners, hit the hostiles he designates with the guns as you drop us."

There was no response for a long moment, then the two railguns mounted on the shuttle's nose opened up. Short bursts, maybe half a dozen rounds at a time, walked across the front of the house. The façade came apart in flaming chunks of wood and concrete as the thirty-millimeter shells carved their way across.

"Fire is suppressed," Romanov reported as the shuttle came to a halt. "We need to move. The interior shell is armored and I doubt we got them all."

Damien was the first out of the shuttle after it touched down, a shield of force moving with him as he charged through the burning wreckage of the SUVs to meet up with Romanov.

The Marine was as ducked behind one of the wrecked vehicles as it was possible for a man in an exosuit to be, his armored body quivering with rage.

"They've got penetrator carbines and an unknown number of troops," he reported shortly. "Kaber and Alstairs are dead. Whoever the fuck these people are, they have damn good guns and are damn good shots."

"Fuck them," Damien replied. "We have two Mages. Tactical shields?"

"Read my mind, my lord."

The Hand smiled grimly, moved his shield forward and extended it to cover the front of the remaining detail. A twitch of power turned the shield translucent, visible to the men behind him.

"Advance by sections under cover of the shields!" Romanov barked.

The Marine suited actions to words, moving forward from the wrecked vehicle behind the shields. His Marines fell in with him, sweeping for targets as they moved into the wreckage of the house. Finally reaching the edge of the original façade, they took what cover they could, and Romanov waved Damien forward.

The Hand waited a moment to be sure the Combat Mage had his own shield up, and then moved forward, carefully, towards the shattered house, Samara and the Secret Service Agents on his heels.

The bombardment from the shuttle had wrecked the exterior section of the house, leaving the armored shell at the core completely obvious. There were bodies scattered through the debris, the men who'd tried to hold off Romanov's people.

They were...more intact than Damien would have expected, but he didn't have time to try and follow the mental alert that raised.

"Find the entrance," he ordered.

"Based off last time, it's over here," one of the Marines replied, poking at a chunk of wall in what had been the kitchen. It resisted and then swung open as she yanked on it.

Gunfire echoed out from behind the metal door. The range was so short, the rounds punched through the shield Romanov had raised in front of the Marine—but the shield absorbed enough force that the penetrator rounds bounced off her armor as she dodged backward, firing her own weapon.

Damien was only a moment behind the Marine, a stronger shield slamming into place to deflect the next burst of rounds. The two shooters were still up somehow, despite one of them having a very large hole blown through their midsection.

Fire flashed from his fingers, arcing across the room behind his companions' bullets. The two attackers were still up, still shooting, and his shield fractured under the pressure. The point Marine was flung back, her armor still absorbing the shots as she and her attackers all went down.

"Son of a bitch," Romanov swore. "Coral, are you okay?"

"Armor is jammed up," the Marine reported. "I'm fine, but this suit is trashed and I'm stuck."

"What were those fuckers?"

Damien shook his head as he stepped into the interior, looking down at the bodies but already suspecting what he would find.

There were the blood and charred flesh you would expect from someone killed by bullets and Mage-fire. There were *also* sparking wires and shattered circuitry woven into their bodies.

"Augments."

The presence of the Legatan Mage killer cyborgs crystallized the fear that had been rising inside Damien since they'd arrived. They were late and Eleanor Meir was in grave danger. There was no time to check if traps were disabled or fight their way through whatever Augments were left.

They had to get into the armored core of the safehouse *now*.

"Stand back," he snapped at Romanov, then gestured at the wall once the Marines were clear. Exploding the wall would risk both his people and the woman they were trying to save. Most of his other options were power-intensive and messy, still dangerous for those around him, except...

He teleported a ten-square-meter chunk of wall into orbit and strode forward into the gap he had opened, fire flashing from his hands at the stunned trio of Augments guarding the corridor on the other side.

One went down to his attack, the others crumpled as gunfire followed from Damien's companions. Then the *other* side of the corridor followed the first wall into space, and the Hand charged forward into the frozen tableau of shocked people on the other side.

Eleanor Meir was back against a wall, her eyes flickering to him with sudden, unexpected hope.

Three Augments were closer to Damien, turning to the sound of the guns as they realized something was happening.

A fifth individual had pushed Meir against the wall but turned as Damien barged through. A smile flickered across the man's lips as he met Damien's gaze, and the two of them recognized each other.

It was the same Mage who'd betrayed Charlotte Ndosi and shot her in the back in the Archive, attempting to kill two Hands with one bullet.

That Mage moved first. Fire flickered into existence around his hands and he slammed a fist *through* Eleanor Meir's chest, crushing the woman's ribcage and smashing her body back into the bookshelves with brutal force.

The closest Augment slammed into Damien as he tried to attack, the cyborg moving with inhuman speed and long training to counter the Mage before he could act. An iron-hard fist slammed into his shoulder, shattering his cast and sending him gasping backward as the cyborgs closed with him.

"I'd love to stay and play," the Mage told Damien, letting Meir's corpse slide off his hand. "But I have other business to attend to. Major, I leave the Hand to you. Mage-killing's your job, isn't it?"

Pinned to a wall by an Augment and disabled by pain, Damien didn't manage *anything* before Meir's murderer flipped him a familiar mocking salute and disappeared in the *pop* of a teleport.

With one Augment holding him, another opened fire on Damien. He managed to yank his wounded shoulder out from under the ironclad grip holding him to the wall, turning a lethal headshot into a painful series of impacts across his armored suit.

Free now, he unleashed a gout of plasma from his hands, hammering it into the Augment standing over him and hurling the cyborg back, smashing furniture to pieces as he incinerated the flesh around the metal.

Even Legatus's cyborgs couldn't survive that—and Romanov's people were only seconds behind him. The last two Augments went down under heavy fire, and Damien struggled to his feet to cross to Meir.

Her eyes were still open, still staring blankly in his direction as if imploring him to act a little bit faster, arrive a little bit sooner.

"Damn it," he swore. Gently, he closed her eyes and stood up to look around.

This safehouse hadn't been a backup archive. There were a few books on the shelves, but none of the papers or storage media it would have taken to contain the Keepers' library. If Meir had known the location of a backup of the data, it was lost with her.

"Wait," he heard Romanov say, the Marine checking over the Augments. "This one's alive—losing blood fast, but..."

"Stabilize him," Damien snapped. "*Somebody* is going to give me some *damn* answers today."

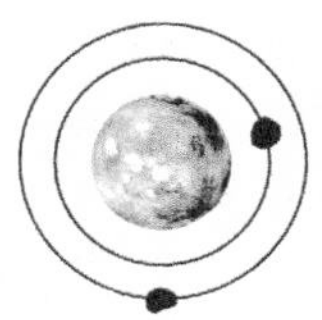

CHAPTER 25

"I FAILED, MY LIEGE," Damien said quietly, staring out the windows of the Mage-King's private office. This sanctuary was buried at the top of Olympus Mons, where the air outside wasn't even breathable by humankind.

Even so, he knew that Royal Guards in exosuit armor patrolled the bleak slopes outside that pane of heavy bulletproof glass, and antimissile lasers and anti-air missiles were hidden just out of sight.

"So far as I can tell," he continued, "Eleanor Meir was the last Keeper. No one else who was pegged as even a possible candidate is alive. I may have gutted their core membership, but someone else cleaned house.

"I failed to save them," he repeated.

"I'll shed no tears for my grandfather's fanatics," Desmond Michael Alexander pointed out from behind his immense, heavy desk. "I can regret that their secrets are lost and I can regret that we end with no answers, but I will shed no tears for the men and women who turned my Hands against me and chose the murder of civilians to guard their secrets."

Damien winced, finally turning to face his King again.

This was an office none but the Mage-King's closest confidantes saw. Hidden safely away from the planet below and paneled with wood brought from Earth, it had originally been the office of the High Matriarch of the Eugenicists, from which that woman had led the plans and schemes that had conquered Mars, triggered a century-long war and created Mage-kind.

And killed somewhere between five and ten million people along the way. They had a rough idea how many tens of thousands of children had died in Project Olympus, the crash force-breeding program that had created the Mages and rediscovered the Gift. The numbers who had died in the War and in the purges of Mars's civilian population...were even vaguer.

But it was a comfortable, quiet office with full modern electronics, tucked away from the hustle and bustle of the Mountain. Here was where the Mage-King of Mars worked in private.

"I promised Meir I would protect her," Damien told Alexander.

"And you wouldn't be the man you are, who I value at my right hand, if you didn't regret failing to keep that promise," his King agreed. "I'd have rather we saved her myself—it appeared she was innocent of most of the Keepers' crimes—but do not *forget* those crimes occurred. They made themselves our enemy, Damien."

The tone of command was unmistakable, and Damien bowed his head in acquiescence.

"I've spent the last couple of weeks trying desperately to find one of them...*any* of them alive so that we could get our answers," he admitted. "I forgot the larger picture."

"It happens, but we need to be careful of it," Alexander warned. "Our job is to see the picture most people are too mired in the day-to-day to catch. Getting lost in the details is a risk we need to watch for."

Damien nodded slowly, turning back to look out over the Mountain again. In the far distance, down the rocky slope, he could make out the glow of Olympus City in the setting sun.

"Twenty Augments," he said. "Fully implanted, fully functional, combat-grade cyborgs on Mars."

"Are we sure they're Legatan?" Alexander asked carefully.

"Not one hundred percent, not yet," Damien admitted. "They're being autopsied as we speak and the hardware examined. We will know with certainty by morning."

"Good. If they are..." he trailed off.

"We also have a prisoner," Damien pointed out. "Dr. Nguyen has him in emergency surgery, but I understand that he should pull through."

"I want you to handle the interrogation personally," Alexander told him. "What we can get out of that man could change everything."

"Just the confirmed presence of a secret cell of Legatan Augments on Mars, caught in an act of terrorism, changes everything," Damien replied.

"Agreed. Prepare your charges, Damien. One way or another, you're going to get your Inquest."

It was almost midnight by the time Dr. Vinh Nguyen finished his work and stepped out of the operating room, a nurse stripping his gloves off into a disposal bag as the door closed behind him. He glanced around him at the hulking forms of their prisoner's guards in exosuit armor and made a displeased grunt.

Two Royal Guardsman and two Marine Combat Mages, all in full armor, stood sentinel outside the OR. There would be no chances taken with a Legatan Augment. The Protectorate's information on the cybernetics those men and women had installed was sparse, but Damien knew their reputation.

The Augments were Mage-killers. That was what they had been created to do. Trained to do. In many cases, they'd been *raised* to do it from an early age.

"How is our friend?" Damien asked.

"He's going to survive," Nguyen replied. "At least for now," he added, looking at the armored guardians. "Is this really necessary, my lord?"

"That man is a combat-grade cyborg we caught in the middle of an act of terrorism," the Hand replied. "He's in no danger of execution, but the precautions are very necessary."

Nguyen snorted.

"Not as much as you think, my lord," he told Damien. "I don't have the codes or enough knowledge of his hardware to do any partial shutdowns of his implants, Montgomery. I had to shut down the whole suite, and his body is dependent on them."

"How bad?" Damien asked, wincing at the thought.

"He'll be blind and partially paralyzed until I either *get* enough software codes or comfort with the hardware to bring at least his eyes and basic limb supports back online," Nguyen said flatly. "He's going to be unconscious for at least six more hours, during which I plan on going over the autopsy results from his friends.

"Continued sensory deprivation of a prisoner is *illegal*, my lord Hand, and for good reason."

"I know. And I want him alive and sane," Damien agreed. "I need to speak to him as soon as possible."

"That'll be in the morning," the doctor told him. "The remaining spells to heal his injuries will take six hours to work, and I'll need to check him over again before I'm prepared to sign off on even questions, let alone interrogation."

"Our time is limited. There was a Mage with them who escaped."

Nguyen held up a hand.

"I'm not being obstructionist here, my lord," he pointed out. "He may be a criminal—a murderer—but he remains my patient and *you* want him alive to question.

"So, give me my time," he insisted. "He'll be better able to answer your questions then."

"All right, Doctor," Damien allowed. "But the situation may change," he warned. "This remains...fluid. We may need to ask him questions sooner rather than later."

"I will inform you as soon as he is ready."

Damien's dreams continually replayed Eleanor Meir's death, intermingled with Charlotte Ndosi's death. Neither woman had had the opportunity to forgive or condemn him for their deaths in real life, but that didn't stop their dream avatars informing him it was his fault.

Over and over and over again.

It was a relief when an alarm finally jerked him awake. The buzzer rang several times before he managed to pull himself out of bed and accept an audio-only channel.

"Montgomery."

"Our Augment friend is awake," Nguyen told him. "I've checked him over; he's in about as good health as you can expect from someone who was shot four times and has had a pervasive set of cybernetics disabled."

"Is he talking?" Damien asked.

"Not really," the doctor admitted. "I don't think he's as groggy as he's pretending to be, though. Assessing the situation. Clever bastard."

"It will take me at least half an hour to get down there," Damien told him. The Mountain was huge, and he needed to shower the fear sweat off.

"That's fine; I want to poke at a few of these systems with a live subject, make sure he's actually as intact as I think he is."

"Be careful, Doctor."

"At least one of your armored mountains has been in there with him since he woke up," Nguyen replied. "I am aware of the threat, my lord, I'll be careful."

"Good," Damien told him, then paused before turning off the channel. "Did the autopsies on the other Augments get finished?"

"Yes," the doctor said crisply. "Legatan. No question about it. It's black parts, no serial numbers, no identifiers, but it's all Legatan hardware, Legatan surgery practices...the samples we've taken agree.

"Your mystery men were Legatan Augment Commandos," Nguyen confirmed flatly.

Damien sighed.

"Thank you, Doctor," he told Nguyen. "It's what I expected. It's even what I needed. But damned if I didn't hope it might be something else."

Not that something else would have changed anything, he supposed. They knew what was going on; all he needed was enough proof to justify an Inquest to tear apart a planetary government.

Those corpses in Nguyen's morgue were that proof.

Showered, dressed in a clean suit, and with Romanov, Samara and two Secret Service bodyguards in tow, Damien arrived at Nguyen's hospital exactly on the half-hour mark he'd given the doctor.

Security had tightened even further since the previous night, with a squad of exosuited Marines blocking the entrance into the hospital complex from the main traffic corridors. They took a moment to scan Damien and his people's ID to be safe, even though they clearly knew who Damien was.

"We appreciate your patience, my lord," the Sergeant told Damien once they were done. "Orders from on high said to be extremely careful."

"Those orders were mine, Sergeant, or near enough as makes no difference," he replied with a grin. "Carry on."

With a nod, the Marine stepped back and waved Damien and his party through. Dr. Nguyen and a pair of nurses were waiting on the other side, the nurses looking intimidated by the sudden appearance of armored Marines everywhere.

"My lord," Nguyen greeted him. "We moved the prisoner to a secure ward before we let him wake up. If you'll follow me?"

"Has he spoken at all?" Damien asked.

"Nothing," the doctor replied. "He's aware of us, reacts to our tests and can clearly hear us. I could tell that even if I didn't have electrodes in his brain to monitor his hardware.

"He is capable of hearing and speech; he is just choosing not to speak," Nguyen continued. "I've also detected at least half a dozen attempts to activate not only his entire implant suite but multiple secondary suites, two of which we didn't even know were there!"

"Has he had any luck?"

"If he'd successfully activated *anything*, I wouldn't be letting you in the same room as him," the doctor said flatly. "Right now, he's conscious and aware but mostly helpless."

"I don't necessarily trust *helpless*," Damien replied dryly. "Guard in the room?"

"Yes, my lord."

"Leave him there. Denis, join me."

"Yes, my lord."

Damien and Romanov stepped into the undecorated recovery room together, though the bodyguard quickly split off to join the exosuited Royal Guardsman against the wall. The door slid shut behind them, locking to impose a further measure of security on the recovery ward at the heart of the main fortress of the Protectorate's government.

The man on the bed looked far less intimidating and dangerous than he had the previous night. With wires and pads attached to half a dozen points on his body and multiple taped-down sections of gauze covering sewn-shut bullet wounds, the impression was more frailty than danger.

That impression, Damien suspected, was false. Blind and injured, the prisoner was still likely more dangerous than most people on the planet.

He checked the screens on the wall and smiled.

"I know you're awake and that you're aware I'm here," he told the prisoner as he grabbed a chair. "I'm hoping you can answer some questions for me."

The prisoner said nothing.

"My name is Damien Montgomery," Damien said. "I suspect you've heard of me—you are, after all, a Legatan Augment on Mars."

That got a reaction, though still only really visible on the monitors behind the man.

Damien waited patiently, sitting and watching the strange man who'd tried to kill him.

"I don't have to tell you anything," the prisoner finally rasped out. "You fuckers took my eyes."

"That is not true," Damien replied. "Your implants are disabled because we can't tell the difference between your combat implants and the ones your body has grown dependent on. There are very few military-grade cyberneticists on Mars. They're coming," he noted, "but they aren't here yet."

He studied the prisoner carefully.

"Now, if you were a prisoner of war, you wouldn't have to tell me anything beyond your name, rank, and serial number," he told the man. "But since we're not at war with Legatus, that leaves you in a messy position.

"You're a civil prisoner, one caught in the act of terrorism," Damien concluded flatly. "That's one of the few things Mars dusts the death penalty off for, though we probably won't in this case.

"Just that you're here is going to cause Legatus all kinds of problems," he continued. "You could answer my questions and perhaps give the bastard who left you to swing against a Hand some problems too, or you can let him get away. I'm still going to hang your government out to dry for your actions either way."

He smiled grimly.

"So, how about that name and rank, soldier?" he demanded.

The silence stretched on for at least a minute, and then the Augment sighed.

"My team?"

"All dead, I'm sorry," Damien told him. "We were trying to rescue Meir; taking prisoners among her murderers wasn't a priority."

The cyborg sighed again, a long, slow exhalation.

"That was her name, was it? Meir?"

"Eleanor Meir. You didn't even know her damned name?" Damien asked.

"Didn't know shit. Fucker showed up with the right authentication codes for full command authority, then treated us like mushrooms. Go here, kill this person. Blew twenty years of pre-work."

Twenty years. The Legatans had been moving against the Protectorate for *twenty years*. It was worse than Damien had been afraid of.

"What's your name, soldier?"

"Major Adrian Kody," the Legatan admitted. "Legatan Augment Corps. No point lying; you've got me wired up six ways to Sunday, and if you've taken any of my men apart, you already knew that."

"LMID?" Damien asked.

"Fuck me," he said with a wince, but didn't confirm or deny it.

"All right, Major Kody. What was your team even doing on Mars?"

"That's classified," Kody told Damien, then laughed, his chuckles rapidly degrading into coughing fits.

When the coughing faded, he shook his head.

"Water?"

Damien carefully filled a plastic cup and placed it in Kody's hand. His fingers trembled weakly, but the cyborg managed to drink and then pass the cup back.

"Look, Montgomery," he finally said. "I have no illusions that just the fact you took me alive means a lot of my government's plans are about to blow up in their faces, but I swore an oath and I owe a duty. I'll give you everything I know on Kay, but I won't betray Legatus."

"Fair enough," Damien allowed. As Kody had admitted, he didn't *need* the Augment to tell him much more than who he was—and anything the man gave him on this "Kay" could be hung on Legatus as well. "How about we start with who 'Kay' is?"

"I don't actually know," Kody replied. "I didn't even know he was a Mage, though I knew he had to be associated with the people whose safehouses we were busting open—all too many of which were Mages."

The cyborg shook his head.

"He showed up...two weeks past now. Had the identification codes, the passphrases, the encryption keys—everything he needed to prove that he was our new control." Kody sighed. "I don't even think they were faked or we were fooled. He got them from our commanders; he was legitimately our new control.

"His objectives were just...so far out of line from what I was expecting. I didn't know why we'd be using Augments for the job, until the first time he sent us after a Mage. He had a lot of data on the people we were going after. He knew where the safehouses were, what the codes were... I presume they were some kind of undercover group, and he had to have been one of them."

"Were you paying attention to the news?" Damien asked.

Kody stared blankly off into space for a moment, then chuckled—which again reduced him to coughing. Damien gave him the water again, and he slowly recovered.

"Shot in the fucking lung," the Augment grumped. "Even your Mage healer can't do much for that."

He paused thoughtfully.

"I hadn't put together the pieces," he admitted. "Should have. The odds that someone *else* was going around wiping out the survivors of a covert conspiracy were pretty low, huh?"

"Yeah. You were taking down the Keepers. Far too damned successfully for my tastes."

"That's life," the Legatan Major said bluntly. "We aren't friends, Montgomery. I may not like Kay or what he asked me to do, but he had the right codes to give me orders, which means my bosses signed off on it and I'll shed no tears for your troubles."

How many of the galaxy's problems, Damien wondered, would be solved if people didn't blindly follow orders?

"And then he teleported out and left you to face a Hand," Damien concluded. "Any idea where he'd have gone?"

"From what he'd said, he had a ship in orbit," Kody replied. "He'd have teleported up there and fled the system. He's long gone, Montgomery. At least if he's got half a brain, anyway, and much as I hate the bastard's guts, he might have been the smartest man I've ever met."

The blinded Augment shook his head.

"You aren't going to catch him. But I got a bone to throw you, if you've anything to offer me."

Damien smiled grimly.

"Right now, Major, you can't even see," he pointed out. "I can easily claim necessity and leave your implants disabled. I don't *need* to call in those cybernetics experts to help us get you functional without being a threat."

Kody coughed.

"Like you said, we aren't friends," Damien echoed.

"Fair," Kody admitted. "Should have known better than to fuck with Darth Montgomery. Kay had the codes but I didn't trust him. I checked him out. I know where his apartment was."

Ignoring the blatant attempt to push his buttons, Damien leaned forward.

"Address, Major, and we'll see about getting at least some of your implants back online," he promised. "*If* you're cooperative."

"I'll play nice," the Legatan told him. "If I'm going to spend the rest of my life in a Martian cell, I'd like to at least be able to see."

CHAPTER 26

THE APARTMENT was in Asimov, a city at the almost exact opposite side of the planet from Olympus Mons. It was a smaller city, built around an air and space transit hub that primarily moved the products of the agricultural fields that stretched as far as the eye could see in every direction around it.

Like any city, it had long grown beyond its original single industry with malls and lawyers and blocks of apartments for the low- and mid-wage employees who kept the service industries running. There were also nicer condo and apartment buildings for the higher-wage employees, but the address that Kody gave Damien didn't take them to one of those buildings.

The building "Kay" had been based out of was a rundown ten-story apartment building that looked like it dated back to the original colonization, built of concrete with smaller windows and obvious marks where airlocks had been changed out for normal doors.

They landed the assault shuttle at the nearest police station, trying to not be *overly* obvious, and were met by a trio of worried-looking women in black police uniforms.

"I am Lieutenant Jeanette Wong," the front woman told Damien. "We weren't warned you were coming, my lord; how may we assist you?"

"Hopefully, we won't need you to do much," he told her with a smile. "I'll need to borrow vehicles for myself and a detail of ten, six of them in exosuit armor."

Wong blinked in surprise but nodded slowly.

"We have a van for our tactical team that should fit six in exosuits," she said after a moment. "We can lend you a couple of unmarked squad cars as well, but the van is marked."

"That will do nicely," he replied. "I apologize for dropping in on you without prior warning, Lieutenant. The situation we are dealing with is fluid, and I'm not sure of the level of danger to the surrounding area.

"I will need you to be standing by for potential evacuations," he continued. "I *hope* not to need you, but the risk is present."

Kay had so far proven willing to accept massive collateral damage in pursuit of his objectives. Damien expected there to be some kind of suicide or self-destruct in the apartment. He was just hoping they could disarm it.

Wong looked uncomfortable.

"My lord, this is a quiet precinct in a quiet city," she said slowly. "I only have about thirty officers on duty and maybe a hundred more I can call up. How large of an evacuation are we talking?"

"At least one apartment building, more likely the entire block," Damien told her. "Call in officers from other precincts if you need them, Lieutenant; you have my authority for that."

She nodded.

"How long do I have, my lord?"

"We're moving out straight away," he said gently. "If I'm reading the navigation software correctly, fifteen minutes?"

Wong swallowed.

"I'll have Sergeant Lindt here show you the vehicles, then," she said, gesturing at one of the women following her forward, "while I go call my fellow precinct heads."

The apartment building didn't look any better in person than it had in the pictures or as they flew over. It was a bleak structure that radiated a hopelessness Damien wasn't used to feeling in the cities of Mars, a generally wealthy planet with a capable safety net.

Arriving in three police vehicles didn't even appear to draw attention from the sparse crowds other than a clear, if subtle, growing distance between the marked van and the scattered individuals on the pathways.

That retreat became far more obvious when Romanov's exosuited Marines exited the tactical van. This was a rundown area used to seeing cops...but it was still a quiet city. Even if it hadn't been, exosuits weren't a tool used by police—they were designed for space boardings and major battles, not arrests and traffic control.

The streets emptied and Damien shook his head as they approached the doors to the apartment building.

"He probably isn't here," he told his detail, "but let's be sure he doesn't make it out if he is. Romanov, have your people cover the exits. If you see the bastard, ping me *before* you engage," he ordered. "We don't want any of you going head to head with a Combat Mage without myself or Romanov backing you up, clear?"

"Yes, my lord."

A wave of the golden hand of Damien's office over the door panel opened the locks. The small icon contained electronics that could, in theory, override every electronic system in the Protectorate. Their actual reach was not quite that complete but was still terrifying to anyone aware of it.

"Sixth floor," he noted. "Watch the elevator, but I think we're taking the stairs."

If nothing else, very few elevators were rated to pack in multiple exosuits.

Damien left checking for technological traps to the capable sensors in his bodyguards' armor and reached out with his own unique senses, looking for magical artifacts, traps or other surprises. There was nothing in the stairwell, at least.

"The building security cameras have been penetrated," Romanov warned him. "By...well, probably every person with less-than-good intentions in a ten-kilometer radius. These systems are not secure.

"Relevant to our interests, though, is that a live feed is being run to a secondary system in the apartment we're heading to."

"Can we spoof it?"

"Already done," the Marine replied. "The shunt was run with Corps software, though," he warned. "Absolute top-of-the-line stuff."

"I'm not surprised," Damien told him. "I'm not sure who this 'Kay' is, but he is definitely a Combat Mage, which leads me to assume Marine."

"There are other people who train Combat Mages," Romanov pointed out. Then he sighed. "Of course, the Marines train the *best* Combat Mages, so you're probably right."

There were no surprises until they reached the sixth floor, but Damien stopped as they were about to exit the stairwell, studying a new feeling in the air.

"Wait," he ordered.

He looked around. He could *feel* magic, but he couldn't see anything immediate. Studying the door leading into the sixth floor, he made sure it was clear, then moved his Sight across the wall.

"Here. Romanov, can you cut the wall open along these lines?" Damien drew a rough square on the wall with his own magic, turning the concrete black.

"Done." The deadly blade concealed in the exosuit's arm served well for rough-and-ready demolition work, and the chunk of wall easily slid out into Damien's hands.

At some point, the wall had been hollowed out from the other side, and the piece of wall he now held had been inlaid with silver runes—runes woven into a spell that was confused by its movement but still functional.

Damien studied it, tracing its lines of power and then shivering slightly as he concluded its purpose.

"Subtle," he noted. "This is looking for someone in an exosuit to go down the hallway on the other side of the door."

"I guess he figured Marines would come after him eventually," Romanov noted. "What does it do if it finds an exosuit?"

"Disintegrates everything in the corridor," the Hand said shortly. "Exosuits, unarmored companions, any poor neighbors who happen to be in the way...gone."

With a slash of power, he carefully severed six key connections, disabling the spell and safely releasing the energy it contained.

"Not going to happen," he continued. "But let's move very carefully as we go further. This was a nasty piece of work, and I'm betting it was only his first line of defense."

The hallway itself proved safe to traverse, with the strange Mage not having left any traps that interfered with his neighbors' lives. The apartment wasn't an end or corner unit, either, which appeared to have prevented Kay from setting up any more traps.

It was the middle unit on the north side, and as soon as Damien reached the door and began to study it, he knew they had a problem.

Magic had been woven across the interior of the door and onto the walls, a floor-to-ceiling network of runic chains that encased the entire apartment in a solid shell of magic that must have taken months of painstaking work, likely done over years and years, to establish.

"This was not a temporary safehouse," Damien said quietly. "I think the entire outer shell of the unit is covered in runes—warning, fire, disintegration. If we open the door without the right token, the entire unit explodes. If we break the rune matrix anywhere else..." He studied the magic as best as he could without being able to see the runes, then shook his head.

"If we break the runes anywhere else, the entire unit explodes," he concluded. "I can't be sure how badly, but I'm guessing the building wouldn't survive."

"It's an old building; they built them tough," Romanov pointed out.

"I was allowing for that," Damien replied. "We're talking barely subnuclear level explosion. Putting this together took a long time and a lot of skill. Less skill, but more time, if someone else wrote the matrix and the Mage doing the work was following instructions."

He shook his head.

"Breaking down the door or coming in through the balcony aren't options," he concluded. "I *want* whatever is inside this apartment intact, which means I don't want it turning into a goddamn bomb."

"So, we can go no further?" Samara asked, the Inspector studying the plain-looking door. "Even if we were to give up on this investigation here, it sounds like this bomb is not something we can safely leave for others to discover by accident."

"It's not," Damien agreed. "But I can't disarm it without be able to actually *see* the runes. The spell is linked to some kind of physical token, I think. Without it, I'm not sure we can get in safely at all."

"Would he have come here after fleeing the Keeper safehouse?" Samara asked. "Could he have teleported directly here?"

"The token wouldn't register from inside the teleport," Damien said absently as he stared at the runes. "He probably went straight to orbit."

"So, he would have to teleport to the hallway and come through the door?" Romanov asked.

"Or would the spell check for the token once he was inside?" Samara said.

Damien looked up at his companions and chuckled.

"That kind of check is complicated," he told them. "It can only do it when the matrix is activated by, say, having the door opened. So, either he would have to teleport to here and go through the door, or..."

"This defense might not stop a teleportation spell," Samara concluded.

"There might be other defenses for that instance," he warned. "But it's our best shot." He shook his head. "That said, I think we're going to need that evacuation we had Wong preparing for. *I* might be able to survive this going off if I'm ready for it, but the neighborhood won't."

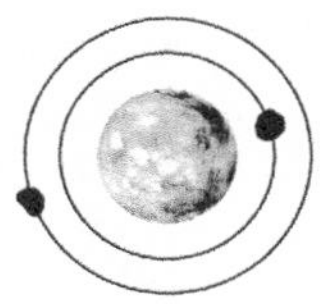

CHAPTER 27

FOUR HOURS LATER, with a police perimeter set up two blocks out and every living thing in that radius evacuated, Damien Montgomery teleported into the center of the apartment safehouse. He froze, remaining completely still as he wrapped the most powerful shields he could conjure around himself.

Nothing happened.

When nothing continued to happen, he released a breath and took a look around. He nonetheless kept most of his body very still as he swept the plain living room with his Sight, seeking the traps and defenses he was almost certain were there.

There was nothing. The outside defenses remained and he could see the silver inlay of the runes that covered every exterior wall of the apartment, but the interior was empty. No runes. No technological traps registered by the scanner harness Romanov had insisted on.

Nothing.

He stood in the middle of a cheaply-furnished apartment, with furniture of the type that inevitably had Swedish names. A small kitchenette occupied one side, sliding doors—with silver runes etched into the glass—led to a small balcony and an open door led into a similarly-furnished bedroom.

If it wasn't for the runes he could see etched on the walls, the apartment would have been completely mundane.

Now, at least, Damien could actually see the runes themselves, not just feel the flow through the walls. Kay had clearly known Damien was a Rune Wright, but now Damien wondered if that had been accounted for when he'd built this safehouse.

No one except a Rune Wright would have been able to detect the defenses from outside. It was even possible that the Keepers didn't realize that a Rune Wright *could* do that; it wasn't an aspect of his abilities that even most of his fellow Hands were aware of.

If Kay hadn't known that, then he might have assumed that even Damien would try to come through the door when they hadn't detected any technological traps—and without proper preparation, the spell matrix that currently surrounded him could easily have killed him.

Now that he was inside it, however, he could see the runes themselves. A regular Mage, trained in reading and modifying Martian Runic, could have read through the matrix and carefully calculated the points to severe it to render it safe.

It would take days to weeks, but it was doable.

Damien, however, studied the flows of magic through the silver and slashed out with his magic after a few minutes. The matrix was complex, intentionally woven to prevent it being broken in only a handful of places...but a few dozen severed links later and the wall around the door was safe.

Another few minutes and the kitchen was safe. Then the balcony door.

Then he *carefully* stepped into the bedroom and safed the last wall, and checked to be sure that the wall and floor matrices were disabled by the removal of the rest.

Finally able to breathe comfortably, he opened a channel to his staff.

"From the lack of explosion, I'm guessing things went according to plan?" Romanov asked.

"So far, so good," Damien agreed. "The matrix is disabled, the energy bled off. The apartment should be safe to enter." He looked around. "I'm not seeing much in terms of paperwork, but there's a wall screen and attached console if nothing else. Hopefully, Samara and her people can pull something out of it."

"If he used it at all, we'll get *something*," the MIS Inspector promised. "We'll be there in five minutes."

Damien very carefully did not touch anything while his investigators and forensics people were on their way, inspecting the plain apartment judiciously after opening the front door.

There really wasn't much to it. It wasn't entirely obvious that this wasn't somewhere heavily lived in—some people simply had austere tastes—but the complete lack of *any* kind of entertainment or personal effects in the one-bedroom suite was definitely a hint.

Other than the runes that had encased the entire unit in magical defenses, there was no more magic or runework in the apartment. Whoever Kay was, he apparently wasn't the type to make a dozen small magical items to handle minor conveniences.

"Huh. This isn't quite what I was expecting," Samara admitted as she strode through the door, a trio of gloved forensics techs on her heels. "I mean, I wasn't expecting a slaughterhouse with plastic on the floors or anything, but this is so..."

"Mundane?" Damien suggested. "This guy is responsible for a lot of death and destruction, including two people he's killed right in front of me. Feels like his home should have a few more skulls and spikes."

The head-scarfed investigator chuckled and turned to her techs.

"Roland, check the bedroom," she snapped. "Biological samples, fingerprints, the works. If he's slept here, we should be able to pull enough to identify him from the RMMC records.

"Aristides, you've got the console and the wallscreen," she continued. "Strip the drives, strip the records. I want to know every file he's looked at on the device and every call he's made. Assume he's wiped them, start on the deep layers.

"Ylka, start in the kitchen and move out from there. General sampling, testing, and checking. Books, cereal brands, anything you can find, tag it for analysis."

The techs split to their assigned chores, and Damien saw Romanov slip through the door after the MIS people.

"We've relaxed the perimeter and allowed people back into most of the buildings," the Marine told them. "I'm keeping this building locked down, regular cops on the ground floor and Marines and Secret Service on this one. We have orbital fire support and a drop battalion standing by if things go sideways."

"That shouldn't be necessary at this point," Damien replied.

"I agree," Romanov said, "but I'm not standing them down until you're back in the damned Mountain, my lord. We almost lost you once; I will *not* risk that happening again. I am not explaining to His Majesty that I let you get killed."

Damien gestured around the empty apartment.

"I'm in so much danger from the cheap Swedish furniture," he replied. "I quiver in the expensive shoes the Chancellor bought me."

"Just because we know there are no more traps here doesn't mean Kay doesn't have an alert for a sniper to set up across the way if someone goes into his apartment!" his bodyguard snapped. "My job is to keep you alive. Don't make it harder than you have to."

With a sigh, Damien nodded, stepping carefully out of the line of sight from the window.

"Fair enough, Denis," he allowed. "I'm not trying to be difficult."

"If you were trying to be difficult, I'd quit," the Marine told him bluntly. "I have to let you do things like teleport into the middle of a *bomb*. I *don't* have to stand down your backup when you're still in a hazard zone."

"We're not leaving until Samara's people have finished taking this place apart."

"Then the Navy and the Corps are on standby until then."

"Most of what we're doing here is just sampling," Samara warned Damien as they waited in the hallway. "It'll take time in the lab—hours, if not days—for us to be able to pull anything from the deep layers of storage on the wallscreen or to ID him from the biological samples he'll have left behind. There isn't going to be a magic bullet here, my lord. There's not much point in you waiting around."

"There's also not much point in my being anywhere else," Damien pointed out. "But I know. I'm not expecting miracles."

"If he is—or even was—a Marine, we'll know who he was pretty quickly," she promised. "I'm not sure how much that will help us, but we'll be able to ID him."

"Knowing who he is helps a lot," he noted. "It gives us a starting point for where he may have been recruited. It'll also tell us where he was assigned if he was still on active duty—twenty Combat Mages died in the Archive and we haven't had them come up missing on any of the Mars bases yet.

"So, they had to be assigned somewhere, and somewhere where they haven't been reported missing yet," he concluded. "I want to know what that assignment is, because it gives us somewhere to look for other Keepers we might have missed."

"Ma'am, my lord," Aristides Ferro stepped out of the apartment. "You need to see this."

"You found something?" Samara asked.

"Most of it was wiped," the tech confirmed as he led them back into the room. "I pulled full copies of everything on the disks before I touched anything, so we should be able to retrieve at least something later on."

Picking up the long black box of electronics he had linked into the half-dismantled wallscreen, Ferro smiled.

"The official recording functions were disabled, but a call was relayed through this unit shortly before the incident in Olympus City."

"If it was relayed, was anything saved here?" Damien asked.

"No, but I had enough metadata to trace the call in the planetary net buffers," the tech replied. "We were lucky. Another few hours and we'd only have been able to retrieve fragments."

"You got the call?" Damien knew that the data buffers that fed a planetwide communication network held and processed a *lot* of data, and bits of it inevitably—and, he understood, somewhat intentionally—ended up being held for as much as twenty-four to forty-eight hours afterwards.

"Most of it, I think," Ferro confirmed. "I haven't played it; I figured you'd want to see."

"Show me," Damien ordered.

The tech tapped a command on his unit and the wallscreen turned on with the image of a pale-skinned, eerily tall man. He wasn't speaking, so presumably the voice that started was Kay's.

"...not my problem if your people stuffed their heads into a meat grinder," he was saying. "All we promised you was ships and guns."

"You would break your sworn word to the Stone and the Void, the Alpha and the Omega?" the man in the image demanded. His voice sounded familiar to Damien, gravelly with the leftovers of vacuum exposure. "We have been betrayed before; we will not tolerate it again, 'Nemesis'."

The image reduced to static for a few moments, and Ferro shook his head when Damien looked at him. That part was lost.

"...provided the ships," Kay was saying when the video returned. "We gave you the target. We didn't have the timing of the Hand's trip in advance."

"The guns you gave us were worse than useless! He turned them on our own ships!"

"He's a fucking *Hand*. I warned you what the limitations of those toys were, 'Alpha'." More static. "...bullied. We are allies, nothing more."

"I need replacement ships and guns," the asteroid miner snapped. "I can find men, but without ships and guns, they can do nothing."

"I'll see what I can do," Kay told him.

"You lie," the other man replied. "Like the Nemesis who came before. We are a tool to you! You will see! The Stone and the Void will bring fire such as you have never seen."

The miner smiled coldly.

"You are not our only ally, Nemesis, and your aid not our only sword. You will *learn*."

The screen turned dark.

"That was the end of the message," Ferro reported. "There were significant time gaps as well, but the buffer drops those first as minimum-value content."

"Can you trace the origins?" Damien asked.

The tech paused thoughtfully.

"Yes," he concluded. "The off-planet side would have had to come in via an orbital satellite; we can trace it back and get a vector of origin. It may take some time," he warned.

"Do it," Damien ordered. "If Kay—or 'Nemesis' or whatever name he's using this time—went anywhere in Sol, the BLF appear to be his only remaining allies, however strained the relationship."

"I wouldn't go to them if I were him," Samara said.

"That's what I'm afraid of," he agreed. "That said..." He waved at the screen. "Those people already almost took out a multi-billion-dollar refinery ship. Who knows what they'll try next?

"They know something about Kay, which means I need to go ask them questions. If I happen to neutralize a dangerous terrorist group along the way, I'm not seeing the disadvantage here."

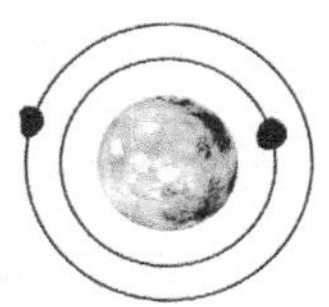

CHAPTER 28

RETURNING TO the Mountain, Damien found himself once again being greeted by a red-armored Royal Guardsman. This time, Dr. Christoffsen was standing with her, and the worried expression on his political advisor's face sent a chill down the Hand's spine.

"Guardsman Han, Doctor," he greeted them warmly as he approached the exit from the landing pad. "The Professor looks like he's seen a ghost." He nodded toward Christoffsen. "What's going on?"

"Nothing good, Damien," his aide replied. "You and I have a meeting with His Majesty in about twenty minutes. Guardsman Han came along to make sure we both made it."

Damien swallowed. That kind of urgency was never a good sign—especially if Christoffsen wasn't willing to give him details.

"The Council?" he asked.

"His Majesty wanted to brief you himself," his aide replied, and Damien nodded.

"All right." He gestured Romanov and Samara to him. "Romanov, you're with me. Samara, get in touch with your people and expedite tracing that location. If I'm not able to go after the BLF, I want enough data to send the Navy after them."

"Of course, my lord," she replied. "I'll make it happen."

His bodyguard stepped up beside him in silence and Damien turned back to Christoffsen.

"All right, Professor. Lead the way."

He wasn't sure if it was a good sign or a bad one that Guardsman Han led them to the very top of the Mountain, to the Mage-King's private office. At least whatever was going on wasn't, yet, a public affair.

Han led Damien and his two companions into the office and then stepped back against the wall. Desmond Michael Alexander the Third stood against the window, his hands crossed behind his back as the gaunt man, seeming far older than he usually did, stared out over the Martian surface.

"Han, Romanov, Christoffsen," Alexander said slowly. "Leave us."

Apparently, the appointment wasn't to include Damien's political advisor after all. In this room, there was no question of authority. Damien's staff bowed their way out after the armored Guardsman, letting the door close behind them and leaving the Hand alone with his King.

Alexander continued to stare out the window in silence for a long time, and for the first time since he'd met his King, it truly sank in to Damien just how *old* the ruler of humanity was. He was well into his second century and had ruled the Protectorate for over three times as long as Damien had been alive.

"My liege?" he said questioningly.

"I have no answers for you, Damien," Alexander said quietly to the window. "Only warnings and premonitions of the end of an era. It is not given, even to my bloodline, to see the future or the past with true clarity."

Damien wasn't sure just what the King was talking about, so he waited in silence.

"I have...journals," the Mage-King continued, "written by my grandfather. Not all of them—he wrote them for most of his life but destroyed many to prevent even his heirs knowing his true thoughts.

"But I know that he wove magic to try and see into the future, to predict the consequences of his actions and guide the creation of the Charter and the nation it defined."

Alexander shook his head.

"Even if his journals hadn't told me he failed, I would have guessed by where we ended up," he concluded. "I can see the logic behind every piece of the Compact and the Charter, and yet the very documents that define the nation I am sworn to rule and defend lay out the fracture lines that will inevitably destroy it.

"No caste system or aristocracy has survived the centuries with its power intact. Humanity kneels poorly as a whole. Setting the Mages apart was necessary to protect them then, but it created the threat we face now."

"My lord?" Damien questioned again.

"Maybe we could have changed things safely when I became King," Alexander told him. "Perhaps my father could have slowly reshaped the Protectorate over his life. I fear it's too late now. The Protectorate will not be reborn around a conference table. I fear the reforms we need will now be bought with blood."

"My liege," Damien repeated, "you've lost me. What's going on?"

Alexander leaned his head against the window, not glass but magically transmuted steel, and exhaled a long sigh.

"The Council of the Protectorate has formally requested that I appear before them," he replied. "While I have been given no official notification of what they want, there are enough loyalists among the Councilors that I know nonetheless.

"Those who would make the Council a formal legislature have made the alliance we feared with the UnArcana worlds. You are a hero who has saved the Protectorate, but they intend to condemn you and demand your resignation—not truly for your actions but because they see an opportunity to weaken the Mountain."

"This is not the only way I can serve," Damien pointed out quietly, watching his King slump against the window with concern. "If I resign, it would short—"

"*No*," Alexander snapped. "I will *not* be dictated to, Damien Montgomery. I will not watch these men and women tear down a man who has saved the Protectorate again and again for their own power."

"My liege," Damien replied. "I serve because I choose to. You did not conscript me. You did not force me to this. You cannot force me to remain."

The tiny office was silent.

"You had a breakthrough on the Keepers?" Alexander asked him.

"On their murderer, at least," he admitted. "Others can follow up. The Belt Liberation Front is tied into this mess, but...the Navy can deal with them. I've prepared the case for the Inquest. Another Hand can serve."

Slowly, with hands that seemed they could not believe what they were doing, Damien unclasped the golden icon of his office.

"My liege, I swore an oath to serve the people, the Protectorate and you," he reminded Alexander. "In that order."

"I do not accept your resignation," the Mage-King said stiffly, coldly. "I *will not*."

"You cannot force me to serve," Damien repeated, laying the golden hand on his King's desk. "And there are a thousand thousand other ways I can serve the people and the Protectorate. I will not be the wedge on which our nation breaks."

Alexander still refused to face him, staring out at Mars.

"You are a better man than I deserve," he told Damien. "May I ask, then, one last service?"

"You remain my King."

"Follow this case to the end," Alexander ordered. "Bear my Voice if not my Hand into the Belt and deal with those who have brought fire and blood to this system.

"Then come to Ceres. If I cannot deny you this sacrifice, then I will by all that is divine shove it down those self-righteous bastards' throats!"

Damien sighed but bowed.

"As you command, my King."

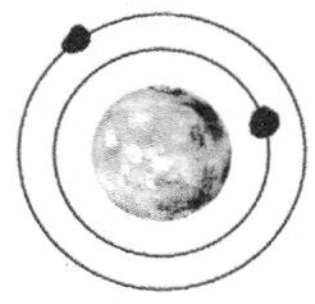

CHAPTER 29

DESPITE ITS dense circuits and weight of responsibility, the golden hand wasn't a particularly heavy object. Damien had grown used to its presence on his chest, but he would never have expected the absence of the small icon to be as obvious as it was.

He left Alexander's office with a folded piece of parchment in the breast pocket of his suit, but that hardly made up for the absence of the golden hand of his now former office. He'd known—or at least been afraid—that it could come to this, but he didn't truly have any plans for what happened next.

Romanov and Christoffsen were waiting for him. The ex-Governor noticed first, his gaze dropping to Damien's chest before he inhaled in shock.

"My lord," Romanov greeted Damien, then fell silent. Something in Damien's expression told him something was wrong.

"Not *my lord* anymore," Damien told him. "I have resigned my Hand. Just...Damien now, I think."

Both men fell in beside him as he continued out in the hallway, waiting in silence for him to get his thoughts in order.

"What happens now?" Christoffsen finally asked as they reached the transit system, a network of trams and elevators that linked the entire immense complex inside Olympus Mons together.

"I have a Royal Warrant," Damien told them. "Denis, you and Munira remain under my command for the moment. I'm charged to complete my investigations into the Keepers, this 'Kay', and the Belt Liberation Front."

He shook his head.

"And that's...it," he concluded. "I don't know what happens after that yet. Robert...your task is complete, I think. I am...beyond grateful for all you have done for me."

"I'm sorry," Christoffsen told him. "That's it, then?"

"His Majesty's sources confirmed it," Damien replied. "They were going to ask for my resignation. His Majesty would have refused, so I pre-empted them."

"It's not right," Romanov objected.

"No. It's politics," Damien agreed. "But...sometimes the best service one can provide is to get out of the way. I'd expected to need your services for longer than this when we pulled you from the Marines. I apologize."

"This is not your fault," the Marine said. "I just can't believe it's got this bad."

"His Majesty thinks...that this was set in motion by the Charter itself," Damien admitted. "It's been coming since the beginning. I've only bought time, but it's time I think the Protectorate needs. Time to carry out the Inquest on Legatus, if nothing else.

"I need you until this mess is over," he continued. "We need to go catch up with Samara, see where we're at on tracking the BLF."

He'd be fine so long as he kept working. He'd keep running until he ran out of road.

Damien wasn't quite sure what would happen then.

"What about me?" Christoffsen asked, the political aide looking almost lost.

"I don't know, Robert," Damien admitted with a sigh. "I don't know where I'm going to be in a month. I'm sure His Majesty will have work for you, or you could even retire." He forced a smile. "We all know you've earned a quiet retirement ten times over."

"If I wanted a quiet retirement, Damien, I'd have one," the ex-Governor pointed out. He offered the younger man his hand. "Good luck."

"The same to you," he replied, shaking Christoffsen's hand. "I don't think this mess is over yet, Robert. It's just...no longer my mess."

Returning to the rooms that they'd been using as a command center for the investigation, Damien couldn't help falling into a leaden, fatalistic walk. The decision to resign might have been his, but that didn't mean he liked it.

He couldn't be sure if it was his step, his face, or the lack of the hand that caused Munira Samara to realize there was a problem, but the woman rose almost instantly as he entered.

"My lord?" she said questioningly, and he shook his head.

"Not *my lord* anymore," he echoed his earlier comment to Romanov. "Just...Damien. I've resigned my Hand, Munira. It appears you may have fallen into one of the shortest 'permanent' appointments to a Hand's staff ever."

He shook his head slowly.

"It's a mess and I apologize for dragging you into it," he told her.

"Politics," she replied. "They always mess everything up. What happens now...especially with this?" She gestured at the screen she'd been working on, which was currently showing the network of communication satellites in orbit around Mars.

"His Majesty and I agreed I would see this mission through to the end," Damien explained. "I hold his Voice and Warrant for the next few weeks, until we get this mess resolved. I *want* this bastard."

He sighed and pointed at the screen.

"How are we doing on a vector?" he asked.

"I've got Daniels and Cook on it," she replied. "They're the best I've ever worked with; I'm expecting some kind of answer soon.

"What do we do once we have the location?"

"The same thing we would have done before," Damien replied. "Romanov and I load up our people onto *Akintola* and head out to investigate as quietly as possible. I no longer have true imperium, so we can't coopt the Navy for it, but with Romanov's people, I still have a full Marine company to call on."

He smiled grimly.

"I may no longer bear a Hand, but *I* am no weaker for it," he pointed out. "Between my own power and Romanov's company, I'm confident in our ability to neutralize the Front and convince them to answer my questions."

"And if this 'Kay' is there?" Samara asked.

"I'm confident in my ability to neutralize him and convince him to answer my questions," Damien echoed. "He's been clever and he's been careful, but he's not in my weight class and he knows it."

"I'll make sure we have an interrogation team ready to go as well," the MIS Inspector told him. "If you can get us prisoners, we can make sure you get answers."

"Let's do it right," Damien agreed. "If I only have one last mission for the Mountain, let's make it worth it."

Damien put the final pieces together in the package he was assembling, then stopped and stared at the computer screen. It was horrifying to see it all listed out like this, the neat little notes—at least one from each of the Hands who'd served in the last five years—on atrocity, murder and revolution.

They'd had enough circumstantial evidence to be certain of who was behind the sudden increase in piracy and weapons smuggling for over a year, but while the Charter gave the Protectorate the authority to intern an entire planetary government and investigate their actions, it had *never* been done to a Core World.

To launch an Inquest of this scale, to take Hands and ships and troops into the home system of the UnArcana movement, was to risk civil war. They'd needed ironclad proof, evidence they could lay in front of the Council that would be utterly damning.

Major Kody and his men were the final link, the incontrovertible proof of a Legatus Military Intelligence Directorate operation on Mars itself. A squad of assassins and spies that had unleashed a terror campaign against the people of the Protectorate on the orders of the Legatan government.

That link tied dozens of potential operations back to Legatus. Pirate campaigns. Armed rebellions. Terrorist movements. The complete devastation of not just one or two but a total of *six* secondary outposts.

Over a million dead.

Damien was grimly certain that some of the conflicts and atrocities wouldn't tie back to Legatus in the end. Humanity had enough scum that at least some of the mess would have grown up on its own.

Whoever was sent to Legatus would have to draw that line, between what could truly be blamed on Legatus and what would have been left uncertain. It wouldn't be Damien now, but he knew the men and women who could replace him there.

He didn't necessarily *trust* them entirely anymore—having two of his former fellows attempt to kill him had eroded the unquestioning trust he'd once had for the Hands—but he knew their skills.

The Inquest would be launched now and the Protectorate would have their answers. The dead would have their justice.

Maybe once they had it, the memory of the shattered ruins of the outposts *he'd* failed to save would haunt his dreams a little less.

"My lord!"

Damien jerked awake, only realizing he'd fallen asleep at his desk when Samara's voice echoed into the office.

"My lord, are you all right?" she asked.

"Just Damien now, remember?" he told her, forcing himself upright. Checking the system, he confirmed that he had at least managed to send the package supporting the Inquest to the Mage-King before he'd passed out.

Shaking his head, he turned his gaze on the MIS Inspector. She'd changed at some point since he'd come in there, switching to a navy-blue suit with a plain white headscarf. Her gaze under the scarf was concerned, though she looked tired herself.

"It's habit already, I suppose," she told him. "Are you all right?" she repeated.

"Just tired," he said. "Nightmares. 'Perk' of the job." He sighed. "My old job, I guess."

"Don't go giving up the mantle just yet, Montgomery," she said sharply. "We still need you on top form if we're going to wrap up this mess with the Keepers and Kay and the Front."

With an only-half-forced chuckle, he threw her a salute.

"Yes, ma'am. What have you got for me?"

"We just finished analyzing the vector we got from the coms satellites," Samara told him. "May I?"

She gestured at the display screen. Glancing at it again, Damien wiped the Inquest file from his screen, then unlinked his own PC and allowed her to access the screen.

"To no one's surprise," Samara noted, "the channel was being relayed from the Belt. We think the origin was relatively close, too. We were losing basically all of the time delay in the distortion on the copy we had, but the satellites' records show the inbound was from about five light-minutes away."

"What's there?" Damien asked.

"Officially?" Samara zoomed in on a section of the asteroid belt on the screen to show to him. "Fuck and all. No ships, no stations; there shouldn't have been anything there during the conversation. So, unless the transmitter was somehow faster than light, which is impossible, or confusing the station..."

"Something is there that's not supposed to be," he concluded, studying the screen. "No chance of it being further out?"

"There isn't anything further out along that line until the Kuiper Belt," she pointed out. "And while we were losing time delay, we weren't losing *days'* worth of time delay."

"How close have you narrowed down the locus?" he asked.

"This area." Samara waved at the screen. "We're talking a cylindrical region of space about a million kilometers long by three hundred thousand kilometers wide. It's not small."

"But by deep-space standards, it's nothing," Damien agreed. "Six significant asteroids?"

"Exactly. My guess? The Front is using one of them as a source of water for fuel and oxygen for their little fleet."

Damien studied the rocks in the arc of space she'd picked out. Everything in the analysis made sense to him, which meant one of those chunks of space debris was almost certainly their target.

"Ready to take another flight, Inspector Samara?"

"I think we can make that happen," she agreed.

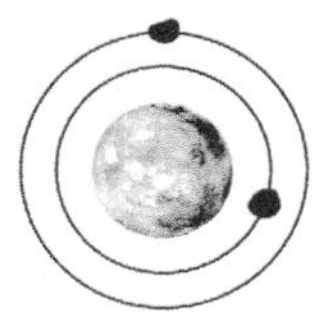

CHAPTER 30

***DOCTOR AKINTOLA'S* BOAT BAY** was already packed full as Damien's pilot neatly squeezed his assault shuttle into the last remaining space. Four Royal Martian Marine Corps assault shuttles already occupied the docking cradles inside the yacht, and the now five deadly small craft crowded a space designed for orbital runabouts and pleasure craft.

The Marine pilots had still managed to leave a clear path to the exit from the boat bay, and at some point between the shuttle touching down and the air and metal outside cooling enough for Damien to exit the spacecraft, the path filled up.

The ex-Hand stepped off the ramp onto *Akintola*'s deck to find himself facing a double file of Martian Marines in dress uniform, stretching from the safety radius around his shuttle to the exit from the bay.

Romanov had been right behind him and had clearly expected this, as neither the Marine nor any of the other occupants of the shuttle ran into Damien's back as he froze, staring at the entire company of men and women drawn up in formation in front of him.

"Company, salute!" a trained parade ground voice bellowed, and the Marines' hands snapped up into perfect salutes.

After two years as a Hand, Damien's response was instinctive as he returned the salute, holding it for a long moment as he struggled to retain some degree of self-control.

"Come on, sir," Romanov whispered from behind him. "We're holding up the line."

The spell somehow broken, Damien dropped his salute and walked forward, passing through the neat rows of saluting Marines as they paid their respects.

"You should have warned me," he whispered back to Romanov.

"My Sergeants barely warned *me*," the Mage-Captain replied. "Not sure if it was their idea or the grunts', to be honest, but I wasn't going to stop them. *You* needed the reminder, if nothing else."

Damien returned another group of salutes, then came to a halt in front of the boat bay doors, where the senior noncoms and junior officers of Romanov's old company, still assigned to his personal escort until his Warrant expired, waited for him.

"Lord Montgomery," the senior Sergeant, a wiry older man Damien had only met a few times, greeted him.

"Not a Lord anymore," he told them. "Just...Montgomery. Thank you."

"Titles change," the noncom replied. "Voices and Hands and Princes and Kings, all just names in the end. The Marine Corps know their own, *my lord*. We repay loyalty with loyalty, duty with duty, honor with honor.

"And no matter what may come to pass, Damien Montgomery, know this: the Royal Martian Marines do *not* forget."

Damien settled into the command chair at the heart of the luxury jump-yacht, feeling surprisingly more calm. He wasn't sure if the Marines knew how much their gesture had meant to him, but it had definitely helped settle his own mood, at least for now.

"What's the plan?" Samara asked as she dropped into one of the observer chairs, studying the screens over his shoulder.

"Find the bad guys, shoot the bad guys, question the survivors, be home for dinner?" Romanov suggested as the Marine turned Secret Service bodyguard took the other chair.

"I don't know about dinner, but that's not a bad summary," Damien replied. He brought up a projection of the Sol system around them.

"Our potential target zone is here." He highlighted the arc of space the channel could have originated from. The midpoint was just over six light-minutes from them. "If we set our course directly for them and burn fifteen gees the whole way, we'll come to a full stop in the middle of that zone in just over fifteen hours—but it won't be very comfortable and they'll see us coming the whole way.

"I don't want to give these pricks that much warning," he concluded.

"Fortunately, right now, one of the trailing Jupiter Trojan clusters is on a near-direct line past them," he noted. "The course to get there would still leave us a few million kilometers off, but being on that course—and publicly filing it, of course—will have us heading in the same direction."

A course lit up on the projection in orange.

"That has us accelerate for seven and a half hours, coast for a day, then decelerate to rendezvous with the Trojan cluster."

Damien tapped the projection. "We'll follow this course until we're about twenty-four million kilometers from the target zone, at which point we'll bring the drive up at fifteen gravities and do a hard deceleration to drop us right into the middle of the zone.

"They'll have about four hours' warning, and we'll be close enough to see where they try and run," he concluded. "I'll want your people in the shuttles at that point, Romanov," he warned. "We may have to try to chase some runners down, make sure they don't get away."

"We can do that," the Marine confirmed. "We'll get these bastards."

"I need them alive," Damien told him. "As many of them as possible. Neutralizing the Belt Liberation Front as a threat is a bonus. I need to know about this bastard they were working with."

He wasn't expecting Kay to be hiding among the Front, though it was possible. He was hoping that they'd be able to tell him more about the mysterious Mage who appeared to have been hunting down the last of the Keepers...*and* working for Legatus.

Even interplanetary flights were long, long endeavors. After the first few hours, Damien found himself calculating whether or not he would save time by jumping *Akintola* part of the way.

He knew the answer before he even tried to calculate. The minimum distance he could jump a starship was about a light-hour. Visiting Jupiter, with Mars as far away as it currently was, could justify it. But the asteroid cluster he was theoretically heading to was less than twenty light-minutes away. His true destination was even closer.

It was an easier exercise than planning for the future. One way or another, the investigation into the Keepers was just about over—either he'd find answers with the BLF...or he wouldn't, and he'd have run out of leads.

Once it was over, he'd return the temporary Warrant he'd been given and then...something.

It had seemed so clear when he'd threatened to retire to prevent the Mage-King trying to keep this mess secret. Then he'd told Alexander he'd go back to Sherwood, take a position with his homeworld's government or perhaps its rapidly-growing defensive militia.

He could still do that, he supposed. Stay "on call" to act as the King's Voice if he needed a Rune Wright's touch for at least some time.

Doing that to defy his King would have been a victory of sorts. His choice. Doing it now felt like admitting defeat, crawling home with his tail between his legs.

That his old girlfriend and her grandfather the Governor would be glad to see him didn't change that.

He supposed he could even buy a ship. Hands were well compensated for their work, and Damien had spent very little of it. His name alone would open options for financing that would be closed to most.

Despite how he'd started, however, Damien couldn't quite see himself as just a Jump Mage or even a ship's Captain anymore.

"You realize, I presume, that you should probably be sleeping?" Samara asked, the dark-skinned Inspector entering the room with silent grace. "The assault shuttles, as I understand, have decent odds against the crap the Front has for warships, but we still need *you* if we're going to carry the day.

"You might have given up the Hand, but you still have the Rune," she noted. "You're still this ship's most powerful armament."

"Four more hours before we even stop accelerating," he replied. "Five after that before we decelerate. So, I have...at least ten, twelve hours to get sleep."

"Which leaves you spending your time staring at a projected starscape and moping," she concluded. "Anything productive coming out of the navel-contemplation?"

"I rose so far above any ambition or dream I had as a child," Damien said after a few moments' hesitation. "I can't go back to being a Jump Mage. I'd be a hazard to any ship I was on, a flashing target to every thug and bounty hunter in the galaxy."

"I don't think there's many thugs or bounty hunters who are that stupid," Samara told him. "I don't suppose 'quiet retirement' is on your list?"

"I'm not even thirty-five, Inspector," he said. "I owe humanity more than that."

"Why?" she asked. "What do you owe anyone, Damien Montgomery? You've given more than most already."

"I have more than most to give," he replied. "There are only a handful of people in the galaxy who share my Gift. I'd be...selfish to turn away from so much need. So much strife."

"Hands don't die in bed," Samara pointed out. "That's the path you've been on. To an early death and a black tomb on the side of the Mountain."

He winced. He'd been there when they'd buried Alaura Stealey, the Hand who'd trained him, in the shadowed basalt tombs at the foot of the field where the dead of the Olympus Project lay. Each Hand had a tomb there.

Many were empty, their occupants' bodies lost to space and war.

"I volunteered," he said. "I wasn't drafted. I wasn't conscripted. They gave me a chance to disappear quietly, but I chose to learn from the Mage-King and enter his service."

He shook his head, studying their course.

"You're right, of course," he agreed. "Hands don't die in bed. I haven't expected to for...four years? Maybe longer. I stopped expecting to die in bed long before I entered His Majesty's service.

"I'm not sure I have it in me to stop," he admitted. "So, when I leave Mars, it will be for one duty or another." He smiled, suddenly a bit more certain of himself. "I don't know where yet," he admitted, "but I know that much.

"I may have resigned my Hand, but I am far from done with the service I owe humanity."

The MIS Inspector didn't say anything in response to that. She just took a seat in the observer chair beside him, leaning back to look up at the stars with him in silence.

CHAPTER 31

DAMIEN DID, in the end, get a little over seven hours of sleep. There was medication involved, a carefully calculated risk, but there was nothing that was going to attack the little jump-yacht in the deep space of the Sol System without at least some hours of warning.

The medication kept the dreams at bay, which meant he woke up feeling more refreshed than he had in several days. A lazy, luxurious shower completed his restoration, and he pulled on his black suit and gloves, feeling somewhat human.

Then, of course, he went to put on his Hand and froze. Eventually, it would be real. Until then... He sighed and shook his head.

"Romanov, anything I need to be aware of?" he asked the Marine over the intercom.

"Things are quiet," Romanov replied. "Training the sensor module on our target zone, though, and I'm not seeing much of...well, anything."

"If you were hiding a secret base for a terrorist organization in the Sol System, how close would we have to get to see it?"

Romanov chuckled.

"Unless someone was arriving or leaving, *inside* the base," he admitted. "Point taken, my lord."

"Commencing deceleration in ten minutes," Damien told him. "Once we're obviously heading their way, that's when I expect to see some activity. I doubt they're up to RMMC levels of competence, after all."

He settled back into the control chair, checking his access to the joysticks for immediate control and the ease of accessing the simulacrum he'd have to defend the ship with. On a screen to his immediate right, the countdown continued to tick away until the moment they would change course.

With a few keystrokes, Damien linked the screens to his right to the yacht's sensors. The feed from the additional sensor module the Marines had mounted on the outside moved into the center of the view, the larger asteroids in the target zone highlighted by *Akintola*'s computers.

"All right," he said aloud. "Let's see how much attention you're paying."

Tapping another series of commands, he opened a shipwide channel.

"All hands, all hands, this is Montgomery," he told them. "Stand by for five subjective gravities in thirty seconds. Secure yourselves and all loose objects. Five subjective gravities in twenty seconds from...now."

The yacht shivered gently as she spun in space, aligning with her new vector, and then Damien grunted as five gravities of force slammed him back into the control couch. The couch was designed for just this purpose, gel pads absorbing the pressure and keeping him functional as his body complained against the massively-increased weight.

They were still almost a light-minute and a half away, and he waited patiently for the time delay to pass. It would take ninety seconds for the light of *Doctor Akintola*'s new course to reach their destination, and ninety more seconds for the light of any response to reach him.

They were still five hours away. He could wait three or four minutes to see what his enemies were doing.

The answer, at least initially, was nothing. He hadn't really expected a group of basically-amateur insurrectionists to do more than that. It would take time for them to confirm that the ship was actually heading their way. Time for them to decide what to do. Even more time for them to act.

And much as Damien was impatient for them to show their hand, the longer they waited to act, the better odds he had of bringing them to bay.

He could wait.

And wait they did.

After half an hour, Damien's estimate of their enemy started ratcheting downward fast. There was reacting slowly, and then there was missing the ship decelerating toward you at fifteen gravities on an antimatter rocket.

By the time they hit a light-minute's separation, though, he was starting to wonder if there wasn't something else going on. Their scans were showing nothing at all. No one was reacting to them. There were no ships there, just dead and silent asteroids.

"Munira, can you go over the sensor scans for me?" he asked the MIS Inspector. "I'm relatively sure I'm not missing any active *ships*, but unless we got the vector on that comm channel wrong, there has to be something there."

Samara had already mirrored the sensor module's feed to her own displays and was tearing into the data with a set of software tools Damien didn't even pretend to understand.

"There is always another possibility," she admitted. "We've been assuming that they were communicating directly with Kay, but they could have been using a relay or transmitting from a ship in transit...or, well, using a mobile relay."

"I know," he said grimly. "It was just all we had. We're going to sweep the area anyway, so we'll see what we see as we approach."

"Wait..." Samara said slowly. "That's odd."

"What is?"

She highlighted a number of objects sharing an orbit with the largest of the asteroids in their flagged area.

"These aren't big enough to be on the regular charts," she pointed out. "I'm not getting great resolution even on them now, but...spectrography says they're artificial."

"There isn't supposed to be anything here at all."

"Exactly. No idea what they are," she admitted, "but they're in the right place and they don't belong. Might just be a relay, which we can strip for more data, but..."

"They might also have some answers of their own," Damien agreed. "Keep on it, Inspector."

The following hours only brought more questions as *Doctor Akintola* drew closer and they got a better look at the strange objects. There were dozens of them, identical skeletal steel cylinders a hundred meters long and at most five wide. Much of their construction was open to space, but solid rails ran the entire length of the objects.

They weren't ships, they weren't habitats, they weren't... Damien had no idea what they were.

"Well, that's at least *one* benefit out of those strange things," Samara pointed out as they crossed the three-hundred-thousand-kilometer mark, still fully half an hour away from their zero-velocity rendezvous.

"I'm listening to any answers and any good news," Damien said drily. "The complete lack of life other than those things is making me twitchy."

"Well, there's definitely a base of some kind on the asteroid they're orbiting with," she replied. "Does that count as signs of life?"

"Yes. Show me," he ordered.

She manipulated the displays, mirroring her screen to one of his and zooming in.

The asteroid was just over a hundred kilometers long, and the base was tucked into the largest crater on one side. It wasn't even a small complex. It was clearly assembled from standard prefabricated modules, a familiar sight in any star system of the Protectorate, but it had been done carefully and well.

A scale dropped onto one side of the screen, helping him judge the size of the base. Forty or so structures, linked together by surface tunnels. Roughly a kilometer or so across.

"That base could hold a thousand, two thousand people, easy," Samara concluded. "Here and here." She tapped a command and several modules flashed. "Those are docking ports. The asteroid doesn't have enough gravity to cause any issues just flying a ship up and linking it."

"But there's nothing there," Damien objected. "How many ships would we be looking at?"

"Hard to say," she said. "Six docking ports. But..." She highlighted a flat portion of the crater. "That spot there is close enough for reasonable access by vac suit and has enough gravity to hold things down. It could easily hold three or four of the transports or thirty to forty of the shuttles we saw attacking *Callisto*."

"So, minimum of six decent-sized ships," he concluded. "Except we saw eight at *Callisto*. Six transports, two mining ships. All of them made it out. Could they have done repairs here?"

"It would be zero-gee work, but they're Belt miners," she told him. "They could do it and the hardware was certainly here, assuming they built those tubes in place."

"Well, I'm only getting more questions at this point," Damien admitted, "and there's only one way to get my answers. Keep working on identifying those satellites."

"What are you doing?"

"Denis and I are going to go invade a terrorist base."

"No," Romanov said flatly. "No, no, no. Not a chance."

Damien looked at the Secret Service Special Agent calmly, waiting for him to get it out of his system.

"You might not be a Hand anymore, but you are my goddamned principal and it remains my job to keep you alive. I am *not* letting you take part in a hostile boarding action!"

"Denis, I am not the Captain of a ship or a pampered diplomat," Damien pointed out. "My *job* is to be in the middle of the action, providing protection and fire support and dealing with problems.

"Not only that, but I need to see what's on this base for myself—and if there is anyone left, I'm more likely to be able to take them alive than your Marines are. And Hand or not, *I* am in charge here.

"So, now that we've established that you don't get to bar me from the operation, what compromise would you suggest?" he asked.

For a moment, Romanov looked like he was going to suggest something along the lines of tying Damien up and locking him in a closet, then the Marine finally sighed.

"You can come on the third shuttle," he said. "It's the same one I'll be on. *I'm* not supposed to lead from the front any more than you are, after all."

"Now, that, Agent, is more reasonable," Damien agreed. As they spoke, he was discarding his suit jacket and dress shirt for an armored vest that covered his torso but left the Runes on his arms fully visible.

There would be no subtlety or concealment today. Not many would recognize the Runes, but exposing them also meant he wouldn't be burning off clothes when he activated them.

The men and women around him clambered into exosuits and slowly boarded their shuttles. Romanov waited for Damien once he'd strapped on his own massive suit of armor.

"That's it?" he asked. "Just the vest?"

Damien smiled and grabbed two more items from the locker—a pistol and a breath mask.

"Not quite, but mostly," he agreed. "If we're dealing with vacuum, I'll consider upgrading, but I don't *need* much, Denis. You know that."

"I know that," the Marine replied, shaking his head. "Still can't help feeling you should wear *something* more substantial."

"I promise to hide behind the men and women in the two-meter suits of armor if trouble starts," Damien told him. "If that makes you feel better."

The Marine shook his head.

"Not really," he admitted. "Our shuttle's over here, my lord."

Damien shook his own head in turn.

"You all really need to stop calling me that," he pointed out.

"No, we don't," Romanov said calmly. "Shall we?"

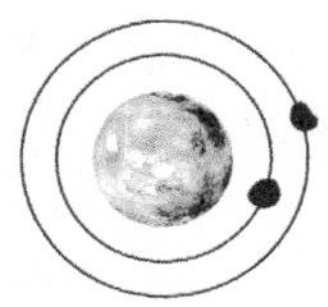

CHAPTER 32

STRAPPED INTO the acceleration couch in the assault shuttle's officers' compartment, Damien watched the sensor feed from *Doctor Akintola* as they drew closer. Romanov was next to him, radiating calm readiness even through the centimeters-thick shell of the exosuit.

If there was any reaction from the hidden base they were approaching, the shuttles would launch immediately. Their weapons systems were light, basically nonexistent compared to a true warship, but they were also primarily designed for ground bombardment.

Against any weapon the Belt Liberation Front might have attached to the base to defend it, the shuttles were a far larger threat than the unarmed yacht carrying them.

The base remained silent as they approached, however, not even so much as a chirp of a traffic controller. If Damien couldn't make out lights in the base, he'd wonder if it had been abandoned long before.

"All right," Samara said over his earpiece. "We are coming to a halt, zero velocity relative to the asteroid, at just under five hundred kilometers. We're only ten kilometers from the closest of those tubes."

"What are the scans showing of the base?" Damien asked. They had a mirror of *Akintola*'s scan data, but Samara had access to the full array plus the yacht's more powerful computers. "If we can spare a shuttle to check out those orbitals, I'd like to get a better idea of what the hell the things are."

"Most of the base is dark and looks like it might have been for years," the MIS Inspector replied. "Cold as the rock around it. The area around the docking ports and between the ports and the landing pad area is still warm; looks like it has power and lights. Looks like there's four standard prefab fusion reactors in the base, but only one is running."

"If the place is mostly empty, we can probably spare a squad to check the satellites," Romanov noted. "Something about them is making me twitchy."

"Join the club," Damien muttered. "All right. Romanov, let's get your people moving. Send a shuttle to the nearest satellite and take the rest of us down."

The Marine started giving orders and Damien switched to a private channel with Samara.

"Are there any power sources on those satellites?" he asked.

"Nothing active," she told him. "If I could trace the power flow, I'd have a better idea of what we're looking at."

The shuttle vibrated as the first of the spacecraft lifted off and drifted out the back of the jump-yacht.

"Can you tell if there's anyone actually on the ground?"

"No," Samara admitted. "I can tell you where they have light and heat, but the sensors aren't refined enough to pick that up. My guess is you're looking at a skeleton caretaking staff, though. Most of them will be on the ships...and I have *no* idea where those are."

"That's what I was afraid of," Damien said as his own shuttle lifted off. "We're back to hoping there's answers down there, because I'm starting to get nervous again."

As Damien had agreed with Romanov, their shuttle hung back as the first pair of landing craft dropped like homesick rocks towards the asteroid base "below" them. A fourth shuttle was beginning the slow and tricky process of matching velocities with the orbiting and gently spinning cylinder they were being sent to investigate, and the last shuttle took up a high overwatch orbit, its missile racks extended to cover the rest of the spacecraft.

The first two shuttles dropped to hard landings on the clear pad the Front had used for much the same purpose, then each disgorged their twenty-strong Marine squads. Exosuited troopers advanced by fire teams across the open area to reach the airlocks.

"Airlocks are active and powered," Corporal Coral reported. "Standard security, the breach package is already through."

"Move in and start securing the modules," Romanov ordered. "Command shuttle is coming in behind you; raise a flag if you hit any resistance."

"Wilco, opening the locks and moving in."

Exosuits began to vanish into the base as Damien's shuttle swept toward the ground itself, rockets flaring to slow it to a somewhat reasonable impact.

"Gravity is..." Romanov snorted. "Point zero three gees. The rock has plenty of iron. Engage your mag-boots and be *careful.* I want High Watch watching for bad guys, not chasing your lost metal asses. Move!"

Damien took the time to put on a vac suit, leaving him the last out, with even Romanov in front of him. For the quick run to the airlock he didn't need the suit, he could hold enough air in with magic, but...if *he* went flying the same way Romanov was warning his men, he couldn't keep himself safe for long enough.

Four exosuited Marines were waiting for him at the base of the shuttle ramp, falling into neat formation as he jogged carefully after the rest of the company. Where they were using mag-boots, Damien was using a spell that kept himself in a small area of artificial gravity.

The clear landing pad area was surprisingly dust-free, any loose debris or grit clearly having been blasted free. Their three shuttles wouldn't have managed that on the way down. It would take a *lot* of launches for an asteroid crater to be this clean.

"Mass launch from here," he murmured to Romanov. "Recently."

"I concur," he replied. "How long ago would it have had to be for us to miss it?"

Damien considered. They'd been watching since they left Mars, but if the Front had been careful, *Akintola*'s sensors might still have missed them leaving.

"Twelve hours," he concluded. "Probably more, but twelve hours ago was the latest they could have snuck out on us unnoticed."

"Do you think they saw us coming?"

"The timing's suspicious, but..."

There was another possibility, one Damien let trail to silence. How much information did the BLF have, he wondered? How much access did they—or this Kay—have?

Would they know that the Mage-King was supposed to be on Council Station in less than two days?

The interior of the asteroid facility looked the same as a dozen other stations or off-world bases Damien had been in. Prefabricated components looked the same no matter where you put them or who used them.

There was some decoration here and there, glorified graffiti really, but enough to make it clear that this part of the base had been occupied. There were rooms with beds that had clearly been slept in, armories that had clearly been used recently. The smell of gun oil and sweat seemed to permeate the entire place when he popped his faceplate.

They clearly hadn't been properly maintaining the air filtration systems, which surprised Damien. These were Belt miners, men who'd been born and raised in artificial environments. Checking on the safety of their air supply should have been second nature.

"No one lived here," Romanov said. "No one ever saw this place as anything except a temporary stopover. Graffiti but no art. Unmaintained life support. Beds but no personal effects.

"Looks like a second-rate barracks," he admitted.

"It wasn't home, so nobody cared," Damien realized aloud. "They'd built it to be more but never had the resources or the will to make it more until—"

"Until they came into ships and guns, apparently through our 'Kay'," Romanov agreed grimly. "But I'm not sure there's anybody here, my lord. I think they all shipped out."

"And left the power running?"

"Keeps the air clean if you end up coming back, and doesn't use that much fuel if you step it down," the Marine replied. "Depending on how much fuel they left, could run for a day, a week, or even a month while waiting for them.

"Does wear your air filters down, though," he noted thoughtfully.

"I'd expect better from miners," Damien replied.

"Yeah, but the kind of guys who get wrapped up in this sort of nihilistic bullshit are not...the smartest or best of their culture," Romanov pointed out. "The usual pattern would say we're dealing with a few charismatic narcissists and a lot of, well, idiots."

"My sympathies for their intellectual shortfalls are limited. Let's see if we can find some kind of computer center," Damien ordered. "That's our best chance for anything resembling answers."

"Sirs, you have to take a look at this," Corporal Massey pinged Damien and Romanov over the company network. "I'm not one hundred percent sure what I'm looking at, but it is definitely some kind of computing setup and it isn't asteroid miner standard prefab. Which separates it from everything *else* on this rock."

"This way," Romanov told Damien, gesturing back down the corridor they'd been traveling through. "I have Massey's location on my screen."

"Lead the way."

While the base itself was huge, less than a fifth of it had been occupied and had an active air supply. It took them only a few minutes to reach the chamber that Massey had found, one of the largest rooms they'd seen so far.

Despite what Massey had said, it clearly *was* a prefabbed module, but not a complete room or setup like most of the pods that had been linked together. The walls and roof were prefabricated, the design normally used for a garage with a floor of native rock.

A pit had been blasted into the rock under it, crudely carved into a series of concentric circles that dropped towards a circular floor four meters across. A large but cheap holo-display had been set up in the middle of that floor, and an assortment of even cheaper consoles had been arranged on the concentric circles.

"Looks like some kind of command center," Damien observed. He studied them, counting, and a thought struck him.

"How many of those satellites were there?" he asked.

"Final count was forty-five," Romanov reported.

"How many consoles do you see, Agent?"

The Marine's helmeted head turned to survey the pit in the middle of the room.

"Son of a bitch. Forty-five."

"Boot them up," Damien ordered. "Let's see what they were showing."

"These models have almost no internal memory," Corporal Massey pointed out. "They run entirely off the user's wrist computer."

"But with our overrides, we can bring up the last thing on the screen," Damien replied. "Move."

He was settling in at the closest console himself, linking in his wrist computer with its standard set of police overrides—no longer the complicated and powerful overrides his Hand had contained, but capable enough for this.

The screen lit up with its last image. Rows of numbers tracked across half the screen, with multiple separate images occupying separate sections, all marked with green lines for projected orbits...and a single red line marked with a set of crosshairs.

"Targeting systems," he said quietly. "Boot the holo-display. I suspect I know what we're going to see."

The main display made it even clearer. Each of the individual consoles had targeted one weapon, but the big display had been used to derive the primary line of attack. Highlighted on one side of the tank was their current location with its forty-five orbiting satellites.

Highlighted on the other side was Council Station.

Damien tapped his wrist PC.

"Samara, have we established just what those orbitals are?" he asked calmly.

"We just finished the data run," she replied, her voice grim. "They're railguns, my lord. Single-shot, capacitor-fed railguns. Firing them threw them completely off course, I can't be certain what the target was—"

"We found the targeting systems," Damien told her, studying the numbers. "If I'm reading these projections right, the projectiles will hit Council Station's defenses in fourteen hours, sixteen minutes, and some change."

His staff were silent.

"We need to get moving," he concluded. "Samara, forward everything you can put together to the Mountain. Alexander *has* to delay his trip."

"What about the Navy?" Romanov asked.

"If I remember correctly, the closest ships are at least sixteen hours from Council Station," Damien told him grimly. "We're just over fourteen if we go fifteen gees the whole way, but it'll take us half an hour just to get the Marines back aboard.

"We can't beat the projectiles there," he concluded. "I need to get aboard *Akintola* and on the coms. If we move fast enough and people *listen*, we might be able to stop this from turning into an abject disaster."

"Understood," Samara replied. "Packaging for transmission now."

Damien turned to Romanov.

"Get your people moving," he said grimly.

"Already on it," the Marine replied. "Only one question, boss."

"What?"

"It wouldn't take these guys twenty-six hours to get to Council Station, would it?"

"It could, easily even," Damien said slowly. "Depends on how hard they were willing to push those ships. However...these railguns could only impart a thousand kilometers a second of velocity. The rounds have a thirty-hour flight time, and these guys could have left anytime from right afterward to about thirteen hours ago."

"So, odds are they went straight to Council Station?" Romanov said. "That makes things simpler, even if they're going to beat us there."

"They had the time to go around a bit to avoid notice, but yes. Anyone who left here after the railguns fired had to have basically gone straight there. That *should* limit their surprises at this point."

His bodyguard snorted.

"Because the bastards *need* more surprises."

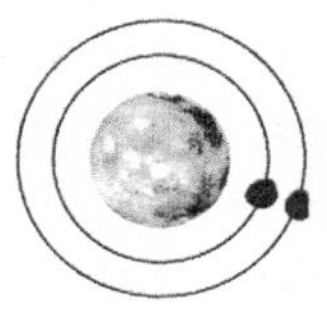

CHAPTER 33

BACK ABOARD *Akintola,* Damien grimaced under five gravities of subjective acceleration as he checked their course ahead, making sure that they were arcing around the inevitable rocks that would orbit into their path.

Even at a thousand kilometers a second, the massive slugs the Front had fired at Council Station were invisible to anyone's sensors. They had minimal heat signatures. No power source. Just a hundred tons of iron slag traveling through space with enough velocity to create the equivalent of a ten-megaton nuclear bomb.

About the only good news was that the data dump they'd taken from the BLF's holo-display suggested that none of the projectiles were aimed at Council Station itself. In an unusual sign of good sense, none of the Station's weapons were mounted on the main hull.

Instead, fifteen smaller defensive stations surrounded Council Station, armed with an array of weapons that had probably been obsolete before the current Mage-King was born. The Belt Liberation Front's attack had three projectiles targeted on each of them—a massive amount of overkill, in Damien's opinion.

He brought up the communications system and *mostly* managed to wipe the grimace of five gravities of acceleration off his face as he recorded a message for the people ahead of him.

"Lictor-Constable Cande Lucas," he greeted the woman he'd argued with once before—the woman in charge of Council Station's defenses and the one he *had* to convince of the danger. "This is Damien Montgomery."

There was no point telling her he was no longer a Hand. It wasn't relevant, and it might undermine his urgency.

"My investigations have discovered an immediate and dire threat to Council Station. At this moment, forty-five one-hundred-ton projectiles are on their way to you at approximately one thousand kilometers per second. They will impact at fourteen hundred hours, thirty-six minutes and some seconds today."

He paused, glancing at the data he had on Council Station's defense and shaking his head.

"They are targeted on your defense platforms. My data informs me those platforms are only capable of basic maneuvering. You have no way to save them. You need to evacuate those platforms *now* or you are going to lose hundreds of people.

"I believe that there is a follow-up wave of at least a dozen ships and several hundred fanatics preparing for a boarding action," he continued. "I suspect the primary target is the Mage-King himself, and I have requested that he abort or delay his meeting with the Council.

"The Council, however, are almost certainly targets in their own right," he said grimly. "I am attaching all of the information I have, Constable. I can't be certain of the arrival time of the second wave of the attack, but we have exact timing on the thirty-second window those projectiles will arrive in."

He sighed.

"I am on my way at the maximum acceleration this ship is capable of," he told her. "Unfortunately, I expect to arrive approximately forty minutes after the incoming projectiles.

"I wish there was more I could give you, Constable. Good luck."

Hitting TRANSMIT, Damien turned to Samara.

"Any response from His Majesty?" he asked.

"A Your-Eyes-Only message just came in for you while you were recording for Lucas," she told him. "Transferring it to your screen."

"Thank you," he told her. "I'm sorry I keep drafting you as impromptu bridge crew; I appreciate it."

"It's the only place on the ship with the data and the analytics package," Samara replied with a grin. "I'll happily pass on your messages so long as I have access to all of these toys!"

He returned her smile, then started the video transmitted from Mars over ten minutes before.

He wasn't entirely surprised to see the King's face appear in the screen, Alexander looking old and grave.

"We've received your transmission, Damien," he said. "I've ordered all nearby vessels to immediately make for Council Station. We're going to violate the shit out of the neutrality agreement I have with them, but I don't care.

"I am transferring from the unarmed yacht I was taking to observe that agreement to the battleship *Storm of Unrelenting Fury*. Given the situation, my escort will not be turning back at the one-light-minute mark and I will be arriving in the company of two battleships and six cruisers."

The Mage-King paused.

"My security is insisting that whichever ship I am on delays, but even if I send part of my escort ahead, Damien, they'll be twelve hours behind you," he said softly. "The nearest patrol destroyers will make a high-speed pass and engage any ships in the vicinity...roughly two hours after you arrive.

"After all that has happened and all that I have asked of you before, I hate to say it, but you are the Council's only hope. Much as they frustrate me, the Protectorate needs them.

"Save them for me, Damien Montgomery. I will make *certain* they understand their debts."

Extended time under heavy acceleration had a strange, uniquely amorphous quality to it, in Damien's experience. Like being five times his normal weight meant that time could be five times faster or five times slower, but not normal.

The human brain didn't handle this type of experience well, which meant he had to check a clock to see how long it had been when he received the response from Council Station. Just over an hour, which, given that the message would have taken six minutes either way, could be a bad sign.

A familiar shaven-headed woman in the white uniform of a Council Lictor appeared on his screen.

"Lord Montgomery, we received your message," she informed him. "I apologize for the delay; certain...elements required that we fully validate your data before accepting your conclusions.

"I have given the order to evacuate our defensive platforms and we welcome your assistance. However"—something in her eyes told him she did *not* like what she had to say—"I must inform you that the Council is not prepared to relax the neutrality zone around Council Station.

"While you and your vessel will be permitted to approach, I have been advised that any decision to allow Martian warships into the neutrality zone would require a majority vote of Council, and we have been unable to assemble quorum."

Damien stared at the recording in horror. Were they idiots? Or, worse, despite apparently hating his guts, did they think that *he* could save them all on his own?

"I am also passing this message on to the Navy vessels that have begun accelerating towards us," she continued, her voice flat but her eyes pleading. "I remind you, Lord Montgomery, that as you once told me, I serve the Council—but we both serve the same masters in the end.

"I ask that you contact the Navy ships as well to...clarify my orders," she finished, and Damien laughed aloud as he realized what she wanted him to do.

"This station's security is my responsibility," she concluded. "I ask you—no, I *beg* you—to provide any and all assistance you can."

The message ended, and Damien kept chuckling for a moment.

"My lord?" Samara asked, looking at him like he was insane. Then she paused, shook her head, and tried again without the title. "Damien, what's so funny?"

"The Lictor-Constable is an intelligent woman determined to do her duty, trapped under superiors who are actively playing power games with their own lives at risk," Damien told her. "What she *means*, my dear Inspector, when she asks me to 'clarify her orders' is that she wants me to tell the Navy warships to completely ignore her."

He sobered, looking at the frozen image sadly.

"Of course, I no longer have that authority," he said quietly. "But then...the Navy Captains don't know that any more than she did, do they?"

"They would not," Samara replied. "Normally, as an officer sworn to uphold the law, I would frown on abusing that lack of knowledge, *Mr.* Montgomery...but given the circumstances, how can I help?"

Seconds might count, but every message had minutes' worth of light-speed delay.

Damien took the time to force himself to breathe, working magic around himself to reduce the pressure for a few moments, and then focused on the camera once again as he exhaled a heavy breath.

"All Navy Captains, this is Montgomery," he told the recorder.

"By now, you have been notified of the incipient attack on Council Station by fringe elements. We have reason to believe these elements have been enabled and armed by outside forces and represent a clear and immediate danger to the safety of the Protectorate and, clearly, of Council Station itself."

The phrasing was formal, stilted...and critically important. By declaring the Belt Liberation Front a danger to the Protectorate, Damien made it a Protectorate problem. A Royal problem.

A Hand's problem—and most importantly, *not* the Council's jurisdiction.

"By now, you have also received orders from Lictor-Constable Lucas telling you to break off, informing us that the Council is not lifting the neutrality zone and therefore Navy warships are not permitted within one light-minute of Council Station."

Damien smiled.

"I am overriding her orders in the Name and the Voice of the Mage-King of Mars," he told them. "In the interests of the security of the Protectorate, I am voiding the neutrality zone around Council Station and ordering all available warships to move to protect the Station.

"The Station will come under enemy fire at fourteen hundred thirty-six hours," he said flatly. "At some point after that, a second enemy assault of ships and boarding troops will commence. You will proceed to the Station and engage those ships, using any means necessary up to and including counter-boarding operations by your Marines.

"The Council may be stubborn and proud, but they remain under His Majesty's Protectorate and we *will* protect them," Damien told the Navy officers. "Godspeed to you, Captains. I have faith in you."

The message went out and Damien leaned back, letting the full force of *Doctor Akintola*'s acceleration crush him down again.

"That's everything," he half-whispered. "Ten hours. Ten hours...and all I can do is hope that the bastards had better aim than I'm inclined to give them credit for."

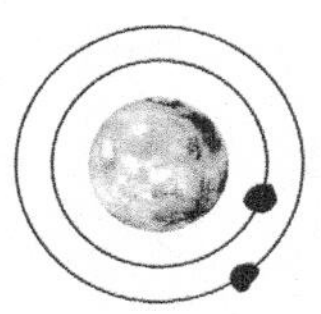

CHAPTER 34

DAMIEN FORCED HIMSELF to sleep. Even under five gravities of subjective acceleration, he could manage it, at least with the drugs he currently had.

He was very careful to be sure that no one else saw him take the medication, though. Romanov knew he had the pills—Damien's desire to keep his weakness hidden fell second to the necessity of his *bodyguard* knowing he was using sleeping pills.

They knocked him out for seven hours, almost exactly, leaving him awake and watching over an hour before the expected impact.

Navy ships were visible for light-minutes in every direction, their antimatter engines brilliant stars that stood out against the night sky as a dozen destroyers burned toward Council Station from as many different directions. Unlike *Akintola*, they weren't even decelerating. Damien would arrive at the Station at a speed where he could engage enemy ships and dock with the station to protect it himself.

The destroyers would pass by at velocities that were frankly *dangerous* inside the asteroid belt. The Belt might not look like fiction made it, but there was enough debris and dust to make speeds of over a percent of lightspeed unwise.

Those Captains didn't care. Duty said they would be at Council Station in time to intervene, and if that meant shooting down an inconvenient asteroid or even taking a meteor strike to the million-ton warships' mighty forward armor, then that was what they would do.

He mentally saluted them. The Royal Martian Navy was a peacetime fleet, with all of the problems that entailed, but its crews and officers *understood* what the Navy existed for.

There was enough civilian shipping scattered around the system that they couldn't be sure they'd picked out the BLF ships. There were at least three clusters of ships of the right size on vectors that could be turned to attack Council Station. Half a dozen ships on similar vectors that were much larger than the vessels they knew the BLF to have, including a *Dealer*-type sublight freighter that resembled his old ship *Blue Jay* enough to bring back a twinge of memories.

"Ninety minutes to impact," Samara told him softly. "No one has even picked up a hint of the projectiles."

"They wouldn't," Damien reminded her. "They're not fast enough or active enough to be picked up with anything except active sensors, and that at only about a million kilometers."

He sighed.

"We'll see them coming," he admitted. "Council Station will see them a good quarter-hour before they hit, but the Station's defenses have *nothing* that can stop a hundred-ton hypervelocity projectile."

"Does anything have a defense that can stop that?" Samara asked.

He shrugged.

"A modern missile defense laser is designed to detonate the fuel supply on a missile," he admitted, "but it would still vaporize enough of a pure iron projectile to force a miss. Mostly, the defense against something like this is to be able to dodge, which the platforms at Council Station simply can't do. They weren't designed for it."

"Seems short-sighted."

"It was," Damien agreed. "But reading between the lines, the first Mage-King *intentionally* crippled Council Station's defenses. I think he figured the only person likely to be trying to break through them was him."

Samara shook her head.

"The more I hear about the Mage-King's grandfather, the more I realize he was a paranoid bastard."

"He was," Damien confirmed. "But he *also* ended a hundred-year-long war, stopped a continuing eugenics project that had lasted just as long, and pulled the Mages out of a forced breeding program. He had a *lot* of credit to spend."

"So, what now?" she asked.

"We wait ninety minutes and see what's left," he said grimly. "Then we go make sure whatever's still intact *stays* intact."

The targeting data they'd found at the hidden launch site was, to Damien's mild surprise, almost completely accurate.

At the exact moment his projections said that Council Station's radar would detect the incoming projectiles, glaring red icons began to flash up on the feed he was receiving from them.

The projectiles were actually closer to *Doctor Akintola* than they were to Council Station, though outside the reach of both the yacht's low-powered proximity radar and Damien's magical power. They continued at the same steady pace they'd maintained the whole trip, while *Akintola* was slowing down, decelerating to allow them to have a useful interaction when they arrived.

Even Damien couldn't reduce the velocity of a full-size starship by enough to have made a high-speed approach worthwhile. Physics left him slowing down as he watched the massive iron slugs ahead of him close with the station he was trying to save.

"Right on schedule," Samara reported. "Vectors are aligned with the data we had. Forty-five projectiles in total, no attrition."

"What was going to take out those things by accident?" he asked bitterly. Still over an hour away from Council Station himself, all they could do was watch.

"Not much," she agreed. "We've confirmed all fifteen defense platforms are evacuated. We still have multiple potential groups of ships," she continued, "but I *think* our problem is these guys."

The approaching BLF spaceships weren't what Damien wanted to look at right now, but her attempted distraction was welcome regardless.

She'd highlighted a group of ten ships, six intra-system transports and four mining ships, that were on a vector that could easily adjust to arrive at Council Station thirty minutes after the bombardment.

"The other three potentials are either too few ships or, well, a big freighter that's on a scheduled flight," Samara concluded, highlighting the others. There was a trio of mining ships in one group and four intra-system transports flying in convoy in the other.

The last of her eliminated options was the *Dealer*-type freighter Damien had noted before.

"The *Dealer* was making a scheduled delivery to Council Station," she told him. "She's been warned off and has adjusted her vector to clear the Station, but her Captain advises that if she doesn't make her delivery, Council Station only has a week or so of oxygen and food."

"We'll worry about that if we're still here tomorrow," Damien pointed out.

"That's what Constable Lucas told her," Samara said. "If those ships are the BLF, my lord—"

"The destroyers will be in range for long-range missile fire before they reach the station," he agreed. "But we don't *know*, Inspector, and I'm not willing to blow apart ships without knowing. None of those ships are responding to hails"—he gestured at the three groups of ships—"and Belt ships are notorious for ignoring authority and having 'broken' radios. The two have something to do with each other," he finished dryly.

Further discussion was cut off as he turned back to the screen and inhaled. The distraction had bought him a few minutes' calm not staring at the inbound bombardment, but time was running out. His image was only a few seconds delayed now, and a sudden sick silence fell over *Akintola*'s bridge as the time ran out.

Council Station's defense platforms were spread across a full light-second, extending the range of their lasers and old missiles across a massive area of space. As the projectiles closed, the lasers opened fire under automated control.

Jets of vaporized metal flared in space, attempts to slow or deflect the massive projectiles...but they were too massive and too fast. The adjustments inflicted were too little, too late, and the closest defense platform lit up with bright sparks as two massive projectiles slammed into it.

The others followed, a growing sphere of destruction around the station as the Belt Liberation Front's hammer came down, shattering platform after platform.

They managed to deflect some of the projectiles, though not enough to save any of the defenses. Each defense platform took at least one hit, but half a dozen slugs went tumbling off into space. Two slammed into the surface of Ceres, thankfully far enough away from the remaining settlements to avoid immediate consequences.

And one, Damien realized a heart-wrenching second before it happened, was deflected *into* Council Station. It was a glancing hit, the projectile hitting at an angle and being smashed aside by the Station's rapid rotation, but the flare of fires and explosive outgassing was visible even from *Akintola*'s hundreds of thousands of kilometers' distance.

His warning had saved hundreds of lives on the defense stations, but that single hit had probably cost just as many lives as had been spared. The ships around the station were buzzing like hornets, some rushing for the assumed safety of the docking ports, others turning to land on Ceres, while still others simply fled.

The ships that fled were the first to come under fire.

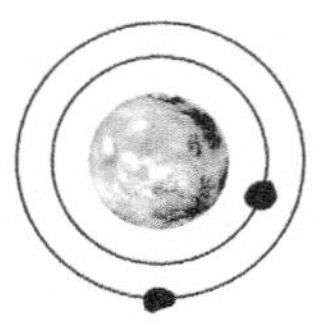

CHAPTER 35

SAMARA HAD assessed correctly. The ten-ship flotilla was clearly BLF ships, the four mining ships opening fire with lasers on the fleeing civilian transports, while the smaller transport vessels launched missiles that had been strapped to their hulls.

Those missiles, Damien noted, were cheap pieces of crap, fusion-drive weapons with accelerations of only a thousand gravities...but they were also far better weapons than the Front had shown in the attack on *Callisto*.

The railguns that also opened fire were what he'd been expecting, fifty-gram slugs accelerated to the same thousand kilometers a second of the more massive projectiles that had just devastated Council Station.

The space around Ceres turned to chaos. There were over forty ships either docked with the Station or in close proximity. None were large, only two were even jump ships according to their beacons, and none were sure of whether they wanted to run or hide under Council Station's skirts.

The ones that had already tried to run died.

A jump-yacht, presumably belonging to one of the Councilors, took a trio of fusion-drive missiles and disappeared in a flash of failing reactor containment.

A quartet of interplanetary shuttles, on their way in from the Jupiter Yards, tried to turn and run. Railgun slugs ripped them apart.

Two orbital runabouts, carrying tourists down to Ceres, caught a laser apiece and came apart above the old mining colony, scattering fiery ash across the dome.

Even the ones that tried to hide were dying, the space around Council Station beginning to fill with railgun slugs and debris. A collision claimed the only jump-courier around the station, an in-system fast hauler loaded with fresh delicacies from Earth slamming into the fragile jump-ship with enough force to split both vessels in half.

It was a disaster in the making, and *Akintola* was diving right into the middle of it.

"I think they spotted us," Damien noted as he picked out six missiles rising *up* out of the chaotic mess, the weapons on a clear course for his jump-yacht. "If they had more missiles, I'd even feel threatened."

The bravado was a frail shield against the dying ships he could only watch.

He tapped a channel.

"Romanov, how do your pilots feel about dogfighting?"

"A lot better than they feel about watching civilians die," the Marine replied gruffly.

"Go," Damien told him. "I think the missiles they've thrown at us are their last bolt; they're down to lasers and railguns...and your shuttles have better weapons than that."

"What about *Akintola*?"

"I'm taking her right at those mining ships," Damien replied grimly. "Those lasers are the biggest threat now they're out of missiles, but I need to get inside fifty thousand klicks to hit them."

"Good luck," Romanov told him. "We're launching."

"Happy hunting, Marines."

Denis strapped himself into the second copilot's seat as the shuttles blasted free. He was in Montgomery's usual ride, since it seemed the ex-Hand would be using *Akintola* for anywhere he needed to go today.

The yacht was still decelerating as the shuttles dropped away, falling behind them as they shot toward Council Station and its attackers. Most of his Marines were still aboard the yacht—the assault shuttle's weapons functioned best with additional gunners, but that still only brought him up to six a ship instead of the usual twenty.

"All right, everybody," he said calmly over the channel to all five ships. "You know how this goes: bad guys to the left of us, civvies to the right, only leaves one place for the Marines."

"Right down the middle, sir."

"Oohrah, people. Hit them hard."

Akintola continued to decelerate. Montgomery might be taking the yacht toward the heaviest concentration of enemy fire he could find, but he *also* needed to be able to dock with Council Station afterward.

Hand or no Hand, the political ramifications of this mess were still apparently Montgomery's problem. So far as Denis was concerned, better the Mage than him!

The assault shuttles aligned themselves on the armed transports and lit off their engines, accelerating into battle. Their weapons weren't much longer-ranged than the ex-Hand's un-amplified magic. They were mostly designed for ground bombardment, but the designers had made sure they *could* all be used in space.

"*Akintola*-Lead," the shuttle's actual copilot announced over the channel, "Fox Three, Three, Three."

Three short-ranged missiles blasted free of the shuttle. They were slow things, only a few dozen times faster than the shuttle itself and carrying fifty-kilo chemical warheads. They were designed to disable tanks, bunkers or anti-aircraft turrets, and the assault shuttle only carried six of them.

Against a military spaceship, their anemic ECM, EW and defensive maneuvers would have doomed them. Against the retrofitted in-system haulers the Belt Liberation Front had brought to the party, the only real issue was their lack of killing power versus a two-hundred-meter spaceship.

Five assault shuttles fired a total of fifteen missiles to announce their arrival into the fight. The hauler Denis had flagged could have survived one hit. Might have survived three, or even six.

It came apart in a cascade of explosions as over a dozen missiles hammered home.

"*Akintola*-Lead," the copilot repeated. "Fox Three, Three, Three."

The assault shuttle trembled as the missiles rippled free again, a moment before the gunner, calling the shots for the entire shuttle force, announced, "Guns, Guns, Guns."

A second armed transport came apart under the missile fire, and then the paired thirty-millimeter railguns mounted on each shuttle began to fire. Like the air-breathing fighters the assault shuttle had inherited its design ancestry from, the ships only carried enough ammunition for about forty seconds of sustained fire.

That allowed for a lot of two-second bursts, and Denis flagged two more of the in-system transports as his shuttles flashed into the middle of the fight. The transports had bigger guns, firing hundred- to two-hundred-gram slugs at a thousand kilometers a second. A single hit would shred any of his shuttles.

His guns were *better*, firing smaller slugs at three times the velocity. The bursts of slugs ripped through both of the flagged transports, ripping the slow, lumbering terrorist ships to pieces.

The Marine shuttles' ECM only bought them so much invulnerability, however, and the two remaining transports filled the space around them with flying debris. Two of Denis's shuttles came apart, men and women he'd known for years dying in sterile flashes of light.

His remaining three ships contorted in space as they flashed through the swarm of vessels around Council Station, continuing to fire bursts at the remaining Front attackers as they had clear lines of fire.

Then his ships were clear, rapidly proceeding out of range as they finally began to decelerate.

All four mining ships remained, now turning their lasers in the direction of the incoming *Doctor Akintola*, but none of the smaller armed transports had survived his pass.

"How long till we come around for another pass?" Denis asked the pilot.

"At least forty minutes," the woman replied with a shake of her head. "We're down to a quarter of our magazines, too—and the Navy should be in missile range by then."

Denis nodded, turning his gaze back to the scope where *Akintola* swooped down on the terrorists.

"Down to you now, my lord," he murmured.

The only reason Damien could see for the Front sending six missiles flying at *Doctor Akintola* was that they'd recognized her. In and of herself, after all, the Civil Fleet jump-yacht was unarmed, mostly unarmored, and in general no more of a threat than the Councilor's yacht they'd destroyed with half as many missiles.

If they had recognized the yacht, though, they'd done an insufficient amount of research. In their place, knowing he was coming, Damien would have thrown *everything* at *Akintola*. The yacht was terrifyingly vulnerable, and he could only do so much without a proper amplifier.

Unfortunately, *Akintola*'s jump matrix was designed to be difficult to access to prevent foolish rich people from damaging their own ships. Even if he *had* been able to get at it, Damien was under strict orders not to convert jump matrices to amplifier matrices.

It gave people ideas.

With an amplifier, he could have wiped all six missiles from space as soon as they'd been launched.

Without, he had to wait until the range dropped and lash out at a "mere" sixty thousand kilometers, destroying the missiles one at a time as they lunged toward him at over a thousand kilometers a second, accelerating the whole way. Destroying a missile took several seconds each—there were enough missiles and they were moving fast enough, the last one actually had him worried before it detonated a hundred kilometers short of the yacht.

"Cutting it closer than I'd like," he said aloud. "I'm glad they misestimated us."

Before the Inspector sharing the bridge with him could reply, he took the controls again, adding a series of barrel rolls and spiraling turns to their course toward the mining ships. He had no idea what range would allow their refitted cutting lasers to damage his ship—and he suspected *they* didn't either.

The attack was a completely different level of both scale and competence than the targeted assassinations Kay had engaged in before. Those, led by Legatan Augment troops, had been small-scale, highly competent operations.

This... The scale was still small, at least by the standards of space combat. A single destroyer would have been a greater threat than the Belt Liberation Front's entire flotilla—but a destroyer would have been spotted long before it reached Council Station.

The scale was clever. It had allowed the attack to take place at all and yet... The Front themselves weren't *quite* a bumbling coterie of buffoons, the long-range bombardment of the Station's defenses proved that, but they certainly weren't trained soldiers.

Lasers flashed through space, interrupting Damien's thoughts. He suspected there was *something* to the different levels of resources of the two operations, a key he was missing...but right now, he needed to stay alive.

Lasers were among the few weapons magic was basically useless against. Without air, he couldn't generate his usual defensive shield around the ship. Without mass or warning, he couldn't deflect, destroy or stop the beams.

All he could do was try and make sure they missed by putting *Doctor Akintola* all over the sky. Damien wasn't an incredible pilot, but he was a perfectly competent one, and the jump-yacht was a stunningly-maneuverable ship.

Even leaving the main program of "decelerate toward Council Station" in place and maneuvering around it with the manual joystick controls, she responded to his commands like an eager warhorse. The general "accelerate halfway then decelerate halfway" flight didn't require these kinds of controls or precision.

They were included in a ship like *Akintola* to allow for flying for fun.

Damien was now using them to fly for their lives.

With one eye on the distance counter to the four mining ships, he put the yacht through a series of twists, keeping them just that one half-second ahead of the flashing lasers.

"They're coming towards us," Samara told him nervously. "Romanov's people have taken care of the transports, but the mining ships are heading right at us."

"I noticed." He danced the entire ship upward, dodging "over" another quartet of deadly beams as the range counter ticked over the hundred-thousand-kilometer line. "I think they've decided we're the biggest problem, for some reason."

"I wonder why," the Inspector said dryly. "Why aren't they firing railguns at us? Those ships have them; they were using them before!"

"They remember us—and they remember what I did to their railguns *last* time," Damien pointed out.

Ninety thousand kilometers.

Avoiding enemy fire now was a matter of luck, and Damien only had so much. A laser slammed into the yacht, tearing through the boat bay in an explosion of vaporized metal and liberated air.

"Please tell me none of the Marines were in there," he said urgently. "Because we sure as hell aren't picking anyone up."

"The Marines aboard are in position to repel boarders throughout the ship in exosuits," she told him. "Two were in the boat bay, but they've reported in as safe, according to Corporal Massey."

"Thank God."

Eighty thousand kilometers.

Damien was barely breathing now as he twitched the controls as randomly as he could, adding layer after layer of twisting to his vector—every additional angle and line of momentum he could add made the Front's targeting computers' job harder.

Sixty thousand kilometers.

Doctor Akintola slammed backward as if she'd run into a brick wall, a laser hitting the yacht dead center as Damien dodged left when he should have dodged right. An engine exploded, failsafes spewing antimatter and debris out into space as the yacht careened completely out of control.

And into the range of Damien's amplified magic.

He let the damage take over making his ship's movements unpredictable and grabbed the simulacrum, reaching out across space to see, to *feel* the four enemy ships desperately trying to kill him and his people.

Even a Rune Wright had limits at this range, only so much force he could inflict, only so much power he could unleash. Normally, he would fight in space with conjured balls of plasma, but without an amplifier, he didn't have the power to do so at this range.

Two hundred grams of matter at the front of the lead mining ship shifted. A simple transmutation spell, the bread and butter of the working Mage that fueled the Protectorate's unending appetite for antimatter, "flipped the polarity" of a fist-sized chunk of the ship's hull.

Most Mages could only change matter to antimatter at a touch. Damien had learned to do it at range a long time before, though never at *this* distance.

The ensuing explosion gutted the mining ship, sending debris smashing into her fellows.

Debris that Damien followed with balls of ghostly witch fire, a sticky plasma that smashed into the holes created by the debris and began eating the hull around them. The two ships jerked away, an instinctive reaction on the part of their pilots trying to save them from the plasma that tore its way through their ships—until it found their fuel cells.

The last ship was intact and he gave her crew a second to see the fate of their friends. Five seconds. Ten.

Then he opened the radio.

"BLF vessel, this is Damien Montgomery," he told them softly. "I speak for Mars...and I offer you mercy. Surrender and submit to interrogation and you will be spared."

"I am the Alpha and the Omega," a familiar voice, gravelly with vacuum damage, responded. "I speak for the Stone and the Void, the People and the Rock that you have denied for so long."

"That's not an answer," Damien replied. "Yield or die. Mars can be merciful."

"I have seen Mars's mercy," the voice spat. "You will see my fire before we are done."

Before Damien could reply, the ship exploded, the fusion core overloading in a crudely rigged self-destruct.

"*Inshallah*," Samara whispered.

Damien exhaled a long sigh, nodding his agreement.

"I do wonder," he said to her, "if the rest of his crew knew he was going to do that...."

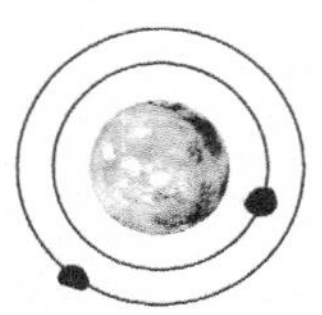

CHAPTER 36

"WHAT IS YOUR STATUS, Constable?" Damien asked Constable Lucas a few minutes later.

"I've got people pulling search and rescue through the Station," she replied. "I've ordered all ships to dock until the Navy can get here and clear up the debris field. I don't have much in terms of spacecraft and less in terms of available hands, but if you're in need of assistance, I'll scrape some people together."

"The explosion helped slow us down," he told her. "We've got one hell of a spin going on, but I'm starting to get that under control, and I'll be able to make a safe docking approach in about ten minutes.

"*Doctor Akintola* won't be going anywhere under her own power *after* that," he admitted, "but I and my Marines and Secret Service detail will be available to assist you shortly."

The shaven-headed woman nodded thankfully with a sigh.

"I appreciate that," she told him. "My bosses are probably going to raise several kinds of havoc, my lord, so let me say this before I get any orders to the contrary: thank you. Your warning and intervention saved hundreds, possibly thousands of lives."

"My job, Lictor-Constable," Damien reminded her. Even with just the Warrant, it was still his job. "I'll be aboard in about ten minutes; my Marine shuttles will be a bit longer. Let me know how we can best assist."

"It's changing moment by moment," Lucas replied. "I'll update you when you arrive. I can guarantee you, though, that *you* are going to have to meet the Council."

"I figured," Damien agreed. "Thank you, Constable."

He closed the channel and glanced over at Samara. The explosion had shaken up the yacht and its passengers pretty badly, and she'd acquired a sharp cut across her cheek. She'd torn off a chunk of her headscarf and was using it as an impromptu bandage as she went through the medkit for gauze and tape.

"Are you all right, Munira?" he asked her.

"I think this might qualify as the most exciting single day of my career," she pointed out, "but I'm fine. Yourself?"

"I'm not sure this even makes the top three yet," Damien replied. "I just wish we'd got more answers."

"This 'Kay' sure had a lot of friends. Legatans on Mars, nihilistic fanatics in the Belt..." Samara shook her head. "And he also seemed perfectly willing to leave them all to die."

"Which tells me that he's neither Legatan nor BLF but a third party," he agreed. "He certainly *was* a Keeper, but I can't help feeling there's more than that."

"The Front was our last link, though," she pointed out. "I'm guessing he fled the system?"

"We'll have to see if we can identify and trace which ship he was on," Damien said, "but yeah. This trail is cold as ice now. I'm not objecting to what it *led* us to—cheap as their gear was, these guys were about to rip the Council of the Protectorate a new one, and *that* wasn't something we would recover from."

He sighed.

"Of course, this links, through Kay, back to Legatus," he admitted. "His Majesty has no choice now but to launch that Inquest."

"That's a good thing, isn't it?"

"It's a *necessary* thing. I'm not sure anything that involves accusing an entire system government of treason qualifies as a good thing," Damien told her. "That it's looking more and more *true* doesn't help."

A final adjustment to the controls finally arrested the last of *Akintola*'s spin.

"There we go," he said aloud. "Next stop, docking. Last stop, too." He shook his head, studying the yacht's automated damage report. "This ship isn't flying anywhere on her own again."

With the immediate crisis over, Denis Romanov's three remaining shuttles were taking a somewhat more sedate pace back toward Council Station than he'd originally been planning—a mere five bone-crushing gravities instead of the utterly devastating, strapped into acceleration couches and missing his exosuit's impact absorption systems, fifteen gravities that they'd made their initial approach at.

"Always nice to know that the Navy wasn't needed," his pilot snarked, eyeing the destroyers still making their high-speed approach. "Do we want to tell them they can slow down?"

"No," Denis replied, studying the simplistic two-dimensional plot the shuttle's screen displayed of the area around Council Station. "The ships that are far enough out that they can actually stop here are already changing their courses," he noted. "Their Marines and search-and-rescue teams are going to be doing a lot of the heavy lifting for cleanup.

"The closer ones..." He ran the numbers. "Starting in about ten minutes, at least one Navy warship is going to be in missile range of Council Station at all times, counting the ones who are going to actually stop here.

"It *looks* like the Front have shot their bolt, but I'm not calling this done until those two battleships over there have settled in on top of Council Station," Denis concluded, pointing at the Mage-King's flotilla still almost twenty-four hours away.

"Besides," the Marine turned Secret Service bodyguard said with a cold smile, "after all of the bullshit the Council has pulled on Lord Montgomery, I think a little bit of twisting the knife on who saved them is entirely justified."

Normally, a ship with as much computer support as *Doctor Akintola* was perfectly capable of making the final docking adjustments herself. Indeed, given the precision needed for those kind of maneuvers, it was generally *preferable* for ships to dock under automatic control.

With the maneuverable little ship missing one of her two main engines and having multiple giant holes in her hull, Damien wasn't particularly willing to trust the yacht's computers to be able to compensate for the damage.

He babied *Akintola* in the entire way, shedding velocity carefully with the one main engine while compensating for the unavoidable rotation with the maneuvering thrusters, then slowly edging the yacht's docking port up to the airlock and making the connection with an audible impact.

Damien sighed aloud.

"And there's the reason we normally let the computers do this," he admitted. "Come on, Inspector. Let's go see if we can help clean up."

His Secret Service detail fell in around them as they crossed through *Akintola*, and the Marines were waiting at the airlock, several teams already having made their way through.

"Place yourselves at Lictor-Constable Lucas's disposal," he told the armored Marines. "The Station has taken a hammering and we want to make certain any survivors are found while we still have time. We probably have more exosuits than the entire Lictor contingent, which means you're the best people for SAR into the damaged areas.

"The *Councilors* may not be my favorite people," he admitted with a smile, "but their staff and the Secretariat remain under our protection regardless. Get them out, people."

"Oohrah!"

"What about us?" the lead Secret Service Agent asked.

"You're with me," he said quietly. "I may have just saved their lives, but I don't necessarily expect the Council to be greeting me with parades and flowers."

Damien's worries weren't calmed by his actual greeting party—a group of eight white-uniformed Lictors, each carrying a black battle carbine with an under-barrel stungun.

None wore the gold medallion of a Mage, but an armed welcome was *never* a good sign. Especially not when he knew that Council Station was dealing with a major catastrophe in several sectors, but they'd instead decided to use eight men and women for a show of force.

"Constable Lucas asked for my Marines to provide assistance," he told them, keeping his voice as calm as he could.

"Of course," the leader, a woman with skin so black her white uniform seemed to glow, told him crisply. "Lictor Lehrer, please guide the Marines towards the damaged areas and link them into our emergency repair channels."

One of the white-uniformed guards bowed slightly to Damien's armed escorts and gestured for them to follow him. Damien made a small gesture he hoped the Lictors didn't catch, confirming that the Marines should go with Lehrer.

His people weren't feeling any more comfortable than he was.

"I am Lictor-Sergeant Ratu," the black woman told him, her tone still crisp and formal. "I am to escort you to the Council. Alone."

She eyed Samara and the six Secret Service Agents accompanying Damien, and he gave her a warm smile.

"I need to speak with the Council, yes," he agreed, "but my escort comes with me. This isn't negotiable, Sergeant Ratu."

Ratu started to respond, then stopped, clearly listening to a voice in her earpiece.

"Of course, my lord," she allowed slowly. "The Constable says your guards are allowed. If you'll come with me, please?"

"Lead on, Sergeant."

Whatever the day still had to bring, it wasn't going to be *boring*.

"Mage-Captain...I think we have a serious problem," Denis's pilot interrupted the Marine with his eyes half-closed, stealing a moment to doze and try and regain energy for the task ahead.

"What kind of problem?" he asked, blinking his eyes open as he tried to study the tactical plot.

"The Inspector flagged two other groups, four transports in one and three mining ships in the other, as potential risks," she explained. "They were ordered off before the Front began their attack, and then everyone ignored them because we knew who the Front ships were."

"I'm not going to like where this is going, am I?"

"None of them have broken off," she confirmed. "All seven ships just adjusted their vectors to target Council Station... and if they're carrying railguns at all, there is *nothing* to stop them bombarding the Station."

"Where's Montgomery?"

"*Akintola* has docked. *Forest Unyielding in Storms* is the closest destroyer. She's in range, but..."

Denis nodded.

A Navy missile had a seven-minute flight time—and while it *had* an abort function, it wasn't the most reliable thing. *Forest Unyielding* could fire on the closing ships, but by the time her missiles arrived, they could have opened fire on Council Station.

If they were terrorists.

If they weren't, there was a roughly forty percent chance *Forest Unyielding* wouldn't be able to stop her missiles from blowing an innocent civilian ship to pieces.

"Is Montgomery available?"

"I think he's already in with the Council."

"*Fuck.*"

Denis stared at the screen. It wasn't his call...but if *Forest Unyielding in Storms*' Captain didn't make the call, Montgomery would have to. And Montgomery wouldn't have an active com in the Council Chamber.

"Get me Lictor-Constable Lucas," he ordered.

Ratu led Damien through the almost-familiar corridors of Council Station to the grand Council Chamber itself, with its massive transparent wall and its rows and rows of desks.

There were Councilors missing from those desks, and Damien found himself wondering, rather uncharitably he knew, if they simply hadn't bothered to get out of bed for something so minor as a major emergency.

Some, however, were almost certainly dead. That thought calmed his ire as he once again strode to the middle of the chamber, looking out past the Councilors at the strip-mined surface of Ceres, now obscured by the rapidly condensing debris field the attack had added. He'd heard no news from the surface, but he doubted the settlements had gone unharmed from the high-velocity impacts.

"The Constable has briefed us on the situation," Councilor Granger told him. "It appears this Council is in your debt, Lord Montgomery."

"My investigations led me to the attack," Damien replied. "Duty would not permit inaction."

"So brave," McClintlock snapped. "So high-handed. Centuries of tradition flouted—and without need, I see. And without authority, I must add, *Mr.* Montgomery."

"My orders were approved by His Majesty," Damien replied with a sigh. Clearly, the Council was aware of his resignation. "Would you have preferred, Councilor, that His Majesty's Navy did nothing but sit by while you were killed?"

"I would prefer that the warships be turning away now the situation is resolved," McClintlock demanded. "Or do you intend to now threaten us with the might of the Martian Navy if we refuse to blithely bow to your demands?"

"Peace, Raul," Paul Newton snapped. "Now is the time for us to recognize that we stand together, not divide ourselves again. I, for one, would rather be alive, which makes me quite grateful to *Voice* Montgomery."

Damien suspected that the irony of Councilor Newton giving him the title he *currently* qualified for, despite his earlier refusal to give Damien any title at all, didn't escape anyone.

"A day ago, this Council was prepared to demand Voice Montgomery's resignation as Hand," Catherine Montague pointed out. "Now we owe him our lives. The situation seems to have...changed."

"His prior actions remain," McClintlock replied. "The high-handed *arrogance* with which he has handled this mess hardly changes my position!"

"I am standing right here," Damien pointed out mildly.

"And if I had my way, you would be in chains!" the Councilor snapped. "Your hands are coated in blood, Montgomery. How many ships and men will die to prove your wild stories this time?"

"Enough!"

Councilor Farai Ayodele's magic slammed McClintlock back into his chair with crushing force, power flaring across the Council Chamber as the Earth Councilor finally ran out of patience and did what Damien couldn't *quite* justify doing.

"Sit down and be silent, McClintlock," the old black man continued as he stalked onto the center floor. "You have gone past rational discussion or reason, and I will not sit here and listen to your poisonous drivel.

"I call for a vote to formally give the Thanks of the Council to Voice Montgomery and to withdraw our request for his resignation as Hand," Ayodele continued, his hand still extended towards the Legatan Councilor and glittering with power as he broke at least three sacred rules of the Chamber at once.

The doors to the Chamber slammed open before anyone could respond, and Damien looked up to see the now-familiar shaven-headed and white-uniformed form of Lictor-Constable Cande Lucas charge through with his wrist computer in her hands.

"My Lord Montgomery!" she snapped. "There's a second wave!"

CHAPTER 37

YEARS OF PRACTICE let Damien read the display the computers threw up in moments. Two more forces, totalling as many ships as had been included in the original attack. If they'd all come together, they might have already won...or have all died when Damien and his people had counterattacked.

Romanov's shuttles were too far away. They could fire railgun rounds and might score a few hits, but the major reason the Martian Navy didn't bother with kinetic weapons was that they were only useful at ranges that were knife-fighting in space.

"We don't know these ships are hostile," Newton said, the Alpha Centauri Councilor staring at the icons flashing orange in the display as Lucas hooked Damien's wrist computer, with its tactical display programming, into the Council Chamber's main projector.

"We don't," Damien agreed, mentally judging the distance to *Forest Unyielding in Storms*. It would take almost the full seven-minute flight time for *Forest Unyielding*'s missiles to intercept the oncoming ships.

"However, they aren't responding to hails and are on an attack approach," he pointed out. "If they're armed, Councilor, it's already too late to stop them firing on Council Station. If the Navy Councilor McClintlock wished to send away intervenes now, they can likely prevent the Station's destruction with all of us aboard."

"Can you stop them, Voice Montgomery?" Councilor Montague asked.

"I can defend this station," he confirmed, "but I can't drive them off. If they attack from multiple angles, I can only defend us from one."

"Then order the Navy to defend us!" Ayodele demanded.

"My lord Councilor," Damien murmured, "if *Forest Unyielding* launches missiles, they *will* destroy whatever they fire at. If we guess wrong..."

The Councilor for Earth nodded, his eyes suddenly dark.

"Can *we* stop their missiles if we are wrong?" he asked after a moment. "Like you, Lord Montgomery, I was trained to use magic for missile defense."

That hadn't occurred to Damien, and he glanced at the time again. They had enough, maybe...

He tapped commands on his wrist computer.

"*Forest Unyielding in Storms*, this is Montgomery, respond," he snapped.

Seconds ticked by.

"This is Mage-Commander Anna Santiago," a Spanish-accented voice finally responded. "Captain of *Forest Unyielding*." She paused. "My lord...have we confirmed hostility on the part of the approaching ships?"

She sounded very young to be commanding a destroyer, likely no older than Damien himself, and he felt a twinge of guilt for having wanted to leave the decision of whether or not to potentially kill over a thousand innocents to her.

"We have not," he admitted. "If they are armed the same as the previous ships, they will be able to engage in three minutes. You must launch now if we are to save the Council."

He heard her swallow.

"My failsafes are not reliable."

"We will not use them," Damien told her. "If their approach is innocent, I and the other Mages aboard Council Station will disable your missiles."

He gave her a few seconds to process that.

"Target the approaching ships and launch your missiles, Captain," he ordered. "We are running out of time."

"Yes, my lord."

The channel cut, but bright green icons lit up on the display as the destroyer began to fire. Three salvos of missiles blazed into space, half a dozen for each of the *probably* terrorist ships closing on Council Station.

"Who else here is trained in missile defense?" Ayodele demanded, looking over the rest of the Council. Six of the Councilors stood immediately. Four more followed a moment later. Another stood, smiling, and shook her head.

"Trained, no," Andrea Tsimote, the Councilor for Míngliàng, told Ayodele. "I was never a soldier. But if you show me the way, I'll do my damnedest."

Guilted by Tsimote's effort, more Mages stood, studying each other's magic as they prepared to defend the Station themselves.

To Damien, the entire Chamber *sang* with power as the Gifts of over three dozen Mages lit to life. It was a sacred rule of the Council that magic was not to be used in the Chamber, that in this space, Mage and mundane were to be equal.

But today, as the Compact their ancestors had agreed demanded, the Mages stepped forward to defend them both.

It was almost a relief when the oncoming ships *did* open fire. Damien had been reasonably sure both that they *were* BLF ships after they'd refused to turn back and that, with the support of the Mage Councilors, he could protect them from the missiles if they weren't...but he still preferred to have ordered missiles fired at *actually* hostile ships.

Of course, that meant that Council Station was once again under fire and he was called on once more to conjure magic in the Council's defense.

The missiles came first, each of the transports and mining ships having half a dozen cheap fusion weapons mounted on external racks. Sixty missiles flashed into space from a quarter-million kilometers away, building velocity as they closed...and then dying as they ran into the will and power of forty Mages determined, no matter what, that they were not going to die today.

Damien took out a third of them himself, but the Council easily handled their fair share. Fuel tanks and warheads detonated in the short-lived fireballs of burning hydrogen instead of the nuclear blasts of hydrogen bombs.

The railgun rounds weren't so easily handled. The counter-missile spell was a simple-enough spell, if draining. Any Mage could do it, though many weaker ones couldn't do it repeatedly.

Conjuring a shield of force of a scale sufficient to help defend a station over a kilometer across without even air to use as a base was an entirely different question.

Even Damien could only cover one side of the station, and he chose to block the side the mining ships were coming from. They had bigger weapons mounted on them and had the lasers as well. He swept a wall of pure telekinetic force into the oncoming fire, throwing the railgun slugs back at the ships that fired them.

They'd seen his trick before, however, and maneuvered to avoid the return of their own weapons—but he'd targeted carefully. He couldn't reliably hit the ships with their own weapons...but he could block their *lasers*.

Even as he filled the space "above" Council Station with spinning debris and vaporizing railgun slugs, protecting the station from everything the BLF's refitted mining ships could do, however, the refitted transports were hammering the other side of the station with their own weapons.

Some of the Councilors were strong enough to protect sections of the Station, but only a handful—not enough to shield the entire ring. The runed carpet underneath Damien's feet trembled as round after round impacted on the hull of Council Station, each hammering home with the force of multiple tons of TNT.

Each of those tremors represented shattered hull plating, broken systems and lost lives...but there was only so much Damien could do. More railgun slugs hammered home into his own shield, and he grimaced. He could do a lot more than almost any other Mage...but there were limits to anyone's power, and he was starting to run perilously close to his.

If only the Mage-King weren't twenty-plus hours away.

The entire Station lurched under his feet as another salvo of railgun slugs hammered home, throwing off his own concentration. He swept power through space, trying to clean up what he'd missed.

Only half a dozen slugs made it through. This time. He twisted his defense back into place, sweeping more slugs back into lasers....

And then *Forest Unyielding*'s missiles finally began arriving. Captain Santiago had targeted the mining ships first, and her initial salvo came crashing down on the crudely-refitted terrorist ships like the wrath of God.

Without point defenses or Mages or amplifiers or even armor, all four ships vanished in balls of antimatter fire. A single sweep of power sent the remaining railgun slugs spinning off into space, no threat to Council Station.

Damien twisted his shield around, interposing it in front of the next salvo from the transports. Two more swarms of metal hammered into the defenses the Mages had raised, but then the rest of *Forest Unyielding*'s missiles struck home, shattering ship after ship as Santiago's fire wiped the remaining terrorists from space.

Leaning on the table he'd so recently given testimony behind, Damien exhaled sharply, letting the shield go as he steadied himself. He could feel the beginnings of a headache as he looked up at the display his wrist computer was still projecting.

Council Station was still there.

That was obvious from the fact that he was still alive, he supposed, but the Station could have been in much worse shape. Chunks of it were flashing red, with oxygen leaking out and almost certainly people Damien had failed to save dead or dying, but the ring itself was intact.

Radiation from the antimatter warheads was hashing the sensor feed the Station was providing him, but the Front's attack ships finally seemed to have been cleared away. *Forest Unyielding in Storms* was past, already growing more distant as she finally ceased accelerating.

He was still breathing heavily, but he wasn't the only one. The Mages had managed to keep Council Station intact, but it had drained a lot of them as they had stepped up to summon magic many of them had never been trained to use.

"My lord..." Montague's voice was soft as she stepped up next to him, studying the projection. "I'm not...very familiar with the iconography of this display, and there seems to be quite some distortion...but I thought that bulk freighter had been ordered off?"

Damien exhaled again, blinking away his fatigue as he focused on where the Tara Councilor was gesturing.

The *Dealer*-type freighter that everyone had assumed couldn't possibly be part of the attack had turned around at some point while they'd been distracted by the Front—and was now accelerating on a collision course for Council Station!

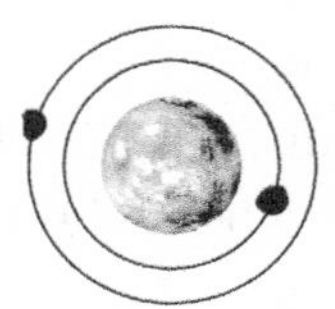

CHAPTER 38

"***TEXAS POKER*** is one of our regular supply ships," Constable Lucas told Damien, staring at the icon on the projected display and reading its details. "I know Captain Marion—hell, her daughter is dating my son!"

"I suspect Captain Marion is dead," Damien replied. He checked the numbers on *Texas Poker*. The ship was currently accelerating at over fifty gravities—*anyone* who was still aboard her was dead. The ship itself wouldn't survive that for long...but it would hold together long *enough*.

"At some point while we were all being distracted by the Belt Liberation Front and their clever assault, someone *else* boarded *Texas Poker* and took control of her, then launched her on an automated suicide course."

That someone might have been a BLF team. It might have been the mysterious Kay. Hell, for all Damien knew, it was the Legatans or a completely unrelated set of attackers!

Certainly, there were enough enemies on the field to leave several possibilities open—and for him to be unsurprised if some new, unknown party were taking advantage of the confusion.

"Can the Navy intercept?" Newton asked, the Alpha Centauri Councilor one of the Mages who'd pushed themselves well beyond their limits already. There were new bags under his eyes, and he was dabbing at a nosebleed with a kleenex.

"Both *Forest Unyielding in Storms* and *Rising Dawn of Freedom* are in range," Damien told the Councilor as he ran the numbers, "but would have four- and six-minute flight times respectively.

"*Texas Poker* is two minutes from impact," he concluded. "The Navy can fire on her, but they won't hit her in time."

He ran one last set of numbers and then stepped away from the projection, looking out the window behind the Councilors for the glittering star he knew had to be there.

The tiny point of light that was going to kill them all.

"We have to do something!"

"She is fully loaded and masses just over five million tons," Damien said. "Her velocity will exceed point zero one cee shortly before impact. It is an impact, Councilors, that would destroy a world.

"I cannot stop her. Even if I weren't already drained, I would never have the power to so much as deflect her alone."

The room was silent. Ayodele stepped up beside Damien, the gaunt Councilor for Earth a head or more taller than the slim, almost tiny ex-Hand.

Damien felt utterly frail in the face of the oncoming hammer, a titanic blow no skill or artifice of his could turn aside. He barely noticed the old man laying a pitch-black hand on his shoulder until the Councilor spoke.

"You're not alone, Lord Montgomery," Ayodele said loudly. "We lack your Runes or your Gift, but we are not weak, and I for one will not die on my knees."

"It doesn't matter, Councilor," Damien whispered. "We can all stand together, weave the powers of forty Mages—hell, Alexander himself could be standing here and we could not turn this aside."

Even from the Olympus Mons Simulacrum on Mars, he couldn't have turned aside the oncoming ship.

"You said it had to be automated," Constable Lucas said aloud. "Can you...move Council Station?"

A moment of hope flared through Damien as he looked back at the projection, studying it, but then it faded as he shook his head.

"We could," he admitted. "But not enough—not when the ship is accelerating at fifty gravities. Unless the people who coded it were fools, it will adjust unless we move much farther than we could."

If the station had an amplifier matrix, he could jump them all...

He looked at the Runes of Power on his arms. At their core, they were same *type* of magic. He'd only ever run his own magic through them, through the cascading sequence of feedback loops carved across his flesh. It wasn't enough to bring his *own* power to a level where he could teleport a kilometer-wide station with no runes in it, but with *forty Mages...*

"You have an idea," Ayodele recognized. "We have no time, Montgomery. No second chances. What do you need us to do?"

"Give me your power," he told them. "As if you were pouring it into a jump matrix...pour it into me."

From the Earth Councilor's expression, he knew enough about just what Damien was and could do to guess what he meant.

"I have studied His Majesty's Gift," Ayodele whispered. "I don't know if you'll survive that."

"One life for many, Councilor," he whispered back. "I chose a duty. I swore an oath."

He strode into the middle of the Council Chamber, facing the growing spark of light that was going to crush them all, and reached out for the power the Mages around him freely gave.

Power flowed through the room in a way he'd never seen before as he dragged it through the air, channeling every ounce of strength and will and Gift the Councilors could spare for him and feeding it into his Runes.

They were warm enough when *he* acted. He could feel his clothes ignite over the Runes and the shocked gasps around him, but he had to focus. Pain was shunted aside. Heat was shunted aside.

Everything was shunted aside except the station beneath his feet and the power he was channeling into the Runes on his skin.

Again and again the power tore through the feedback loops, doubling and tripling as he ran the power of forty Mages through an artifice designed not only for just one Mage but for one *specific* Mage.

It wasn't enough, but the gravity runes were touching his feet and he struck at them, draining their power as he encased Council Station in a bubble of his will.

He had no simulacrum. No runes or connections to channel his power.

Just his will, his Gift, and the power he was given.

He focused everything into a single searing moment and *stepped.*

He had enough time to see the spark of light he'd been watching change as Ceres shrank from filling the entire screen to a tiny orb a million kilometers distant.

Then the pain exploded through him and Damien Montgomery fell into darkness.

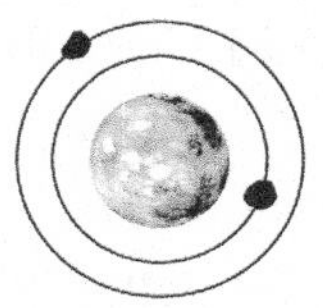

CHAPTER 39

DAMIEN WOKE UP.

Waking from black-out unconsciousness was becoming a disturbingly common experience for him, though the splitting migraine and searing pain in his forearms were new. It took him a moment to be sure that, yes, he *could* open his eyes and see; it was just that the room was dark.

"You, my young friend, are far too cavalier with your own skin," the familiar, if tired, voice of the Mage-King of Mars said in the darkness. "Your eyes need a few moments; they, um...exploded."

"That bad?" Damien asked.

"Your forearm Runes are...gone," Alexander said quietly. "Your eardrums exploded. You bled *through* your eyeballs, destroying them almost completely. Your left lung failed and your heart stopped beating on at least two occasions."

"Fuck." No wonder he hurt.

"And to be clear, you *melted the silver* out of your arms," the King pointed out. "You almost lost your left arm. You would have if I'd been any further away. You owe Councilor Ayodele your life, Damien. He was the only Mage-Surgeon on Council Station.

"If he hadn't been here and placed you into magical suspension, you would have died."

"Will I heal?" Damien asked.

"I've rebuilt your eyes and your eardrums," his ruler told him. "Ayodele is a better Healer than I am, but I have more power. Combined, we managed to fix your lung and save your arms."

The room was silent for a moment.

"But the Runes are gone," Damien echoed.

"And the scar tissue is...ugly," Alexander admitted. "Your glove habit is going to have another purpose for a while. I..." He sighed. "It might be possible, between you and me, to restore your Runes. But that's a question for another day, once everything has healed more completely.

"For now, you only have three Runes of Power," the King told him. He sighed. "I wish I could say you shouldn't have done it."

"How many people are on this station, my liege?"

"Over seventeen thousand. Eight hundred died in the attack, but there are over sixteen thousand people left alive who would have died with you had you done nothing."

"I knew the risks," Damien replied. "Painful death in exchange for sixteen thousand innocent lives was a trade I was prepared to make." He chuckled softly.

"Would you have done anything different, my King?"

"No." Alexander sighed. "We managed to capture *Texas Poker*," he admitted. "All of her crew were still aboard. It's...not possible for us to tell if any of them were dead when the ship started her charge."

Fifty gravities for an extended period wouldn't leave the bodies in an autopsiable state.

"Inspector Samara's assessment is that the ship was boarded, the bridge was captured, and then whoever set the program teleported off," he concluded.

"The modus operandi is familiar," Damien said. "Kay. Or Nemesis. Or whoever the *fuck* the son of a bitch is."

"He covered his tracks well. *Texas Poker* wouldn't have survived the impact, but her surveillance cameras were destroyed and wiped anyway."

"My Warrant was to pursue him," Damien said determinedly. "I will keep pursuing him."

"That Warrant has been given to Munira Samara now," Alexander told him. "I have another task for you, Damien Montgomery, if you're fit for it."

"My head feels like someone took an ax to it and my hands feel like they've been dipped in molten silver," Damien replied. "But I am your man, to the end. You know that."

"I'm going to turn the lights on and call in a doctor," the Mage-King of Mars told him. "Once he's cleared you, your people are waiting. Let them know you're all right, Damien. Lady Inspector Samara seems especially concerned.

"Once that's done," Alexander's voice turned grim, "it remains necessary for me to appear before the Council. I have insisted that you be with me."

"My liege?" Damien asked slowly.

"You will see, Damien Montgomery. I will not permit what has happened to go unremarked, to the good or the ill.

"We will have work to do."

Alexander had left the room by the time the lights were fully on, and Damien, blinking against the pain in his repaired eyes, finally looked at his hands and forearms. The sight caused him to inhale sharply, setting off a cascade of pain throughout his body that forced him to close his eyes again.

Breathing slowly, he forced himself to open his eyes again and look at the ruin he'd made of himself.

From the elbow down on both arms, his skin was blackened and twisted. He could tell that it was already partly healed, vast amounts of magic having been poured into his flesh to keep *anything* intact, but his arms looked more like lightning-struck branches than human skin.

He tried to move his hand, only to find himself whimpering in pain, which distracted him from the door opening and someone else entering the room.

"Damien."

Dr. Vinh Nguyen looked down at him with an unreadable expression on his face.

"I prefer to see my patients on a more irregular basis than this," he said softly. "His Majesty and Councilor Ayodele saved your life and your eyes, but...even they couldn't do much for your arms but halt the damage sufficiently to preserve your limbs.

"I..." Nguyen sighed. "I'm not sure it was worth it," he admitted. "Try and make a fist for me."

Damien's fingers twitched, the blackened claws barely twitching toward each other. Nguyen shook his head and held out a plastic cup.

"Grab this," he instructed.

Damien managed, barely, to wrap his uncooperative fingers around the cup and get a grip on it. He could tell that even the slightest problem would cause him to drop it.

"His Majesty saved the tendons in your arms," Nguyen told him as he took the cup away. "But they were badly damaged. Reconstruction and regeneration of muscle and tendon is not a straightforward process and is definitively not one where sheer power can make a difference."

Damien blinked back tears of pain, staring at the ruins of his hands.

"Will I ever—"

"Recover full function? No," the doctor said flatly. "Partial function, yes. Rapidly, actually. In a month or so, you'll be able to hold a glass or cup without too many problems. Give us six months to a year, and you'll probably be able to use a computer or fire a gun again.

"Both...may require modification of the hardware," Nguyen admitted. "You will never have full dexterity in your fingers again.

"It's rarely something I would recommend, but I'm not certain that amputation and cybernetic replacement isn't the best option here," he continued.

"What about the Runes?" Damien asked. Cybernetic replacement would cause issues with the remaining ones, but given how many he'd lost...

Nguyen sighed.

"I'm...probably the closest thing there is to an expert on the interaction of Runes of Power and the human body," he noted. "Your interface runes, your projector rune, and the Runes of Power on your forearms were destroyed. The polymer melted and ran into your flesh. There are still fragments of silver embedded throughout your arms. There always will be."

He shook his head.

"I believe you could safely restore your interface runes and likely the projector rune," Nguyen told him. "I... am not certain your body would tolerate the strain of those Runes of Power again."

"And we couldn't mount them on cybernetics," Damien pointed out.

"So far as I understand, no," the doctor agreed. "I will give you something for the pain," he continued, "but I would warn that even that will only reduce over time. Your arms will *always* hurt now.

"You *badly* damaged your body, Damien. The consequences of that will walk with you for the rest of your life. Neither I nor the Mage-King nor every doctor in the Protectorate combined could heal you entirely now."

Damien sighed and nodded.

"Then I'll live with it," he said, his voice breaking as more pain wracked his body. "One way or another."

"Fortunately, you still possess magic that will assist you in the fine manipulation your hands are no longer capable of," the doctor continued. "I would recommend practicing both magical manipulation and voice control of computers for the near future. Becoming reliant on those tools risks your long-term recovery, but..."

Nguyen shook his head sadly.

"You'll need to do it anyway," he concluded. "Wherever duty takes you from here, Damien, I suggest you take the best physiotherapists you can find with you. You're going to need them."

If his Warrant had been given to Samara...

"I'm not sure where I go from here, Doctor," Damien admitted.

"I doubt his Majesty intends to leave you on the sidelines for long," Nguyen replied. "Honestly, I'd rather lock you in the Mountain for a year and hover over your damned hands myself, but I suspect we need you for more than that."

He stepped up to Damien with a hypodermic, pressing it to the injured Mage's shoulder.

"This is as much as I can give you for the pain right now," he noted. "There are clothes in the other room. I can have one of my nurses help you dress..."

"No," Damien told him. "If I must learn to dress with magic, then I may as well start now."

"I'm sorry, Damien," Nguyen whispered. "I wish we could do more."

"I made my choice, Doctor," Damien replied. "I was prepared to die to save these people. This is an improvement from that plan."

Magical telekinesis was one of the first things any Mage learned. Damien had used it over his life for everything from a personal gravity field to preserving air when dumped into deep space to inlaying silver directly into his skin.

He had never used it to *dress*, and the process did not go smoothly. When Samara and Romanov entered the room, he was decent...but had failed to put on gloves, his Mage medallion or even his suit jacket.

"You look like shit," the Marine said bluntly, picking up the medallion on its leather collar and helping Damien put it on. "Like you shoved your hands into a forge."

"The comparison is...apt," Damien admitted with a wince. "How are you holding up?"

"I lost twelve people," the Special Agent replied. "I've had better weeks. If not for the man I'm helping dress, however, I would have had a ringside seat to over fifteen thousand deaths in one of the biggest man-made fireballs of all time.

"I can live with the end result," he concluded, holding up the jacket for Damien to slide his arms into.

Samara was waiting with the elbow-length gloves, an affectation that was now going to be a requirement, and carefully helped him slide his destroyed hands into the supple black leather.

"*Inshallah*," she finished Romanov's comment, "I would have been one of those dead, Lord Montgomery. You saved my life along with thousands of others. Thank you."

"The job," he replied, more than a little embarrassed. "A job it seems you inherited. His Majesty told me he passed the Warrant to investigate Kay on to you?"

"He did," she said softly. "There are a limited number of ships he could have teleported to from *Texas Poker*, my lord. I *will* find him."

"Pretty sure I'm *definitely* not a 'my lord' at this point," Damien told her. "No Hand. No Warrant. I am neither a Hand nor a Voice now, *Lady* Samara."

Only years of practice with the mixed-ethnic skin tones common to Mars allowed him to pick out Samara's flush.

"I didn't mean to steal anything—"

"You're better qualified to chase an interstellar fugitive than I," he pointed out. "Just make sure you have a Combat Mage with you when you catch up to him. Are you inheriting Romanov?" he gestured to the ex-Marine.

"I've been advised that I and my detail will be remaining assigned to you for the foreseeable future," Romanov replied. "Whatever His Majesty has in mind for you, my lord, it appears a Secret Service detail will be required."

"Not sure what Alexander will want with one crippled Mage," Damien said, shaking his head. "We've apparently finally managed to pass that wonderful afternoon on Andala for worst day ever, have we, Denis?"

"If we can avoid being at ground zero of major kinetic impactors for the rest of both of our careers, I will be extremely happy, my lord," Romanov replied.

"So will I, Denis," Damien admitted.

"Now, I understand that His Majesty is waiting on me?"

"And we have orders to make sure no one rushes you," Samara told him with a smile. "In answer to your question, I am being assigned a Marine Combat Mage strike team as escorts. Since, unlike Hands, I lack any magical abilities of my own, His Majesty feels I need powerful magical support and protection."

A Combat Mage strike team had three members. Between them, they could probably hold off a Hand, at least long enough for their charge to escape. His newest recruit would be well served.

"Good," he allowed. Glancing around the room, he sighed.

"Tempted as I am to abuse your orders, I think it will be better all around if His Majesty and I go deal with the Council," he told them. "Are you with me for this?"

"I am," Romanov confirmed. "Samara has...paperwork."

The investigator smiled. It was a cold expression.

"I may still have research to do," she said softly, "but I promise you, Damien Montgomery, the bastard who tried to destroy this station *will* be found."

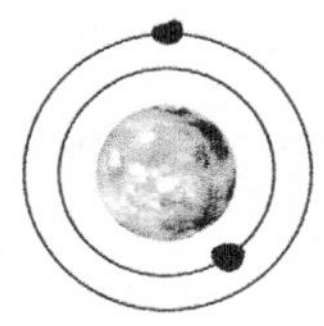

CHAPTER 40

"YOU KNEW."

Damien wasn't asking his King a question. The first words out of his mouth as he met Alexander in the office the Mage-King had commandeered were a statement of fact.

From the way the older man immediately looked down at Damien's gloved hands and sighed, he was completely correct.

"Yes," Alexander admitted. "Partly, I figured it was better for you to hear how bad it was from the actual doctor. Partly...I was too much of a coward to be the one to tell you."

Damien held his hands out, his nearly frozen fingers uppermost as he studied them. The black gloves at least covered the visible portion of the injury, though the tremors in his wrists and the immobility of his fingers told the story to those with eyes to see.

"I was prepared to pay a higher price," he finally said. "But it's going to take time to truly sink in."

"Whatever treatment you need, whatever care is necessary, we will provide," Alexander told him. "Though I know Dr. Nguyen suggested cybernetics..."

"They would require reworking the remaining Runes of Power," Damien replied instantly. "I know."

The Runes were unique to a person. Adding cybernetic limbs would change enough about him to require them to be redone...and an incorrect Rune of Power could easily be fatal.

"The risk is too high," he continued. "This is...unpleasant, but I am all too aware of the alternatives."

Alexander laid his hands on the cheap desk and looked straight at Damien.

"There are prices to be paid for what I have asked you to do, asked you to become," he stated. "You have paid them again and again. Three times now in less than as many months, you have lived only because a Mage-Surgeon was to hand, and that is a skillset only barely less rare than our own."

Alexander paused, seeming to marshal his thoughts and words.

"You have given enough," he finally continued. "Bled enough. If you want to go on medical leave, even retire...you've earned it."

Damien was surprised. His understanding was that he was currently *unemployed*, with his Warrant passed on to Samara to complete his task. Medical leave would have been a best-case scenario, but...

"You wouldn't be saying that if you didn't have a job for me," he pointed out.

"Over one hundred systems look to Mars to shield them from evil," the Mage-King replied. "Almost one hundred billion souls." He shook his head.

"I can turn aside few tools in the struggle to keep them safe, but I cannot help but feel that you have given enough."

"But you need me."

"But I need you."

Damien held up his ruined hands.

"Even as a cripple?" he asked bluntly.

"A cripple." Alexander snorted. "A cripple who remains one of only four adult Rune Wrights in the Protectorate. A cripple who, even weakened and injured, is the fourth most powerful Mage alive.

"I need you," he repeated with a nod. "I need your power, your Sight. I can send others in your place, yes, but there are few I trust as much and fewer who can *do* as much."

"Last I checked, I was unemployed," Damien pointed out.

"Medical retirement is hardly unemployment," Alexander told him.

"I would see you given a generous pension."

Damien laughed.

"You realize it works better if you offer me the money to stay, right?"

"My conscience says I should let you go," the Mage-King of Mars admitted. "But that ironclad sense of duty says I should draft you."

"Duty," Damien echoed. "I didn't learn that set of shackles from you, my King. Crippled or not, so long as you serve the people of the Protectorate, I am your man."

"I'm sorry," Alexander said with a sigh.

"I'm not," the younger man told him. "I believe we have a meeting to get to?"

Romanov and two Royal Guardsmen, all clad in combat exosuit armor, were waiting for the two Rune Wrights when they left the office. The three armored men fell in behind Damien as he followed the Mage-King through the corridors of Council Station.

The two with them weren't the only Royal Guardsmen around. They passed at least a dozen of the powerful exosuit-clad Mages as they made their way towards the Council Chamber as well as Marines and Secret Service Agents.

All of them were helping, assisting with repairs, coordinating search and rescue, providing security...but it was also very obvious who was in charge. And it *wasn't* the Council of the Protectorate.

When they reached the doors to the Chamber, there were six armed Lictors barring the way. Damien doubted it was unintentional that they were all obviously carrying the overpowered carbines the Secret Service had developed to fight exosuits.

Nonetheless, at the approach of the Mage-King of Mars, they stood aside and allowed all of them to enter, including the bodyguards that had always been barred when Damien alone appeared before the Council.

Desmond Michael Alexander the Third led the way into the room, age and weariness seeming to fall away as the gaunt old man in the plain gray suit strode to the center of the room, standing straight with his hands behind his back as he surveyed his Council.

"Much has happened since this Council requested that We appear before them," he told them. "But here We are."

The silence stretched out.

"Speak," Alexander ordered. "Enough blood has been shed for Us to stand here that We *demand* it."

It was still a good ten, fifteen seconds before Councilor Paul Newton rose.

"We requested Your presence to demand the resignation of Hand Damien Montgomery," he admitted. "A request that now seems... short-sighted. I am certain that You knew why we asked You here, so I believe it is necessary for us to state this:

"We have voted and this Council no longer desires Hand Montgomery's resignation," Newton stated. "We understand that Hand Montgomery has already resigned and I and my fellows"—he gestured around at the other Councilors—"also wish to make it clear that we have no objections to the restoration of Damien Montgomery to the responsibilities and privileges of his prior role."

The white-haired Councilor for Alpha Centauri met Damien's gaze levelly.

"For myself, Lord Montgomery, I owe you my life—and far more importantly, the life of my wife and daughter," he said softly. "I am in your debt beyond words."

From the uncomfortable shifting at many of the desks, few of the turnabouts had been as complete as Councilor Newton's. But they had been complete enough for them to change their minds.

"We are pleased by this news," Alexander said softly into the silence. "But We cannot ignore where We were.

"For Our entire reign, We have sought to compromise and cooperate with this Council," he reminded them. "We have argued, We conflicted, but We believed We had found a balance that worked for Us—and, more importantly, worked for the Protectorate.

"And yet."

The words sank into the quiet of the Council Chamber like a stone.

"And yet," he repeated, "you strike at a loyal servant and friend to strike at Us. You undermine Our Hands to weaken Our power and expand your own. We are prepared to compromise, Councilors, but We will not be attacked."

"We did not—" Newton tried to object.

"You did," the Mage-King of Mars replied coldly. "You used *this man*"—he gestured at Damien—"as a vector to undermine the very structure of Our Protectorate."

Newton wilted. The Council Chamber returned to silence, and Alexander smiled. It was a thin, pale thing.

"We are not blind to the needs of the Protectorate nor the desire for compromise," he finally said. "So, here We are. We have asked much of this Council in recent years. We will ask more of it in the days and years to come.

"We have long regarded this Council as a necessary advisor. We have long leaned on this Council to study and review the laws that We seek to lay on the Protectorate.

"So, let it be said and let it be done," Alexander said, his voice rising in volume. "We declare before this body, this Council of the Protectorate, that We shall pass no law binding the worlds of Our Protectorate that has not been approved by this Council.

"We reserve to Ourselves the ancient right of veto and command of Our armies and navies, but We have long turned to this Council to draft Our legislation and law. We declare what has been tradition...to be law."

It was odd, Damien realized, how even *silence* could have different tones. One moment terrified, the next stunned.

"Compromise, Our Councilors, is a question of give-and-take," the Mage-King noted. "We have given what you desire, and now you will learn what We require.

"A shadow has fallen across Our Protectorate. A shadow cast at the highest levels, a conspiracy of Hands and worlds and lies and darkness. Worlds have been torn apart in war, outposts seared clean of life.

"Even in the darkest hours, We cannot leave the Sol System," Alexander concluded. "So, We have always had Our Hands, to reach out where We cannot. But even Our Hands have limits, have been subject to this Council's oversight.

"An oversight that you have *abused*," he said flatly, "but one the Protectorate cannot afford for Us to take from you. But We have always had one more tool in Our arsenal. Those men and women We have charged for investigations of the highest of treasons, to lead the Inquests of entire worlds.

"Damien Montgomery," Alexander continued, "kneel before me."

Damien was mostly lost at this point, feeling like he'd wandered into the middle of a stampede—and he suspected most of the Council didn't feel any more certain of what was going on.

"We had to have this cast anew," the King said conversationally as he pulled something from inside his suit. "Only two of these have ever been given. One was vaporized with the man who wore it. The other's was buried with her."

It was a Hand on a chain, the same icon that Damien had given back to his King a few days before, but...

The Hand Damien had returned with his resignation was cast in gold. This was cast in *platinum* and Damien wasn't even sure what a platinum Hand *meant*.

"Damien Montgomery, We declare you Our First Hand," Alexander said softly as he draped the chain around Damien's neck, allowing the platinum icon to drop onto his chest. "We charge you to stand at Our right hand, above all others. We once made you a Hand, a Judge of men and nations.

"We now declare you a Judge of kings and stars."

Damien exhaled, meeting Alexander's gaze and nodding. He thought he understood now.

"And We charge you, as We did before, to root out Our secret enemy and end this shadow war."

Damien rose carefully, the new Hand on his chest heavier than the one he was used to and his limbs still feeling weak. Alexander kept his hands on the younger man's shoulders after draping the chain around his neck, subtly helping him to rise.

He traded a nod with his King and began to marshal his thoughts. He'd drafted an entire report to allow someone else to do what had to come next, but if it fell to him, he knew the whole mess better than anyone at this point.

"This is ridiculous!" a voice snapped.

Damien wasn't surprised that when he turned to face the Council, Councilor McClintlock had risen to his feet.

"This man and our King have run roughshod over the authority and protection of this Council," McClintlock snarled. "There are warships at our door, Marines and Royal Guardsmen throughout our Station, and you expect us to applaud you raising this man, whose hands are drenched in blood, above even the limited oversight we have over your Hands?"

"Raul, Montgomery just saved our lives," Ayodele told him sharply. "The vote against him was a kangaroo court and we all bloody knew it."

"The King gives us one carrot and we're expected to just roll over like happy dogs?" the Legatan Councilor replied. "I refuse. We were at risk because his people failed to identify a clear threat in advance. I, for one, find it suspicious that the Front was allowed to—"

"Sit. Down," Damien ordered, magic augmenting his voice to cut over McClintlock's rant.

"I will not be—"

"I said sit down, Councilor McClintlock," Damien snapped. "I don't think we're done speaking just yet, and I suspect you should stop digging."

He was trying to project threat in his voice and managed it, apparently, well enough that the Councilor sat. Damien glanced over at Alexander, who gave him a small "go ahead" gesture, then inhaled.

"For five years now, we have seen a shadow war waged across our worlds," Damien told the Councilors. "You've all been aware of it, at least peripherally. So many of you...so much more than peripherally. Ardennes.

Sherwood. Míngliàng. Panterra. Oberon. New California.

"A litany of names," he said softly. "Each of those Councilors knows of what I speak."

Each of those Councilors had visibly reacted when he'd spoken.

"There are a dozen others among you I could name," he noted. "Fire and bloodshed have been brought to our worlds, and again, and again, the Hands and the Navy have arrived to turn the tide."

McClintlock was staring at him and Damien could *see* the sinking realization behind the Councilor's eyes.

"We have seen the wreckage of these conflicts, and we have seen the common threads, the common paths," Damien continued. "We long ago realized there was one actor behind so many of these. And a powerful actor it had to be, to send ships and spies and weapons to so many worlds.

"And now that actor has struck on Mars itself, with assassinations and bombings and even the very attack on this Station itself," he told them.

Damien waited, letting the silence linger as the Councilors stared at him, waiting for the only thing he could say next.

"But in that overreach," he finally resumed, "they have revealed themselves. So, I stand before you today and I tell you that the Protectorate finally knows our enemy.

"Based on the arms used in Ardennes, Panterran, Oberonian and New Californian armed revolutions, the ships used to attack Antonius and burn the Greenwood colony to the ground, the Augment agents present on Ardennes and other worlds"—he *heard* the shocked inhalation of breath as he gave them enough to guess—"and the testimony of Major Adrian Kody of the Legatan Military Intelligence Directorate, I accuse the Legatan government of Grand Treason.

"I accuse your world, Councilor McClintlock, of waging war against the other worlds of the Protectorate in the shadows, of espionage and mass murder."

He couldn't really point, not with his fingers refusing to move, but he did his best and watched the Councilor turn white.

"I formally declare an Inquest and will proceed to the Legatus System with a team of investigators backed by a Navy task force to investigate your government's files and prove, before all the galaxy, their guilt or innocence."

The Council Chamber was silent and every eye was on Raul McClintlock, waiting to see how the man would respond.

They'd all guessed, at least in quiet conversations out of the light, that Legatus had been behind the attacks. They'd all known Legatus had the resources and the will—but also that Mars would have to wait until they had unquestionable evidence to lay any charges.

The UnArcana World's relationship with the Protectorate was fraught. Trapped and exposed as traitors and murders...what would Councilor McClintlock do?

As it turned out, he would laugh.

He rose to his feet, laughing and shaking his head.

"This is what we come to, is it?" he demanded. "This kind of sick joke? Kangaroo courts and false charges to smear the name of my world? Legatus not merely required to kneel but to grovel on our bellies and beg?

"We will not simply roll over and submit," McClintlock told them all. "You say there is proof! I do not believe you!"

"Then you are a fool," Damien told him. "Recordings of my interview with Major Kody will be distributed to the Council within the hour, along with the details of the investigations on *nineteen worlds*, showing that Legatan arms and Legatan agents were involved in the conflicts and terrorist movements.

"We will gladly share the proof of Legatus's crimes with the Council," he continued. "And when the Inquest is concluded, if your world is truly innocent, then your assistance would be critical in finding the truly guilty parties."

"No," the Legatan Councilor said, shaking his head. "No, Hand Montgomery, I think we will not be party to your witch hunt or subject to your inquisition."

He reached inside his suit, pulled out a small package neatly wrapped in parchment, and laid it on the desk in front of him. In front of the confused gaze of the Council, he unwrapped it to reveal a single black datachip marked with the seal of the Legatan Legislature.

"We knew, on Legatus, that one day Mars would come for us," McClintlock said, his voice strained but level. "We knew that one day there would be false charges leveled and a Hand would be sent to bring us to heel, to teach us that we should serve the Mages instead of turning them away.

"We knew that one day Mars would attempt to complete the Eugenicists' work," he spat.

"This"—he tapped the chip—"is our formal notification that we are withdrawing from the Charter, the Compact, and the Protectorate. No, Lord Montgomery, you will not be investigating my world to find your imaginary enemy.

"Legatus will no longer bow to your authority."

Damien would have expected Legatus seceding to surprise him less. It had been discussed again and again as a threat, a possibility, yet to see Raul McClintlock stand in the Council Chamber and declare that his world would break with Mars and the Mage-King was a shock to the system.

"Very well." Alexander spoke for the first time since laying the Hand on Damien, his voice calm and even as he stepped up to face McClintlock.

"If Legatus would walk alone, then Legatus will walk alone," he told the Councilor. "You and your staff have twenty-four hours to pack your things. We will then provide a Navy vessel to transport all of your personnel back to Legatus, where the ship will pick up all Royal personnel in that system.

"No Royal ships will visit your system after that," he continued. "Once you have arranged some deal for transportation with the Mage Guilds, you may send a representative here to discuss a trade treaty with Us and Our Council.

"We will have no slaves, no conquests, in Our Protectorate," Alexander told them all. "If you wish to leave, leave. But know that We will not force the Mage Guilds to deal with you. You may find yourselves more isolated than you expect."

The Council Chamber was silent again.

"Go," the Mage-King told McClintlock. "If Legatus is no longer part of the Protectorate, then you are no longer part of this Council."

The ex-Councilor nodded sharply, rising slowly and striding from the room.

Damien wasn't surprised, this time, to see several other Councilors from the other UnArcana worlds follow him.

"And so it ends," he heard his King murmur.

"If we're lucky," Damien replied. "If we're lucky, this is the end...but it could all too easily be only the beginning of the end."

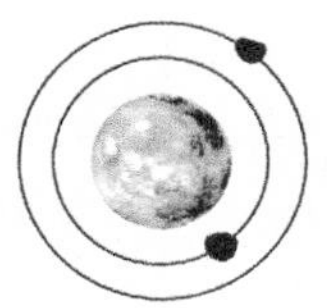

CHAPTER 41

WINTON HAD spent a great deal of time, when the Legatans had first given him the Link communicator, learning how it worked and checking over its system. The old man was far too familiar with the ways these kinds of games were played, and he'd been unsurprised to discover that the communicator had been set up to inform his Legatan partners if it was moved.

He'd disabled that functionality before he'd brought the Link aboard his ship, and the system was happily telling the President of Legatus that the old ex-Keeper remained in orbit of Alpha Centauri, even as his ship drifted in deep space a mere light-year from Sol.

"This is a disaster," George Solace admitted bluntly. "McClintlock did the right thing—we gave him that writ for a reason—but the timing could not be worse."

"I gave you the technology you need over a year ago," Winton pointed out. "Surely, you're not entirely without capabilities now."

He knew *exactly* how many of the new carrier groups Legatus had commissioned, but the "mere" mercenary Solace believed him to be wouldn't.

"We have some ships," Solace admitted. "Less than ten percent of our target strength. There was debate over how to acquire the...core units for the engines."

"If Alexander attacks now, are you in danger?"

"No, Partisan, Alexander won't move so obviously," the Legatan replied. "He's already signaled his choice of weapons: the Mage Guilds and economic warfare. He'll try to starve us out, deny us shipping."

Solace shook his head.

"It will only strengthen our will," he concluded. "He will hand me the hammer I need to finish the debates and accelerate the collection of the core units. We will have our new fleet before the Mage-King decides to stop pretending to be gentle."

Winton carefully did not smile. It took quite a leap of mental logic to classify the Mage Guilds refusing to ship to the UnArcana Systems without protections as economic warfare on the Mage-King's part, though he wasn't surprised that Solace had made it.

"How soon will the Republic be born?" he asked instead.

"We're waiting to hear back from the last systems," Solace told him. "Some have decided to lick the Mage-King's boots like beaten curs, but I think we'll have ten systems to form our Republic of Faith and Reason."

"What do you need from me?" Winton asked. "My resources are limited, but what aid I can give, I will."

"Are you certain no one will be able to recognize what the engines are?" the President asked.

"There are no more Keepers, Mister President," Winton replied. "Their order is done and their secrets died with them. Only I and your production teams have enough information to realize what fuels the Republic Fleet."

"Good," Solace said with a firm nod. "I will not see the Eugenicists win, Partisan. If there is anything else in the Keepers' archives that could aid us..."

"I do not believe so," Winton told him. "I will check. If I find anything, I will let you know."

"Otherwise..." The President shrugged. "Our own information networks in Sol have been damaged, and McClintlock, quite sensibly, destroyed all of the Link systems before being expelled. Your assistance in keeping us informed will be invaluable...and will be appropriately compensated."

"Of course. My services are yours, Lord Protector."

Solace smiled coldly.

"I am not Lord Protector yet, Partisan. But soon."

The Link systems retracted back into the roof, and Winton turned to look at Kent Riley.

"You played a dangerous game, my protégé," he pointed out. "I don't think Solace realizes why his people were blamed for the attack on Council Station, but you placed us at risk."

"I didn't expect to be caught by Montgomery," the younger ex-Keeper admitted. "Nor did I expect the Augment to roll over so easily, but I must admit it worked out perfectly. Legatus was blamed for both the annihilation of the Keepers and the arming of BLF. Anyone who has ever heard the code name Nemesis Sol is dead."

"His Majesty has sent a Voice after you," Winton warned him. "They picked her well; her record is intimidating and she was a good chunk of why Montgomery managed to catch you at all. She will not be easily shaken from the trail."

"The trail leads to nowhere," Riley pointed out. "Even if she identifies the ship, I didn't take it all the way to Tau Ceti. Let her hunt me, boss. It'll drag their resources and evidence against us into the open—without threatening *you*.

"I am expendable."

"Not forever," the older man replied. "I am very old, Riley. You and you alone of my allies know enough to even begin to replace me. Your carelessness in Sol, however..."

"I expected Montgomery to be more distracted by the threat of losing his job," Riley conceded. "I won't make that mistake again. Our new First Hand is a dangerous foe."

"He is but one man, and what has been set into motion will grind him up like so many others. Montgomery will be useful to us in the long run, I think, our unwitting ally more than our foe."

"Perhaps we should recruit him?" Riley suggested. "Injured or not, he remains powerful."

"And straightforward, painfully so," Winton replied. "No, Montgomery is most useful when our targets are the Protectorate's enemies.

Remember, when the dust settles, it is the Protectorate we want to preserve.

"I want Montgomery alive. Let's not send any more assassins at him, shall we?"

"I didn't," Riley admitted. "Took me a good couple of days to even work out who had."

"If you didn't attempt to assassinate him, Riley, who did?" Winton asked. He believed the younger Mage, and from that base he could learn who *had* tried, but if Riley had already learned the answer...

"I only confirmed it just before I left Sol, and I think it's something we may be able to find value in," Kent Riley, known as both "Kay" and "Nemesis", told his mentor. "It seems that certain of Alexander's allies saw the Hand as a detriment...one that would go away if said Hand was dead."

A string of Hindi curses echoed through the dark office as the light switch failed to work.

"I must apologize for that, Councilor Granger," a smooth voice said in the shadows. "We need to speak, but I would prefer not to be identified. We're also being jammed, if you're thinking about your panic button."

"This is Council Station," Suresh Granger, Councilor for Tau Ceti, snapped. "You will not get away with this!"

"With what?" Winton asked, amused. "I'm no threat to you, Councilor, I just wish to have this conversation without interruption or identification."

"I will neither be bribed nor threatened," Granger replied. "What do you want?"

"It's not necessarily what I want, Councilor Granger, but what I know...and what *you* might want."

Even in the dark, Winton could see the other man freeze.

"What do you mean? Who are you?"

"The important thing today, I think, is that I am the man with the proof that *you* attempted to have Damien Montgomery murdered."

Granger's continued stillness was all the confirmation Winton needed.

"And since I am certain that you do not want *that* information to reach the Mage-King or the new First Hand, well...then I guess what I want *does* matter, doesn't it?"

ABOUT THE AUTHOR

GLYNN STEWART is the author of Starship's Mage, a bestselling science fiction and fantasy series where faster-than-light travel is possible–but only because of magic. His other works include science fiction series Duchy of Terra, Castle Federation and Vigilante, as well as the urban fantasy series ONSET and Changeling Blood.

Writing managed to liberate Glynn from a bleak future as an accountant. With his personality and hope for a high-tech future intact, he lives in Kitchener, Ontario with his partner, their cats, and an unstoppable writing habit.

OTHER BOOKS BY GLYNN STEWART

For release announcements join the mailing list or visit **GlynnStewart.com**

STARSHIP'S MAGE

Starship's Mage
Hand of Mars
Voice of Mars
Alien Arcana
Judgment of Mars
UnArcana Stars
Sword of Mars
Mountain of Mars
The Service of Mars
A Darker Magic
Mage-Commander (upcoming)

Starship's Mage: Red Falcon

Interstellar Mage
Mage-Provocateur
Agents of Mars

Pulsar Race: A Starship's Mage Universe Novella

DUCHY OF TERRA

The Terran Privateer
Duchess of Terra
Terra and Imperium
Darkness Beyond
Shield of Terra
Imperium Defiant
Relics of Eternity
Shadows of the Fall
Eyes of Tomorrow

SCATTERED STARS

Scattered Stars: Conviction

Conviction

Deception

Equilibrium

Fortitude (upcoming)

PEACEKEEPERS OF SOL

Raven's Peace

The Peacekeeper Initiative

Raven's Course

Drifter's Folly (upcoming)

EXILE

Exile

Refuge

Crusade

Ashen Stars: An Exile Novella

CASTLE FEDERATION

Space Carrier Avalon

Stellar Fox

Battle Group Avalon

Q-Ship Chameleon

Rimward Stars

Operation Medusa

A Question of Faith: A Castle Federation Novella

SCIENCE FICTION STAND ALONE NOVELLA

Excalibur Lost

VIGILANTE

(WITH TERRY MIXON)

Heart of Vengeance

Oath of Vengeance

Bound By Stars: A Vigilante Series

(With Terry Mixon)

Bound By Law

Bound by Honor

Bound by Blood

TEER AND KARD

Wardtown

Blood Ward

CHANGELING BLOOD

Changeling's Fealty

Hunter's Oath

Noble's Honor

Fae, Flames & Fedoras: A Changeling Blood Novella

ONSET

ONSET: To Serve and Protect

ONSET: My Enemy's Enemy

ONSET: Blood of the Innocent

ONSET: Stay of Execution

Murder by Magic: An ONSET Novella

FANTASY STAND ALONE NOVELS

Children of Prophecy

City in the Sky

Made in the USA
Coppell, TX
09 September 2022